THE
CARDORIAN
COMPLEX

THE
CARDORIAN
COMPLEX

J. TAYLOR BAKER

Eagle Cliff Press

THE CARDORIAN COMPLEX

Cover & Interior design by Eight Little Pages

Eagle Cliff Press LLC

This book is dedicated to the many wonderful people who helped me through my teenage years, especially...

My parents, John and Deborah,
who always believed I would do something great one day,

Michaela,
who taught me how to be a good friend,

Lydia,
who tutored me through school,

And Christina,
who changed my life by giving me Alicia

Table of Contents

PART ONE

PRITCHARD HAVEN

Chapter One

The Skydiver Incident

The Donnigan Boys would never see him differently. Jeremiah had only just begun to accept this now that his four years at Laronna were almost over. His chest weighed heavily on the rest of his body anytime he saw them together, smiles spread across their bland, happy faces while he trudged along from class to class by himself, going numb with each and every step he took. In their eyes he was still the same as he'd always been, only taller, and with a deeper voice more fitting for someone months away from going off to college. He was still the quiet one of the group, the sort of person who never spoke unless spoken to first, always getting lost in his daydreams while everyone else was busy living life in the real world, going to parties and passing time with a few of their friends. Their beliefs hadn't changed in four years and wouldn't change in another ten, no matter how many nights he fell asleep with his face buried into his pillow, hoping everything would change when he woke up tomorrow.

"You're an INFP," Tom had said the first time Jeremiah visited the school. "This is also known as the Dreamer type, if you'd rather call yourself that."

Jeremiah had been fifteen the first time he met Tom, unaware of how much time he would spend with the counselor during the next four years. Tom was a tall man with a lean figure, and a soft, boyish face that often made him look like a younger man in a stretched body. He was either in his early forties or early fifties, but he had the spirit of someone half his age. They each sported brown hair that matched the color of their eyes, although Tom managed to keep his mostly straight, while Jeremiah's always looked like it needed a few extra seconds of combing.

Jeremiah could still remember his first visit to the school's counseling office. It was less than half the size of a standard classroom, just big enough to fit two padded chairs, a small desk, and a large wooden cabinet propped against the wall across from the door. There were no windows to be found, and so the only light came from a single bulb buried into the ceiling. Jeremiah had been given a pencil, a clipboard, and a list of questions Tom referred to as the Myers Briggs Type Indicator. He had spent about thirty minutes answering these questions before handing the clipboard over to the counselor, who only needed two minutes to review the answers and tally the results.

"The first section shows whether you lean more toward being an *introvert* or an *extrovert*," the counselor explained. "Extroverts, marked with the letter E, are highly social. They are often very outgoing, and love to be with their friends. On the other end of the spectrum, we have introverts, which is what you are. Introverts, marked with the letter I, will often prefer to spend most of their time alone. They will often engage in private activities, like writing or drawing, that allow them to be with their own thoughts and ideas, and they tend to prefer small groups of friends instead of large ones."

Before meeting with Tom, Jeremiah had never heard of these terms. Now at eighteen, he could only see the world as split between introverts and extroverts, the people like him who never looked like they had much to say and people like the Donnigan Boys who never stayed quiet. He could still remember the last time he ran in the field at his old middle school, a day in late October when the autumn leaves lay scattered across the ground and crackled under the weight of his feet. He'd been twelve years old at the time. He'd been playing in his own imagination, fighting dragons with an enchanted sword and piloting starships to the furthest boundaries of space, acting out his own private fantasies while the other students saw some deranged child running and shouting at invisible people. He immediately stopped when he noticed the other boys eating lunch by the tetherball court, talking and laughing while he stood alone with blades of grass rubbing against his ankles. It was like waking up from a dream, buried beneath the sheets in deep sleep until the rising sun dragged him out onto the cold, rough ground, and just like that, his last adventure was over. One look across the field, and everything inside his head meant nothing.

"The second section tells us how we prefer to learn new information," Tom continued. "*Sensory*, marked with the letter S, means you focus on details you can see, hear, count, or observe as part of your surroundings. At the other end of the spectrum is *Intuitive*, which is marked with the letter N. These people focus more on patterns and possibilities. They pay more attention to how something feels, and how things should be instead of how they are."

Jeremiah had lost plenty of things in his time at Laronna, but he'd earned a lot back in exchange. His love of daydreaming had been replaced by a skill in curiosity, as he chose to call it. Instead of wasting his time making up names and stories for the imaginary creatures he drew in his sketchpad, he would watch his classmates with incredible focus. He would study the way they spoke, the way they dressed, the way they acted, whether he was far away or standing right next to them. He remembered sitting down one morning in Mr. Dawson's history class, looking around the room and suddenly noticing for the first time that he was the only boy dressed in khaki shorts, and tall dress socks like the kind most people would only wear to church and funerals. One week later, he stepped back into that class wearing jeans and a normal pair of socks. He sat down at his desk with a confidence he hadn't felt in years, then looked around and saw he was the only boy in the room wearing muddy hiking shoes rather than a pair of sneakers, and realized he still had more work to do.

It took a few tries before he found a style that suited him. He owned two hooded sweatshirts that he wore interchangeably, often times with the zipper undone. One was navy-blue, and the other was black. He rarely wore T-shirts, opting to stuff his closet full of shirts with long sleeves to help conceal his thin arms. Most of the time he wore collared shirts with buttons all the way down the front, but only if they looked casual enough so he could go to school and not look like he was on his way to a wedding. He always wore jeans that were the same dark shade the Donnigan Boys liked so much, and athletic shoes to make him look more sports-oriented than he actually was.

"The third section is about decisions," Tom continued. "*Thinkers*, marked with a T, usually make decisions based on reason and logic. *Feelers*, marked with an F, make choices based on values and beliefs."

The last few years had kept to a steady routine, with each day coming and going like the one before and the one to come after. Jeremiah rarely had to deal with tough choices, but he knew even without the Myers Briggs that he was more of a feeler than a thinker. The voice in his brain was never as loud as the one in his gut. Every decision he'd made for the last four years came from a need to be liked and a fear of going back to the blind, foolish boy he used to be. He did whatever felt right, whatever felt safe, whatever felt like the right step to take if he wanted the Donnigan Boys to respect him.

"And lastly, the fourth section is for Judging vs. Perceiving," Tom announced. "*Judging*, with a J, means you tend to stay organized and like to follow a firm routine. *Perceiving*, with a P, means you prefer to deal with problems as they happen, and don't care so much about keeping things in order. Perceivers usually wait for things to happen and don't try so hard to change the way things are."

The messy state of the desk in his bedroom made a strong case that Jeremiah was more of a P than a J. He'd worked hard during the last few years to be more organized and proactive, finding ways to keep track of school projects and solving problems on his own rather than waiting for help. He'd become much more reliable over the last few years, now that he was more in touch with the real world and not so caught up in daydreams. Considering how much had stayed the same, this was one of the few changes he could be proud of.

"Introvert. Intuitive. Feeling. Perceiving," Tom repeated as he handed Jeremiah the clipboard. "INFP for short. Does that sound like you?"

"Yeah, I think so," he replied. He took a moment to review the last page before he gave back the clipboard.

"Do you like what it says about you?" Tom asked. "Is there anything you wish could be different?"

"Not me," Jeremiah answered. "But my parents would probably want me to be an E. They don't think I talk enough. They say I spend too much time alone instead of talking to other kids and playing with them—that sort of thing."

"So, they don't think you're a social person?" Tom said, nodding as if he'd heard this same response from other students. "That's why they want you to come to Laronna. Is that right?"

"Yes, sir."

"And do you agree with your parents?"

"Which part?" Jeremiah asked. "That I don't talk much or that I should come to Laronna to get help?"

"Both," Tom replied. "I have a feeling they might have the same answer."

"I don't mind being quiet," Jeremiah said, after a long stretch of silence. "I like doing things alone so no one can bother me, but sometimes I also wish I had more friends. I like watching the other kids talk to each other, and sometimes I wish I could join them. I just don't know how."

"But you want to learn, right?" Tom asked, leaning further into his seat, with his hands clasped in his lap.

Jeremiah offered a feeble nod as his response, and Tom shot back with a warm, tender smile, the kind that made the dark, dim room feel a little bit brighter.

"I'm glad to say you've come to the right place," the counselor said. "You're not alone, Jeremiah. I know it might seem that way, but I've been a counselor at this school for six years now, and I meet with kids every day who want all the same things as you. They all want something to be different. They just need a little help. That's what

Laronna is meant to do."

It was a school where students learn to grow. That was the line that stuck with Jeremiah when he read the brochure his mother slipped into his lunchbox. It was a tiny place in the middle of nowhere, less than half the size of his old school, with barely a hundred students and a staff of no more than thirty people. While most schools were made from brick or concrete, Laronna was mostly made out of wood, which often made it look more like a long house instead of an actual school. It felt a lot more like a summer camp, especially since the whole place had been built on a large field of lush grass and was surrounded by a forest of tall trees that cut them off from the rest of Pritchard Haven.

"Do you think this place can help me?" Jeremiah asked the counselor.

"I do," Tom replied, gently nodding his head. "But it may not be easy. Change is always hard, but it's usually much harder to grow up and stay the same year after year. There's a story I always like to tell my students that I think does a good job of showing what I mean. Would you like to hear it?"

"Sure. That's okay," he replied.

Tom set the clipboard back on his desk and leaned back in his seat, before he hunched over once again and continued to speak.

"Let's say it was your dream to become a professional singer. You perform a song for your mother without taking one lesson and she thinks you sound terrible, but because she's your mother, she doesn't want to discourage you, so she lies and says you were wonderful. You feel proud of yourself, so you audition for your school choir. Your instructor also thinks you're terrible but doesn't want to discourage you, so she lies and lets you join the rest of her students. Two months later, you're performing a solo in front of hundreds of people in a packed theater, and everyone in the audience thinks you're the worst singer in the world, so they shout at you as loud as they can until you get off the stage.

"Does that sound like a good story for you?"

"No," Jeremiah admitted. "I would rather someone tell me I wasn't good so I could take lessons and get better. Then I wouldn't embarrass myself in front of all those people."

"But what if I told you it may take years before you're ready," Tom continued. "You may have to train and practice for a very long time before you're ready to perform in front of a crowd that big. Would that stop you?"

"No."

"Why not?"

Jeremiah wasn't sure what to say at first. The room fell silent as he stared at the floor, searching for his answer, while Tom sat patiently in the other chair.

"Well, because, in this story, it's my dream to become a famous singer," he began, "and obviously, that's not going to be easy. If I want to be a good singer, I'll have to work and I'll have to practice, and then one day I'll be ready."

The glint in Tom's eyes and the smile on his face made it clear Jeremiah had chosen the right answer. The counselor looked as if he wanted to jump out of his seat and celebrate with a round of applause, but nevertheless he stayed in his chair and kept his pride quiet.

"That's a very mature answer," Tom said. "Not a lot of men your age would've said that. You see, I've found throughout my life and career, that whenever we're unhappy with the way things are, our first reaction is always to wish for change to come. People are very good at *wanting* things; *doing* things is when we start to feel a little overwhelmed. You said earlier that there are some kids at school you wished could be your friends. Have you ever gotten out of bed one morning, got ready for school, and just hoped one of them would come and talk to you?"

"Yeah, I have," he muttered. The actual number of days he'd done this was much higher, but he chose to keep that a secret for now.

"Has it ever worked?"

"Not really. I'm sitting here, right?"

Jeremiah smiled as the counselor let out a faint laugh. "Yes, you are," Tom said. "And you're probably going to be here again. But that doesn't have to be a bad thing. You said it yourself: Change isn't easy.

We can't make people talk to us, and we can't make them like us. All we can do is decide who we are, and who we want to be. That doesn't happen by snapping our fingers. It takes time, it takes work, and it takes help."

"Your help?" Jeremiah asked.

Tom nodded. "That's what I'm here for," he said with a smile. "That's what I do as a high school counselor. When you need advice, when you need support, or when you just want to talk, all you have to do is knock on my door. I promise I'll do whatever I can to help, as long as you're willing to try with me."

— — — —

The counselor had never betrayed his promise over the last four years, despite how often Jeremiah thought of begging his parents to let him switch to the public high school. His many failed attempts at impressing the Donnigan Boys and Donnigan Girls had led to some of his most discouraging memories, but the promise of Tom's unyielding support always filled him with a sense of hope that kept him going to school each morning, ready to try again. He trusted Tom now more than his own parents, who had come to respect and admire the counselor for the help he'd given their son.

He was a kind, compassionate man who always put the needs of the students ahead of his own, and until today, Jeremiah had always been happy to see him.

It was the last Saturday of April, a few weeks before graduation, when thoughts of summer break were fresh in everyone's mind. Jeremiah rode his bike down the empty roads and through the hiking trails in the nearby woods until he arrived at Tom's house at 448 Erikson Road. It was a lonely neighborhood, deep in the far northwest part of Pritchard Haven, surrounded by dense thickets of trees with no neighbors, apart from one who lived in a small red house at the opposite side of the street. Jeremiah wondered why someone as friendly as Tom would choose to live in such a lonely, dismal part of the town, especially since he didn't have a wife or kids to keep him company. It seemed like a strange place to live for a man who was so good with people, but Jeremiah knew better than to assume he or anyone else would always do what was expected of them. The Skydiver Incident had proven this.

His hand shook as he knocked on the door. He shut his eyes and drew in short, heavy breaths while he waited, trying to stay calm while the memory of Alicia cut deeper into his chest, punishing him with a never-ending stream of guilt. He could barely look Tom in the eye when the counselor opened the door to welcome him inside. He kept his head low as he followed Tom to a nearby room. A pair of chairs had already been set up, stationed at opposite ends of a coffee table and right beside a burning fireplace. Even with the sound of crackling embers filling the air, Jeremiah still felt cold and numb. His line of vision rested somewhere between the counselor's face and the carpet beneath their feet. His heart raced as he prepared to speak.

"I'm sorry to come here like this," Jeremiah said. "I couldn't wait until Monday. I had to talk to you as soon as I could."

"I'm always here to help," Tom replied, speaking in a soft, nurturing voice. "What can I do?"

"Something happened on Friday during the Sharing Circle," Jeremiah explained. "I didn't do it on purpose, I swear, but I really messed up, and I don't know how I can fix it."

Jeremiah could see the irony as well as anyone. The Sharing Circles were meant to bring everyone closer together, and somehow after all his years of practice, this one had only made things worse. Once a month, the students would get together with everyone else from their year and go to the library. For Jeremiah and all the rest of his twelfth-grade peers, this meant he'd have to wait until the last Friday of the month. The chairs and couches would all be arranged in a circle, and all the windows would be covered to keep the room dimly lit. Once they all took their seats, the teacher put in charge of running the Circle would pick up the white conch shell from its place on the shelf and ask a question. It was always a personal one, something that pried at their memories, their hopes for the future, their biggest regrets, or something about their current lives they wished could be different.

Some were difficult to answer, others were easy, but each one served a purpose. Every answer told a story, and everyone in the room could hear it.

It seemed like such a childish idea, the sort of thing Jeremiah would expect to see in a kindergarten class as a way to introduce all the kids to each other, but Sharing Circles had become one of his favorite parts about Laronna. Even the Donnigan Boys seemed to like it, if only because it took up time they would otherwise spend in class. They didn't need any help talking about themselves, but Sharing Circles were the only way Jeremiah could talk and be listened to. He needed the structure, a system where everyone had a turn to speak and wouldn't have to fight for attention in a sea of cluttering voices. His classmates would always hear him, and up until yesterday, this had always been a good thing.

"Ms. Meehan asked us if we would ever go skydiving," Jeremiah said to Tom. "The shell went around the Circle and we all said yes. At least, I think we did. I only remember what Alicia said. She sort of perked up in her seat and said that was a really interesting question. She was smiling, too; she usually smiles whenever she answers. Anyway, she said she didn't really see the point of skydiving and that it seemed silly to risk our lives over something that didn't have any real purpose, and before she finished her sentence, I laughed. It was just for a second. It was quiet, like I was sneezing, but the whole room heard it. Alicia looked at me, and then she started crying. She rushed out of the room before anyone could say something."

Jeremiah could barely keep eye contact with the counselor as he spoke. His head bowed further with each word until he was staring at the floor, overwhelmed by guilt over what he'd done to his closest friend. He could see Alicia sitting across from him, the smallest hints of tears resting around the base of her eyelids, the stunned silence she wore on her face for a fraction of a second before she stood up and stormed away, not turning back.

"Why did you laugh?" Tom asked. He leaned further into his seat. "What was so funny about what she said?"

"I don't know," Jeremiah answered. "I honestly don't. It just sort of happened. I guess it was something about the way she was talking, or the way her voice sounded. I just laughed, and I don't know why."

"I think I know," Tom muttered. "But you might not like the answer."

Jeremiah drew in a deep breath, trying to steady his heart, bracing himself for when the counselor spoke again.

"There's an old friend of mine," Tom began, "someone I knew before I moved to this town ten years ago, who believed the recipe for comedy was normality in the presence of absurdity. I don't know if this is his original saying, but I learned it from him. This means we subconsciously decide what's funny by, first, having a firm understanding of what's normal in our culture, and second, by being exposed to something that is not normal.

"Let's use me as an example. I come to work each day dressed similarly to how I am now: green collared shirt, brown slacks, and maybe a jacket if it's a little cold. But what if I came to school wearing a mask and a long red cape? What do you think would happen?"

"Everyone would probably stare at you like you were a freak," he answered.

"Most likely," Tom said, easing his way into a quiet chuckle to lighten the mood. "Now, suppose I wear that same cape and mask at a carnival and I'm surrounded by clowns and street magicians. If I looked more like everyone else, would I really be that strange?"

"No, I guess not," Jeremiah replied, rising up in his seat to finally look Tom in the eye. "but I'm still not sure what this has to do with Alicia."

"Well, then let me ask a different question," Tom continued. He leaned back in his chair, as if trying to give Jeremiah some space. "How different would you say Alicia is compared to the rest of your classmates?"

"A lot different," he answered, knowing most people would agree.

Alicia's family had been living in America for only two years. They'd moved away from Germany to start a new life on the other side of the world. They had a new home in a small town with its own set of rules for what was right and wrong, and Alicia had yet to learn them all. She would raise her hand in class when asking for permission to speak while Ethan Kantzton, Casey Marsley, and all the other Donnigan Boys would just blurt out their answers. She sat perfectly straight in her chair while they slouched, and she spoke clearly and eloquently at all times while they mumbled. She was a punctual young girl, the sort of person who would say "lovely" or "splendid" when everyone else would say "cool" or "awesome." She'd always seemed to be one or two decades too old for how young she really was. She dressed like a grown woman, behaved like a grown woman, and spoke like a grown woman, despite having the warm and innocent spirit of a young girl.

"How many friends does she have—apart from you?" Tom asked.

"Not many. The other girls don't talk to her much. She always tries talking to them but they don't listen."

"Sort of like you and the Donnigan Boys. Are you still calling them by that name?"

"Yeah, I am," Jeremiah answered. "I know it's a little mean, but I think it fits them nicely."

"Well, let's talk about them while we're here," Tom said, leaning in closer. "By my count, I've spoken to you in my office twenty-seven times within the last four years, and you and I have talked about these boys every single time. You've talked with me about how they ignore you, how they never listen to you when you're standing right next to them, and how they've never invited you to do anything with them outside of school. And yet, despite this, you always come asking me for advice on how to be their friend. Why do you care so much about impressing them?"

The painful stretch of silence that swept into the room was a stronger answer than anything Jeremiah could put into words. He sat stiff in his chair, his body numb and cold while his head hung down. A long sigh burst from behind his lips. He saw no way out of this question that made any sense, considering it still didn't make any sense to him either. He cared more about Alicia than he cared about any of the Donnigan Boys, and yet his actions always said the opposite.

"Because it's what I came here to do," Jeremiah said finally. "I need to know these things. Spending time all by myself was fine when I was twelve, sure, but what happens when I start college in a few months? What happens when I start looking for jobs, or when I want to have a family and I can't even get someone to talk to me? I have to learn how to follow everyone else's rules, and I thought these guys would be a good place to start."

Another long pause echoed through the room as the counselor nodded his head. A dreary look appeared in his eyes, as if he were sharing the cold sense of emptiness Jeremiah felt in his veins as he spoke.

"You remember the story about the singer, right?" Jeremiah asked. "The one you told me the day we met?"

"There's an amendment I would like to make to it," Tom replied, speaking now in a soft, somber voice. "Sometimes the audience is wrong. Even the best singers have their critics. That's what I think is happening now. You're a good singer, Jer, but they're a bad audience."

"But they're the only audience I have."

"Not for long. Graduation's only a few weeks away. Then you'll be off to college. You'll make plenty of new friends once you start school again."

"How do you know that?" Jeremiah asked, speaking with a raised voice that quickly settled into a weaker tone. "What if they're all just like the Donnigan Boys? How do you know they'll be any different?"

"I don't," Tom admitted, after a short pause and a heavy sigh, "but the odds are in your favor. You can't go somewhere with thousands of people and expect they'll all think the same way. If you look hard enough, you'll find your friends, and if they're any good you won't have to change to impress them."

The left side of Jeremiah's mouth bent upward in a partial smile, the way it often did when a funny thought jabbed its way into his mind. "Aren't you the one who always says that change is a good thing?"

Tom smiled back, aware of the irony. "It usually is, but sometimes you also have to know when to stop." His eyes darted off to the side.

"Do you see that red house across the street?"

Jeremiah turned his head to look out the window. "Yeah, what about it?"

"That place was empty the first year I lived here," Tom said. "One day, someone bought it and moved in while I was off at work. I went over that evening to knock on the door, hoping I could introduce myself, maybe invite this person over to my home for some drinks or a late dinner, but no one ever came. I tried again the next day, and the next day, and the day after that, but each time I just stood by that door and waited for someone who never showed up. To this day I don't even know what this person looks like. I could have kept on knocking, but at some point, I had to tell myself that some doors, real or metaphorical, just aren't meant to open for you."

Jeremiah turned away from the window. Tom gazed at the red house a while longer, and once he looked away, they both locked eyes with each other.

"I know it's frustrating," the counselor said, "but the truth is, no matter how hard you try, you just can't control what someone else will or won't do. Do you see what I mean?"

"Yeah, I think so," he muttered, sighing again as he'd done so many times today. He looked away from Tom when he felt a few tears beneath his eyes, and looked back once he pushed them down.

"It's just hard, you know? It's hard when you want something so simple and everyone keeps acting like it's something you have to earn, and right when you think you know what they want, they find something else for you to do. It's hard when you think you've finally figured out what's been going wrong, and then waking up one day and seeing you've just been wasting your time, or that they were all just tolerating you until you went away. It's hard being eighteen and feeling like you're twelve years old again, when everyone expects you to know this stuff and you've run out of time.

"I'm not ready to be grown up yet. I thought I would be by now, but I'm not.

"And I don't know what I can do about it."

The counselor sat with his head hanging low, hands clasped in his lap as a sad look began to brew in his eyes. He opened his mouth as if he were about to speak, but then he closed his lips and remained silent. He opened his mouth a second time, his eyes darting across the room as if he were debating whether or not he should say something, but then he stayed quiet. He kept this up for such a long time that Jeremiah eventually perked up in his seat, so puzzled about what was going on in Tom's head that he almost forgot about everything else.

"There is something I might be able to do," Tom said finally. He leaned further into his seat and kept his voice soft and quiet. Jeremiah leaned closer as well, wondering what the counselor was about to say.

"I'll make a deal with you. I want you to come to the counseling office two weeks from now on Friday, after school when all your classes are done. At that point, if you still feel like you haven't finished what you set out to do four years ago, I will offer you something that might act as a second chance."

"What is it?" Jeremiah asked.

"I can't tell you just yet," Tom replied. "That's your end of the deal. I want you to spend these next two weeks preparing for graduation. Whatever you think will help you walk away from this place with a good memory of these last four years, I want you to find it. You can interpret that any way you want. You can spend that time trying to impress those Donnigan Boys, or you can apologize to Alicia and spend this time with her. I won't tell you what to do, but if you're still unsatisfied two weeks from now, I can offer you something that just might do the trick. Does that sound fair?"

Jeremiah wasn't sure how to respond at first. For a moment, he sat stiff in his chair like a statue, his eyes gazing down at the floor once again. The tears around his eyes were gone, and the pain in his chest was slowly fading away. His skill in curiosity was already at work. He couldn't stop wondering about Tom's mysterious offer, even when he had more pressing issues to focus on. Alicia was still out there. Sooner or later, he would have to face her again, and he had no clue what to say. Making amends with his friend was still his top priority, but until he had his answer, his mind could never rest.

"Yeah, it does," Jeremiah said at last, finally ready to speak. He felt the urge to ask one last time if Tom could explain his end of the deal, just so he could leave this session with some kind of closure, but Jeremiah knew the counselor wouldn't budge. As kind and caring as Tom was, he still had his principles. He'd always tried to show Jeremiah the value of patience, and this was no exception. So instead of prying for answers, Jeremiah nodded his head, cracked a faint smile, and joined Tom for a quick hug before he began walking to the door.

"Thanks for talking to me about this," Jeremiah said. "I still have no idea what I'm going to do next year without you. You know me better than anyone else."

"If only I were enough," Tom muttered, a bleak look in his eyes as Jeremiah shut the door and left.

The Four Sections of the
Myers Briggs Type Indicator

Section One: "A Person's World"	
Introverted (I) vs. Extraverted (E)	
Preferring to spend time and energy focusing on thoughts, ideas, and one's own inner world.	Preferring to spend time and energy focusing on friends, socializing, and one's own outer world.
Section Two: "Receiving Information"	
Sensory (S) vs. Intuitive (N)	
Paying attention to what can be seen, heard, touched, or easily observed as a fact.	Paying attention to instinct, impressions, and possible outcomes.
Section Three: "Decision Making"	
Thinking (T) vs. Feeling (F)	
Making a decision based on logic and reason.	Making a decision based on personal beliefs and values.
Section Four: "A Person's Structure"	
Judging (J) vs. Perceiving (P)	
Preferring to stay organized and follow a consistent routine.	Preferring to be flexible and adjust plans depending on current situations.

The Sixteen Personality Types According to the Myers Briggs Type Indicator [i]

ENFJ The Teacher	INFJ The Confidant	INTJ The Strategist	ENTJ The Leader
ENFP The Speaker	INFP The Dreamer	INTP The Engineer	ENTP The Inventor
ESFP The Performer	ISFP The Artist	ISTP The Craftsman	ESTP The Persuader
ESFJ The Helper	ISFJ The Protector	ISTJ The Inspector	ESTJ The Enforcer

---

[i] There are many variations of the secondary names that accompany each type. The names given in this diagram will not be consistent across sources.

Chapter Two

The Girl in the Cabinet

The Scheinbachs had lived in Pritchard Haven for nearly two years, and in all that time, Jeremiah had never been to their house. His friendship with Alicia mostly rested on conversations that took place during school, whenever they were sick of playing sidekick to the rest of their classmates and wanted to spend their time with a genuine friend. He had always wanted to visit her house one day. Now he stood looking at the front door, gritting his teeth in a state of panic, wishing he could leave and save his apology for Monday. But leaving wasn't an option. He refused to be both a lousy friend and a coward, and so instead of turning back, he stared at their house, walked up to their front porch, rang the bell, and waited until Alicia's mother came to the door.

"Hi—hello, Mrs. Scheinbach. My name's Jeremiah Carso. I go to school with Alicia."

"Oh yes, I remember you from the school play," the woman replied. She spoke in a soft, soothing voice with a thick German accent.

"Is Alicia here now?"

"Yes. I'll get her," Mrs. Scheinbach said. She turned around and shouted something in German to the upper floor of the house, where Alicia was undoubtedly cooped up in her bedroom. Jeremiah waited patiently as they continued to speak through the ceiling, wishing he understood what they were saying, and trying to judge by the tone of Alicia's voice how nervous he should be. When their conversation ended, Mrs. Scheinbach said Alicia would be down in a moment. Then she disappeared into the kitchen, leaving Jeremiah alone on the doorstep.

He nearly froze when he heard her coming down the stairs. His heart beat faster with every footstep, reaching its critical mass when Alicia finally arrived at the door. Apart from the flat, disappointed expression she wore on her face, she looked the same as ever. Her skin was astonishingly pale, whiter than that of anyone else he'd seen in Pritchard Haven. She had a strong, prominent chin and soft, round cheeks, a pair of beautiful dark blue eyes, and long blonde hair that shimmered like brass and hung down just past her shoulders. She wore a pair of light blue jeans, a white cable knit sweater, and a pair of brown penny loafers—her favorite type of shoe.

"I'm really sorry about what I did yesterday," Jeremiah said. He spoke faster than normal, the way he often did when he was anxious. "I don't know why I did that, but I don't want to make any excuses. You didn't do anything wrong. It was my fault, and I'm sorry."

He waited for Alicia to speak, his heart racing faster every second she stayed silent. Thankfully, she didn't react to his apology with the look of spite he'd been expecting, which meant there was still hope. She looked down at her feet, then to the right side of her body, and finally, with a gentle sigh, she looked up at Jeremiah.

"Well, thank you for saying that," she replied. She spoke at a low volume, the sort of mumbling tone Jeremiah often used when he felt sad but pretended to be fine so nobody would ask any questions. This meant his road to forgiveness wouldn't end here. He would have to prove himself as a true friend with his actions and with the respect he would show her from now on. Luckily, he knew just where to start.

"I want to make it up to you," Jeremiah said. "How about we go to Shangrin Lake again? I know a lot of good hiking trails I didn't get to show you last time. There's one that leads to this spot by the shore with a really good view. If you have a bike, we can ride down now and I could show you."

Jeremiah didn't have much else to offer, considering how Pritchard Haven was such a small town that seemed to be made entirely from trees, parks, and tiny shops that left very little room for adventures. It was also a gentle, peaceful town with hardly any crime, and gorgeous weather for most of the year. It was a place Jeremiah had always been grateful to call his home, but there was only so much time he could spend stuck in such a small place when the rest of the world was his to explore. He was eighteen now, after all. The idea of leaving his small town wasn't as scary as it had been a few years back. Pritchard Haven was starting to feel stale, but his love of Shangrin Lake could never go away. He loved the look of nature, and the solitude that allowed him to be quiet without the usual consequences.

He began to lightly tap his foot while he waited for Alicia's reply, and then unleashed a sigh of relief when she smiled and left to get her bike.

Once they arrived at the entrance to the hiking trail, Jeremiah and Alicia secured their bikes to the rack and began walking. This was the first time in months they'd done something together, and still they behaved the same as ever. Alicia did most of the talking, while Jeremiah settled into his usual role as the listener. This was why he always thought they made such a good pair. Alicia always had a lot to say while Jeremiah usually spoke in weather-watcher comments, as he called them. These were the things people said when they had nothing important to say but still wanted to break the awkward silence, and so they'd resort to talking about the temperature or how nice and blue the sky looked that day. Jeremiah never had anything interesting to say unless he was with Tom, whereas Alicia was always ready with stories about her old life in Germany, performing in dance recitals, acting in school plays, or hiking across mountain trails and rowing down rivers in kayaks.

He led Alicia off the hiking trail and down to his private spot by the shoreline. He sat beside her on the ground, buried himself in the shade of nearby trees while the dry dirt and rough grass rubbed against his pants. He looked to the shallow part of the water by the shoreline and saw a rock he'd tossed in the lake about four years ago.

He remembered the way it felt in his hands, its rough edges scratching against his skin as he rubbed it with his fingers, and now it seemed all that time in the water had made it smooth and glasslike. He decided to call it the Smoothing Rock, and he looked at it for as long as he could before the peaceful silence stumbled its way into awkwardness. He felt the urge to talk, to say something to Alicia besides his usual weather-watcher comments, and before he had a chance to think, his lips burst open with the first meaningful subject his mind could come up with.

"I was at Tom's house earlier today," Jeremiah said. "Tom Berrinser, from Laronna. I wanted to talk to him about yesterday, and at some point, we started talking about the Donnigan Boys."

"The Donnigan Boys?" Alicia said, smiling as if she were about to laugh.

"That's what I call them when I'm with Tom," Jeremiah responded. "I like making up names for things, in case you haven't noticed."

"Well, that name certainly fits them rather nicely," Alicia said. "Still, it's not the way I would talk about my friends."

"They're not my friends," Jeremiah said. "That's what I wanted to tell you. I'm not going to talk to them anymore. You're the one who's really important to me, and I want to start acting like it."

"Well, you're off to a decent start," Alicia said, taking a moment to gaze across the placid water. She smiled, then turned back. "Why were you friends with them before?"

"That's the problem. I never was. I just wanted to be."

"Why?"

"It's complicated," he muttered, then tried to think of a better answer when Alicia mockingly rolled her eyes then looked away. "Do you remember the monologue?"

She turned back. "Excuse me?"

"Do you remember the monologue from the school play last year?" Jeremiah asked. "The one nobody else could memorize except you, so you got to play Olivia?"

"Yes, I do," Alicia said, "but how does that have anything to do with what I asked?"

"I know—bear with me for a minute," Jeremiah said. "What would you have done if you messed up all your lines on the first try? Would you have given up?"

"No. I would just try again."

"And what if you still messed up? How many times would you try until you gave up and said you're just not good enough to play the lead?"

"I would keep trying until I ran out of chances," Alicia replied. "I wouldn't quit unless I had to. I'm much too stubborn for that."

"So am I," Jeremiah said. "That's why I didn't quit before now. They all kept acting like I wasn't good enough to be with them, and I was going to prove that I was, no matter what it took."

"Is that why you spend so much time with Tom?"

Jeremiah nodded. He leaned to the side and pressed his hand against his cheek, overcome by a sudden numbness that made him want to hide his face. He felt embarrassed, sitting next to his best friend, admitting he still needed a grown man's advice to help him master the basic social graces most people seemed to know from birth.

"He's taught me almost everything I know," he admitted, his voice fading into a dull, quiet mumble. "I have no idea what I'm going to do without him next year. I'm really going to miss him."

"I'm sure he feels the same way about you," Alicia said. "My dad says he always gets a little anxious at the end of the year when his students leave the school."

Jeremiah looked puzzled. "How does your dad know that?"

"Because they're friends," Alicia answered. "My dad went to school with Tom in America before he met my mom. They've known each other for years. That's part of the reason why we came to Pritchard Haven when we moved."

"Wow. I had no idea," Jeremiah said, his eyebrows raised in surprise. "Your dad's from America?"

Alicia nodded. "His parents emigrated from Germany before he was born. That's why neither of us has the accent. My parents raised me in the U.S. until I was seven."

"How come you never mentioned that before?"

"I don't know, really," Alicia admitted, smiling at how peculiar this was. "I guess it just never came up in conversation. Honestly, I'm rather surprised Tom never mentioned it to you. He never said anything about my family when we moved here?"

"No, he didn't," he replied. "He doesn't like talking about himself. We usually just talk about me."

"Well, he is a counselor. I suppose that's his job."

Jeremiah nodded. "Have you ever talked to him before—I mean, in his counseling office? Have you ever had a session with him?"

Alicia glanced up at the sky, scouring through her memory until she found something to say. "Well, I had to take that Myers Briggs test when I enrolled, just because it was required by the school. Besides that, I've only been to his office one other time: last September on the week after my birthday party."

"That's all?"

Alicia nodded. "If I'm being honest, I wish I had spoken with him a lot more. My dad promised Tom would help me adjust to America, and that if I were having any trouble at school, I could always go to him for advice. And I never did."

"Why not?"

"It's like I said," Alicia responded, "I'm much too stubborn. My parents warned me that making new friends would be difficult, but I insisted I could handle myself. I changed the way I dressed, watched all the shows those other girls talked about, listened to the music they liked, but it just wasn't enough. When I was ten, I remember watching this girl Frederica walk to school in the rain. She slipped and all her supplies fell out of her book bag and landed in a puddle. I ran up to her while she was crying and I lent her a spare notebook and a few pencils. That same day, she sat next to me in class and asked if I wanted to visit her house during the weekend. All of a sudden, I had a friend, just because I did something good. But good isn't good enough anymore. Now it's nothing but rules: learning what to wear, what to talk about, how you ought to look, how you ought to behave, and if you aren't a perfect match, you're a bad one.

"It's a bit silly, I think. When did making friends start to be so much work?"

"Your guess is as good as mine," Jeremiah said, who'd been quietly asking himself the same question for some time now. "Don't worry. We're only here for about another month. Then you're going to college, right?"

"Yes, I am," Alicia muttered, not sounding very excited. "I just wish I could get there sooner. A month is still a long time to spend all by myself."

"You won't be," Jeremiah said. His voice was calm but firm. He looked at Alicia and held his pose until she turned around and locked eyes with him. "I'll be here. I know I haven't exactly been there for you lately, but I promise that won't happen again. You're the best friend I've got, and now I'm going to start acting like it."

—— —— —— —— ——

Jeremiah meant every word of his promise, but as he rode home from Shangrin Lake a few hours later, he wondered if he had the strength to keep it. His doubt stuck around as the next several days dragged on, reminding him of all the promises he'd failed to keep during these last four years, scolding him for how little he'd changed with all the time he was given.

He fell asleep the next several nights with his face buried into his pillow, tossing and turning under his sheets as the pain in his gut grew stronger. He wondered if all his work had been for nothing. He asked himself if he'd really changed at all within the last four years, or if it was all nothing but a convenient lie. For almost two weeks, he crawled out of bed with the same dull, beaten look in his eyes, wondering if things could ever be different for him. Then the answer struck him over the head like a bolt of lightning, and he raced to school as fast as he could.

Jeremiah stopped by the counseling office before class and asked Tom if he could retake the Myers Briggs to see if his score would look any different. The counselor looked hesitant, but he eventually said yes, and Jeremiah agreed to come back after he finished his final class. Jeremiah waited out the next several hours until the bell rang, at which point he rushed back to the counseling room. He sat in his usual spot while Tom fetched the question sheet from the bottom left drawer of the cabinet.

"Before I give this to you," Tom said, "I have to remind you to be honest when you're picking your answers."

"Why wouldn't I be honest?" Jeremiah asked, puzzled why Tom would assume otherwise.

"Because you're hoping to see a different result than what you're expecting," Tom explained. "The test only works if you can look at yourself objectively and admit who you are even if you don't like it. Our minds have a way of tricking us into seeing what we want to see. The final score won't be any use to you if it's all based on lies. You know that, right?"

"Yeah, I do," Jeremiah promised.

"All right then," Tom said as he handed Jeremiah the clipboard. "You can leave your answers on my desk when you're finished. Make sure you close the door behind you when you leave. It will lock automatically. I'll tally the results tomorrow, and then maybe we can talk about that offer I mentioned earlier."

Jeremiah's eyes shot open as if he'd seen a rat scurry across the carpet. So much had been on his mind lately that his memory of Tom's mysterious deal had faded. Now that he remembered, his mind began to drift, pulling him away from his current task so he could try to figure out the answer. When Tom left the office, Jeremiah shook his head and took a deep breath to regain his focus. Then he looked down at the clipboard in his lap, grabbed hold of his pencil, and began answering each question as honestly as possible.

He moved at a quick but efficient pace, putting himself in the scenarios described on the paper until he reached a rigid conclusion on the choice he would make. He didn't worry about his hopes playing tricks with his mind. He was too good at self-criticism to show pride now, and the results of his first time had been wiped from his memory. He knew he was a Dreamer and an INFP, but he'd forgotten the answers he chose and the score that illustrated the strength of the four trait categories. His time at Laronna might have taken him from being a deep introvert with a score in the twenties to now being partially introverted with a score of maybe fifteen or sixteen.

He tried his best to remember the original numbers, but gave up every time he looked down at his clipboard and realized he'd dazed off for too long. He kept his head down, locking his eyes on the pages in his lap, answering as many of the questions as he could before the daydreams took over and pulled his head up to look around the room. Even after he gave his final answer, he remained in his seat, digging through his own memory while he stared at the walls, the ceiling, the door behind him, and Tom's cabinet in the back of the room, where his original copy was tucked away in one of the drawers.

Jeremiah suddenly realized he had never truly noticed the cabinet until now. Tom always sat in the middle of this space, his back to the cabinet while his calm eyes lay steadily on Jeremiah, who always had other things to think about instead of what was right behind the counselor. Now there was nothing else in the room to block his view. He thought about taking a look inside for his old results. He set the clipboard on Tom's desk and debated if he should seize the opportunity or wait to ask the counselor tomorrow. He stood up from his chair and decided it was best to leave. He reached out to grab the doorknob, knowing he was making the right choice, and yet he couldn't open the door. Stepping out of the office meant he'd be locked out until tomorrow. He needed to be extra sure of his choice while he had the time to make one.

He stood by the door while looking across to the cabinet, wondering what he should do until he realized that his files weren't the only ones inside. He had the chance to look at the test results for all the Donnigan Boys. He could learn what was so different about them, and maybe understand a little better why they'd found him so unappealing. He had the chance to learn more about Alicia, take a tiny peek inside her mind and maybe discover more about the way she thought, what she believed in, what she considered important, and how he could be a better friend to her.

There was no better way to keep his promise to Alicia than to learn as much about her as he could, and no worse way to break it than to violate her privacy. He knelt by the base of the cabinet, breathing heavily as his hands began to shake, gazing down at the carpet as the dueling voices in his head made their final orders. Once he found his strength, he looked up and pulled the doors open in one swift motion, promising he would only stay for five minutes, and that anything he learned in that time would stay private and be used for a good purpose.

Jeremiah pulled open the bottom left drawer and found Alicia's old test results. She was an ISFJ, or at least she had been two years ago at the time of her transfer. He saw the description stapled to the back page and read it aloud:

"Known also as the Protector type, ISFJs are fiercely loyal people who are kind, quiet, and honor traditions. They value stability and are sensitive to other people's needs due to impeccable skills of observation. They are often driven by a strong desire to be needed, and to prove themselves as reliable members of society.

"That certainly sounds like her," Jeremiah whispered. He scanned the inside of the drawer for his own results, but he couldn't find them. He pulled open a few other drawers until he found his original answer sheet resting on top of a picture frame. The girl in the picture looked to be about eighteen years old, with eyes the color of caramel, tangled brown hair that stretched down past her shoulders, and pale white skin that could have matched Alicia's. She appeared to have a thin, healthy body, but otherwise she did not strike him as being particularly beautiful. This might have been due to her sullen, dispassionate expression rather than the composition of her face, which was gentle-looking with soft cheeks and a slender jawline.

Jeremiah didn't recognize her face from pictures he'd seen of past students, and he knew Tom didn't have a daughter or any family he was still close with. He looked for clues by searching a few other drawers, and soon he found a small wooden chest that was roughly the size of a shoebox. It was bound shut by a lock, making it the only item in the cabinet Tom had bothered to keep extra secure. He shook the box and heard something rattle inside, but he couldn't tell what it was. He studied the box closely but gave up after a few minutes, understanding there was nothing he could do without the key.

He put everything back in its place then stepped out of the office. He shut the door, hopped on his bike, and went home.

——— ——— ——— ———

The sealed box and the girl from the picture stayed fixed in his mind during the night, and all throughout the following day. He stayed with Alicia, sat by her in class and talked with her during lunch, trying his best to be a good friend while his own curiosities rattled in his head, swaying his focus hour after hour until he went back to the counseling office. He sat down in his chair, looking away from the cabinet as Tom handed him the clipboard. He turned to the last page to see his new typing.

"INFX?" Jeremiah said, looking puzzled. "What does that mean?"

"X is a letter that means Personal Balance," the counselor said proudly. "That's what I was taught to call it. Personal Balance means that you do not have a dominant trait in that category. Instead of being on one end of the spectrum, you're somewhere in the middle."

Tom reached across his desk to review Jeremiah's original results. "You were an INFP four years ago. The P means Perceiving. The opposite trait is Judging. This means you are more organized, more proactive, and more likely to take control of your actions than wait for the right time."

"Is that a good thing?" Jeremiah asked.

"In my opinion, yes, it is," Tom replied. "Personal Balance is usually a sign of growth. It shows you've learned new skills, but still haven't lost your grip on who you used to be. That's what a positive change is all about. That's what I wanted for you ever since you first stepped into my office. It seems I haven't been as much of a failure as I thought."

"Tom, don't say that," Jeremiah said. He spoke softly while the counselor sat with a blank look on his face. "You've helped me more than anyone else. I don't know who I'd even be now without you. You've done everything you could for me."

"Not yet," Tom said. His voice rose from a whisper to its usual tone, and the whole room went stiff right as he spoke. "There is something else I could do. It's something I've considered doing for a long time, but I've never had a good reason for it until now."

This was the moment he'd waited for. After two weeks of waiting and countless hours of racking his brain for answers, he was about to hear Tom's offer.

"Do you think you've kept up your end of the deal?" Tom asked.

"Yes. I do. I've stuck by Alicia every day for the last two weeks. I'm happy with her, I really am, but I still have a lot of work to do before I start school again. I'm not ready yet."

"So, you want to hear my offer?" Tom asked. "That's your final answer?"

Jeremiah paused to review his answer one last time. He could see Tom's body stiffen as he waited, bracing himself for either answer, hiding his breath behind his closed lips.

"Yes."

Tom nodded. He stood up from his chair and walked to the back of the room. He opened the cabinet as he released his breath, and Jeremiah instantly knew what was about to happen.

As expected, Tom returned to his chair seconds later with the wooden box in his hands.

Jeremiah's Myers Briggs Scores

Original Results							
3	24	4	18	8	12	11	16
E	I	S	N	T	F	J	P
Score	Score	Score	Score	Score	Score	Score	Score
(E or I) I		(S or N) N		(T or F) F		(J or P) P	

New Results							
10	17	8	14	8	12	13	14
E	I	S	N	T	F	J	P
Score	Score	Score	Score	Score	Score	Score	Score
(E or I) I		(S or N) N		(T or F) F		(J or P) X	

Chapter Three

The Aurascope

The room felt darker when Tom returned to his chair even though the lights hadn't changed. The walls seemed to close in even when they were as far apart as always. Even the sounds of strong winds and footsteps that Jeremiah would sometimes hear outside had vanished. He was stiff in his chair, speechless as he wondered what the counselor was about to say.

"Can you promise me you'll keep this to yourself?" Tom asked.

"Yes, sir," Jeremiah replied. He realized this was the first time he'd referred to Tom as "sir" since the day they met. It had been so many years ago and yet the word flew out of his mouth so naturally. He expected Tom to react to this in some way, but instead the counselor thanked him for his promise, and released a heavy sigh as he caressed the lid of the wooden box.

"Before I was a counselor at Laronna, before I even lived in Pritchard Haven," Tom began, "I belonged to a very reclusive group of people who call themselves the Auralites. Have you heard of them?"

"No, I haven't."

"I wouldn't think so. I barely know what they are myself. Some say they're teachers. Others call them philosophers. Some call them mentors, scientists, pagans, but to me, more than anything else, the Auralites are students of people. They devote their lives to learning more about the human personality, what it is, how it's made, and how it changes or stays the same over time. They know more about the science of people and the social world than anyone else you'll ever meet, and it's all because of what's in this box."

Time seemed to go by slowly as Jeremiah watched the counselor pull a key from his pocket. He gritted his teeth to stifle the sound of his breathing, and he felt his hands quiver as Tom unlocked the box and slowly pried it open. Nestled inside was a smooth glass ball that resembled a large pearl. With a closer look, Jeremiah could see it wasn't made from pure glass. The inside seemed to be filled with some sort of white crystal that had been sculpted into a round, edgeless shape. He decided to call it crystal-glass, a name he found rather fitting for a substance so alluring he couldn't look away from it.

The counselor gently took it out of the box and held it in the space between them. From the moment Tom's hand touched the edge of the crystal-glass, the strange item glowed from the inside in a dazzling display of bright, colored lights.

The coldness went away. His chest felt warm. His tense body melted like wax when the glow pierced his eyes and showered his face. Jeremiah sat with his eyes and mouth wide open, as quiet as if he were asleep, so entranced by what he saw in the counselor's hand that everything else in the room disappeared.

He took a moment to marvel at this strange item, letting his mind get lost in wonder until his usual skills of observation took over. As Jeremiah looked more closely, he discovered the lights stayed trapped behind the crystal-glass without producing a halo. He also noticed that the colored lights were divided into rings, like ripples stretching across a pool of water, or the stump of a fallen tree. The rings mostly shifted between yellows, blues, and greens, and only in the very center was a small mass of white light.

"What is it?" Jeremiah whispered, barely able to speak.

"It's called an Aurascope," Tom replied. "It's used to show a person's Aura. Have you heard of that word before?"

"Yeah, I have," Jeremiah said. "I'm not sure if I could tell you what it is, but I've heard of it."

"It's a word with a lot of meanings," Tom admitted. "You've probably heard it described as a sort of spiritual energy, or a light that inhabits the soul of all living things. I've also seen it used artistically, like when poets or writers need a pretentious way to describe something so they'll look at a flower and say it has an Aura of peace and tenderness—something like that. It's an empty word in a lot of places, but with the Auralites, it's something very specific. In their eyes, Aura is a science. It shows us who we are at a deeply intimate level that we could never see with any other method."

"Not even the Myers Briggs?" Jeremiah asked.

Tom nodded. "An Aurascope has three distinct advantages over the Myers Briggs that make it infinitely better. First, it examines sixteen trait pairings instead of only four. Second, it gives you feedback instantly instead of forcing you to tally the score yourself. Third, and most importantly, it's always right. These self-report surveys like the Myers Briggs rely on your own perceptions, and perceptions can be wrong. If you don't have a strong level of self-awareness, or if you're just too stubborn to admit there's something you don't like about yourself, you'll end up with a different score just by lying to yourself too many times. That's a weakness it can never get rid of, but the Aurascope always shows the truth, whether you like it or not."

Tom placed the Aurascope back in the box. As he lifted his hand, the colored lights vanished, leaving only the bulb in the ceiling shining down on them.

"How does it work?" Jeremiah asked.

"It's not as complicated as it looks," Tom promised. "It follows most of the same rules as the Myers Briggs except it uses colored lights instead of letters. The only tricky part is figuring out what they mean. Here, let me show you."

Tom reached across to his desk and grabbed a set of colored pens, and then proceeded to draw three circles in a row on a blank sheet of paper. The circle on the left was blue, the one in the middle was green, and the one on the right was red. The sides of the circles overlapped, creating two new spaces for the counselor to mark with additional colors. The section between the blue and green circles was teal, while the section between the red and green circles was yellow.

"There are three primary colors of light," Tom said as he slid the drawing to Jeremiah. "The same is also true for Aura. Red is known as the color of passion, because it deals with traits like adventurousness, creativity, sociability, sensitivity, and abstract thinking."

Jeremiah remembered seeing only one red ring in Tom's aura. He assumed it was a mark of sensitivity, since the counselor's job was rooted in his sense of empathy. He remembered seeing rings of mostly blue and green with an occasional yellow, and the speck of white light at the core.

"Blue light is known as the color of order," Tom continued, using his pen to point to the circle on the left of the page. "Blue is for traits that deal with logic, introversion, restraint, linear thinking, and following rules."

"And what about green?"

"Green is the color of Balance—Personal Balance. That's why I drew it in the middle. A green ring means you aren't on one end of the spectrum or another; you're somewhere in between."

Tom asked Jeremiah to hold the Aurascope. Jeremiah's hand drifted around the surface of the strange object before he finally grabbed it, and with this exchange of hands, a new pattern of light appeared. He looked at it with the bewildered innocence of a much younger boy, clueless and curious all at once.

"You see this ring here?" Tom asked, pointing to the outermost section of the light, pressed right against the underside of the crystal-glass and furthest away from the white core. "This is the part of your Aura that shows Introvert vs. Extrovert. If you were a highly sociable person who loved to talk and loved being with your friends, this section would be pure red."

"But I'm not," Jeremiah said, acknowledging the ring was blue, not red.

"If we were having this conversation four years ago, this ring would be pure blue," Tom said. "You would be deeply introverted. You would be quiet, reclusive, and you would always be off in your own little worlds far away from everyone else. But now, if you look closely, you'll notice this part of your Aura isn't pure blue anymore."

Jeremiah perked up in his seat when he leaned in for a closer look. His eyes widened with joy. "It's teal."

"Cyan is the technical name for it," Tom corrected, "but yes, you're right. It's the color halfway between the blue on the far left and the green in the middle. This means you are moderately introverted. You're still a bit on the quiet side, but you are way more sociable now than you were before."

Tom shifted his focus and pointed to the tenth ring. "This section is Practical vs. Imaginative. Four years ago, this would have been pure red, showing that you were a serious daydreamer. Now it's yellow, halfway between the green and the red, meaning you are now moderately imaginative. This shows me you still have a shred of that old daydreamer in you, but you've gained a little more focus now that you're becoming an adult. You've gotten closer to that perfect balance—closer to the green light."

"But I can't be blue," Jeremiah said. He meant to phrase this as a statement, but the inflection in his voice made it sound like a question.

"Right," Tom said. "That's important to understand. Our personalities don't ever flip from one extreme to the other. We can't become someone new, but we can learn to be different. That's really what you want. The best kind of change is the one that helps you grow into someone better, but still lets you hold onto the parts of yourself that are crucial to your identity.

"That's what Personal Balance is about. That's what I've always wanted for you."

Tom abstained from saying anything about the remaining fourteen rings of the Aurascope, but he promised there would be a time for that in the future, if Jeremiah accepted his impending offer. Jeremiah tilted his head away and looked to the counselor, not sure whether to be anxious or curious.

"There is a place, about a day's drive north of here, called Parliss County. It's where I lived when I was part of the Auralites, and where many of my old friends still live. Everything I've ever said to you, any advice I've given you, is something I learned when I was there. A lot of them have lived difficult lives. They've all struggled with change, growing older, fixing things they thought were broken—all the same issues you've had for a long time now. And I think you could learn a lot from them if you came back with me this summer."

Jeremiah had never known so much about the counselor's past despite all the time they'd spent together; now he knew so much he barely knew how to handle it. Half his mind was still caught on the Aurascope in his hand while the rest was drowning with questions about this strange place in the north. It seemed too good to be real: a town full of Toms, men and women who were just as wise, if not wiser, who knew about everything he'd puzzled over for the last four years. The chance to talk with just one would be worth the long drive, and he had the chance to meet several.

And yet, his heart still beat with uncertainty. His body numbed as the weight of Tom's offer pressed down on him. He'd spent months wishing he could be free from Pritchard Haven, but this dream was much scarier now that he had his chance.

"Do I have to decide now?" Jeremiah asked. "What about my parents?"

"I already told them," Tom replied, shocking Jeremiah once again. "I never showed them the Aurascope, but I told them everything I knew was important. I told them you were worried, that you didn't think you were ready to move on just yet, so I asked them if I could spend a little more time with you this summer and introduce you to some new people I thought could help."

"What did they say?"

"They said it was your choice. They know you're old enough to make your own decisions. They trust me to look after you, and they trust you even more. They'll support whatever decision you make, as long as you think it's the right one."

— — — — —

Tom told Jeremiah to think about his choice over the next few days, but asked that he have an answer ready by the end of next Friday. As he rode home on his bike, Jeremiah felt like he'd woken up from a dream and only had a slight grip on his own real world. Hours later, he lay awake in his bed after a long talk with his parents, unable to sleep with the echoes of Tom's voice and the image of colored lights flooding his mind.

He woke up the next day on a Saturday afternoon, his body wrapped in bed sheets after hours of tossing and turning. He got on his bike and rode back to Shangrin Lake, hoping a little time at his private spot by the Smoothing Rock would do him some good. He stayed perfectly still, trying to steady his mind with long, cleansing breaths as he looked out across the water.

He remembered when he brought Alicia to this place just a few weeks ago, the first time he'd ever shared a moment like this with a friend. He could hear her voice ringing in his ear, and the longer he gazed across the lake, the more he imagined reaching out and touching her hand, until he finally looked away and saw he was alone. His only friend was gone, and all the rest of his classmates would never dream of wasting their precious Saturday by sitting near a lake. By now they were probably at Casey's house, playing video games, practicing skateboard tricks in the driveway, or chatting about all the fun stuff they were going to do this summer once they graduated.

On any other day, thinking about the Donnigan Boys would be enough to set his blood on fire, to force his hand into a fist as he spat at the memory of everyone who'd left him to rot for the last four years. Instead, he shut his eyes, lowered his head, and turned the blame on himself. He had four years to learn, four years to figure out how to kill his shy, quiet ways, and even with Tom's help, he'd failed. He only had one friend, and he almost lost her.

If nothing changed before September, the next four years would be no different. He could already see the future ahead of him, sitting down at his desk, introducing himself to his new classmates, trying to forge a bond that would only last a few days before he ran out of things to talk about. Then he would fall back into his quiet ways, and they would find new friends who shared their interests and told better stories. On Friday nights, he'd leave his dorm and go on a walk to clear his head. He'd see house parties on every block, kids in their twenties out on the porch drinking beer and dancing to the music playing in the nearby room, and once in a while, he'd see a young couple making out by the edge of the street, so overwhelmed by lust and joy they wouldn't care who saw them.

Tears began to form around his eyes as Jeremiah looked down the path in front of him. He felt the cold rush down his spine, numbing his body every second he sat face to face with the years of never-ending loneliness that awaited him. Unless something changed, this would be his future: watching life happen from the side of the road, and not being a part of it.

"I have to grow up now," Jeremiah whispered, talking to himself as he usually did when he was alone, and simple thoughts weren't strong enough to inspire the right actions.

He left his spot by the lake without waiting another minute. He climbed onto his bike and rode to Tom's house as fast as he could.

"Have you decided?" Tom asked when he opened the door.

Jeremiah nodded. "I want to go, but I was wondering if I could make a small request."

Tom winced. "And what's that?"

"I was wondering if Alicia could come with us."

The stunned look on Tom's face made the whole house go quiet. This was not the reaction Jeremiah had hoped for, but he preferred it to the sound of the counselor saying "no" right away. He still had a chance.

"Jer, with all due respect, that's asking quite a lot of me."

"I know," Jeremiah said, feeling guilty for even asking. "I know it's not fair for me to ask this, but she needs this just as much as I do. You're good friends with her dad, right?"

"I see him once a month or so," Tom replied, "but I don't know how safe he would feel about me taking his daughter away for the summer. Why do you want her to come?"

"Because she wants the same things I want. She's just too proud to admit it. That's why she doesn't like making appointments with you.

She acts like she's fine but I know she's doubting herself, and I think this place you're taking me can help her a lot."

"Jer, that's very nice of you, but it's not that simple."

"I know, but it's important. She needs this."

"Does she?"

He spoke with a hint of accusation that shocked Jeremiah into a moment of stunned silence. He could tell Tom regretted speaking this way by the fragile look in his eyes that appeared right after. He looked as if he wanted to apologize, but instead he let the moment pass.

"Jer, I need you to be honest with me," he said, returning to his usual soft, nurturing voice. "Who are you doing this for? Do you want her to come because she needs it? Or do you just not want to be alone?"

Jeremiah broke into a short pause as he tried to find his answer. "A little bit of both, if I'm being honest," he admitted. "I know she acts like she's fine, but I know just from talking to her that she's been lonely for a while. And I know a lot of that is my fault. I was her only friend and I was never around when she needed me. I just want to make things right with her."

Jeremiah couldn't tell if it was his choice of words, the way he spoke, or some combination of the two, but Tom was noticeably affected by this response. His face was free of any emotion. His body went stiff as if all his muscles had turned to stone, and a long stretch of time passed before he spoke again.

"All right, then," Tom said after a heavy sigh. "I'll see what I can do, but I have my own request I need to ask from you."

"Sure. Anything," Jeremiah said.

"Promise me you won't tell her about the girl in the photo."

It took a moment for Jeremiah to see what Tom meant, and once the pieces fell together, his eyes flashed wide open as if he'd seen a bug crawling up his arm. He froze, barely able to draw another breath while his heart beat faster and faster.

"You put your old test results back in your folder when I knew I left them in the drawer with the picture frame," Tom explained.

"I was just trying to look for my old score," Jeremiah said. He spoke faster than normal, as he often did when he was afraid. "I swear I wasn't trying to snoop around."

"I know," Tom said, speaking in his usual calm, assuring voice. "I'm not upset. You were going to learn about her eventually, so I guess you saved me a bit of extra work. Think of it like that."

Jeremiah nodded. "Who is she?"

"Her name is Alexandra Cardor. You'll learn more about her once we get to Parliss County, but right now, I'd rather not talk about her."

Jeremiah could see the bleak look in Tom's eyes when he muttered her name. Even with his quiet voice, the words carried so much weight that Jeremiah almost wished he hadn't asked. He wanted to know more, but he didn't push the counselor to say anything else. He had no room left to ask for favors after his request with Alicia and his benign trespassing in the office cabinet. A less forgiving man would have lost his patience by now. Whatever story there was behind the girl in the picture, it was surely too long and intricate to be told on Tom's doorstep. He remembered how he felt during his last visit to this house, when Tom first told him about the deal, and he tried to find that same level of patience. If he wanted his answers, he'd have to wait until they got to Parliss County.

Jeremiah promised he wouldn't say anything about Alexandra until the time was right. He caught a palpable look of relief in Tom's eyes as he left the house and rode away on his bike. Jeremiah had never seen Tom look and act so vulnerable. Tom was a man who had always been a voice of strength and resilience each day for the last four years, but this had only been one side of him. He was clearly a different man than the one who left Parliss County. He wasn't just the counselor of Laronna anymore, and Jeremiah knew he needed to get used to this. After all, he was leaving for college in just a few months. He needed to learn how to manage himself without Tom whispering advice in his ear every step of the way.

He hoped that a summer with the Auralites would help him get there, and that Alicia would be right by his side.

Chapter Four

The Shrugging Man

There had been a time not too long ago when Tom considered the hardest part of his job to be the first meeting with a new student, and now these days it was the easiest. His many years of practice had sharpened his skills in winning trust, selling himself as a caring, intelligent man who understood and respected the troubles of young people. He knew by now this was his greatest talent, and worried he was about to spend the next few days abusing it.

There was every reason to suspect Alicia would choose to stay in Pritchard Haven for the summer, and yet he wasn't worried. He had the advantage of being an old friend of Alicia's father, a man who already knew bits and pieces of his old life and trusted his skills as a guardian. Tom visited the Scheinbach house after school the following Tuesday to talk with the family. He saw the concern rise in Alicia's eyes as he told them about this strange place up in the north, but the more the counselor spoke, she began not to look so doubtful, and within the hour she agreed to join them.

At first, Tom was impressed by how quickly he'd settled all of this. He marveled in his remarkable success for only a moment as he left the Scheinbach house, but right as he waved goodbye and shut the front door, his pride disappeared and turned into guilt. He felt the cold air racing down his spine as he drove away in his car, and a rotting pain in his gut whenever he thought about Jeremiah or Alicia.

They trusted him, they believed in him, and he had lied his way into a promise he knew he would break.

Tom didn't change his mind as the last few days of spring dragged on. There was too much at stake to turn back after all the work he'd done, so he made all the necessary arrangements and phone calls for their upcoming trip while Jeremiah and Alicia endured their final days at Laronna. He attended their graduation ceremony on the first Sunday of June, alongside his fellow staff members and the many proud parents who clapped and cheered for their sons and daughters. Most of them would be going off to college, forced to wait a few more months in their small town before Autumn came back around to mark the coming of a new adventure, while Jeremiah and Alicia would only need to wait three days.

On Thursday morning, Tom drove to each of their houses and helped them load their bags into the trunk of his car. One by one, Jeremiah and Alicia said goodbye to their parents then piled into the backseat, ready to leave Pritchard Haven. They were half-asleep and barely conscious from waking up so early, their eyes pinned to the nearby windows, watching the trees fly past them as they drove. They kept their eyes open until the forests vanished into a landscape of plains and wheat fields. Signs and billboards began popping up from the sides of the road, which became more common as they drove past the more urban parts of the state.

It wasn't until the sun went down, when the road was lonely and the landscape was once again lush with trees, that Tom knew the drive was almost over. He drove down one empty street after another, with nothing but the light from the nearby lampposts to show him the way. The car shook to the rhythm of the cobblestone road beneath the tires, waking up Jeremiah and Alicia after several hours of resting. Tom kept on driving until he saw a sign for Corraine-Callister Road, which was commonly referred to as Cor-Cal, or the Wide Road. He left the car in a parking lot near a small apartment building, a dirty and unsettling place where they might have been forced to stay if it weren't for the generosity of Gerald Zeeger.

Tom was careful to stick to the eastern side of the Wide Road as he led Jeremiah and Alicia down a few blocks to the Broken Cottage pub. The sign above the door displayed an image of an old grey bird perched in a nest, which had been built in the crevice of a house that was split down the middle. Tom peered through the windows and saw nothing but a pitch-black room without a single customer inside. He knocked on the door, gently at first, but louder after a moment of waiting in the cold air. Then suddenly the lights flashed on and his old friend opened the door to let them inside. He looked about the same as Tom remembered. He was a large man with a big round belly. His hair had lost most of its color, giving him the appearance of a man ten or so years older than Tom, even though they were the same age.

"This is Gerald Zeeger," Tom said. "This is the man I was telling you about. He's letting us stay upstairs in his loft while we're here. Gerald, this is Jeremiah and Alicia."

"It's a pleasure to meet you both," Gerald said, his voice still as gruff as Tom remembered. He shook hands with Jeremiah and Alicia, and then he led them all up the nearby stairs to the loft above his pub.

The loft appeared the same as it had almost a decade ago, further cementing Tom's belief his dear friend hadn't changed much in their years of separation. It was nothing much more than a few bedrooms, a couch where Tom would be sleeping for the next few days, a kitchen for making food, a wooden table for eating said food, and a large cabinet of old books resting against the wall in a spot where most people would have put a TV. The windows at the opposite end of the room offered a great view of East Parliss, where Tom had lived and worked during his time with the Auralites, and had missed dearly in his ten years of absence.

"I can't thank you enough for letting them stay here," Tom said, once he was sure Jeremiah and Alicia had fallen asleep in their new bedrooms. He spoke quietly so he wouldn't wake them up.

"I'm sure you'll try anyway," Gerald said, laughing quietly as he fetched a bottle of red wine from his kitchen then sat across from Tom at the dining table. "That is what you do best: doing what you ought to do no matter how much the rest of us say it can't be done; putting yourself in debt to numbskulls like me who owe you more than we could ever give."

Tom couldn't keep himself from smiling when Gerald spoke the way he did with a few drinks in him. He'd always had an unconventional sense of humor about the sort of things Tom never seemed to notice, and had ways of getting wiser with each sip of alcohol while most men would get dumber.

"Well, what you've done tonight wipes your slate clean, as far as I'm concerned," Tom said.

"Thanks for that," Gerald replied. "I'll take your thanks when thanks aren't worth giving. It's good of you to say it anyway, I suppose. It's the polite thing to do, isn't it? It's funny that we always ought to say 'thanks' and 'sorry' even when we don't need to. That's never felt right to me. Men like you shouldn't be expected to act so low to folks like me who stick to the things we know are easy. Why are we all so damn ashamed to have a bit of pride?"

Tom smiled. "Didn't you tell me once it's always the people who don't apologize who need to the most?"

Gerald glanced off to the side for a moment, searching his memory as best as he could. "It sounds more like one of your little sayings, but perhaps you're right. I might not have the best memory, but when I say something, you can be certain I know what I mean. So, you remember this, Tom, just for my sake: you don't ever need to be shy about asking me for favors. You've got no reason to feel guilty coming here.

"So why are you so guilty?"

Tom had tried to keep his stress hidden behind a blank face and a look of drowsiness he'd achieved after several hours of driving, and yet somehow Gerald was still able to see through his act. His dear friend had always been curiously observant for a man with his drinking habits, which would have been a serious concern of Tom's if he weren't somehow still able to speak and think like a sober man. He would speak at a low volume, like a man who was always tired and at the cusp of falling asleep, but his drinks would never dull his senses.

"I'm about to do something wrong," Tom confessed, lowering his head and resting his clasped hands on the table. "It's irresponsible, it's dangerous; I'd even say it's a little selfish. I thought about it for a long time but I've made my decision, and now I can't turn back."

"I'm listening," Gerald said after a quick pause, a curious glance, and another sip of his wine.

"When I called you a few weeks ago, and I asked if you would mind letting the three of us stay with you, there's something I didn't mention: I won't be staying here. I'll be gone. I don't know for how long, but I know I won't be around enough to look after these two. I'll need you to watch over them for me."

"Why? Where are you going?" Gerald asked, finally starting to show signs of nervousness.

Tom reached into his coat pocket and pulled out an envelope with no return address. He gave it to Gerald, who then reached inside to take out the letter, and read it out loud in a quiet voice:

To the dearest Tom Berrinser,

If you are reading this, you know that I have discovered your new home. I assure you that any sense of dread and panic you might be feeling as a result of this news is completely unwarranted, since I have every intention of being on your side. I suspect you have now looked to the end of this letter for my name and see that I have not given it to you. There's a certain safety in keeping secrets that I don't wish to be rid of until you prove yourself worthy of my trust and patience. I promise there is no need to be afraid, since I am writing this letter as a request for your help, for a cause I believe you will find very intriguing.

I have information about Alexandra Cardor. She and I were close at a time you and she were not, and there are things I know about her that have been a mystery to you for a long time. If at any point you choose to come back to Parliss County, I will share what I know with you, and if you are willing to do the same for me then perhaps you and I can go much further together.

If you decide to come back, call the number written at the bottom of the page. An old friend of yours will be waiting to give you further instructions. All I ask is that you come alone. If I have any reason to suspect you're up to something clever, I'll have no choice but to take back my offer. I promise that is not something you want.

I eagerly await your arrival, whenever it may come. I have nothing but time.

Sincerely,

The Second Counselor of Alexandra Cardor

The letter still stung even when read aloud in Gerald's familiar voice, in one of the few places in Parliss County where Tom still felt welcome. He took the letter from Gerald and stuffed it back in his coat pocket. He didn't want to look at it again for the rest of the night.

"How long have you had this?" Gerald asked.

"Nine years. I found it in my mailbox one morning and never did anything about it until now."

"What's so special about now?"

"I'm not the only one who needs to be here," Tom said, gesturing to the other side of the loft where Jeremiah and Alicia were asleep in their bedrooms. "I've always wanted to come back. I've always wanted to know what this person could tell me, but I always found a way to say no. I told myself for nine years that Pritchard Haven was my new home. I had a job I loved and dozens of students who needed my attention, and I had to put their needs ahead of mine."

"So, you're doing this out of charity?" Gerald asked, with a discernable level of doubt in his voice.

"I'm saying there's a common interest," Tom replied. "All three of us could get what we wanted if we came here. There's no reason why any of us should go home unhappy."

"But the letter told you to come alone."

"Which is why I can't be seen with Jeremiah and Alicia while I'm here. I can't give this person any reason to suspect I broke this one rule, or the deal is off. That's why I need your help."

"I'd say you need a bit more than that," Gerald said, taking another sip of his wine and looking across to the bedroom doors. "Do they know anything about this?"

"No."

"And you're leaving them with a stranger?"

"I'm leaving them with you."

"Is that much better? They don't know me."

"And we have three days to change that before I go," Tom said. "They're old enough that they don't need that much supervision—just someone to give them a place to eat and sleep while I'm gone. Please, I know it's an odd request, but I need your help. I have to do this. I have to know what happened to her."

"Do you?" Gerald asked.

Tom said nothing. Gerald stood up and tossed his empty bottle into the sink, then wandered into the kitchen to fetch another.

"Let me ask you a question," he said, popping the cork as he returned to his seat. "Why are you here? Is it for her or for them?"

"Is there any chance you would let me say both?" Tom asked, afraid of what his honest answer might be if he took the time to think.

"Not this time," Gerald answered. "For your sake, I'd better make sure you pick one."

Tom couldn't remember the last time he'd heard Gerald speak this way. In all their past interactions, Tom had always taken on the role of reason and sensibility, spending his time focused on the important issues of the day while Gerald would find comfort with nothing but a shrug of his shoulders and a drink in his hand. His old friend rarely cared enough about anything to steer away from the lax, carefree nature that governed his life, but even he could make an exception once in a while.

"Didn't you tell me once that picking sides when you don't have to will always lead to trouble?" Tom asked.

"I did, but that's not the only reason they call me the Shrugging Man. Do you know the other one?"

"I do, but I have a feeling you still want to tell me."

Gerald smiled while he raised his bottle in the air as if he were making a toast, and then sunk right back into a reserved and serious demeanor.

"I reckon there are three ways we deal with the things that trouble us," he began, after taking another swig of his drink. "There's your method, which is to solve the problem. The second way, the least healthy way, is to tolerate it no matter how much it hurts you. The third way, my way, is to simply stop caring about it. I find that to be the most helpful. Do you really think the man or woman who sent you this letter is going to help you find Alexandra? Is it worth it to put yourself through all this grief when it might all be for nothing? How do you know this road you're on won't take you somewhere worse?"

"I don't," Tom confessed, before Gerald had the chance to keep talking. "But isn't there just as good a chance this person knows where she is and how I might see her again? Isn't that worth giving it a try?"

"Not when you have them," Gerald said, looking to the bedroom doors across the loft. "They need you, and I think you need them more than you realize. It's not good for you to waste your time thinking about what used to be when there's so much you have now."

"I know," Tom muttered, bowing his head even further, his hands still clasped together. "I shouldn't be doing this, and if this were about anyone besides her, I would agree with you. But it is her, and that changes everything. She was like a daughter to me. I can't go another ten years knowing I had a chance to find her again but I was too scared to take it.

"I'm not asking you to agree with me, Gerald. I'm not even asking for you to understand. I'm just asking that you let me do this."

"Then I will," Gerald said, after a long pause that ended when his mouth bent up in a half-smile. "For all I know, this might even be the right choice. I wouldn't be the one to know. I've never been much good at making up my mind."

Tom shrugged. "You chose to live here. Does that count?"

"Not in Parliss," he grumbled. "You're not exactly standing up for much when you choose to live on the Wide Road. I thought living on the barrier would help me get away from all this nonsense, but I'm not sure that's the case. I still hear those East Parliss and West Parliss talking points from my customers—the same ol' arguments you hear everywhere else. It's the same story every year—everyone trying to prove their decision is right and putting down anyone who says otherwise. That's not the life I intend to live, so I won't be the one to get in your way."

Gerald got off his chair and waddled over to Tom, a strong scent of wine on his breath. There was a tender look on his face as he locked eyes with Tom, then set his hand on the counselor's shoulder.

"I want you to do what you think is right," he said, "just as long as it's for the right reason. Remember that, my friend."

———————

Tom spent the rest of the night on Gerald's couch with anxious thoughts and dreams traversing his mind until the sun came up in the morning. He'd planned on spending these next few days teaching Jeremiah and Alicia how to read an Aurascope, but he decided to let Gerald deliver these final lessons instead, hoping a little extra time with the Shrugging Man would help them adjust to their new caretaker. He expected it would take the full three days before Gerald was no longer a stranger to them, and somehow it only took two. By Saturday night it was as if Gerald had been a distant uncle to them both, and one night later, Tom was confident all three of them would be fine without him.

He waited for Jeremiah and Alicia to fall asleep before he set the final stages of his plan into motion. He opened his bag and withdrew a stack of envelopes, each one containing a letter he'd written over the last few weeks. He kept one for himself but gave the rest to Gerald, who quickly tucked them away in a drawer in his bedroom. Tom pulled the letter out of the envelope in his hands, and then read it one last time.

Jer and Alicia,

I am sorry I didn't tell you about this earlier. I'm rather ashamed of myself I never discussed this with you before we left Pritchard Haven, but I always found a reason to put it off until I gave myself no other choice but to leave you this letter.

There is something I need to do while I'm here in Parliss County.

It's not something I can explain in sufficient detail with just this letter, but I promise I will tell you everything before we return home. I don't know how often I'll be able to see you both, which is why I arranged to have you stay with Gerald, who is a close friend of mine, and a man I would trust with my life. He will look after you while I am away. He will keep you safe, and he will make sure you always have a place to eat and a place to sleep while you're here.

At this point you are both probably wondering what you're supposed to do while I'm away. Don't worry. I've taken care of that. I've spent the last few weeks talking on the phone with all my old friends who live in East Parliss. These are the Auralites I believe you have the most to learn from, and they have generously agreed to meet with you during your stay.

Each Monday for the next three weeks, Gerald will leave both of you a letter. By reading each letter, you will learn information about the person, or people, I arranged to meet with you, and you will also find instructions on how to find them. Your only task is to spend the next seven days learning about the Auralites you meet, listening to their stories, and discovering who they are and who they have become during their time in Parliss County. What you take away from this experience is entirely up to you. As long as you learn something, that is all I can ask for.

I sadly do not have any friends who live in West Parliss, where I would like you to explore during the last three weeks of our stay. Because of this, the only assignment I can give you is to wander around, find a place you like, and try to have a bit of fun with the locals. Hopefully, this little bit of freedom will make up for leaving you so suddenly.

I understand I have no excuse for dropping this news on you without any warning, but I promise I would never abandon either of you if this weren't serious. I will explain everything later, and when I do, hopefully you will understand my point of view.

Best wishes,

Tom

He set the letter down on the couch and threw the envelope in the trash. He stared at their bedroom doors one last time, and then he and Gerald walked down the stairs and stepped out onto the sidewalk. They stood side by side under the dangling sign for a moment as they traded goodbyes and wished each other luck, and then Tom started walking away.

"Wait."

Tom stopped and turned around.

"I just realized you never answered my question," Gerald said. "Why are you back? Her or them?"

"You're not going to like the answer," he replied. "It's both, but not for the reason you think."

"Then what is the reason?"

Tom looked to the nearest window above the Broken Cottage. He thought of Jeremiah and Alicia, who by now were fast asleep in their new bedrooms, and when the moment passed, he looked away and turned back to his old friend.

"I've known these two for a long time now, and none of my advice has gotten them where they want to be. There's nothing else I can do for them, but there might be something I can still do for her. So, I might as well give all my old friends a shot at what I couldn't do and focus my time on the one thing I still might get right."

Gerald looked puzzled. "So, you're leaving to help them?"

Tom nodded. "I was never going to be their counselor forever. At some point, they'll need to know how to go on without me. And I think Parliss County is a good place to start."

Tom said nothing else. He turned around and kept on walking to Allport Drive, while Gerald went back inside to get some sleep.

PART TWO

EAST PARLISS COUNTY

The Colors of Aura

SPECTRUM COLORS

BLUE	CYAN	GREEN	YELLOW	RED
-	-	-	-	-
Deep Order	Moderate Order	Personal Balance	Moderate Passion	Deep Passion

IRREGULAR COLORS

MAGENTA	WHITE
-	-
Color of Conflict	Unified Balance

The Sixteen Rings of the Aurascope: [ii]		
	BLUE-SIDED TRAITS:	RED-SIDED TRAITS:
Ring Sixteen	Attached to the Familiar	Open to Change
Ring Fifteen	Conscientious	Expedient
Ring Fourteen	Forthright	Shrewd
Ring Thirteen	Trusting	Suspicious
Ring Twelve	Confident	Apprehensive
Ring Eleven	Independent	Dependent
Ring Ten	Practical	Imaginative
Ring Nine	Concrete Reasoning	Abstract Reasoning
Ring Eight	Relaxed	Tense

[ii] Based on Raymond Cattell's 16 Personality Factor Model.

Ring Seven	Emotionally Stable	Neurotic
Ring Six	Forceful	Submissive
Ring Five	Tough-Minded	Sensitive
Ring Four	Serious	Carefree
Ring Three	Restrained	Spontaneous
Ring Two	Reclusive	Adventurous
Ring One	Introverted	Extroverted

Chapter Five

The Jennabelle Kids

Part One

Tom was gone when Jeremiah crawled out of bed the next morning. He'd woken up around the same time as Alicia, with the help of the blinding light of an early sunrise, and the sound of Mr. Zeeger rummaging through his cabinet for a bottle of his morning liquor. He saw a letter resting on the couch. He picked it up and read it out loud to Alicia while Mr. Zeeger poured maple syrup on their pancakes. When he finished he felt as if all the breath in his lungs had vanished. He locked eyes with Alicia and found a similar reaction. His legs felt weak, like he could fall onto the couch at any moment, but he stayed standing, wondering where Tom was and why he'd left.

"Where's Tom?" Jeremiah asked as Mr. Zeeger placed the syrup pitcher back on the counter.

"I'm afraid I can't tell you," he replied. "He asked me to keep it private, and I've got to respect his wishes. He's trusting me to look after you two, and I've got to prove his faith in me is well placed."

Jeremiah's chest felt lighter than usual, like someone had sucked the air and blood from his body. For the first time in four years, he couldn't speak to Tom. He couldn't walk to the counselor's office or ride his bike to stop by his house. He was all on his own, a strange fact that weighed heavily on his mind as he looked around Mr. Zeeger's loft.

"Can you at least tell me why he left?" he asked. "Is he in trouble?"

"I'm sorry; I can't say anything. I really wish I could, but Tom asked me to wait until he came back, and that's what I'm going to do."

Jeremiah wanted to stand his ground and ask again and again until he got an answer, but when he opened his mouth to speak, he imagined Mr. Zeeger lashing out at him for his rudeness, and for having the gall to throw a temper tantrum while he was a guest in another man's home. He fell silent as these visions cut into his head. He tried to hold onto the fire he felt brewing in his gut, that fierce curiosity that drove him into the cabinet, but the idea of confronting another person was too much to handle. He had always been a submissive person. During his three days in Parliss County, he'd discovered this trait was represented by the red light that filled the sixth ring of his Aura.

He hoped Alicia would be the one to pressure Mr. Zeeger for answers, but she fell back into silence as well. At that point, he accepted there was nothing else he could do but trust that Tom was doing fine wherever he was, and then try to move along with his day.

He did his best not to think about Tom as he and Alicia enjoyed their breakfast. When they finished eating, Mr. Zeeger gave them each a letter from Tom with instructions about how they would spend their first full week in East Parliss. He returned to the kitchen a moment later after he fetched a pair of shoulder bags from his bedroom, a brown one for Jeremiah and a green one for Alicia. Inside each bag was a journal and a pencil, which they would use to keep notes about the Auralites they met. Each bag also came with a map of Parliss County, but most importantly, they each came with an Aurascope. Tom had given his to Jeremiah, while the one in Alicia's bag had once belonged to Mr. Zeeger, and had spent several years locked away in a box in his bedroom until just a few hours ago.

Jeremiah walked alongside Alicia as they made their way toward the center of East Parliss, spouting his usual weather-watcher comments at each block just to fill the gaps of silence. His weather-watcherness was mostly justified in this one case, since the town streets and landscape came with such a distinct appearance it would be impossible to walk a few steps without mentioning the cobblestone roads, the tall black lampposts on the sidewalk, or the resounding absence of cars or traffic that made it look as if the Auralites only traveled by walking. Small shops and restaurants littered the streets, while all the tallest buildings reached about four or five stories up, each one made from bricks in warm shades of red, brown, and orange like autumn leaves.

It wasn't until they reached the entrance to Littelbine Park that they went their separate ways. Jeremiah stood by for a moment and watched Alicia saunter off down a nearby road to wherever it was she'd been told to go. He then followed the instructions from his own letter and walked to a fountain in a secluded part of the park surrounded by trees and drenched in cool shade. There were two men and two women waiting for him, who all looked to be somewhere in their early thirties. They introduced themselves before suggesting they all go for a walk along the nearby hiking trails that snuck through the park, and Jeremiah agreed without any hesitation.

The four stayed unusually quiet as they all made their way along the trail. They mentioned they were from a nearby town called Sedderberg, and that one of the men, Collin, had once been the captain of their high school's soccer team. In one hour of walking, that was all they said. They walked with their backs perfectly straight, their hands in their pockets, and their heads staring perfectly ahead into the distance like they were statues.

Tom said in his letter that they were all good friends, but from the way they acted, Jeremiah would have never believed it. No one even bothered to make the usual weather-watcher comments he would have made to end the painful silence. He wanted to say something, but each time he opened his mouth, he couldn't find the right words, so he just stayed quiet.

He studied each little detail of their movements just as he'd done with the Donnigan Boys. He mimicked them until they all stopped at the edge of a small pond, at which point he sat down beside them by the shore. He continued to join their silence until Sandra spoke up.

"Hey, look what I found here," she said. Jeremiah leaned forward to get a better view and saw she was holding a small bag about the size of her palm.

"What's inside?" Fletcher asked.

"Just rocks. Little ones," Sandra replied as she pulled one out. "I guess someone left them here and forgot about them. What color would you say this one is?"

"Looks red to me," Collin answered.

"Red," Melanie answered.

"Same here. Red," Fletcher answered.

"Red," Jeremiah replied, even though to him the pebble looked more like light brown.

Sandra pulled a second rock out of the bag. Jeremiah thought it looked turquoise, even though the other four seemed to agree it was normal blue. Jeremiah studied the rock at a few different angles to see if it looked any different, but the color stayed the same in his eyes no matter how he positioned his head. In the end, Jeremiah said it was blue. He figured they could see something he couldn't, and he didn't want to embarrass himself by proving it.

It wasn't until Sandra took a seventh rock out of the bag that the four stopped agreeing with each other, and the more they disagreed, the safer Jeremiah felt giving his honest answers. He didn't understand why they were so interested in these rocks, but he said nothing about it. This little game of theirs was better than sitting around and saying nothing for the whole day, so he took his blessing and followed their lead until the bag was empty.

"How 'bout we all play a game of Silent Captain?" Collin suggested. The other three said that sounded like a great idea, and Jeremiah joined in their chorus of approval as Collin withdrew a deck of playing cards he'd been carrying in his coat pocket.

"Do you know how to play?" Fletcher asked.

Jeremiah came within milliseconds of saying yes, but changed course just in time to say no. There was no use pretending he knew the rules when they were about to play a game. Getting caught in a lie so quickly would just make things worse.

"I wouldn't think so," Collin said. "No one plays it anywhere else but Parliss County. I thought Tom might've played a few games with you before you came here. He was really good at it."

"He didn't," Jeremiah said. "How do you play?"

"That's the tricky part," Collin said with an amused smile. "We can't tell you. That's one of the rules. You have to learn how to play without anyone teaching you."

Jeremiah asked if he could watch them play a game before he tried, but this apparently went against the rules as well. He wondered if this was actually a rule or something they were making up to mess with him, but he joined them for a game anyway.

He quickly discovered the game was a lot like poker, except the hands were different and the players gambled with their own cards instead of chips. They all shouted "Foul" whenever he made an illegal move that needed to be undone, and he quickly lost the first few games before he had a firm enough grasp on the rules and patterns. He finished in third and fourth place for the next few rounds, and he finished second on the last game they played before they decided it was time to go back.

————

They fell into silence once again as they made their way back to the fountain, walking with the same rigid posture despite how friendly and personable they'd all been at the pond. Jeremiah felt as sheepish and awkward around them as he normally did with the Donnigan Boys. The feeling stayed even after he left Littelbine Park, walking back to the Broken Cottage disappointed by his first day out in Parliss County. He hadn't learned anything interesting about these four people, and he had nothing to write about in his new journal apart from the rules to Silent Captain, or at least, all the rules he knew.

Jeremiah wasn't sure what Tom expected him to learn from a day of aimless wandering and playing card games, but he still went back to Littelbine Park the next morning, hoping today might lead to something different. He parted ways with Alicia at the park entrance then walked to the fountain, surprised to see Fletcher was the only one waiting for him. He wore a grey collared shirt and a pair of glasses, while his curly black hair blew to the side in the gentle breeze. He smiled when he saw Jeremiah, which he had not done yesterday.

As Jeremiah walked closer, he saw something behind Fletcher. He leaned to the side to get a better look, and saw a doll sitting on the edge of the fountain. Her skin was made of beige felt, with small green buttons as eyes, and hair made from strands of red and purple yarn tightened into one long braid that hung down to the heels of her feet. She wore a bright blue dress and black plastic shoes, and as her mouth, she had one thin strand of black yarn stitched into a U shape, making for a silly but endearing smile.

"You probably noticed we were all acting a little weird the other day," Fletcher said. "That's because yesterday was all part of a test. You just didn't know it was happening. We wanted to see how you responded to situations that promoted conformity."

A spark went off in Jeremiah's mind as he watched Fletcher pull the bag of colored rocks from his pocket. Second by second, the pieces all fell together, as Jeremiah looked back on yesterday's events and understood what he'd missed.

"You were lying about the colors."

Fletcher nodded. "Sandra had the bag with her the whole time. The goal was to see if you'd give your honest answers, or if you'd lie in order to fit in with the rest of us. The long, silent walks were supposed to ramp up the pressure. We wanted to see how you'd react to being the odd one out, if you'd embrace it, or try to match the rest of us."

"And what about the card game?"

"That was just for fun," Fletcher said, smiling. "Though, I suppose it went along with the same theme: noticing patterns and following rules—all that stuff."

A heavy sigh escaped through Jeremiah's lips as he lowered his head, embarrassed by all the clues he'd missed. "I'm guessing I didn't pass any of these tests, right?"

"These tests aren't about passing or failing," Fletcher replied, smiling once again to help lighten the mood. "They're built to show you what that kind of pressure does—good or bad."

Fletcher sat down on the edge of the fountain and tapped the spot next to him. When he insisted this wasn't a test, Jeremiah wandered over and sat beside him.

"Let me ask you a question," Fletcher continued as he adjusted his glasses. "What does conformity mean to you?"

"Giving up on what you like and what you value just to fit in with a group of people," Jeremiah answered.

"And how do you know your values are the right ones?" Fletcher asked. "What if I don't like the way you look and I decide to kick you in the knee just because of that. Would that be fair?"

"No, of course not," Jeremiah said, stammering while he tried to rephrase his answer. "I guess what I meant was that you should be who you want to be as long as you don't hurt someone else, and you shouldn't let other people decide what you do."

"Fair enough," Fletcher said. "So, if you're in school, and the teacher wants you to raise your hand to ask for permission to speak, is it okay to ignore this rule and blurt out your questions whenever you want?"

"No," Jeremiah replied, already seeing how the rest of this conversation would go. There was a counter point waiting on the edge of Fletcher's tongue for every answer he could give. "Look, I'm a little confused. What are you trying to say?"

"I'm saying there's no real answer. Like I said, this isn't about passing or failing. Most people see conformity as a bad thing, like you're giving up the most important parts of yourself to fit with what the rest of your culture expects from you. And sometimes that's true. It can kill our sense of independence, or tell us that what we believe is wrong. But that's the tricky part: Sometimes, we are wrong, and if no one else is around to let us know that, we just keep making the same mistakes until we pay for them. That's why it isn't always such a bad thing. It's how we learn manners, and how we learn to deal with other people who are different from us. We conform every day just by walking on the sidewalk instead of down the middle of the road. Conformity isn't all bad. We're just trained to think it is."

"But it's not always good either," Jeremiah said, remembering his time with the Donnigan Boys.

"I know," Fletcher said. "That's what makes it so tricky. How do we know when it's right and when it's wrong? How do we find the good inside the bad? How do we strike the right balance? It's not easy, but it's a good skill to have, and it's a skill the four of us have been practicing for years. Do you have Tom's Aurascope in that bag of yours?"

"Yeah, I do."

"Let me hold it for a moment," Fletcher said. "Then you'll see what I mean."

Jeremiah dug the Aurascope out from the bottom of his bag and gave it to Fletcher. Once again, a dazzling array of bright, colored lights appeared behind the crystal-glass. Jeremiah reached inside his bag a second time for his journal and pencil so he could make a detailed record of the colors of all sixteen rings, despite being told to focus only on the four that were green: Introvert vs. Extrovert, Relaxed vs. Tense, Forceful vs. Submissive, and Tough vs. Sensitive.

"Green light is a sign of Personal Balance," Fletcher said. "That's what the Auralites call it. I wasn't always like this. If you looked at my colors about fifteen years ago, you would think I was a whole different person, and the other three would say the same. We all helped each other get where we are today, and that's the story we're here to tell you.

"My part of the story comes first. That's why I'm here today."

———————

Before Fletcher began his story, he suggested they go for a walk down one of the trails in Littelbine Park. He picked up the doll and gave her to Jeremiah, who took a moment to admire the strange little thing once he finished tucking his journal and the Aurascope back inside his shoulder bag. As they started to walk, he held the doll with one hand and let his arm dangle as if he were carrying a briefcase, but as he looked down and saw he was holding her by the neck, he decided to hold her up against his chest with both arms as if he were carrying a toddler.

"Her name's Jennabelle," Fletcher said, once they escaped the shade of the trees and could feel the sun shining down above them. "I made her when I was fifteen—when all four of us were starting high school."

"Why did you make her?" Jeremiah asked, curious as to why a fifteen-year-old boy would have any interest in dolls.

"She was a birthday gift for Sandra," he replied. "I'd been friends with her for years before we ever started high school, but I never fell in love with her until I turned fifteen. Something in me just snapped, you know? I can't really explain it, but it was real. I just started seeing her differently—the way she walked, the way she smiled, even the way she dressed. I couldn't stop thinking about her, and one day, just a few weeks before her birthday, I decided to do something about it."

Jeremiah looked down at the doll in his arms. "Did she like her?"

"She did for a while, but, as you can expect, there's only so much fun you can have with a doll when you're that old. She hugged Jennabelle when I gave her away, smiled about how cute she was, but, eventually, the novelty wore off. Sandra just put her on the bookshelf and stopped paying attention to her a few days after the party."

"Did you ever say anything to her?" Jeremiah asked.

Fletcher shook his head. "I was too scared. That's why I made Jennabelle in the first place. I was really shy when I was younger. People said I was super quiet, even when I tried not to be. I was one of those kids who always sat around lots of people and wanted a bunch of friends, but I never found anything clever to say when I needed to, so I always ended up on the sidelines until they got bored of me. I was built to be alone, but Sandra, she was the opposite. People always liked to be around her. She had that kind of spirit that just drew people in. She was always laughing, always smiling, and she was never alone. We balanced each other out pretty nicely as kids, but as we got older, once our little world opened up and threw us both into our teenage years, we slowly started going our separate ways. I thought Jennabelle was a sure way to win her over, but my plan didn't work."

Jeremiah understood all too well how it felt to be the one in this spot. He didn't have to look too long to remember just one of the many times he'd walked past Casey Marsley or Ethan Kantzton on his way to class, raised his hand to wave hello and then segued into brushing his hair when they ignored him, trying to salvage what credibility he had by pretending this was his plan all along. Most of his conversations with the Donnigan Boys were nothing more than long hellos and quick goodbyes. On a lucky day, they would notice him when he said hello, and Jeremiah could sit with their group and listen to them chat about their day, laugh at their jokes, and chime in with a weather-watcher comment whenever he saw an opening, but when their conversation came to an end, when the bell rang and a new class was about to start, Jeremiah was alone again. Nothing he ever said or did remained a part of his permanent record. He had to win them over every day, and most of his work never paid off.

"I think you and I would've gotten along pretty well," Jeremiah muttered.

"So do I," Fletcher said, grinning slightly. "Tom said you used to be a very talented artist. He said when you were in seventh grade, you liked to draw weird creatures in your sketchpad. You'd give them names and come up with all these facts about where they lived, what they ate, and other little details like that. Is that true?"

"Yeah, it is," Jeremiah said, though he hadn't seen that old sketchpad for several years. As far as he knew, it was hidden somewhere under his bed or inside his closet back home.

"People always assume that artist types are very sensitive," Fletcher said, looking away from the path to stare at Jeremiah. "Are you an exception to the rule?"

"I'm afraid not," he replied, looking back on a long list of experiences he could have used as proof. A single disappointment could linger on for a whole day, whether it came in the form of a low grade on a test or getting snubbed by Ethan Kantzton on their way to class. One misstep could haunt him for hours, dragging him down into the pit of doubt that surrounded him every day, stirring up the sort of glum and dour attitude that most adults would dismiss as melodrama.

"It feels real, doesn't it?" Fletcher said. "That's the tricky part when you're that young: People don't think it's real. Some say it's nothing but angst. Some tell you just to hang in there, and they promise it'll get better when you're older. It's not until you're older that most people start thinking about your problems the way you want them to. That's when they start looking for the real solutions. Not a lot of young people get real solutions. I loved Sandra a lot, I really did, and when I knew she didn't feel the same way, it was like my wife had left me after we'd been married for all these years. That was how it felt to me, but not to anyone else."

"I'm sorry. I'm sure that was hard," Jeremiah said in a soft, muted voice, barely louder than a whisper. "But, I guess it all worked out in the end. You're both friends now, right?"

Fletcher smiled. "Yes, we are. Very good friends."

"How?" Jeremiah asked. "How did you get over her?"

"Collin helped me," he replied. "Aside from Sandra, I've known him longer than anyone else. One day, we were walking home together, and I started rambling on and on about her. I'm not even sure what I said, but it doesn't matter, because before I talked for too long, he did the nicest thing he'd ever done: He told me to shut the hell up."

This wasn't the friendliest bit of advice, or the most supportive, and yet Fletcher smiled as the memory came back to him. Somehow, the last several years had made this difficult time in his life more bearable.

"That seems a little rude of him, doesn't it?"

"Yes and no," Fletcher said.

Jeremiah never liked these kinds of answers. He nearly rolled his eyes but he stopped himself just in time as Fletcher kept talking.

"Friends are there to support you. The good ones listen, the better ones listen longer, but the best ones help you get better when nothing else is working. Sometimes that means being a little too honest. He said we can only tread water for so long before we swim out of the pool, and if I couldn't do it myself then he was going to help me."

"But it's not that easy," Jeremiah protested, remembering all the times he'd come home from school after a lousy day, when his parents told him to stop being so upset, as if he could change his mood by flipping a switch. "People can't get happy just because they want to. It's harder than that."

"You're right," Fletcher said. "It's like I said earlier: When you're young, most of your problems don't feel real to anyone but you. They can weigh on you a lot, and not a lot of people will pay attention. It's hard to deal with, but it's even harder when you're not even trying to help yourself. That was my biggest problem. I wasn't helping myself. I was too focused on the bad and not on something better. That's where Collin came in. I needed something else to focus on, and he helped me find it. He convinced me to join the school soccer team."

For the rest of their walk, Jeremiah listened as Fletcher spoke about his time on the team. He'd gotten off to a rough start, labeled as the weakest player on the team, distracted by thoughts of Sandra cutting into his head whenever he stepped onto the field. He constantly wanted to quit but he always found a way to stay and support the team, and Collin was always with him. He was never without the help of his best friend, the voice of discipline, the only one who could strike the right balance between kind and tough. He could give Fletcher a shoulder to lean on, and then rush him out onto the field to do his job.

Fletcher said it was a long and difficult road, one filled with plenty of low points and game-losing errors that broke him down one after the other, but day by day, things started to get better. His head felt clearer, his legs felt stronger, and the will to win was greater than ever. Soon enough, any and all thoughts of Sandra disappeared the moment he set his sights on the ball. His once broken heart put itself together when the coach blew the whistle, refusing to let anything distract him from the task at hand.

With time and practice, Sandra became nothing but a memory, and he began to accept he was just one of the millions of men who would grow up to never marry his high school sweetheart. The truth didn't hurt so much, and as the months went by, it hurt even less.

"How did you become friends with Sandra again?" Jeremiah asked, still wondering how this strange group of four ever came to be.

"That's a story for another day," Fletcher said. Jeremiah had a feeling this would be his answer. "My story doesn't go that far."

"Then how far does it go?"

He shrugged. "I suppose it ends here. There isn't much else I can say that would add to my journey. I played soccer for almost two years, learned how to toughen up a bit, and then I quit the team."

Jeremiah looked shocked. "You quit? How come?"

"I got into a bad fight with Collin," he replied. "It was just a few days after he broke up with Mel, but you'll hear more about that later. That's not my part of the story to tell."

———   ———   ———   ———

Jeremiah had several questions he wanted to ask by the time they'd made a full lap around the park, but he knew each of them would have to wait until later. He let go of Jennabelle and gave her back to Fletcher, and then he waved goodbye and walked back to the Broken Cottage.

He came back to Littelbine Park the next morning and saw Sandra by herself in a red summer dress. Even from a distance, he was able to spot her long black hair blowing in the faint breeze, and her rich brown skin that glistened like copper when she stood in the sun. Once again, Jennabelle was resting by the fountain. He admired the doll a second time as he reached into his bag and took out the Aurascope, and then he gave it to Sandra.

As her fingers wrapped around the crystal-glass, Jeremiah could see her imagination, her social nature, her passion for adventure, and all the other lovely traits he'd learned about the other day. She directed Jeremiah's attention to the third and fourth rings of her Aura, the places that measured Restraint vs. Spontaneity, and Serious vs. Carefree. These were the rings Sandra said had once been pure red but were now a vivid green, marking the end of a journey as a wild, careless young girl, who became a woman with the capacity for restraint and empathy.

"I was full of energy when I was a kid," Sandra said once they began their walk around the park, as Jeremiah held the doll close to his chest. "I was always laughing and giggling about something, and I could never sit still for too long without wanting to go somewhere else. I never could tell when people needed time alone, or when they just weren't in the mood to do what I wanted. When I was ten, I would drag Fletcher out with the rest of our classmates to play our made-up games when we had time off from school, and I never noticed when he was feeling shy. I was always off having too much fun to see it. I was a kid who always had something to say, and he was always there to listen. That's why I liked him so much."

"But you were different," Jeremiah said, already aware of this part of the story from yesterday.

"Yeah, we were," Sandra replied. "It just didn't matter to me yet. It wasn't something either of us did wrong. We just slowly ran out of things to talk about. He was always fine being by himself; I always wanted to be with people. One day, I picked up on this and just didn't bother asking him to play with us. I didn't ask him the next day either, or the next day, and pretty soon I had a whole new set of friends without him."

"I'm sorry," Jeremiah muttered, doing his best to stick with Sandra while his mind drifted off to thoughts of Alicia, taking him back to how close they'd been during her first few months at the school, before he fell back into the lap of the Donnigan Boys.

"Friends don't always last," Sandra continued, "but like I said, it's not always someone's fault. I had my own friends and they were the people I liked to be with. The part I regret is that I stopped caring about him completely. Losing him was like losing a nice scarf, or a keychain. I didn't care that I'd lost him 'cause I had ten other friends I could be with any day I wanted, but losing me was hard for him. He made Jennabelle for me 'cause I was still important to him, and I put her on my bookshelf and never bothered to look at her. My friends would even tell jokes about what a weird gift she was, and I would laugh with them."

The more Sandra spoke, the more Jeremiah felt like he was talking with one of the Donnigan Girls, the sort of person who could always find a way to laugh and be happy, and who spent most of her time caught up with her friends while blind to everyone else. She wouldn't notice the people like him, the Fletchers and the Alicias, those who wanted nothing more than a friend and would take any chance they could to find one.

He remembered the first time he laid eyes on Alicia, the pale-skinned girl with the brass blonde hair he once only knew as the girl who'd moved to the United States from Germany. She'd been standing outside the school auditorium on a cool September morning, holding the door open as all the other students drifted inside to gather for their start-of-the-year assembly. She was the new girl in school, a girl with no friends, already doing her best to earn some good will by letting everyone else in before her. Jeremiah knew she would have stayed outside until she was the last one left, but he didn't feel right about leaving the new girl out in the cold, so he waved to get her attention and pointed to the doorstop next to her feet. He kicked it down to prop the door open, and then he went inside with Alicia.

Jeremiah didn't know at the time how much this moment would set the tone for the next two years Alicia would spend at her new school. Dozens of students had entered the room before her. Any of them could have seen the doorstop and kicked it down, but no one did. They'd been too busy chatting with their friends to notice a fellow classmate standing out in the cold autumn breeze, generously letting them go inside ahead of her, not getting a shred of gratitude from those she hoped would one day be her friends.

He imagined Sandra's younger self sitting next to the Donnigan Girls, chatting away in a small cluster, paying no attention to the new girl holding the door open, and she seemed like a perfect fit. She would have been a great addition to their club, but he had to remember Sandra was not the same woman she'd been her first year of high school. All four of them had changed, and Sandra's story wasn't over yet.

"Did you know he used to be in love with you?" Jeremiah asked.

"Not for a long time," Sandra confessed. "I didn't know about that or any of the drama with Mel until this one day when I saw Collin eating by himself in the school cafeteria. I sat with him and I asked why he looked so glum, and then he told me everything."

"How did you react to that?" Jeremiah asked, wondering how he would handle this sort of news if he wound up in this position one day.

"It didn't mean much to me at first," Sandra said. "Ironically, that was part of the problem. We used to be friends. He made a doll for me as a birthday gift, and I didn't care at all that I'd broken his heart. I shrugged it off like it was nothing, but over the next few weeks, I started to feel differently."

"Why?"

"Because of Jennabelle. From that day on, every time I was in my room, I started to notice her more. She didn't look any different, but she felt different. She didn't feel like a doll to me anymore. She started to feel like a living thing, like a baby I'd stuffed inside my closet and was leaving to die. I felt guilty, and it got worse every single day for almost two months. And then I had the dream."

Jeremiah's eyes widened. "The dream?"

Sandra nodded. "I'd just come back from school and saw someone had broken into my room. The windows were shattered, my clothes were all torn up, and somehow Jennabelle was on the ground. She was on fire. She was talking, too. Her lips didn't move but I could hear her voice from inside. She was begging for help, but all I did was hide in my closet and let her burn until the voice went away.

"I woke up immediately after the fire was gone, and I ran to my closet to see if Jennabelle was okay. I know this might seem silly, but as soon as I found her, I picked her up and told her I was sorry, and I spent the rest of the night sleeping with her in my arms."

Jeremiah could hear the sound of Sandra's voice deepen with each word, until they were left in silence. He watched as a small tear emerged from her right eye and trickled down her cheek, proving the night of the dream was still a hard memory after all these years.

"It was a long night," Sandra muttered, starting to rebuild her composure. "But I'm glad it happened, because the next morning I told myself I could never let that happen again. I had to start caring, not just for Jennabelle, but for everyone. So, I started spending a little less time with my old friends and tried to make room to hang out with Collin. I was the only friend he had left at the time. He didn't have Fletcher, or Mel, or anybody else from his soccer team. He needed me, and I promised I would be there for him. By the end of that year, he was my new best friend."

Jeremiah looked out at the path in front of him. He imagined the younger versions of Sandra and Collin walking side by side, all alone in a desolate park while the rest of their classmates were off somewhere else. They had no one but each other, but that was all they needed. He thought about Alicia standing by the door, and he smiled.

"Were you still happy?" Jeremiah asked.

Sandra nodded. "Yes, I was. Why wouldn't I be?"

"Well, it just seems like you had such a good life until all this. I mean, you had all the friends you could want, everyone liked you, you were happy all the time; why did you want all that to change?"

"I didn't," Sandra said, with a bright smile. "I'm still the same girl I used to be, just better. I still love to have fun, I still tell jokes, I still go to parties, and I want everyone around me to be having a good time. The only difference is that the old me didn't have the patience to be with people who didn't already feel like that. If I had to go out of my way to make someone happy, it wasn't worth it. I couldn't be a good friend unless it was convenient for me. That was what needed to change.

"That's why I came to East Parliss. That's why I tried to be a good friend to Collin. That's why I took care of Jennabelle for as long as I could, until I eventually gave her away."

"You gave her away?" Jeremiah said, raising his voice out of shock while he wondered why she would do something like this.

Sandra nodded. "I gave her to Mel. She needed her more than I did, but she'll tell you about that later."

Chapter Six

The Jennabelle Kids

Part Two

Jeremiah didn't know the difference between being tense and being apprehensive, and felt a little cheated to see two bright crimson rings in his Aura when one would have been plenty. He could only guess that one had to do with a lack of confidence while the other was a sign of internal stress, both of which had raised a cloud above his head for far too long.

He remembered the first time he and Alicia went to Shangrin Lake together. It was an early December day. The Scheinbachs had lived in Pritchard Haven for about three months, and Alicia's father had recently bought a canoe at a yard sale. Alicia had asked if Jeremiah wanted to take it out on the water, figuring it would be a fun way to spend a few hours of the upcoming Saturday. Jeremiah may have said yes right away if this were any other time of the year, but winter had begun to show itself in the cold winds and cloudy skies. One misstep or a strong breeze at the wrong moment could send him into the icy water. He felt his skin turn cold as he imagined his rise to the surface, gasping for breath as he reached out with his shivering hands for the side of the boat, and even when he climbed back aboard, he would be forced to sit in soggy clothes until they returned to shore.

Despite this, Jeremiah agreed to go. He rode his bike to the lake that following Saturday, pleased to see the blue sky above him, and to feel the calm winds brushing against his hair. The cold winter air had taken a break this one day, as if the invisible nature spirits of Pritchard Haven were rewarding him for his small act of courage. He and Alicia cruised off the shore and paddled out toward the center of the lake, listening to the leaves blow in the wind, and watching the fish swim under the boat. Alicia kept him entertained with stories about Germany, and as usual, Jeremiah chipped in once in a while with his weather-watcher comments.

It'd been a rare occasion when something good came from doing something he had originally not wanted to do. If it weren't for Alicia's love of adventure, his fear of falling into the frigid water would have gotten the best of him. This great day would have never happened, and he and Alicia may not be the friends they were now. Ironically, he'd also repressed the same emotions to follow the Donnigan Boys, and he had suffered because of it.

He thought about what Fletcher said about the fickleness of conformity. He wished there were a way it could be easier to know when it was right and when it was wrong.

— — — — —

When he returned to Littelbine Park the next day, he found Collin waiting for him by the fountain. He was easy to spot because he was the tallest of the four, and had bright blonde hair that stood out in the shade. He asked for Jeremiah to lend him the Aurascope, and then to pay close attention to a specific group of rings that had changed during his time in East Parliss: Serious vs. Carefree, Tough vs. Sensitive, and Forceful vs. Submissive. As Jeremiah expected, these rings had slid to the middle of the spectrum and were now infused with green light.

Jeremiah made his notes and then tucked his belongings inside his bag. He took Jennabelle and held her against his chest, as he'd done the last two days, and then followed Collin down a nearby path.

"I was a lot more competitive than the other players," Collin said, once they began their walk down the nearest path. "That's why most of them didn't like me that much. Playing wasn't enough by the time I was fifteen. I needed to win, and I didn't have any patience for people who were only there to have fun. Even when I was too young to be captain, I still acted like I was in charge. I'd always let the coach know when the older kids were screwing around, and I always made sure our breaks didn't last too long."

"Did you have any friends on the team?" Jeremiah asked, figuring he already knew the answer.

"Not until Fletch came along," he replied. "I didn't care much about friends back then. He was the only one I needed."

There was a short pause before Jeremiah spoke again, as he noticed the sullen look taking over Collin's eyes and the deepening of his voice.

"He told me you two had a fight."

"I've been in fights with a lot of people," Collin confessed, his voice filled with regret as the memories came back one by one. "It didn't matter if I was on or off the field. I was a competitor, and I always wanted to win."

Collin released a heavy sigh, and the long gap of silence that followed was a sign this part of his story was the hardest to tell. For Collin, this was the September of his second year in high school, the time when the signs of adolescence crept into consciousness, stealing his focus away from his lifelong passion for soccer and onto the world of women and dating. He said he'd grown close to a girl named Melanie, who sat next to him in his biology class. After a few months of meeting up at a nearby café, they committed to a long-term relationship, which came with the unfortunate consequence of leaving Fletcher at the bottom of their little group.

Collin confessed he didn't understand how lonely his friend felt at the time. He could still remember kissing Melanie at her sixteenth birthday party, and the sound of shattering glass as Fletcher accidentally smashed a nearby jar of candy in frustration.

"Mel and I used to fight all the time," he said. "To be honest, I barely even remember what they were all about. I'm sure if I could remember, I'd think they were pretty stupid. But maybe that was the problem all along. I thought they were dumb and she thought they were important. I remember one time she got some really bad grade on a math test and I told her she was overreacting, and that this was nothing to be scared about. That really made her mad, but, again, I didn't see that. We just saw the world a lot differently than each other. That's how all the arguing started."

"Did you ever love her?" Jeremiah asked.

"I think I did at first," Collin said, pausing for a moment to consider his answer. "But honestly, I think I stayed with her just because I didn't want to be alone. That's why I was so angry when we broke up. I acted like it was all her fault. Fletcher confronted me about this, and said I needed to stop acting like a brat, but I was too damn defensive to listen. I lashed out at him for taking her side instead of mine. We traded a few insults back and forth, and from that point on, he didn't want anything to do with me. He quit the team, he stopped talking to me, but that wasn't even the worst part."

"What happened next?" Jeremiah asked, holding his breath in anticipation.

Collin smirked. "A few weeks later, he and Mel started dating."

"Ouch," Jeremiah said, trying his best to grasp how hard it would have been for Collin to see these two together, holding hands and kissing by one of their lockers, while he strolled past all by himself.

"I can't begin to tell you how much I hated him," Collin said, "so I'm not going to try. You get the idea. In just a few days, he went from being my best friend to my sworn enemy. I lost my girlfriend and my best friend all at once. I was all on my own."

The sad look on Collin's face was so infectious that Jeremiah felt his stomach grow cold as they continued to march along the path. His chest stayed warm with the help of Jennabelle nestled between his arms, but the rest of his body felt stiff and numb, as if he'd just climbed out of bed and wanted to go back to sleep. He thought about the Skydiver Incident, the closest he'd ever come to losing a good friend. He'd never heard Alicia shout once in their two years of friendship, and yet the sound of her screaming felt too precise to come from nowhere. Second by second, the fight he'd been lucky enough to escape came back. He was losing his best friend, his only friend, and as the pain in his stomach grew worse, he shut his eyes and remembered Collin and the rest of his friends standing by the fountain, and then he didn't feel so bad. It was the one central theme to all of their stories. Somehow, despite whatever happened in high school, they were all still friends today. They'd found their way back to one another, and they were better people because of it. Their story wasn't over.

"How did you and Fletcher become friends again?"

"It was because of Jennabelle," Collin answered, now speaking in a gentler voice. "This was around the time when Sandra was really protective of her. She started talking about her a lot more and I got really sick of it. I was sick of anything that reminded me of Fletcher, including Jennabelle. One day I got so angry I almost did something Sandra never would've forgiven me for. She invited me to her house one day after practice to study for a test. I snuck into her bedroom and stuffed Jennabelle in my bag when she wasn't looking. I was going to throw her into the lake by my house. I was just about to let her go, but then I stopped. I don't know how to explain it. It was like she came alive, like I was about to drown a child over some stupid feud with my best friend. My hands started shaking, and before I even knew what I was doing, I just stepped back and held Jennabelle close to me. I looked at her, and then I started crying."

"What happened with Sandra?" Jeremiah asked. "Did you ever tell her?"

Collin nodded. "I kept waiting for her to say she didn't want to be my friend anymore, but she forgave me anyway. I thought that would make everything better, but it just made me feel more ashamed of myself. I couldn't fall asleep that night. I kept thinking about Mel. I wondered if all our fights really were my fault, and if Fletcher was right all along to say that stuff about me. I went to school the next day and saw how happy those two were together, and suddenly I wasn't mad at them anymore. I was just mad at myself. I didn't like who I was, and I knew if I wanted to be happy, I needed to change."

Collin said he knew it wouldn't be easy to change his reputation with his teammates, and yet he promised to try anyway. He spent the next several months acting like a true member of the team, putting aside all his old rules about the importance of discipline and switching his mind to the purpose of having fun and offering support when it was needed. He cheered with the rest of the team when a player scored a goal or made some other spectacular play, and by the end of the season he'd taken up the coach's job of giving pep talks at the start of each game. His reputation began to shift as the months dragged on, and at the start of his fourth and last year of high school, he'd been named captain by a unanimous vote.

"What about Fletcher and Melanie?" Jeremiah asked. "How did you fix things with them?"

"That's not my part of the story to tell," Collin replied. "You'll hear about that tomorrow."

Somehow, Jeremiah already knew this would be the response, but he figured it was worth a shot anyway. He was too curious for his own good. Unanswered questions and unfinished stories were the two best ways to keep him awake in bed at night. Tom had given him plenty of these in just the last few days. Nevertheless, when they arrived at the fountain, he thanked Collin for this story, let go of Jennabelle, and said goodbye as he left Littelbine Park, already counting down the hours until his next visit.

— — — — —

The next day, he saw Melanie waiting for him by the fountain. She was dressed mostly in black, and her auburn hair glistened in the sunlight shining down from an opening in the nearby treetops. She asked for the Aurascope and pointed Jeremiah to the rings that had turned green since her time in high school. She had found Personal Balance in the rings of Toughness vs. Sensitivity, Relaxed vs. Tense, Confident vs. Apprehensive, Independent vs. Dependent, and Stable vs. Neurotic. It was the highest number of changes he'd seen so far, leading him to suspect this fourth and final story would be the best of them all.

Once again, he found Jennabelle sitting by the fountain, and held her tight within his arms as he and Melanie began their walk. She chose to begin her part of the story with a brief but efficient summary of her lonely childhood. She shared a few memories of her bickering parents and her father's abusive behavior, both of which had left a mark on their daughter that would show in her later years. From a young age, she'd been forced to abandon the childish behavior her father found so irritating, sculpting her into a woman in the body of a child. Days had gone by when she never uttered a single word while inside her house, afraid that stepping out of line for even a moment could end with reduced time with the TV or a smack in the face.

"I didn't expect a lot from my parents," she admitted, "but I expected a lot from my friends. I kept my home life a secret from almost everyone, but when I did let someone in on my secret, it was only because I trusted them, and because I needed them. I needed their love and attention, and I was willing to do anything I could to get it, even if I had to rely on sympathy. When I felt like I had no choice, when I couldn't go anywhere else, I just dumped all my problems at their doorstep and hoped they would know what to do."

"I'm guessing Collin and Fletcher were some of those people, right?" Jeremiah asked.

Melanie nodded. "I told Collin about my father after we started dating. One day I told him I didn't want to talk about my childhood, so we didn't. The next day I waited for him to ask anyway just to see how I was doing. The day after that, I accused him of not caring enough about me, so then he started coddling me like I was a baby and making sure I was fine and happy, but I got sick of that in just two days. By the end of the week, we were right back where we started. That's how it always was. Not just with him, but with everyone."

"That sounds rough," Jeremiah said. "For both of you, I mean. My parents don't fight that often, so I don't really know what it's like to see something like that."

"It's not easy," Melanie said. "But it's also not an excuse for the way I acted. I was sixteen. I was old enough to know how to talk about my problems. I should've known to take responsibility for my actions, but I never did. Nothing was ever my fault; it was always someone else's."

According to Melanie, the time she'd spent with Collin reached its limit within four months, while her time with Fletcher stretched out more than a year. Fifteen months went by before any real tensions emerged between them, quickly setting the record for the longest amount of time someone had gone without disappointing her in some way. Fletcher had reached a standard that had never been set, and with that came higher expectations he couldn't reach.

"I would talk to him anytime my parents were fighting, and he would listen. I would talk to him whenever my parents got mad at me, and he still listened. When I was sad and miserable, he was there to let me cry without judging me, and when I was angry he was always right there. I took all my frustration out on him, and when he tried to comfort me, I would shout back and tell him he didn't know how hard it was to live like this. One day he got sick of being my punching bag, and that was the day he finally pushed back. The last thing he said to me before he left was that I was going to end up all by myself one day, crying in some dark corner with no one around to love or help me, and I would have no one to blame but myself."

Melanie said it didn't take too long for Fletcher's parting words to show some hint of truth, since her dad left their family just one month later, and a family that had lasted more than eighteen years together at the edge of a cliff had finally toppled. Her brothers dealt with their father's absence by staying away from their house and spending as much time as they could with their friends, while her mother had taken to drinking any day she came home after an extra shift at work. Whatever friends Melanie used to have were gone by the time she needed them most, and so she was left with no one but herself.

She lay down in her bed with the lights on so Fletcher's vision of the future couldn't come true entirely, but in the absence of all her friends and family, she finally began to question how much of this was her own fault. Her body shook with guilt when she looked into her past. Tears slid down her red, shattered face as she screamed into her pillow, seeking forgiveness from those who weren't around to listen.

Jeremiah remained patient as Melanie shut her eyes and fell into silence. He could feel the weight of her memories, the pain she wore on her face as she relived this night, trying her best to stay strong and finish her story no matter how many ghosts she took with her.

"I didn't blame myself for my dad leaving," she muttered, once she felt ready to speak. "That's no one's fault but his own. But I blamed myself for everything else. There was one night when I was lying awake in my bed, and I heard someone knock at the door. I hoped Fletcher had come back so I could say how sorry I was. I would've even liked if Collin came back so I could do the same for him. But it wasn't either of them. It was Sandra. She came up to my room with a doll and asked if I was doing all right. She told me how sad she was to hear that my dad left. She told me about this doll that Fletcher made her a few years back as a birthday gift, and how he would want me to have it now. I told Sandra I didn't want it, and I told her to get out, but she didn't leave until I took Jennabelle."

Melanie said she'd set Jennabelle on the top shelf of her closet, the place she would have kept her dolls if she'd grown up with any. She then lay down in her bed with the lights off as she tried to fall asleep, but she always wound up with her eyes wide open and the rest of her body tangled in the sheets. She walked over to the closet, took Jennabelle from her place on the shelf, then climbed back in bed and cuddled the poor thing in her arms, whispering into her felt ears that she would take care of her.

She went on to sleep with the little doll each night for the next few months, like a young girl taking on the role of a mother to offer a home to something so small and helpless that needed a grown woman's love and wisdom to stay alive. She wished Fletcher could see her as she was now, if only to prove she wasn't so heartless, and had the capacity to love without asking for anything in return.

"I skipped school one day in spring, a couple weeks after Sandra came to see me," Melanie said. "I needed a day off in order to get my thoughts straight. I took a bus up north, and I brought Jennabelle with me. I took her to this spot right here."

Jeremiah was so caught up in Melanie's story he hadn't bothered to pay attention to where they were until now. They were standing a few steps away from an empty playground, complete with swings, a slide, and a set of monkey bars that were too high up off the ground for a kid to reach without the help of a parent. He sat down with Melanie at a bench by the side of the trail as she explained how her family had come to this park several years ago on their way home from a camping trip. It was one of the rare times when her family felt healthy, when arguments weren't so common and her father seemed like a decent man. If she was going to be a good mother for this poor doll, there was no better place to practice than here.

She'd been lucky to come to the playground at a time when no one else was around, giving her the freedom to push Jennabelle on the swings without anyone staring at her. Her privacy only lasted a few minutes before a man walked by on the nearby trail. She immediately stopped pushing Jennabelle, worried the man would laugh at her for playing with a silly doll. Instead, the man smiled and promised not to bother her, and explained he'd only come this way to catch some fresh air and gather his thoughts.

"I probably would've stopped playing with Jennabelle if it were anyone else but him," Melanie said. "But somehow I felt like I could trust him. So, I kept pushing Jennabelle on the swings while he stayed sitting right where we are now. He kept to himself for a few minutes before he asked about her. I told him she was a gift, and when he asked who gave her to me, I started crying. I tried to stop, but I just couldn't help myself. He stood up and apologized for his question. He told me it was fine if I didn't want to talk, but I knew I couldn't walk away. I had to learn how to talk about my problems instead of yelling about them. This was my chance to start a new path, so I did what I had to do. I brushed the tears off my face, I took Jennabelle off the swings, I sat down next to the man on the bench, and I asked if I could talk to him."

"Did he say yes?" Jeremiah asked.

Melanie smiled. "Of course, he did. When has Tom ever shied away from helping someone?"

Ever since his day with Fletcher, Jeremiah wondered how and when Tom would enter their story. He froze as this piece of the puzzle slid into place, but when the shock subsided, he smiled, knowing that if anyone could help pull Melanie out of the darkness, Tom was the man for the job.

"What did you tell him?" he asked.

"Everything," she replied. "Fletcher, Collin, my dad, the girl who gave me Jennabelle as a gift. I didn't even know he had a background in mental health counseling, but that didn't stop me from dumping everything right at his feet. It was pretty good timing, too. He told me he'd also fallen out of touch with someone recently, and that the last few weeks had been one of the hardest times in his life. He felt as lonely as I did, and I told him I'd try to help any way that I could."

"Who was this person?" Jeremiah asked, though the answer came to him right as the words escaped his mouth. It came to him like a flash of lightning. He remembered the cabinet, the picture, the girl with the pale skin and the tangled brown hair.

"Her name was Alexandra Cardor. Do you know about her?"

"Not really," he replied. "All I know is her name and what she looks like. Who was she?"

Melanie glanced away for a moment. He could see the reservation in her eyes, wondering if she had the right to divulge this information. Jeremiah held his breath in suspense, hoping she wouldn't prolong his quest for answers any longer.

"She used to be Tom's patient," she began, "back when he was working as a therapist. He brought Alexandra to East Parliss when she finished high school."

"Did something happen to her?"

"They got into a fight—a really bad fight, and one day she ran away from Tom and went to live in West Parliss. That's all he told me when I asked. He tried not to talk about her. He tried to keep the conversation about me and all my problems."

Jeremiah grinned. "Go figure. He never puts himself first."

"No, he doesn't," Melanie said, losing herself in her memories once again. "I was really lucky. I needed someone like him that day. I didn't know where to go, or how I was going to fix my life, but he knew. He always knows."

Jeremiah wanted to ask if she knew anything else about Alexandra, hoping he could add a few more details to this story before he left Littelbine Park. Maybe she knew why Tom left Parliss County, or why he had to leave him and Alicia at the Broken Cottage. But as Jeremiah looked down at Jennabelle, as he felt her felt skin brush up against his body, he knew these answers would have to wait. He had to let Melanie finish her story.

"What did Tom say?" he asked.

"He asked why I chose to keep Jennabelle even though she had so many bad memories tied up with her. I didn't know how to answer, but he did. He knew because he had a Jennabelle of his own—a picture of Alexandra he kept in his coat pocket. He told me that when you love someone more than you love yourself, you keep them with you anyway you can. It didn't matter that Alexandra was angry with him. It didn't matter she was gone. He still treasured the time they got to spend together, so he kept her photo, and hoped one day they might see each other again.

"I'm not sure if it was what he said or the way he said it, but it really struck a nerve with me. I held Jennabelle tight in my arms. I realized how much I really loved her, but more importantly, I finally understood why I did. She gave me hope. She was proof that a stranger could still love me enough to leave me a gift, even when I wasn't kind to her. She reminded me I still had a chance to fix my life. All the people I hurt were still back in my hometown, and if I were brave enough and if they were kind enough, then maybe we still had a shot at staying friends."

"Looks like you were right," Jeremiah said.

Melanie smiled. "Tom told me it wouldn't be easy, but he also told me that was why I should try. I had a chance to do something he might never be able to do. I had the chance to fix something I'd broken, and I could make sure it didn't happen again. That was when he told me about the Auralites, and that I had unknowingly come to the place where they all lived. He told me it was a place people came when they wanted change and had run out of places to look for it. He called it a place people came to be better, where I could teach myself to not be so reactive, or so hostile. When I left, I promised him I would come back one day, but not quite yet. I had some work to do back home."

Despite all the bad luck that had befallen Melanie these last several weeks, her meeting with Tom could not have come at a better time. Collin had let go of all his old feuds, Fletcher was no longer mourning the collapse of his old love affairs, and by handing over Jennabelle, Sandra had proven she would sign on as Melanie's friend at any given moment. So, when Melanie asked if all four of them could meet that following Saturday to talk, all of them promised they would come.

According to Melanie, they'd spent hours telling their sides of their stories, apologizing for their actions, and thanking one another for helping them grow. Jeremiah did his best to imagine what it must have been like by the end, as though he'd been a fifth member of these Jennabelle Kids, as he called them, watching four years of bad history vanish one second at a time, all because of a little doll.

Melanie had brought them all to Parliss County that summer. She introduced them to Tom, who showed them all how to read the Aurascope, and helped them learn about the many different, fascinating people who lived in this strange place. He taught them the importance of Personal Balance and offered his services as a counselor whenever they were needed. They would all go their separate ways in the fall, right when they had to leave for their first year in college, but in the summer, they'd meet up once again and spend six weeks in a shared apartment on the east side of the county. They came back even when they discovered Tom left to go work at a school in a small town in the middle of nowhere called Pritchard Haven, and they had yet to spend a summer anywhere else since.

"Is it hard being friends with each other?" Jeremiah asked. "After everything you all went through?"

"Sometimes," Melanie confessed. "I'd be lying if I said otherwise. The past never goes away forever, but there's no use looking back when you can look forward. That's really the only place you can go."

"Do you ever think about what would've happened if you never met Tom that day? Do you think the four of you would still be friends?"

"Probably not, but I don't think it's impossible. You'll find as you get older that the people who change your life the most have a way of sticking around. You just don't always know how they'll do it."

——— ——— ——— ——— ———

He didn't want to let go of Jennabelle when they returned to the fountain. He felt his fingers dig into her felt skin as he lifted her away from his chest, and the slightest possible ache in his stomach when Mel pulled her away and held the doll with her own, loving arms. He waved goodbye as he made his way out of the park and returned to the Broken Cottage. He sat down at his bed. He opened his journal and began to write about the day's events, laying down the final piece of the puzzle. He looked back on all four stories, experiencing each and every moment of loss, regret, redemption, and forgiveness a second time. His memory of the Skydiver Incident grew like wildfire, burning him from the inside as he imagined how such a small, careless act could have cost him his closest friend, while at the same time, reminding him that a wounded friendship could heal. He and Alicia could survive. The Jennabelle Kids were living proof.

The same bittersweet emotion stuck around during the next two days. Jeremiah returned to Littelbine Park on Saturday and Sunday to pass time with the Jennabelle Kids until their allotted seven days were over. There were no more stories left to tell, no more tests, silent walks, or bags of colored rocks. Instead, they all sat by the fountain and played Silent Captain, cracking jokes and swapping stories to lighten the mood, as any good group of friends would do. They even brought Jennabelle to come and watch.

Chapter Seven

The Dining Game

Tom was already gone when Alicia crawled out of bed the next morning. She felt the breath drain from her body as Jeremiah read his letter out loud, and her chest go numb when he set it back down on the couch. She wasn't afraid, or anxious, but a sense of emptiness consumed her as Jeremiah tried to ask Mr. Zeeger for answers. It was like she'd woken up in her own house without the soothing presence of her father, which was a strange way to feel about a man she'd barely known or spoken to until the last few months.

She had always done her best to avoid visiting the counseling room. She thought it was the mark of a mature woman to show strength and confidence at all times, and that asking for help was a sign of weakness. She wanted to believe she was tough, but the Aurascope said otherwise. Her fifth ring burned with yellowish-red, placing her on the side of the spectrum that leaned more toward a sensitive soul, proving she was open to moments of frailty despite her best efforts to stay calm and resilient.

She had visited the counseling room for the first time near the end of last September, in the weeks following her birthday party. She'd invited all the other girls in her class to her house for a formal dinner. She'd asked them to wear their nicest dresses and to come prepared for a night of exotic food and classical European music. It was the perfect plan, she thought. There could be no better way to impress her classmates than by throwing the most elaborate, sophisticated dinner they'd ever attended. She remembered going to school the following Monday, head up high and a smile on her face as she arrived at her first class dressed in some of the clothes she'd received as gifts from her parents—a cashmere sweater that matched the hue of her eyes, a wool scarf, and a lovely pair of brown penny loafers—her favorite type of shoe.

Her heart beat with the utmost confidence when she sat down beside her new friends, but as the day dragged on, the more they turned their heads away when she spoke, the more she wanted to lock herself in the girls' bathroom and wait for the final bell to ring. She remembered the tears dripping down her face when she overheard Gabby Milles chatting about how lame the dinner was, and when she heard the rest of them laugh, she decided maybe one trip to the counseling office could do her some good.

"Were you trying to impress them?" Tom asked.

"Yes, I suppose I was," Alicia said. "I haven't known them for very long, and they don't know much about me. I thought this would be the right way to change that."

"Is there anyone here you would consider a friend?"

"Just one. Jeremiah Carso. I didn't invite him just because he would be the only boy and I thought that would be a little awkward for him."

"That was very wise of you," the counselor said. "This is a good sign. This shows me you do have a sense of how certain types of people will feel if they're put into a difficult situation. So, let's see if we can use that way of thinking to look at all these girls. Tell me, how do you think they felt coming to your dinner party? How happy were they?"

"I'm not all that sure," Alicia replied, her voice even softer than usual. "They all seemed like they were having a good time."

"Well, let me get a little more specific, then," the counselor said, "because I think I see what your problem might be. Tell me, how often do you hear these girls listening to that sort of music you had playing at dinner?"

"Not ever."

"And when you tried talking with them about all the concerts and dance festivals you'd been to in Germany, how many of them had something to add to the conversation?"

"None of them," Alicia confessed, starting to grasp the counselor's point. "I thought they might be curious about where I came from, so that's what I tried to talk about. Is that a bad idea?"

"Not always," Tom answered, "but I think it's a sign you may not be paying close attention to what they are looking for. I think that might be where your problem is coming from. Can I give you another example?"

"Yes, of course," Alicia muttered.

Tom reached across to his desk and pulled his cell phone out of the drawer. He turned back to Alicia, clutching the phone in his right hand and holding it up in front of his face.

"Let's say we were in Germany together. I find you out on the street and I want to convince you to buy this new phone. What language should I be speaking to you?"

"German."

"Exactly. Now, suppose I tried to sell this phone to an American girl. What then?"

"You would speak English."

"And why is that?"

"Because most people here don't know German. You want to use the most popular language wherever you are to reach the most people."

"And that's the important part," Tom said. "It's always about the culture of the buyer, not the seller. See, right now, Alicia, you are a salesperson. You're thinking of how to convince others that you have something to offer: your friendship, your good company, your sense of humor—anything that makes these girls think they have something in common with you. Do you see what I mean?"

"I suppose so," Alicia muttered. Her hair began to fall over her face as she lowered her head in discouragement. "But it still doesn't seem fair to me. Why should I be expected to put aside what I care about to impress people who wouldn't do the same for me?"

Tom smiled for a moment while he released a heavy sigh, and then he went back to his more reserved, thoughtful expression. "That's the frustrating part, isn't it? It's always the people who know these rules that end up making all the compromises. It's the rude ones who get to do whatever they want, the ones who keep getting excuses made for them 'cause people like us know to bite our tongues and not start any trouble. You're right, Alicia. It isn't fair, but it's the way things are. People like us have to play their games by their rules before we're important enough to start influencing the way they behave. If we do a good job, and enough people start caring about our likes and our values, then maybe one day, you'll get the dinner party you've always wanted. But for right now, if you want to get close with these girls, you'll have to make the first few compromises."

— — — —

Tom's voice snuck back into her head as she sat down for breakfast with Jeremiah and Mr. Zeeger. She tried her best not to think about her birthday party, which became a challenge once she read the letter resting next to her plate. She was supposed to spend her first week with Bianca Bellanessa, a woman Tom knew from his brief time as a member of the Parryrose Club. The green ticket inside the envelope granted her the privilege of eating with some of the most well-respected Auralites in East Parliss for the next seven days. Her task was to find her place in the club, learn as much as she could about Bianca, and to try her best to get to the Head of the Table.

Alicia wasn't sure what Tom meant by the Head of the Table, but the rest of the letter was such a dream come true she didn't think on it for long. As strange as it may have seemed to anyone else, Alicia had always loved the company of adults. Even as a young girl, she'd loved dressing up in her nicest clothes and following her parents to grown-up parties where she was the youngest attendee. Her curiosity over Tom's current whereabouts vanished in an instant when she imagined sitting down for brunch and dinner with the other members, and the exquisite food and lovely dresses she'd find everywhere she looked.

She devoured her breakfast as fast as she could, growing impatient while she waited for Jeremiah to clear his plate. She left Mr. Zeeger's loft with nothing but her new green bag slung around her right shoulder, equipped with a private journal, a pencil, a map of Parliss County, and her very own Aurascope.

She parted ways with Jeremiah at the entrance to Littelbine Park then followed her own map down a few roads and around a few corners until she found the restaurant called the Grand Burnett. She gave her ticket to the man in a blue collared shirt standing by a podium, and then followed him up a flight of stairs to a private dining hall that belonged to the Parryrose Club.

Light rained down on her face when the doors swung open. Her eyes grew wide as the breath escaped her body, leaving her in a state of wonder while she stepped inside. The room was roughly half the size of a school gymnasium, furnished with a red velvet carpet and matching drapes that hung by the few windows on the surrounding walls. Chandeliers hung from the ceiling, casting light across the dozens of circular tables scattered across the hall, each with only six or seven seats and a single burning candle in the middle.

It took every bit of strength she had to restrain herself from gazing in awe like a child. She knew she had to maintain a sense of grace and stature if she wanted to look the part. She was the youngest one in the room by a substantial margin, drawing the attention of all the older men and women right as the door shut behind her. The only person who appeared to not be surprised was a woman sitting at a table near the end of the buffet line. She was about as tall as Tom, with a lean and elegant figure, smooth white skin nearly as pale as her own, and brunette hair that curled at the base of her neck. She was quite beautiful, so much so that Alicia felt a little disoriented as she made her way over to the table. She assumed this was the woman from the letter. She approached the table and was about to ask if this was Bianca Bellanessa, but the woman spoke before she had the chance.

"Everyone, this is my niece, Alicia. She's visiting from out of town while my sister is away on business."

"Pleased to finally meet you," said one of the men at the table as he extended his arm for a handshake. "We took the liberty of saving you a seat by your aunt over here."

Alicia took her place at the empty chair. She wondered why Bianca introduced her as a niece, but she knew better than to ask. She wondered if perhaps there was something Bianca knew that Tom neglected to put in his letter, and if this harmless lie was somehow in her best interest. In the weeks preceding their arrival to Parliss County, the counselor mentioned he'd left the Auralites with a number of bad memories in his footprints. It was possible this bad history involved some drama within the Parryrose Club, and Bianca was protecting her with this false identity.

Alicia's guess appeared to be a decent one, considering whenever someone asked a question about her family or hometown, Bianca was ready with an answer. Alicia only spoke for herself when they asked about her own private hobbies and interests. She answered these questions honestly, figuring it wouldn't help to lie about something that had no connection with Tom. She kept up this façade until Bianca announced it was time to leave. She led Alicia out of the dining hall, down the steps and out to the sidewalk where no one could hear them.

"You were marvelous back there, darling," Bianca said, reaching into her purse for a cigarette. "I was rather worried that little charade wouldn't work, but you played along beautifully."

"Right, thank you," Alicia said. "But would you mind telling me just exactly why that all happened?"

"It's a bit of a long story," Bianca replied as she lit her cigarette. "But to be brief, there are quite a few people in the club who might think poorly of you if they knew you had some connection with Tom. You would have seen it eventually. I figured it was right to give you a fair chance. Reputations are much easier to make than change."

"Well, thank you then, ma'am; I appreciate that a lot," Alicia said.

"It's no trouble, darling. There's nothing I would rather do. I don't have any children of my own; playing auntie for a week is something I've always dreamt of doing. Besides, he told me a lot about you when we spoke on the phone. I have a feeling we might be good friends once all this is over."

Bianca lowered her hand and released her first puff of smoke.

"Did he tell you anything about me?"

"No. Just your name," Alicia responded. "He did tell me that I was supposed to try to get to the Head of the Table. Do you know what that is?"

Her eyes widened. "The Head? In just one week? My goodness, he certainly has high expectations of you, now doesn't he?"

"But what is it exactly? The tables in the dining hall were round. How do you tell where the Head is?"

"He's not talking about our morning brunch," Bianca said. "Come back to the club for dinner at seven. Then you'll see what he's talking about."

Alicia nearly stomped her foot on the pavement when she heard this. She was tired of all the secrecy that had been stirring around lately. She wanted Bianca to explain what all this was, but each time she found the nerve to raise her voice, the fire inside her died out, and soon she agreed to meet Bianca at the dining hall later without any protest.

Alicia returned to the Grand Burnett later in the evening. The small round tables were gone, and in their place was a single giant table that reached across the full length of the room, meticulously crafted with ornate, regal carvings that made it look as if it belonged in a palace. The end closest to the door was mostly empty with just a few of the older people helping themselves to plain dishes of mashed potatoes and mixed vegetables. The better food was stationed at the higher end of the table, where the younger, chattier members of the club feasted on seared scallops, filet mignon, and chocolate custard. A woman with a lit cigarette tucked between her fingers sat at the far end of the table, surrounded by a cluster of men and women dressed in magnificent clothes. Alicia figured this woman must be sitting at the Head of the Table. She tried to get a better look before she spotted Bianca waving to her from the middle of the table's hierarchy next to an empty seat.

"I'm afraid I couldn't get you a seat higher up," Bianca confessed once Alicia sat down. "They wouldn't let you sit further up than this. I wouldn't be too upset about this if I were you. Most people always have to start at the bottom when they're new. Not to brag, but the fact I got you this far up is somewhat of a miracle."

"Well, thank you for that," Alicia said, smiling to show her gratitude. She helped herself to a glass of water since she was too young for the wine. She leaned in closer to look at the higher end of the table. Their side of the room echoed with loud, boisterous voices, catching the attention of most of the other members and making it difficult for her and Bianca to speak in private.

"The Head is where the club's founder used to sit while he was still a member," Bianca said as she poured herself a glass of white wine. "He was a man we all looked up to until he was arrested for suspected tax evasion. Now his old chair is up for grabs and everyone wants a piece of it. That woman has been there for about three weeks now. Before her, those two men sitting by her would switch back and forth each week, and that man you see with the apple crisp was there for two weeks before then."

"What about you?"

"I had my turn a few months ago; haven't gotten it back since then," Bianca groaned. She took a sip of her wine. "That's the way it works. Everyone wants it for as long as they can, and the longer you have it, the more people want it. Stay at the top too long, the rest of us find ways to knock you down a few seats. Those people you see up there, the ones I usually sit with, they take turns every few weeks."

"I suppose it wouldn't be possible for me to sit up there, would it?" Alicia asked.

Bianca set her wineglass down by her plate and wiped her lips with a napkin. "It won't be easy, but I would say it's possible, just considering the sort of people you're here with. You're much younger than the rest of us. Several women here might love to spend time with someone young enough to be their daughter. You're from out of town, very bright for your age, a lot more promising than some of their own children. You're also quite beautiful for a growing girl. You have a lovely face and very pretty eyes. I think a lot of people would find you to be very interesting. I think perhaps if you and I put our minds together, we could come up with a way to get you up there. You'd be the youngest person ever to sit at the Head of the Table. Wouldn't that be exciting?"

"Yes, it would be," Alicia said, doing her best not to blush as she pictured herself sitting at the Head, dining and chatting with the most prestigious members of the Parryrose Club.

"I'll help you any way I can," Bianca said, "but you will have to promise to do exactly what I say without question. I know my way around these people, so you'll have to trust that I know what I'm doing."

"I will. I promise."

"Very good," Bianca said, taking another sip of her wine. "I quite like you, Alicia. You remind me a little bit of myself when I was your age. I think with a little work, you could feel right at home here."

Bianca insisted they stay and eat for as long as they could, warning Alicia that any minute spent away from the club was time gone to waste. She introduced Alicia to everyone sitting around their part of the table and ensured they both talked as much as they could before they left.

Alicia met with Bianca the next morning a few blocks away from the Grand Burnett, and then they walked up to the dining hall together as aunt and niece. The giant dinner table had vanished overnight, and in its place were dozens of small round tables with a limited number of seats.

"You have to play the part of the prodigal daughter," Bianca whispered, speaking to Alicia as they made their way down the buffet. "That's what I want you to keep in mind at all times. You're young, you're pretty, you're smart, you're talented, and you love your family. Everything you say or do has to stay in line with that. Show them how remarkable you are but be careful not to brag. Arrogance is not something they want to see in a young girl."

"How can I do that?" Alicia asked, wondering how she was supposed to sell herself and stay humble at the same time.

"There is a trick that might help," Bianca replied. "I thought of it last night on my way to bed. Tell them your mother is teaching you how to paint, and you are in the process of making a painting like the one she gave to me as a birthday gift several years ago: a young girl on a hill releasing a bird into the sky."

"You want me to lie to them?" Alicia asked, as an uneasy feeling swelled inside her body.

"It's not really a lie," Bianca said. "I did actually once own a painting that looked just like that. We're just embellishing the truth a bit. Everyone does it. It's the perfect story to tell. It shows you're smart, that you're talented, and that you care about your mother and me, and you can say all that without bragging. Trust me, darling, they'll fall in love with you in an instant."

"All right, I'll do it," Alicia said, nodding hesitantly while mustering up the nerve to do what she needed to.

"I've already found a table for us right near the middle of the room," Bianca said, pointing with the tip of her foot so she wouldn't arouse any attention. "You see that man in the brown vest? His name is Charles Durham. He's a retired lawyer who recently took up gardening as a hobby. He has four sons who never went to law school like he wanted. He'll ask if you have any interest in the legal practice, and when he does, just say you're considering it, and ask him for advice. He'll do the rest of the talking. Just nod and find a way to compliment him every few minutes."

"Right," Alicia muttered. "What about that woman with the glasses?"

"Susan Huang," Bianca whispered. "Very unfortunate woman. She's always wanted to have children of her own but could never get pregnant. She'll want to talk to you probably more than anyone else here. She'll want to know if you've started dating; she'll want to know about your friends. Tell her as much as you can—she will bend any rule she has to in order to sit next to you if you treat her like a mother.

"Lastly, that man on the right is George Henry. He's a single father with a daughter about a few years older than you. She hasn't been talking to him much lately. Make sure you show him empathy. Also, if you can, find a way to mention how much you can't stand the interior color of the Red Basket Bakery. He talks all the time about how *garish* it is. Be sure to use that word. He uses it all the time even when it doesn't make sense."

Each of these predictions came true within twenty minutes of Alicia taking her seat at this table. George and Susan were fascinated with her adolescent life, barraging her with endless questions about her experiences with boys, what it was like to be in school, and what she liked to do with her free time. She expressed a vague interest in studying law and Mr. Durham went on to talk about his college experience for ten full minutes with no interruptions. When asked about her plans for the summer, Alicia took the chance to use Bianca's painting story, which won the praise and affection of everyone at the table. She saw Susan shed a small tear and whisper something in private when Bianca mentioned how proud she was of her lovely niece, which left Alicia feeling a little guilty for lying.

She eased her conscience by staying honest about everything else. She mentioned her struggles with the girls from her old school, hoping it would earn a little sympathy without seeming too melodramatic. She told them about her love for acting and the world of theatre. She mentioned how just last year she'd played the lead role of Olivia in Samuel Callingston's *Candlelight Palace,* which seemed to earn more praise than anything else she'd said before.

"I'm not sure if we need to use that painting story anymore," Alicia said to Bianca, once brunch was over and they were alone on the sidewalk.

"We do," Bianca insisted, reaching for her box of cigarettes as they marched down the street. "Trust me, with this crowd, it works better than anything else."

"Do I have to? This doesn't feel right."

Bianca stopped walking. She set her purse down on the pavement and placed her hand on Alicia's shoulder.

"Alicia, darling, I know this is difficult, but I need you to trust me. I wouldn't ask you to use this story unless it were absolutely necessary. It's all a part of being the prodigal daughter. You have to show your talents in a way that reflects your love of your family. There's no better way than this. I know it might seem odd, but I need you to trust that I know what I'm doing. Can you promise you'll trust me?"

Alicia paused. She nearly sighed out of exasperation, but she stopped herself. "Fine. I'll keep using it."

"Splendid. Thank you, darling," Bianca said, removing her hand from Alicia's shoulder as a smile burst onto her face. "I assure you it'll work wonders while you're here. Oh, and also, don't go talking anymore about those girls who weren't nice to you in school; it doesn't reflect well on you. Always look like you know what you're doing even if you don't."

"But what about Susan and George? They didn't seem to mind."

"Susan and George aren't everyone. The rest of them won't be so quick to show pity. Staying near the top end of the table means letting a few people sink so you can keep climbing. They keep the interesting ones close; the ones they think have something to offer. That's what you need to be."

Alicia thought back on her session with Tom. She could hear the soft echo of his voice like it was a fly hovering by her ear. She remembered what the counselor said about the frustration of compromise, and the importance of fitting expectations in order to be a part of something bigger. She was starting to see why Tom was friends with this woman. They seemed to share many of these same observations on social customs, though they differed greatly in how they spoke about them. Tom had always shown a high degree of empathy, understanding how hard it was to play another person's role just to find some sort of acceptance. Bianca, however, had proven herself to be more disciplined in this world. She was a force to be reckoned with, the sort of person who knew what had to be done and didn't have the patience for those who needed a gentle hand to show them the way.

Alicia tried to copy Bianca's mindset during the next few days. She chided herself for being so afraid of a simple lie, and reminded herself she was not a little girl who needed anyone's help. She carried herself with poise and confidence at each meal. She sat the way Bianca did: her back perfectly straight, her right leg crossed over her left, and holding a glass in hand at all times. She pushed through the uneasy feeling of the painting story until it felt natural, and she stayed honest about everything else.

She tried her best to talk about *Candlelight Palace* as often as possible. This was partly because she loved to talk about theatre, but mostly because everyone was so impressed to hear she had played the lead role. She would talk about her love of acting for as long as she could before a new subject eased its way into the conversation. She upheld the same role as the prodigal daughter, and found herself sitting just eight seats away from the Head after four days, surrounded by her own collection of minor colleagues.

She'd reached the higher end of the table in less than a week, but she wasn't at the Head. By day six, she was still sitting where she'd been on day four. She only had one more night to get to the Head, which felt less and less likely with each passing hour. Even with her distinct role as the prodigal daughter, the Head seemed almost too prestigious for someone so new and young. She figured Bianca had a good chance to get there now, since she was back in her usual place at the high end of the table, and because the blonde woman who'd been sitting there for the last few days was gone.

Alicia looked around for this woman but couldn't find her. She thought maybe this woman had taken a break for the night, until she looked around and saw her sitting at the lower end of the table, just three seats below the halfway point where the food was better than decent but less than remarkable. Alicia nearly spilled her drink in shock upon this discovery, stunned by how a person who'd been so high in stature just a few days ago could fall so low in just a few nights.

Alicia turned around to ask Bianca how this happened but saw she'd left to use the bathroom, and so she turned to Mr. Durham instead.

"Do you know who that woman is over there?" Alicia asked. "The one with the blonde hair, holding the cigarette."

"That's Sofia Agniss," the old man said. "Why do you ask?"

"Why is she sitting so far down today? Did something happen to her?"

Mr. Durham looked surprised. "Did Bianca not tell you?"

"No, she didn't, I suppose," Alicia replied. "Would you mind telling me?"

"Well, it goes back quite a few years," he said, setting his glass down by his appetizers. "How much do you know about a man named Tom Berrinser?"

"Not a whole lot," Alicia said, trying to keep a straight face. "Bianca mentioned him once but never went into much detail."

"He was a member of the club a few years ago. So was this young woman named Alexandra Cardor, who was a patient of his at the time. Tom was her therapist, you see. To put it simply, this young girl caused a lot of trouble in East Parliss and eventually left to live on the West side. About a year later, Tom moved away to some small town in the middle of nowhere, but no one here has talked to him since. At least, that was what we thought, until Ms. Agniss started this rumor that your aunt was still talking to him even though he was banned from the club."

"What made Sofia think that?" Alicia asked.

"That painting she had in her apartment," Mr. Durham answered. "The one your mother made, with the girl and the bird. Ms. Agniss started a rumor that this was actually one of Alexandra's works. She visited your aunt's apartment once for tea and claimed she saw Alexandra's signature by the bottom end of the frame, but that it had been covered up with paint. Most of us believed her, since your aunt and Tom were fairly close back when he was still a member. Your aunt insisted it was your mother, her sister, who made the painting, but no one believed her. Before you came along, she was stuck sitting by the middle, but now you've given people proof that Ms. Agniss was lying this whole time. She moved down, and Bianca moved back into her usual place."

On any other occasion, Alicia might have kept the old man's attention a while longer to ask more questions about Tom, or this Alexandra Cardor, but she lost focus once she felt her blood begin to boil in her veins. She sat perfectly still in her chair, narrowing her eyes in fury as she grappled with the unsettling truth of Bianca's tricks. It was like watching a priceless vase shatter on the ground and reassemble itself like a puzzle, putting the missing pieces of Bianca's story together until Alicia had a clear, pristine view of what this entire week had been about.

She stormed out of the dining hall right as Bianca came back from the bathroom. She marched down the stairs and left the Grand Burnett, making her way back to Mr. Zeeger's home while Bianca pursued her.

"Alicia! Where do you think you're going?"

"You lied to me!" Alicia shouted. She stopped dead in her tracks and turned around, staring down her former teacher with a look of pure, unfettered disgust. "Mr. Durham told me about Ms. Agniss! This whole time you were using me to get a better seat! You made me tell that story because it would help you!"

She smiled. "Alicia, darling, this is no reason to lose your temper," Bianca said. She didn't appear the least bit upset, which only made Alicia that much angrier. "I was doing what I could to help you move up but I couldn't have done that if they didn't trust me. This was just as much about you as it was about me. Darling, don't look so angry."

Bianca reached out to pat Alicia on the shoulder, but she pushed her hand away. "Don't touch me! I can't believe you would use me like this! I trusted you! I did everything you said, I admired everything about you, and this whole time you were just thinking about how to use me!"

"I will not let you patronize me this way!" Bianca demanded. "I've taken care of you this entire week. I helped make everyone in that room fall in love with you. How could you be this ungrateful?"

Alicia didn't listen to her. "Tom trusted you! He trusted you to look after me while he was gone, and you completely threw that away!"

"So, you're taking his side?" Bianca sneered, speaking now with a bitter look in her eyes and a cold, ruthless voice. "Do you know how much trouble I've gotten into because of him? Do you want me to tell you what happened with him and Alexandra?"

"I'm not trusting a word you say."

"I have a feeling you want to know."

"It doesn't matter. I'm not letting you tell me what to do," Alicia said. "You're not my real aunt. You're barely fit to be a mother."

Bianca slapped her across the cheek. Alicia staggered back and nearly fell down on the sidewalk, but she managed to keep her balance. She could feel her skin burn and sting all at once as she looked across to Bianca, afraid, but doing her best to look unfazed. The look on Bianca's face was a mix of sadness and quivering anger, her cold and heartless eyes piercing through Alicia with pure resentment as tears began to trickle down her cheeks.

Alicia tried not to show any signs of sympathy, but she struggled to keep her bitter spirit alive as Bianca placed her hand on her own face to cover her tears and ruddy cheeks. She looked scared. She looked guilty, as if she wanted to take back what she'd done. For a while, Alicia thought Bianca might actually apologize, but she never did.

"Well then," Bianca said with a heavy sigh, wiping away the last of her tears and forcing a cold, bitter look into her weakened eyes. "I suppose we won't be able to meet again tomorrow. I can't have my niece showing up and spoiling our secret, now can I? I've worked too hard to lose it all now. I can make things very hard for you if you somehow find a way to tell anyone about what just happened. I know where Tom is. I can let the entire club know he's back and make sure he has a very rough stay here.

"And I could do it anytime I want, so don't give me a reason."

Bianca left without saying another word, leaving Alicia by herself at the edge of the road until she looked up to the Grand Burnett and walked away. Bianca was right. She wasn't going back to the club. She didn't care about the Head of the Table, or anything she'd learned from Bianca during the last six days. She wanted to go home, to run away from Parliss County and have a simple dinner with her mother and father back in Pritchard Haven, but settled for her room in the loft above the Broken Cottage. She brushed aside her tears and massaged her cheek to do away with the pain and the red mark so Jeremiah and Mr. Zeeger wouldn't ask any questions. As far as they would know, her first week in East Parliss had been a perfectly enjoyable experience.

Alicia didn't realize until the next morning she'd left her bag at the dining hall. She made her way to the Grand Burnett hoping someone from the club had been generous enough to leave it behind, and thankfully, the man in the blue collared shirt was waiting out by his podium with the green bag by his feet. She thanked the man and checked to see if any of Tom's supplies were missing. She unleashed a deep sigh of relief as she felt the spine of her journal, and when she saw the faint burst of light as her skin brushed against the Aurascope.

She suddenly realized she hadn't used it during her time at the Parryrose Club. Bianca had never offered to reveal her Aura—a massive red flag Alicia wished she'd caught before. She wondered what her former teacher's Aura might have looked like, but it didn't matter. The lies, the slap, and the tears said everything she needed to know.

Alicia sauntered off to the other side of the road and turned around for one last look at the Grand Burnett. She thought about running past the man in the blue collared shirt and taking her place at any one of the brunch tables, just to show Bianca she wasn't a coward. But she had no choice other than to stay outside. If Bianca had been honest, if she really knew where Tom was and had the power to hurt him, then Alicia knew she had to stay away. She still had no clue where Tom was or what he was doing, but it was clearly something very important, and she knew the counselor needed to stay alone and unbothered no matter the cost.

Chapter Eight

Mothcatcher

As Tom walked away from the Broken Cottage, he felt something tug at his collar. He nearly turned around expecting to see Gerald standing behind him, urging him to come back, but his dear friend was nowhere to be seen. He stood alone on the Eastern side of Corraine-Callister, mere footsteps away from the Western side of the county, but he refused to cross. He stayed to his side, and kept on walking under the pitch-black sky, with only the lampposts to guide his way.

On a summer night, the air was warm enough so most wouldn't shiver as they walked outside, but Tom was an exception. He felt the cold race down his spine, the same way he'd felt when he finished his meeting with the Scheinbachs. His hands quivered with mild guilt the further he walked, but he kept walking nonetheless. He'd waited nine years for this night. Not one more day could pass.

He stood along the side of Allport Drive. He gazed up at an apartment building, one that was five stories tall and made from brick, as most were in Parliss County. The door opened shortly after he rang the buzzer, and then he climbed the staircase until he reached the third floor. He quickly made his way to room 316, and before he could even knock to announce his arrival, the door swung open.

"Well, well, look who finally came by to say hello," Bianca said, as she leaned against the side of the doorway with a cheeky smile across her face. "I was starting to think you'd forgotten about me."

"You do an exceptional job of making that impossible," Tom said as he regained his composure, trying his best to contain the exasperated sigh he felt in his lungs. "May I come in?"

"Did you do what I asked?" Bianca said, clogging the doorway with her body as she awaited her answer.

"I'm not sure *asking* is the right word for what you did."

"Neither would I, but I suppose it's the polite thing to do. Didn't you once say the illusion of respect matters more than the real thing?"

Tom shrugged. "That sure does sound like me. You'd be amazed how much better we remember lessons when they come in those quirky little phrases. You've heard the old saying that you catch more bees with honey than vinegar, right?"

Bianca raised her eyebrow. "Are you suggesting I haven't?"

"I'm suggesting you might get more favors if you asked for them instead."

"What good is doing favors when there's no promise you'll get one in return?"

"Not everything needs to be a deal, Bianca."

"Maybe not where you live now, but over here, it absolutely is. Putting food on someone else's plate just means less for you, and if there's not enough to share then I'm not giving away any peaches unless I get the cobbler two days later. People don't respond to beggars; they respond to sellers. Modern friendship has outgrown the need for kindness."

"I highly doubt that's the case," Tom said, fully aware this was a lost cause, but trying nonetheless.

"Then it's probably a good thing you left the club," Bianca said. "And I can't help but notice you still have not answered my question. Did you do what I *needed* you to do?"

"Yes, I did," Tom said reluctantly. "Alicia will be at the Grand Burnett tomorrow morning in time for brunch. May I come in now?"

"Well, since you asked nicely."

She winked at Tom and smiled as she removed herself from the doorway. He sat on the couch while Bianca disappeared into her bedroom to make a phone call. He took some time to admire the rest of the apartment until she returned. It was surely the most lavish apartment in Parliss County. Everything from the carpet to the coffee table looked expensive, like something he could've seen on the cover of a magazine. It looked just the same as he remembered, until he noticed that Alexandra's painting, the one she'd given Bianca as a birthday gift, was missing. It used to hang on the wall right above the TV set, but some cubist piece had usurped its spot.

"I just called to let him know you're here," Bianca said once she stepped out of the room. "Someone will be here shortly."

"Where's her painting?"

"Pardon? Oh, don't worry. I gave it to him. It's still in good shape."

"It was a present for you," Tom said, raising his voice. "She made it herself."

"It was causing some trouble over at the club," she insisted, pouring herself a glass of chardonnay, and preparing a second glass for Tom. "I'd rather not get into this story again. Look, it's better off with him anyway. Can we please not make a fuss about this?"

Tom closed his eyes and sighed. This was so typical of his former friend. Not even a birthday gift was sacred to her. He tried to stay focused as Bianca finished pouring her drinks and sat down on the couch beside him.

"As I was saying, someone will be here soon to escort you," Bianca promised. "Until then, you and I will just have to pass the time. Maybe you can tell me a little more about this girl while we wait. What's her name again?"

"Alicia. Alicia Scheinbach," Tom said as he took his glass. He had no plans of drinking, but he knew Bianca would make a big issue out of refusing her hospitality, so he held the glass anyway and pretended to be thankful.

"What are her hobbies? What's she interested in?"

"She loves theater," Tom replied. "She's a very talented actress. She played Olivia in the production of *Candlelight Palace* we did at our school this year. She speaks German, too. I'm not sure if I mentioned that on the phone. She once threw a dinner party on her birthday and played classical European music while they ate. I think she'll feel right at home with the Parryrose Club."

Bianca smiled. "Well, she sounds lovely."

"She is," Tom said as he faked taking a sip of his wine. "You promise you'll take good care of her, right?"

Bianca smirked. "You seem a little suspicious."

"I have a pretty good reason to be," the counselor said. "I called you weeks ago asking if you can introduce me to this man who wrote that letter, and the one thing you ask for is to chaperone one of my guests around the club for a week? What exactly do you get out of this?"

Bianca didn't answer right away, which by itself was enough to prove the answer was rather serious. A blank, almost sad look appeared on her face. She set her glass of wine down on the coffee table, then lay her arms on her lap and clasped her hands together.

"Well, if you must know, I've been thinking about having children."

Tom froze. "You have?"

She nodded. "A lot of the other women I know are getting married. I'm getting older, and frankly, the thought of having a daughter look up to me for support does sound rather nice. I'm thinking it might be time I settle down."

Tom felt guilty for being so suspicious. He'd assumed Bianca was planning to use Alicia as a way to manage her status in the Parryrose Club, and that her place at the Head of the Table was still her governing focus. Raising a child was never something she would have considered ten years ago. He thought perhaps the time Bianca spent with Alexandra at the club had set this in motion, and all their years apart had left her with a cold, numbing pain that could only be filled by another bright young woman who could play the role of a stand-in daughter.

While they waited, Tom and Bianca exchanged a few stories about all the notable things they'd done in the last ten years. It was three o'clock in the morning when the buzzer rang again, so late into the night and so early in the morning that both the night owls and the early birds were in bed. Tom felt his heart race faster the moment he heard the sound. He set his glass down on the coffee table, stood up from his seat on the couch, and walked over to the nearest window. He looked down at the street beneath the apartment and saw two men standing on the sidewalk. They were waiting for him.

"How do you know this man?" Tom asked, curious why he had chosen Bianca as his personal messenger.

"I asked him for a favor once a long time ago," Bianca answered. "I've been finding ways to pay him back ever since. He reminds me of you in some ways. He's very perceptive, very smart, and he will help you if you help him. But you have to be careful. He knows how to get what he wants. He knows how to win people over, but he's not always the right person to trust. Remember that. Don't let him stab you in the back with the knife you give him."

Tom drew a heavy breath and let it out as he turned from the window, taking one last look at the two men standing on the sidewalk. He said goodbye to Bianca, thanked her for her help, wished her luck, then left the apartment to see what the rest of the night had waiting for him.

He made his way back down the stairs without wasting a second, his heart beating and hands quivering long before he stepped outside. The men waiting for him were much younger than they had appeared from Bianca's window. They could have been the same age as Jeremiah and Alicia, which left Tom with a perverse, unsettling feeling as he looked into their eyes, and let them show him the way.

They said nothing as Tom followed them away from Allport Drive. They walked in silence, leading him back toward the Wide Road, a few blocks north of the Broken Cottage and all the way to the Canmark Theater, which Tom recently learned had been closed for the last few years. It was a sad thing to hear. So many Auralites had once described it as the heart of Parliss County. It stood on the Eastern side of Corraine-Callister Road, right in the center of the county on the invisible line that split the West from the East. It had been a place of joy and unity, and now his eyes hurt just looking at it. He scowled at the weeds and fallen branches smothering the promenade leading up to the entrance, mourning what had become of this place after a decade of neglect. The only remnant of its former beauty rested in the white poppies that grew in a garden box by the front door, which thankfully, someone had bothered to take care of.

A third young man with dark, unkempt hair and hazel eyes stood by the entrance. He led Tom and his two escorts through the auditorium that had once been able to sit a thousand guests, up to the stage and behind the curtain, where a lonely door stood waiting for them. The three young men each made a silent gesture toward the door, which Tom perceived as more of an invitation to enter rather than an order, as if they were allowing him the chance to turn back while he still could.

He wrapped his hand around the doorknob and resisted turning it for only a moment before one strong, heavy breath brought him the courage to step through.

He descended a flight of stairs as the three young men stayed up top, listening as the old steps creaked under his weight and the force of his footsteps. He slipped on a wet step near the end of the stairwell but managed to land in the hallway below with his balance intact. He would have been surrounded in complete darkness if it weren't for the scarlet ambience of the candles hanging from the walls, all the way down to the other end of a corridor and into a room, where more young men and women sat at a wooden table. Tom guessed there were about ten of them—thirteen counting the boys upstairs—their heads bowing down and obscured by shadows as if trying to keep their identities secret.

Tom did not look at them for long. His focus rested on the man sitting at the end of the table. He looked to be about Tom's age and height. He had a slender chin and slick blonde hair that was starting to turn grey.

"Ah, he is finally here," the man said, raising his hands in celebration. "The famous Tom Berrinser. What a pleasure it is to finally have you grace our presence. Please, might you do me the courtesy of having a seat by me? Saves us the trouble of shouting across the room. Voices have a way of echoing in these lower rooms, as you'll soon discover."

Tom's experience as a counselor had trained him to make assessments very quickly. He was always the first to notice the way people spoke, how they communicated with hand gestures and facial expressions, and whether or not they looked him in the eye. The man at the other end of the table spoke in a vibrant, cheery voice that most people would reserve for telling jokes, possibly as an attempt to unnerve Tom by acting in a way that contrasted the eeriness of the setting and circumstance. He spoke with a hint of sarcasm, giving Tom the impression that he was rather arrogant, the sort of person who would smirk at his own witty remarks, and perhaps had a little too much pride for his own good.

Tom could tell he was going to detest this man very soon, not because of the way he spoke or behaved, but because the only unused chair in the whole room was at the lower end of the long table. This meant even though this strange man had intended for them to sit together, he had not bothered to move the chair so Tom would have to do it himself, a subtle way of establishing dominance without saying a word. It was a sly tactic he both loathed and respected.

He picked up the chair, set it down next to his host, and took his seat. He made sure to keep a stern but calm expression on his face, a look that said he could be reasoned with but not deceived.

"I take it you found your way to Ms. Bellanessa's place without too much trouble," the strange man said. "Did she by chance say anything about me?"

"We spoke about you on the phone, before I came back," Tom replied, speaking in an uncommonly gruff voice. "She told me your name—your real name—is Simon Falzoga, but people here have referred to you as Mothcatcher. You're a self-described expert in the field of what you call the science of persuasion, but I suppose a few others can attest to your skill. They say you can convince people to change their minds and beliefs, not by tricks or deceit, but by friendly arguing, helping them see what they simply weren't looking for."

"Well, that is what I would like to think of myself," Mothcatcher said as he reached under the table for a bottle of chardonnay. "We'll have to see if I can meet your expectations. Care for a glass?"

"I'd rather not," Tom said, knowing it would be foolish of him to dull his senses at a time like this. "I'd like to know what you wanted to show me in your letter."

"Very well," Mothcatcher said, setting the bottle down without pouring a drink for himself. "I don't like wasting time either. I only asked what you knew because I thought it might help demonstrate what I'm about to ask of you."

"What do you mean?"

"I have done my best to surround myself in secrecy. I've made sure you know the most basic details of who I am, but a curious and observant man such as yourself surely wants more than that. You have been studying my names, learning about my reputation, trying to build some sort of role for me to fit, and now that you're here and you're watching me speak, you're trying to see if your expectations are correct.

"Are they?"

Tom observed the strange man one last time before giving his answer, closing his mind to Bianca's stories and rumors so his early bias wouldn't sway his focus.

"I would say you're like I expected you to be."

"And would you consider yourself good at reading people?"

"Very. It's part of the job."

"Then surely you wouldn't mind a demonstration, would you?"

Mothcatcher slipped a silk glove onto his right hand and reached down to grab an Aurascope that had been resting beneath the table. The layer of silk between his skin and the crystalline glass kept the Aurascope from bursting into color. His true character remained invisible, but that would soon change.

"You're an extrovert. That I'm nearly sure of," Tom began. "Anybody who's built such a legacy for himself as a master of persuasion has to be a natural speaker, and good with people; not to mention I've been here for less than five minutes and not one other person at this table has spoken except you or me, which either means they trust you to speak on their behalf or you have convinced them you can do a better job speaking for them. Either one seems likely to me."

Tom looked to the other end of the room for a quick glance at the shadowy figures sitting at the table, then turned back to Mothcatcher.

"They expect certain things from you—ways you can help them or give them what they want, which likely has conditioned you to fit the role of a leader. But do you consider yourself a leader or just play one for their sake? That's what I'm curious about. I can see evidence for both. For example, while I've been talking you've kept steady eye contact with me and haven't blinked once, which, to be honest, is a little unnerving. Would you mind?"

Mothcatcher blinked, and Tom went on.

"Thank you. Now, as I was saying, this unyielding focus, I would say, is a sign you don't get nervous too much, but the fact you've also been tapping your left foot this whole time suggests that you're actually trying to hide how anxious you are at the moment. Whenever you speak you make gestures with your hands, but now that you're quiet, you're moving your fingers a little, which tells me you are trying to show restraint even though you are a spontaneous person. You like to make your own rules, you like to break all the other rules, and you understand how appealing it sounds to call yourself a rule-breaker. That would explain why all your followers here are around that eighteen-to-twenty-year-old range—the same as Alexandra was when I first brought her here—the age when we're still challenging who we think we are but have the illusion of power and freedom that comes from adulthood. You make them feel that sense of freedom. You're used to being a symbol of unconventional authority and getting what you want in a different way than anyone else, which I would say makes you extremely confident. In that case, your foot-tapping is probably connected to something else besides anxiety. You have a tough mind, but you have a bit of an ego that makes you defensive at times when your greatness is questioned. You will smile and laugh when you feel threatened but will let these taunts consume you until you find a way to even the score.

"So, I will make my last observation and phrase it in a way I believe will not upset you. You are, more than anything else, a brilliant, cunning, and shrewd man. That is not to say you're a liar, but you don't speak a language of gifts and rewards—you think of the world in deals, bargains, and trading favors for bigger favors. Anything you do for me will somehow find its way back to you, whether I know it or not."

Mothcatcher grabbed hold of the Aurascope with his naked hand. The young men and women sitting at the table were all amazed to see that most of Tom's assumptions were right. He was shrewd and suspicious, but also highly confident. He was an extrovert without much value for rules and conscientious behavior. The biggest of Tom's missed predictions was that Mothcatcher actually showed a high degree of restraint despite his constant gesturing, while the rest of his Aura looked a way Tom could have expected.

"Well done, Mr. Berrinser. Not bad for a man who's known me for one night. You didn't disappoint, not that we expected you to. We all hoped you would pass this little test of mine, because you will need to pass a second one. That is why I asked you to come."

Mothcatcher stood up from his chair and gestured for Tom to do the same. The counselor watched as the strange man grabbed onto a set of drapes hanging from the wall, and then pulled them apart to reveal a painting.

Alexandra's painting.

It was mounted on the wall behind Mothcatcher's chair, so close to the ground that both of their heads were above the top edge of the frame. It was a picture of a young girl in a green dress kneeling down at the top of a hill, releasing a purple sparrow from her clasped hands into a bright blue sky.

He admired its detailed beauty for a brief moment before Mothcatcher grabbed the right side of the frame and pulled it across to the left as if he were opening a door, revealing a dark compartment that looked just large enough to fit a child of ten or twelve years old. Tom bent down for a better view and saw a large chest that looked to be made of brass, or some other metal with a golden sheen, sealed shut by a combination lock with eight digits.

"You were a lot of help to Alexandra in your time with her," Mothcatcher said. "We admire you for that, but I offered her something she never had with you. I offered her a place of comfort, a place without expectations, and as a symbol of my companionship, I gave her this: a place where she could keep her most precious belonging safe."

"And what was that?" Tom asked.

"Her journal. The same one you gave her when you first brought her here; the place where she kept all her thoughts and memories about her time in Parliss. They were memories that needed to be kept away from people like us—the men who were too driven by curiosity to respect that basic need for privacy. So, I gave her a box only she knew how to open, so she could keep her book in a place where no one else could touch it."

"Not even you?"

Mothcatcher shook his head. "That is the price of privacy, and that is the gift I was willing to give. I gave her that freedom, and all I wanted in exchange was her companionship. That was our unspoken deal, but as you can see, she broke it. I want to know why she left, what I did wrong, and how I could have stopped it. Everything I need to know is somewhere in that journal, and I need your help to get it."

Tom had no clue how his skills in reading people would offer any help opening this box. That was until Mothcatcher pointed to the sheets of tattered paper that were pinned to the backside of the painting. Written at the top of each page was a personal question about Alexandra, and below each question was a list of ten possible answers with a single-digit number written next to each one, starting at zero and ending at nine.

"She hid the combination right in front of us," Tom whispered.

"She didn't leave these clues so we could open the box," Mothcatcher said. "She left them so we could try to, and fail. What better way is there to spite men like us than to test our knowledge and show us just how much we didn't learn? I've tried to crack this code more times than I care to remember, each time more confident than the last that I'd figured it out, and the damn thing stayed shut each time. It's maddening, I tell you, like slamming against a glass window that won't break. It's frustrating, but even I can't help but admire how clever she was with this little game. In order to take what's inside, we have to open the box, but the only way to open the box is to have the knowledge that comes from the book that's in the box we can't open. It's rather cruel, but it's the best kind of cruel, if you ask me."

"And now you want me to try opening it," Tom said. "That's what this is all about?"

The man nodded. "We know her better than anyone else alive today. We've loved her the most, we've ached the most, and we've spent too long asking ourselves what we did wrong to push her away and how it could have been stopped. Now we have the chance to fix that. With our combined knowledge there won't be an hour of her life we don't know about, and you and I can finally be at peace."

Tom felt the inside of his body swell with a sort of hope he hadn't felt in a decade. He felt half his normal weight as his fingers shook at the thought of opening this box, but he hesitated when he stepped back to reality. He wondered if it was right of him to violate her privacy even if she was gone, doing the very thing that had warranted a sealed box in the first place. He had already shirked one of his moral responsibilities by leaving Gerald's home. A second selfish act might be one too many.

"Is it right?" Tom asked. "You wouldn't pick through a dead girl's grave just to find some spare coins, would you?"

"She isn't dead, Tom," Mothcatcher said. "She's gone. She left us, all of us, and as long as we have no idea why she left, you and I will keep making the same mistakes and others will suffer."

He turned around. "They will suffer."

Tom turned around to face the young men and women sitting at the table, their heads still bowed down and shrouded in shadow.

"Who are these kids?" Tom asked, wondering why he hadn't bothered to ask this until now.

"They are the Cardorians," he answered. "That is what I call them, and it's a name that suits them perfectly because they are just like her. They came to Parliss County hoping to find something they never found. They were left with no place to go except here, and if I fail them, they will have nothing. They're just like her: alone, unwanted, angry, guilty, still learning how to hope for a bright future even when the world keeps them stuck in one place. I tell them stories about Alexandra and they have chosen to mold themselves after her, living by her example, hoping they could succeed where she couldn't.

"To put it simply, Tom, these are our grandchildren. And they don't want to end up like their mother."

Whether it was his intention or not, Mothcatcher had found Tom's crucial weakness and was exploiting it perfectly. An awful feeling of guilt swelled inside him each time he turned his back on a child or young person who needed his help. His chest would feel cold and the muscles in his face would sag. Only the promise of Mothcatcher's letter had numbed this guilt long enough for him to leave Gerald's place tonight. He thought about Jeremiah and Alicia, wondering if he might have been able to help them more if he had learned from his past mistakes, and would send future students down a similar path without the secrets from Alexandra's journal. He had gone from one moral dilemma to another, asking whether opening the box was truly for the benefit of others or an excuse to justify his own curiosity. The end result would still be the same: an open box with Alexandra's journal in his hands.

He had already come this far. He figured he might as well go as far as he could while he still had the chance.

"Who would keep it?" Tom asked. "If we open the box, who gets the journal?"

"I will let you have it," Mothcatcher replied. "I only ask that I get one day to read it all by myself so I can have the answers I need. After that, it is yours to keep if you want it. That is my solemn promise."

"All right then. I'll do it."

"Wonderful," he said, raising his voice to convey his excitement before he settled down once again. "You've made the right decision, Tom. We will have to make the most of the six weeks you have here, and there is not an hour to waste. You will sleep here at the theater. We've already set up a bed for you in the costume room. You will tell me what you know about our beloved Alexandra, and I will tell you what I know. On Saturday night six weeks from now, we will attempt to open the box, and when we succeed, I will take the journal to read for the following Sunday. Then it will be yours to keep, permitted you do what I say."

"Do you really trust me that little?" Tom asked, speaking in a benign, taunting manner with just a hint of accusation.

"On the contrary. I trust you quite a lot. I just can't give you the chance to prove me wrong."

Chapter Nine

The Painter of Besalbee Road

It was such an unusual name that Alicia couldn't help but smile as she read Tom's second letter, which she found resting at her seat next to her breakfast when she woke up the following Monday. She split up from Jeremiah as soon as they stepped out of the Broken Cottage, heading up north and waving goodbye as her friend walked away in the other direction. She followed her map up a few blocks until she saw the sign for Besalbee Road, then followed the sound of beating drums and whistling flutes from around the corner.

It was half the width of all the other streets she'd seen in East Parliss, packed with dancers, musicians, and street performers from one end to the other. A pair of gypsy women danced within earshot of a man playing a flute, and after a moment of scouring the crowd, she finally found the man she was looking for. He was sitting on a frail wooden stool, perched in front of an easel with a paintbrush in his hand. He looked to be about fifty years old, with dark skin and curly grey hair. He wore a brown fedora, along with a white collared shirt that would have made him appear rather distinguished if it weren't covered in splotches of paint.

He asked Alicia if he could hold the Aurascope. As expected, he was a sensitive soul with a wide imagination and an abstract method of thinking, each apparent by the yellowish-red light that appeared in each of these rings. The light blue from the outer rings meant he was an introvert, as Alicia would expect from someone with such a solitary hobby. A green ring marked him as someone both serious and carefree, a man with a firm commitment and a rigid set of beliefs about his work but with a boundless energy that still let his mind run wild with ideas.

"Would you like to see mine?" Alicia asked as she looked at the Aurascope, figuring it would be polite to return the offer.

"I appreciate you asking, but I'd rather not if that's fine with you. I prefer to live with my disadvantage."

"Disadvantage, sir?"

"I find it to be the responsibility of any true artist to live beyond truths. My disadvantage is the same as that of the people who live in the rest of the world; folks who think what they see is true when it might be a lie. What makes me happy might make another sad; I'll find hope in what you think is a sign of death and melancholy. I don't need any fancy trinkets to tell me what I should believe. If I did, I would be a dismal artist, now would I?"

"Yes, I suppose so," Alicia said as she tucked the Aurascope into her bag. "But then why did you let me see yours?"

"I thought it might help you trust me a little more," the Painter replied. "I am a stranger after all, friend of Tom's or not, but hopefully from this point on we can learn more about each other the way we should: through time and talking. I'd prefer that much more. I don't have many people to talk to. This road is most of who I am now, and while I may love it, I would sure like having someone to share it with."

The Painter had been generous to bring a second set of art supplies and a proper chair for Alicia, along with a smock so she wouldn't ruin her nice clothes. The Painter asked Alicia to spend the next seven days painting something to represent herself ten years in the future. She wasn't as afraid of this question as most of those her age would have been. Her mother often said she had the soul of a grown woman, wise and well-mannered beyond her age, and the adult world was never something she felt was far away.

It seemed like a simple task, considering how much time Alicia had spent these last few months thinking about her future, waiting to see what she would become once she left Pritchard Haven. She remembered visiting Tom's office only one week after moving from Germany, taking the Myers Briggs for the first time—as was required for all incoming students. She'd left the counselor's office as an ISFJ, the Protector type, a person defined by a fierce sense of loyalty, keen skills of observation, a need to be reliable, and plenty of other good traits she did not want to outgrow.

She'd taken the test a second time just a few days before graduation, curious, like Jeremiah, to see if she had changed. Now she was an ISXJ, more of a thinker and less of a feeler, more inclined to follow logic than the whims of her emotions. She'd considered this to be a step in the right direction, though as she walked away from Tom's office, she felt empty knowing her identity as a Protector was damaged. She had achieved Personal Balance, as Tom called it, but at the expense of a title she was proud to bear, and a title she would have loved to carry into her future.

Alicia set her paintbrush down and studied some of the Painter's other works for inspiration. Three of them rested by the edge of the sidewalk. The one on the left featured a white porcelain doll with a large crack in her head, standing against a black and violet background. The one on the right portrayed a girl standing in a desert at the edge of an oasis of palm trees and fresh lakes. Alicia noticed after giving it a closer look that the trees were transparent, a mirage, starting to fade from sight and leaving the girl lost in the desert again. The painting in the middle was the one that caught Alicia's attention the most: a young girl hugging a giant bear against a blank white background.

She turned to her own blank canvass and made a quick sketch of her twenty-eight-year-old self crouched down in the middle of a hiking trail, caring for some poor injured animal she had yet to create. She couldn't decide what animal it was, so she decided to leave the space empty until she made up her mind. It was a perfect depiction of the sort of woman she wanted to be: an adventurer with a love of the wilderness and a tender spirit to comfort the poor and helpless. It suited her old Protector type rather well, which led Alicia to wonder if perhaps this was a job she would like to have someday.

She kept her easel turned away from the Painter to hide her work until it was good enough to be seen. She sat with her head bowed down, doing her best to ignore the masterpiece being made just one step away. She refused to walk away from Besalbee Road at the end of the week with a piece of art she'd be ashamed to call her own. She took three days just to finish painting her crouching body, paying close attention to each and every detail, trying to stay focused despite the music and dancing that surrounded her every day. She worked as long as she could until the pain in her wrist forced her to take a break, and when that time came, she would sit and watch the gypsy dancers across the street and listen to the clarinetist just a few steps to her left. She would also take this time to talk with the Painter, who somehow could still manage to hold a steady conversation without taking his focus away from his work.

He was a rather proficient speaker, capable of stretching the answer to any question into long stories and anecdotes of when he was a younger man. Alicia learned he'd once been a history professor at a college in a town called Wittendale. He would come to East Parliss in the summer to paint and be free from the pressures of work. Since his retirement, he'd lived in a small house just a few blocks south of Besalbee Road. He was not married and had no plans to be, claiming his constant distraction and lack of interest in most things outside of art and history would make him a poor husband.

Alicia wanted to ask if he'd ever been with a woman before, but decided that would be intrusive of her, so she put her mind back to the task of finishing her painting. She chose a sloth as the wounded animal her older self would be saving. She had always loved sloths because of how funny their faces looked, and they were fairly easy to paint since they were so round and fluffy. She drew the poor creature with a pencil to establish its shape and size. Then she began retracing the lines with her thinnest paintbrush to make the image pop. About a day later, she was ready to add the color and the shading, a process that was only halfway done when the sun began to set.

She thought it was funny to see how much more effort she was putting into the sloth than she was putting into herself. She figured this was probably a good sign that she cared more about the welfare of a wounded animal than her own. She wondered if this really was the way she would behave a decade from now, whether her Protector spirit would endure for that long or if this caring woman was just an illusion of her own blind faith.

"Can I ask you something, sir?"

"You just did," the Painter said with a cheerful smile. "But yes, you may. What's your question?"

"Well, it might be a little too late, but I was wondering something about my painting. Did you want me to paint what I *hope* I'll be in ten years, or what I *think* I will be?"

"Either is fine with me," the Painter said, not taking his eyes off his work. "I have a feeling they won't be that different."

Alicia continued to paint for another few minutes before she asked the Painter what he meant by this.

"Expectations are most often the first step to reality. That's the lesson my life has taught me. I remember being sixteen and finding my love of art. I thought after just a few days of practice and all the blind praise of my parents that my work was destined to be in museums across the country. It wasn't until I was about twenty, when I was a little older and smarter, that I started to think I wasn't all that good. I was meeting people who were better, and they're still better than I am today. I was quite depressed thinking I could never be the best. Doubt made me weaker. I expected less of myself and became a lesser man because of it, and I stayed as that man for an unhealthy length of time before I grew the courage to try again. Now I am a new man. I don't waste my time with thoughts of greatness so there's no room for doubt."

The Painter looked away from his easel for a moment so he could lock eyes with Alicia. "Do you doubt yourself often? Surely you must have seen it by now. The young either doubt themselves too much or not enough. Which are you?"

"Well, I'd like to think I'm neither," Alicia replied, knowing this answer was a little too easy. "I've never been scared of being an adult. I've never worried about taking care of myself, or what job I would have. Getting there is what scares me the most. Sometimes I feel like I'm just stalling time and dodging bullets until all this teenage nonsense just goes away."

"It will one day," the Painter said, turning back to his work. "It will when everyone else starts thinking the way you do. People tend to be bored when things stay the same for too long."

"Is that what happened with you?"

"I suppose so," the Painter said after a short pause. "Doubt gets a little boring after it stops feeling so dreadful. I am a firm believer in change. That's what East Parliss is about, and that's what my work is about as well."

The Painter gestured for Alicia to look at the three paintings resting by the edge of the sidewalk. "These were inspired by one young woman I knew many years ago. They are different because she was different. She was a broken young girl at eight, a comforted young woman at eighteen, and a lost young woman not too much later."

"Who was she?" Alicia asked, even though she already felt like she knew the answer.

"Her name was Alexandra Cardor. Have you heard that name before?"

"Once last week, but I didn't learn much about her."

"Tom brought her to East Parliss about twelve years ago," the Painter said. "She's the only other person I've painted with besides you. Tom thought it would be therapeutic for her—a good way to cope with her anger. She made one of the most exquisite pieces I've ever seen. It was a young girl kneeling down on top of a hill, with her arms reaching up in the air to release a small bird from her hands so it could fly away."

"That sounds lovely," Alicia said, trying to block out her memories of the Parryrose Club. "It sounds almost like my painting, now that I think about it."

"That doesn't surprise me," the Painter said. "I gave you the same challenge I gave her. I asked her to make something to forget about who she was and help her see what she could become. That's the place where all young people go in their own minds, and I make myself responsible for helping them make it a good thing."

"Did painting help her?" Alicia asked.

"I suppose it did for a while," the Painter said after a long sigh. "I'm not sure it matters that much now. She doesn't like East Parliss anymore. She's not very popular around here either. I'm one of the last few left who still remembers her fondly. That's why I have these three paintings out for the rest of us to see. They remind us all of the good we don't see in her anymore."

"Why do people here not like her?"

The Painter looked down at his feet. "A lot of us helped her when she needed us, and one day she just left, like we meant nothing to her. She had a special talent for getting people to love her. It was not a sexual love, or a romantic love, but the way you might feel about a daughter or a sister. A day with her would often feel like a week, and a week with her would feel like a month. In half a year, she could make anyone feel like she was part of their family, and watching someone like that walk away from you leaves a terrible sting."

"Yes, I'm sure that would," Alicia muttered, carrying on with her painting as she wondered how this must have affected Tom, and whether it was why he left Parliss County all those years ago.

"That's a common flaw you will notice in people as you get older," the Painter said. "We are only as good as our worst moment. One crucial mistake can tear down friendships no matter how many great and pleasant memories you have together. One act of carelessness can leave the drop of ink that spoils the drink. I can't let myself fall into these traps. I leave these three paintings with me to keep the good close by, and the sting as far away as I can."

The skin around the Painter's eyes began to quiver as if he were about to cry, and Alicia decided it was best not to ask any more questions.

She spent the rest of the day painting in silence and left Besalbee Road at the cusp of sunset, walking with her head down as she thought of what it must have been like for Tom and the Painter to lose someone so important to them. Coming to America had forced Alicia to cope with a similar kind of loneliness. It had grown worse with all her time with the Donnigan Girls, and although she'd only been free of them for a few weeks, she felt as strong and sure of herself as she once had as a young girl. Laronna felt like a lifetime ago, some memory that became more and more of a dream with each day she spent in Parliss. Jeremiah and Tom were all that had stuck with her, the only two people from her current life that would drag back memories of this odd past for many years to come, and somehow that didn't feel so bad to her.

"Can I ask you something?" Alicia said to Jeremiah, while they were alone in the loft and Mr. Zeeger was downstairs helping his customers.

"You just did," Jeremiah said, grinning. Alicia rolled her eyes. That joke was getting old very quickly.

"Very funny," she said. "So, can we have a real conversation now?"

"Sure. What's up?"

"Do you know what you want to be when you're older?"

"Not really," he replied, after a short pause. The cheery look that had been in his eyes a moment ago was gone. "Why do you ask? Is this about your painting?"

"A little bit."

"Are you having any trouble?"

"No. It's going well. I'm almost done. It's just given me a lot to think about lately."

"Like what?" he replied. "Do you have a plan?"

"Not exactly," she confessed, after a heavy sigh and a short pause of her own. "All I know is that I don't want to commit to something just yet. I want to spend some time traveling. I don't think I'll ever know what I really want unless I see a bit more of the world first."

"Well, in that case, you're pretty lucky," Jeremiah said. "You've already seen more than I have."

"I guess so," Alicia muttered. "It just doesn't seem like enough."

"Don't worry. You'll be fine," Jeremiah said. "Trust me, you're a lot better off than I am."

"How so?"

"Well, if I'm being honest, I think you're a lot tougher than I am. I don't think I could handle moving to another country when I was that young. I needed Tom's help just to feel safe going to school each day, but you did his job all by yourself. If you can do that, I don't think there's a whole lot you have to worry about."

Alicia smiled. "You really think so?"

He nodded. "You don't need to have a plan right now. You just need to know what feels good and what doesn't. If you can do that, then when the time comes, you'll know where to go."

For the rest of the day, Alicia couldn't stop thinking about everything Jeremiah had said. She crawled into bed with the memory of their talk still fresh in her mind, keeping her awake deep into the night until she finally dozed off.

Alicia went back to Besalbee Road the next morning, parting ways with Jeremiah outside the Broken Cottage just as they'd done every day of this week. She secretly wished they could go to Besalbee Road together, curious to see how he would have followed the Painter's challenge and what he hoped to be in the future.

She finished the painting on Sunday evening with barely a minute to spare. She called it *The Protector*, and wrote the title at the bottom right-hand corner just above her signature. Proud of her work, she turned her easel around to let the Painter see it at last. A warm smile appeared on his face as he admired his student's work, gazing upon it with the sort of awe and wonder most people would save for watching a sunset. Alicia nearly blushed when she saw the glint appear in his eyes, but as usual, she kept her giddiness to herself, trying to look professional.

The Painter returned the favor and allowed Alicia to see what he'd made during the last seven days. It was a picture of a young girl in a green dress, tossing a clean, unused knife into a roaring fire so it would melt before having the chance to kill. The Painter had named this piece *The Protector*.

"It seems I have judged you well," the Painter said, smiling as Alicia carefully picked up her finished painting and walked back to the Broken Cottage.

Alicia's Myers Briggs Scores

Original Results							
10	17	14	8	8	12	22	5
E	I	S	N	T	F	J	P
Score	Score	Score	Score	Score	Score	Score	Score
(E or I)	I	(S or N)	S	(T or F)	F	(J or P)	J

New Results							
11	16	13	9	10	10	22	5
E	I	S	N	T	F	J	P
Score	Score	Score	Score	Score	Score	Score	Score
(E or I)	I	(S or N)	S	(T or F)	X	(J or P)	J

Chapter Ten

Lola and the Berryserpent

There were days when Jeremiah was fine being alone, free to roam about his thoughts and daydreams without the pressure of conversation to get in his way. There were also days when being alone was the last thing he wanted, days when he would've traded anything he had for a bit of company, some friends to take him out to parties and concerts and give him the memories he would cherish until his death. His state of mind could change as easily as the wind.

He didn't know why he was like this, or why he'd always been like this, and hoped the Aurascope could help him find the answer.

He looked at the eleventh ring of his Aura, where blue light was a sign of independence, and a dependent nature was shown in red. He was curious to see which side was stronger, and he was surprised to see this ring was magenta: a perfect cross of red and blue with no side winning against the other, the one color Jeremiah knew nothing about.

"It's known as the color of conflict," Mr. Zeeger said. He sat at the table with a bottle of white wine in his hand, while Jeremiah stood by the kitchen.

"It's known as an irregular color of Aura, since it isn't part of the usual blue-to-red spectrum like the others. Magenta is a color that shows up in places where we feel lost. It's different from green, which represents balance—two opposite ends working together for a greater good. Magenta is a sign of some internal fight, like two halves of your soul debating which side is right and which is wrong."

Mr. Zeeger asked to look at Jeremiah's Aura for a more detailed view. "Ring eleven," he said. "That's a common one for young people. We all have days we think we don't need anyone else, but it doesn't take long at all before we wish we had friends by our side. There's always a balance. Too much self-reliance means you wind up sheltered in your home with no one to talk to; depend on others too much and you can't take care of yourself. There's always a middle ground, and it's different for each person. That's why they're so hard to find, but you'll learn more about that later."

——— ——— ——— ———

Jeremiah wasn't sure what Mr. Zeeger meant by this. He hoped that Tom's second letter, which he found resting by his plate at the kitchen table, would help make this a little clearer. He parted ways with Alicia once they were outside the pub. He said goodbye as he watched his friend saunter off to some place called Besalbee Road, and then followed the counselor's instructions to a lonely house in the southern part of East Parliss. It looked to be only one story high. It stood at the edge of a massive field of wheat on a road with no neighbors. The road was made from asphalt rather than cobblestone, showing just how separate this place was from the rest of the town.

A woman came to greet him when he knocked on the door. She smiled as she reached out for a handshake and introduced herself as Gretchen Salcott. She looked to be around Tom's age, though she was a few inches shorter. She had a soft, childlike face with gentle features, light hazel eyes, and short brown hair that barely reached past her ears. Her house was fairly tidy, with the exception of one room next to the kitchen where sheets of paper, old essays, and news articles lay scattered across her desk and the carpet. A degree from Princeton hung from the wall. Books and awards sat on dusty shelves, without any pictures of friends or family.

Like the Jennabelle Kids, Gretchen's Aura was composed of

moderate colors with hardly any deep reds and blues. Whatever traits were more dominant had only won by a small margin. She leaned slightly more to the side of sensitive instead of tough, suspicious instead of trusting, reclusive instead of adventurous, imaginative instead of practical, and carefree instead of serious. The only rings that appeared unbalanced were her first, showing she was an introvert; and her fourteenth, which was red as a sign of her shrewd, cunning nature, a trait Jeremiah did not expect to see given the woman's benign, friendly appearance.

"I was the youngest of four kids, with three older brothers who never had a hard time getting attention," Gretchen said as she sat down with Jeremiah at the kitchen table, right beside a window with an excellent view of the prairie that was her backyard. "They were all gifted athletes, very handsome, and my parents expected more out of them than me. I always had to be clever if I wanted them to notice me. My teachers always said I was an excellent writer. That was the one skill I had that my brothers couldn't compete with, and boy did I take advantage of it. I wrote stories up in my bedroom any chance I could. Unless I was eating, studying, bathing, or sleeping, I was busy scribbling down short stories as fast as I could until my hand was too sore.

"Do you have any of them?" Jeremiah asked, curious to see just how good she'd been at such a young age.

"The good ones are lying around my office somewhere in a pile. Most of my early stories were fantasies about girls who flew on the backs of dragons and red eagles the size of horses. They were always about fighting witches and evil sorcerers, or finding some ancient sword of some made-up name to save her village, but my father didn't seem too invested in them. I didn't learn until I was fifteen that he didn't love fantasy worlds the way I did. That's when I tried writing more contemporary stories that focused on real world problems. They were just as long, but they were much harder to write."

"How come?"

Gretchen shrugged. "They were a lot darker than what I was used to. Most of them were about young men and women living in poverty or coping with mental illness—the kind of stories that tug at your emotions until you just want to lie down and go to sleep. Those types of stories seemed to impress him more, so I wrote more of them. I started to lose my grasp on fantasy when I was seventeen, to the point where I almost lost my love of fiction. When I started working as a journalist a few years later, I wrote articles about domestic violence, drug addictions, and child abuse. By the time I started writing stories again, I'd seen too much of the world to go back to my dragons. So, I wrote this instead."

Gretchen reached across to the kitchen counter and handed Jeremiah a copy of a children's book entitled *Lola and the Berryserpent.* There was a little girl on the front cover, with a purple snake draped across her neck and shoulders like a scarf. Gretchen said this was the book she was the proudest of compared to all her other works, despite its lack of popularity. Children had found it dull, tedious, and way too long, while adults had protested to remove it from schools for its dark themes they deemed unsuitable for young boys and girls.

"What's it about?" Jeremiah asked.

"That's for you to find out," Gretchen replied. "I want you to read this book during our week together. I want you to read it and see what it makes you think about. You can take it back to Gerald's place if you want, but if you'd rather not walk that far, you're welcome to stay here."

Jeremiah chose to read in the old rocking chair on Gretchen's front porch, on the side of the house that granted him a pleasant view of tall trees and a cloudless sky that distracted him several times from his reading. His habit for daydreaming and getting lost in his own thoughts had always been his weakness in reading, despite how engrossed he became in Gretchen's book. He cared for Lola in just the first few chapters as he imagined her walking alone down a quiet street in the middle of the night. She had run away from home for a reason the book kept as a mystery for now, and she was off in search of a new home. She grew hungry after walking for so long and stopped at a nearby park to pick blackberries. She ate some and put the others in her coat pockets for later, since she didn't know when or where her next meal would be. She staggered back when she heard a rustling sound from inside the bush, and was terrified to see a large purple snake crawl out from between the branches. Lola picked up a rock and threw it at the snake. She missed her shot and cowered in fear that the hideous creature would devour her whole, but instead the snake turned around and began eating blackberries.

Lola had never heard of a snake that ate berries before. She had always seen snakes as vicious killers who ate mice and poisoned people with their sharp teeth, but this one was different. It was lost and all by itself in the wild, just like she was, and she felt guilty for trying to hurt the poor thing. She apologized by giving the snake some of the berries she'd stashed away in her pockets, and by promising she would take care of it from now on. She decided to call this new friend of hers the Berryserpent, and offered to carry it across her shoulders like a scarf while they traveled together in search of a new home.

It took Jeremiah a few more days of reading to understand why such a charming story of unlikely friends was banned in so many schools. He got his answer about one-third of the way through the book, in a later chapter that explained Lola had run away from home because of her father. He'd come home late one night many weeks ago, drunk and tired and furious after a long day at work. Lola had woken up when she heard the sound of her parents bickering down in the kitchen. She'd crept out of her room and stood at the top of the stairs, just in time to see her father smash a bottle against the counter and stab her mother with the shards of glass. She'd put her hands over her mouth before she could scream then ran back to her room and climbed out the window to escape. She'd reckoned the cops would be looking for her, which meant she needed to go far away so they couldn't find her and take her back.

"I can never go back," Lola said to the Berryserpent. "I have no parents anymore. You're the only family I've got."

She promised the Berryserpent she would find a new home for them in no time at all, which proved to be much harder than expected. She would walk to nearby towns and find people on the street. She would ask if they could take care of her, but the Berryserpent always frightened them away.

Sadly, Lola didn't notice this was the reason nobody wanted to talk to her, and so she spent the next few chapters wondering what she was doing wrong and why no one cared enough to give her a chance. She slept under a park bench with the Berryserpent nestled against her body, sobbing at the dreadful thought they would never find anyone who would love them both.

It was a picture as clear as any Jeremiah could see in a painting, so strong he shut the book as all his old memories of the Donnigan Boys came rushing back. He remembered one time when Roy Garson sat next to him in English class, but only stayed at his desk for a moment until Ethan and Casey walked in, at which point he retreated to the back of the classroom to join the rest of his posse. He thought of all the times he'd joined them for lunch, and how rarely they'd paid attention when he spoke or tried cracking a joke. He tried to remember a time when any of them reached out to him first, but not one example came to mind.

He thought back on what Gretchen said about her three brothers and wondered how much of Lola came from her own struggles for love and attention. All of Jeremiah's time spent writing stories and poems for class assignments had taught him that authors always found ways to put themselves into their work, whether they tried to or not. Lola had to come from somewhere.

Jeremiah came back to Gretchen's house early the next morning to continue his reading. He sat back in the rocking chair and rejoined Lola as she crawled out from under the bench and startled an old woman who'd come to the park to feed the birds.

"Young girl," said the old woman. "Why do you carry that hideous thing around your shoulders?"

"He's my friend, ma'am," Lola said with an innocent smile. "I look after him because no one else will, and I love him 'cause no one else does, and he does the same for me. I'm his mother now, ma'am. He's my responsibility, and I have to find us a new home."

"Well, darling, I'm sorry to tell you this, but no one is going to let you into their home with that thing on your shoulders. You'll have to get rid of it and get rid of it soon."

The old woman told Lola to leave the snake at the park and then go to the police. Lola did neither of these things. Instead, she refilled her pockets with blackberries and rushed out of town as quickly as she could before any cops had the chance to spot her. She told the Berryserpent she would never abandon him, but she struggled to keep her promise when she set foot in the next town and watched more people run away from her before she could even speak. Now she understood why she was having so much trouble finding a new home, and she wondered if she would be better off without her new friend.

She would sneak away at night while the Berryserpent was asleep and try to run to a new town all by herself, but she would always stop after running a few blocks and turn back to be with her friend. Each new day she promised herself she would stick by the Berryserpent, and each night she would change her mind and run away only to turn around just a few minutes later. She could never fully decide to do the right thing or the smart thing, whether she trusted herself and the Berryserpent to depend on each other, or if she might be better off alone.

Gretchen's book took a dark turn when a pair of police officers found Lola one night while she was alone. They took her to the station before she could run back to the Berryserpent. She started to cry, begging them to let her go, but they wouldn't listen. The local sheriff asked where her parents were and where she was from, and Lola said she'd run away from home after her mother's death to escape her cruel father. She said she met a friendly purple snake along the way who had been her trusty companion for many months, but the sheriff didn't believe this part of her story.

The next day, Lola was sent to live in a nearby foster home owned by a man named Mr. Green. There were three other kids who lived in this house, but Lola didn't bother making friends with them. She was still determined to find the Berryserpent and bring him to live with her at the foster house. She snuck away one night and ran to a park with a patch of blackberry bushes and called out for the Berryserpent. She stayed until the eastern sky started to turn rosy pink with the rising sun, and then she ran back to the foster house before Mr. Green could wake up and see she was missing.

Lola came back to this same park each night for the next two months, hoping her friend would slither out from the blackberry bushes like he'd done the night they met. Lola called out for hours before she started to believe the Berryserpent was gone, and just as she started to cry, she heard a noise from behind her. She turned around and saw Mr. Green. Lola was afraid she was about to be in a lot of trouble, but the man smiled and asked if they could talk for a moment.

"He's real!" Lola shouted. "I know you don't believe me. I know none of you believe me, but he was my friend and I abandoned him."

"You didn't abandon him," said Mr. Green. "You were taken from him."

"But I tried to leave him," Lola protested, sobbing more than she'd ever done before. "I got caught when I was running away from him. He's all alone, and it's all my fault. I have to find him, sir. He's my only friend."

"He's not your only friend anymore," said Mr. Green. "You have me. You have Benny, you have Emily, and you have Jimmy. We're all your friends now, and we love you very much."

"But I can't leave him alone," said Lola. "I need to say I'm sorry. I need to find him a home."

"What if he already has a home?" Mr. Green asked. "Snakes don't belong in houses. They belong out in the wild. That's not a place for little girls. Do you think your friend would want to live in a place like this?"

Lola took a moment to think of an answer. "I guess I never really thought much about that. But why would he stay with me for so long if he didn't want to live in a house?"

"Maybe he wanted to see you find a home," Mr. Green suggested. "Maybe, from his point of view, he was the one looking after you, and now that you have a home he doesn't need to protect you anymore."

"Maybe you're right," Lola admitted, "but I still can't leave him. He's my friend. I have to see him at least one more time just so I can say goodbye."

"I know you want to," said Mr. Green. "I know it hurts, but sometimes we don't get to say goodbye. Sometimes we're just taken from our friends when we don't expect it. You didn't get to say goodbye to your mother, right?"

"No," Lola said, burying her face into Mr. Green's coat as she continued to cry. "It's not fair."

"I know it isn't fair," said Mr. Green. "But fairness isn't something we can control. All we can do is control what we do when the world doesn't spin the way we want it to. Your mother loved you very much. The Berryserpent loved you very much. I love you very much. And even if those other two aren't around anymore, those memories can keep them with you for years to come."

Lola nodded. She kept her head down as the last few tears dripped down her cheeks, and then she wiped them all away with a stroke of her hand.

"Can I ask you something, sir?"

"Anything at all, darling."

"Can you promise you'll always be my friend?" Lola asked. "I mean, I know I'll move out when I'm older, and I'll get my own house and my own job, but can you promise we'll always be friends even when we're apart? And can we say goodbye to each other all the time so that if you die or I get taken away, then at least we still got to say goodbye? I can't lose any more people without saying goodbye."

"I promise I'll always be your friend," said Mr. Green, as Lola began to smile for the first time in months. "And I'll look after you for as long as I can. Now, let's get you back home."

— — — — —

139

It was Saturday when Jeremiah finished reading these final pages, leaving just one more day to spend with Gretchen before his second week was over. As much as he loved her book, he understood why it wasn't very successful, or why so many parents sought to keep it away from their children. A story with so much death, loss, and loneliness might have sent his eight-year-old self sobbing into his pillow by the final chapter, a reaction that would have given any good parent a reason to be concerned.

With every step he took on his way back to the Broken Cottage, Lola was with him. He could see her on the other side of the road, beneath the lampposts, looking down on him from the nearby windows, marching alongside his shadow even as he returned to his bedroom.

He wondered why Gretchen had asked him to read this book in the first place. He lay in bed and gazed up at the ceiling, asking himself what he was supposed to take away from Lola's journey, what Gretchen wanted him to learn, and why Tom devoted seven days of his summer to reading a children's book. He opened his journal and wrote down everything he remembered from the story, looking for symbols and deeper meanings in every quote, character, scene, and subplot. He nearly dropped his pencil when he took a more critical look at the Berryserpent and asked himself why Gretchen chose to make him purple. Then the answer was clear: Purple. Magenta. The color of conflict. Something Lola carried with her wherever she went. A part of her identity that always brought her trouble. A problem she loved, but a problem that had to go if she wanted to be happy. A dirty color that had to be replaced with the color of Personal Balance. Green. Mr. Green.

With hindsight at his disposal, Jeremiah wanted to bury his face in shame he hadn't seen the subtext all along. Now that he knew, his memory of Lola was sharper than ever. He saw her when he went to sleep, when he woke up the next morning, and as he walked back to Gretchen's home for his final day. He saw the former journalist sitting in the rocking chair out on the porch, a book on her lap and a cup of coffee in hand. He heard the wood creak beneath his feet as he stepped onto the porch and locked eyes with her.

"Mr. Green is Tom," Jeremiah said. "And Lola is Alexandra Cardor. Is that right?"

She smiled. "What gave it away?"

"The Berryserpent. You made him purple for a reason. I just didn't see it 'til last night."

"Well, you were right," Gretchen said. "I knew Alexandra once, a long time ago when Tom brought her to this place. It was like having my own daughter for a short time. She was just like how I remember myself at that age, just with a few more troubles than my own family squabbling."

"Like what? What happened when she was young?"

He realized the answer as soon as he spoke, but he let Gretchen tell him anyway.

"When she was eight years old, Lola's age, she woke up in the middle of the night when she heard her father stumble into the house. He was drunk and angry, and when he got into a fight with Alexandra's mother, he knocked her to the ground and stabbed her four times with a broken wine bottle. Alexandra saw the whole thing while crouching down at the top of the stairs. She snuck out of her bedroom window to run away, but she didn't get very far before the police found her. When she told them what happened, they rushed to her house and arrested her father."

"Jeez," Jeremiah said, wondering how a kid that young could deal with something so terrible. "What happened to her after that?"

"She was sent to live with her aunt and uncle—on her mother's side. They didn't have a lot of money. They didn't have any kids of their own and had never planned to, but they didn't trust anyone else to look after her. They felt responsible for her, so they agreed to look after her even though they never wanted to be parents."

"Were they good to her?"

"They were," Gretchen said with a little hesitation. "They were kind, but a little impatient, from what I've heard. I suppose that's something you can expect from parents who never wanted to be parents. They weren't used to making compromises with children.

They were very pragmatic. They didn't buy her any toys except for a few plush animals because they thought toys were a waste of money. They gave Alexandra only what she needed, but that was it. Sometimes a child needs a little more than that."

Gretchen said she'd always seen Alexandra as a girl from two childhoods. One was decent, safe, but without the luxuries most kids her age took for granted. The other was full of love and affection until one night destroyed it all, and now cast a dark shadow on her years as a growing woman. She had a mixed and messy identity that showed itself in her adolescence. On any day she might prefer to study hard for school or work long shifts as a waitress at a nearby restaurant. The next day she might receive a bad grade on a test and decide she was an awful student, and that her time would be better spent smoking in the parking lot and skipping school to quash her stress with the soothing taste of alcohol. She would come home one night and endure a harsh lecture from her aunt and uncle about her childish behavior and the importance of having a good career, and by the start of next week she would be studying again.

"The only time her aunt and uncle paid any extra money was for psychiatric help," Gretchen said. "They were concerned something wasn't right with her. They swore she was bipolar, had PTSD, or some sort of mental illness that was keeping her this way, but all the doctors and therapists said she was fine. They wouldn't diagnose her with anything, but her aunt and uncle still heard her talking to herself in her sleep while she rolled around in her bed. They knew she needed someone to help her. They just didn't know who it would be and what needed fixing."

"And that's where Tom came in, right?"

Gretchen nodded. "He was the last of Alexandra's therapists. She was a patient of his for two years before he ever told her about Parliss County. He encouraged her to come live with the Auralites when she turned eighteen. He promised he would help her learn Personal Balance, and that with his help and counseling, she would feel better about herself. He promised to do whatever it took to keep her safe and happy, just like Mr. Green."

Jeremiah opened his mouth to ask where Alexandra was now, but Gretchen kept talking before he could make a sound. "And Tom still loves her very much, even though most of East Parliss resents her now. To him, Alexandra will always be like my Lola. That's how I wanted you to see her before you learned anything else about her. That's why I asked you to read this book."

"Why do people here not like her?" Jeremiah asked.

"She left us," Gretchen answered. "That's the simplest way to put it. A lot of people here in East Parliss worked very hard to help her, and we had so much faith in her. Then she started having disagreements with Tom and took out her frustration in a way that hurt a lot of us, and then one day she left. She walked across Corraine-Callister one night and went to West Parliss. No one on this side has seen her since."

"That doesn't sound so bad," Jeremiah said. "Maybe she just wasn't happy here anymore."

"That's how I see it now," Gretchen said. "But it's not that easy when someone you care about rejects you so harshly. You're still upset with those boys from school, aren't you?"

Jeremiah's head quickly jerked to the side, as it often did when he heard something that surprised him. "How do you know about them?"

"Tom mentioned them when he called me a few weeks back," Gretchen replied. "He told me you would see a lot of yourself in Lola, and that you were used to being alone even when you didn't know why. He wanted this to be the way you learned about Alexandra, and when he told me about those boys, I knew I had to share her story with you."

"Why?"

"I wanted to help you learn how to forgive them."

Jeremiah did his best not to scoff, laugh, or roll his eyes in disbelief. He skipped down his list of reactions until he just glanced away for a moment, and then turned back to face Gretchen with a doubt-ridden look in his eyes.

"I'm not saying they were right to do whatever they did," Gretchen clarified, before Jeremiah could say anything else. "I'm saying it's the right thing for you. Nothing good ever comes from moving forward with anger. If you want proof, just look around the rest of East Parliss and you'll find it.

"Or you can look around right here."

Jeremiah glanced off to the left side of the house, then to the right, then to the trees from across the other side of the road. He realized once again how alone they were. She was alone, in a house made for one person.

"I haven't seen my family in years," Gretchen muttered, speaking in a cold, fragile whisper with her eyes still aimed to the ground. "I thought getting back in touch with them would be easy, that I could step in anytime I wanted and it would be like nothing happened, but I waited too long. They all had their stories. They all had their own memories, their own lives, and I was never around to be a part of any of them. They tried to bring me in, they really did, but I'd been gone so long that I didn't fit in their set anymore. I waited years until I finally told the teenage girl in me to stop dragging me down with all her fears and her anger, but I had already run out of time."

"I'm sorry. I'm sure that was hard for you," Jeremiah muttered, wishing he had something better to say.

"I swore I would never let that happen again," Gretchen said. "I swore I'd never waste my time feeling alone, that I'd never take people who loved me and turn them away. That's why I wrote Lola. She may not mean much to everyone else, but she means everything to me. She keeps me whole. She makes me better. Maybe, when you find a Lola of your own, you'll know what I mean."

As Jeremiah saw the sad, broken look buried inside Gretchen's eyes, he wondered if maybe forgiveness was the right choice for him after all. Gretchen suggested that he write his own story, that he devote a few of his free hours to getting inside the heads of his old classmates until he could turn them into good, complex characters with their own lives, ideas, fears, and hopes, but he only managed to scratch down one sentence with Ethan Kantzton's name on the paper before he tore the page out of his journal and threw it away. He couldn't do it. He'd given them plenty of chances for redemption, and they had all been spent.

He knew a day would come when he could forgive them, when Laronna was nothing but a distant memory, when he was bored of wasting time on old grudges.

One day, he would want to learn more about his classmates, dig into their childhoods, unmask their hopes and fears, and wonder what might happen to them in the future, but their time would have to wait.

Alexandra was first in line.

He had to know who she was.

He had to know what she wanted.

He had to know why she left.

Chapter Eleven

An Invisible Switch

During his second year of high school, a few days after his sixteenth birthday, Jeremiah saw the Donnigan Boys standing by the water fountain. Off to the side, Mike Harver stood with his hand pressed against his throat, not saying a word while the rest of his friends talked and talked like they always did. Casey explained once they all sat down for class that Mike was recovering from a throat infection and was trying to stay quiet for the whole day so he wouldn't experience any pain. He remained silent throughout the rest of the week, and yet he stuck by his friends every day. When he returned to school the following Monday after a final trip to the hospital, he was back to his old self, as if nothing had happened. He'd been socially absent for a whole week, and yet all his friends still wanted him around.

"There's a question I've been meaning to ask you for a while," Jeremiah said, in a session with Tom that had taken place during Thursday of that week. "You said a long time ago that extroverts were people who were socially outgoing and loved to talk, right?"

"Yes," Tom said, leaning forward in his chair with his clasped hands resting between his legs.

"But what if this person couldn't speak?" Jeremiah asked. "What if he *wanted* to talk, and be social, but he just *couldn't?* Would he still be an extrovert?"

"That's a very good question," Tom said, glancing off to the side, looking as if he didn't know the answer. "Is this about Mike?"

Jeremiah nodded. "I talked more than he did all last week, and they still liked him more than me. It just got me curious, that's all."

"It should. That's a very interesting question. I don't know if you're aware of this, but you've actually addressed an old concept known as the Three Facets of Identity—sometimes called the TFI Principle."

"What is it?"

"It's an idea that claims our identities are composed of three individual parts: our skills, our choices, and our birthright. If we're given certain privileges from birth—being wealthy, for example—we might grow up to demonstrate a kind of carelessness or arrogance that we wouldn't have if we were born to poorer parents. If we have a talent for painting, we would probably fall in love with art because of the attention we get from it, even though we probably never would have developed that passion if we, say, happened to be born blind. The aspect of choice, simply, is how we choose to behave once the rest of our identity is established. Does that make sense?"

"Yeah, I think so," Jeremiah said. It didn't really answer his question, but it was interesting nonetheless.

"It gives you a lot to think about, doesn't it?" Tom continued. "It's a good question: How much of one's personality is determined by choice, and how much is determined by skill? Suppose Mike had been born with a speech impediment of some kind. Do you think he'd be the so-called golden boy he is now? What if he lost his voice permanently? Do you think he could keep all his friends, or would they all move on without him?"

Jeremiah knew that whenever Tom asked this many questions in a row, he didn't mean for any of them to be answered, only pondered. Jeremiah stared down at the floor, running down the list of all the Mike Harvers that appeared in his mind, and the counselor let him sit in silence for a while until he bothered to speak again.

"You've always wanted to be more outgoing, right?" Tom said. "What's stopping you? Are you choosing to be more reserved? Is that how you were born? Or are you simply just not very good at making conversation?"

"I don't know," Jeremiah muttered. He spoke even though he was fairly sure Tom intended these questions to be rhetorical, but the words slipped out of his mouth too quickly for him to stop. He knew one thing for sure: he was not this way by choice, even if the Donnigan Boys thought he was. He would've gladly thrown away his old sketchpad with all his drawings if it meant he could have their special gift for speaking, the one that helped them magically generate new jokes and topics of conversation from thin air, and never resort to weather-watcher comments to break the silence.

— — — — —

Tom never said where he learned about the Three Facets of Identity. A few more years would have to pass until Jeremiah got his answer. He was living in the counselor's past while paving the way for his own future, and yet his old problems still followed him every step of the way. He'd often asked himself if he would make the trade, if he would swap his I for an E, lose everything that came from his quiet habits so he could reap all the costs and benefits of being a Donnigan Boy. His answer changed every day, but none of them ever mattered, since he would always be the same in the world outside his own head. He'd always be stuck as a quiet kid with the dream of being a loud one, and he had the Aurascope to prove it.

He'd expected something to be different after his week with the Jennabelle Kids, but nothing was. He'd expected something to be different after his week with Gretchen, but nothing was. His blues and reds were still alive. His cyans and yellows hadn't taken their last few steps to the green light at the center. His magenta-colored ring still haunted him. His colors remained the same, and as depressing as it was to see his lack of progress day after day, he still couldn't stop looking.

He looked at himself in the Aurascope every night, in his bedroom under the sheets while the others were asleep. He couldn't help himself. It was too addicting. He'd spent years learning how to study people, how to spot the winners from the losers, the parts of people that made them great and the parts that needed fixing. Now he finally had the answer in his hands, and he never wanted to let it go. He had to study it every day and stay true to his stubborn belief that one day he would be a new man.

— — — —

He expected to see another pair of letters waiting at the kitchen table when he crawled out of bed on the first day of his third week, but instead he only found one. He discovered as Alicia read the letter out loud that they would be meeting the same Auralite this week. He hoped Alicia felt as happy about this news as he was. Jeremiah had hoped this would happen eventually, considering half his reason for coming here in the first place was so he could spend more time with his dear friend. They hadn't done much together apart from eating dinner at the end of the day and sharing stories about their experiences with the Auralites. Now, at last, they had a chance to make a new memory together.

The man they were supposed to meet this week was Howard Granzill. The letter mentioned he was an actor who used to perform at the old Canmark Theater. As a boy, he'd watched his older brother die from an overdose of heroin. Once as punishment for shouting back at his parents, his mother slapped him across the face until his cheek was red, and he'd been left to spend a night sleeping in the yard after being whipped across the back with his father's belt. He had fallen in love with a woman who years later would leave him at the altar on their wedding day, a loss that left him clinically depressed and sent him down a path that led to his own addiction. He spent nearly five years hooked on cocaine until he found help in East Parliss, and quickly rose to fame as one of the Canmark's best performers.

Jeremiah's heart sank just from listening to Alicia recite these facts from the letter. His sense of pity only grew worse when Mr. Zeeger informed them the Canmark Theater had been closed for nearly a decade, which meant the one silver lining of this man's life was dead.

They were supposed to meet this man at the Broken Cottage. Mr. Zeeger gave them permission to sit at a private table by the bar despite being below the drinking age. They waited for Howard Granzill while they listened to the comedian who was performing from a tiny stage in the back end of the pub. He was fairly short with broad shoulders and a stocky physique, and he had a loud, booming voice that could have carried across a city block. Half the people in the room were bent over laughing when Jeremiah and Alicia sat down, and the other half would take their turns as the act went on.

The bar erupted in applause when the comedian announced his act was over, at which point he grabbed his coat and briefcase as a folk singer took his place on the stage. Jeremiah thought of asking one of the other customers for his name, and might have done so if the comedian hadn't come to sit down at their table. The man's name was clear the instant he asked if they were the Jeremiah and Alicia he'd come to meet.

"I reckon you weren't expecting this," Mr. Granzill said once he led them to a booth in a quieter section of the pub. "I certainly wouldn't blame you. I never would've thought I'd be the kind of person who could make people laugh. There was a time when I thought these kinds of entertainers were the scum of the earth—all caught up in their happy lives and their jokes and distracting the public from the real problems out there. Little did I know I was going to be one of them someday, and I'm a much healthier man because of it."

A comedian was the last profession Jeremiah would expect from a man who'd lived such a hard life. He was stunned by how much this man had changed after so much hardship, but the feeling quickly died away when Howard asked to borrow Alicia's Aurascope, and revealed he was still in many ways the same as he'd always been. Many of his rings still burned red with apprehension, sensitivity, and neuroticism. A stark, fiery magenta appeared in many rings as well: Trusting vs. Suspicion, Conscientiousness vs. Expedience, and Forceful vs. Submissive, proving the wounds of his childhood had yet to disappear. He fit the mold of a scared child from an abusive family who'd endured the loss of a brother and fiancé, and yet he behaved just the opposite.

"I lie for a living," the comedian said. "That's what acting is, but it's a good kind of lying you should never feel ashamed of. We lie because we all have this dream of an invisible switch. We live as who we are but wish we could be something better. We will always want to be somewhere else, and we dream of an invisible switch inside our minds to do that. But these switches don't exist, so we settle for acting, hoping that just maybe we can trick ourselves into thinking it's real."

The comedian reached inside his briefcase and set a stack of papers on the table. They were monologues, long and theatrical speeches to be spoken by a single character. Each script came with a title named after its one character, as well as a brief description of the sort of person they were, how old they were, where they were from, and any other piece of information that served a crucial part in their identity. Anything else was left for their actors to create. In this case, that responsibility went to Jeremiah and Alicia, who were each asked to pick one speech and spend the next seven days rehearsing these lines and creating these characters, and then perform in the pub on Sunday evening.

Alicia chose one about a young woman who came from a wealthy family, who from a young age had been groomed and dressed like a doll, made to smile and act perfectly respectable in every way, but had a secret love for the woods and would often lie to her parents about going to the library to study when she would actually go walking along the nearby hiking trails while taking photos of birds and collecting leaves to keep in her closet. The role was so perfect for Alicia that Jeremiah felt the script must have been written for her, but she would still need practice to get it right.

"I once spent a full month confined in an empty room living off rice and water so I could play a man stranded on an island," Howard said. "They told me I didn't have to, but I told them I did. A good performance takes work and discipline, and that's what I want to encourage."

151

Alicia, being the seasoned young actress she was, didn't protest this idea of extra work, and left the booth minutes later for Littelbine Park with her script, her phone for taking pictures of birds, and a paper bag for collecting leaves. Jeremiah knew she would spend hours getting in touch with her new character and studying her lines, and that she wouldn't stop until it was so late she had no choice but to put her work aside until the next morning.

The script Jeremiah chose was about a boy he didn't like at all, which made for a great but difficult role to play. His character was a perfect fit for the Donnigan Boys. He had Mike Harver's cockiness, Casey Marsley's love for crude humor, and Ethan Kantzton's irritable nature. Just reading some of his lines left Jeremiah with a lingering taste of disgust on his tongue, but he spent the rest of the day memorizing each word until the acting was all he had left to work on. This was bound to be the hardest part. He was so different from this boy, and he was nowhere near as talented as Alicia that he could disappear into the skin of his role without the comedian's help.

Jeremiah found Howard sitting in the pub the next morning at a table in the more crowded part of the room, where the voices of the other customers were loud and distracting. He asked if they could move to a quieter table but the comedian said no, insisting that dealing with crowds and distractions was an essential skill to a performer.

"You'll need to get used to talking a lot," the comedian said. "This is a social character. He talks a lot more than he listens and he has a lot of friends to talk to. You and I will have to talk a lot, and you'll have to get more used to crude humor. This is fairly simple, since all we need to do to practice is talk about something. We can do that right now, about anything you want. What's on your mind?"

Jeremiah didn't waste any time thinking of a response. He already knew what he wanted to talk about. "Well, actually, there is something I've wanted to ask you for a while."

"And what's that?"

"How much do you know about Alexandra Cardor?"

Howard's body went stiff for a fraction of a second as he took the time to process what had just been said. He looked as if he regretted his question, but after a sip of his lager, and a moment of silence to take a breath and clear his head, the fear in his eyes passed away.

"I actually know quite a bit more than most," he began, setting his cup down with a loud thud. "You picked a good person to ask. I was, at a time, closer with her than anyone else apart from Tom. There's nothing quite like the bond you make with someone who's also dealt with... *difficult* parents. You know about her father, right?"

Jeremiah nodded.

"I was one of the few people Tom trusted who could get inside her mind as well as he could. He called me on the phone back when he was trying to convince her to come to Parliss. He asked me if I had any interest in teaching her about acting. He told me she was a good girl, just someone who was lost and didn't know what she wanted— never felt like she had much of a place in her town and needed to start somewhere else, and I promised to help in any way I could."

"So, she was one of the Canmark actors?" Jeremiah asked.

"One of the best we ever had," Howard replied. "Back in my time, method acting was considered the best way to pursue Personal Balance. It gave you lots of opportunities to look into the souls of those who were different from you—really get inside their heads and see what they see. I thought maybe I could help this poor girl. I would look after her anytime she was at the theater and Tom would look after her everywhere else. He'd take her to eat at the Grand Burnett. He'd introduce her to all his friends, like this one old history teacher, and a journalist who lives in the southern part of town. Basically, anything you and Alicia have done the last few weeks, Alexandra did also. The only difference is that you two are only going to be here for a few weeks. Alexandra was in East Parliss for a year."

"And then she left," Jeremiah said. "That's the part I don't know. Why did she leave when she and Tom were so close?"

"They stopped being close," the comedian said, after another sip of his drink. "But, obviously, you're going to want a more detailed answer. Let me start by asking you a question instead: Do you know what made Tom different from all the other counselors, doctors, and therapists she'd seen before him?"

Jeremiah glanced off to the side to gather his thoughts, but he turned back when the comedian spoke out again. "Say whatever comes to mind. We're still training you for your speech on Sunday. You have to be more impulsive. You don't need to think. You know Tom. What made him different? Say it."

"Empathy," Jeremiah blurted out. It flew out of his mouth like a bullet, but as he stopped to consider his response, it made perfect sense.

Howard nodded. "It's one thing to nod your head and say you feel sorry for someone. It's another when you really feel that person's pain, when you're so good at getting inside their head that you start to feel like you've shared a life together. That's what made him different. In her view, Tom was like a second father, a better father, and someone who actually wanted to help out of compassion and not because it was his job. Tom was the first person to make her feel like she didn't need to pretend anymore—that it was all right to show a little weakness. She thought she'd found someone who wouldn't be so intrusive, but she was wrong."

"That can't be right," Jeremiah argued. "She wasn't wrong. That's the kind of person Tom is."

"That's one side of the person Tom is," Howard corrected. "You have to remember that before he was your counselor, he was an Auralite of East Parliss. He was a strong supporter of Personal Balance—the green Aura—our natural responsibility to be better people and seek out positive change. He believed in accountability and discipline, and he was an actor, just like me. He just never went on stage."

Howard downed another swig of his drink, as Jeremiah sat and let these words dig into his head.

"He convinced Alexandra to come to Parliss when she turned eighteen. He brought her to East Parliss and promised to help her even though he was trying to fix her instead, like he was teaching her to ride a bike but lied about having training wheels. He had all the best intentions for her, make no mistake, but it was this sort of mild deception that Alexandra despised. She didn't want someone to treat her like a broken toy that needed fixing. She wanted a new father, and every day, Tom drifted further from that role."

"She just didn't see it yet," Jeremiah said, putting parts of the story together now that he could see more clearly. "But she saw it eventually, right?"

Howard nodded, with a sullen look in his eyes as he returned to his drink. "I should've seen it coming. She didn't love acting the way the rest of us did. There were certain roles she liked—the characters that felt like her, but it was the ones she had nothing in common with that were the hardest for her. They made her feel dishonest. They made her say things she didn't believe. Like I said, she despised that kind of mild deception."

"But that's what acting is," Jeremiah said. "A good kind of lying."

"Yes, indeed," the comedian said. "And that's exactly what she despised about it. She got tired of lying, and all the time she spent with me taught her how to see it. She could see fakeness very well, and after some time, she started to see it in Tom. She started to doubt if Tom really was that different from all the other therapists. She grew suspicious, and then one moment came that proved to her that Tom wasn't the man she thought he was."

"What happened?"

"She asked Tom if she could go to West Parliss, and he said no," Howard replied. "He told Alexandra that just one week on the other side would undo all the progress she'd made. That was the word that tipped her over the edge: progress; like she'd been a part of some experiment this whole time when she thought Tom was looking after her as a second father. She started to see Tom as being more loyal to East Parliss than to her, and soon she began to see all of us in that way. She got angrier, more frustrated, and within just a few weeks, she started picking fights with Tom, with me, the people at the Parryrose Club, and all her other friends until the night she left. She walked off into West Parliss, and we haven't seen her since."

Jeremiah sat in his chair without saying a word, his eyes glaring down at the table while flashes of Alexandra's rage and Tom's sadness ran through his mind as if they were his own memories. He was grateful that Howard allowed him a moment of silence, knowing this was hard to take for a young boy who loved the counselor like his own father. He didn't feel disappointed in Tom. He wasn't upset by any mistakes the counselor made, but he didn't resent Alexandra either. He felt sympathy toward them both, as if the crumbling of their friendship had all just been some colossal misunderstanding with no true villain, but Jeremiah knew deep down they both couldn't be entirely innocent. After all, Tom had left Alicia and him just days into their stay in Parliss County with no warning, for a personal matter they still knew nothing about, but it was clearly more important to him.

"That's why Tom left Parliss County," Jeremiah muttered. "He couldn't deal with losing Alexandra, and he couldn't live in a place with so many memories of her, so he left."

Howard nodded. "He stayed for one more year to help these four kids who came that next summer, but then he left. I honestly never thought he would ever come back, but I guess he thought you and Alicia needed a little time with the Auralites. Either that or he saw a chance for redemption."

"Maybe both," Jeremiah said, still trying to speak in Tom's defense. "He's letting Alicia and me go to West Parliss. That's where we're spending the second half of our stay here. He's learned from his mistakes. I know he has."

"I'm sure he's trying to," Howard replied, "but you'd be surprised how often we all make mistakes we promise not to make a second time. He might let you go into West Parliss but I know he isn't happy about it. He's never liked the Western end. He went across only one time to look for Alexandra, but he couldn't find her. He's never been back since."

"Do you know where Alexandra is?"

"No, I don't. Honestly, I've said more about this matter than I should. We should get back to the script before we waste too much time. How 'bout you try reciting it while I order another drink?"

— — — — —

Jeremiah did as he was told, just as he continued to do over the next several days. Each morning, he recited his speech right as he sat down in the pub and a second time before they left. The time in between was spent talking, telling jokes and fake stories about parties and skipping school to help Jeremiah see more of his character. Each day, he had some new question about Tom or Alexandra, and the comedian always indulged him with one or two quick anecdotes about old performances at the Canmark Theater, or games of Silent Captain they'd all played with each other, but he would stop before he got too distracted and bring them back to their real task, no matter how little Jeremiah cared about it.

He didn't care about his speech anymore. He couldn't rehearse his lines for even a minute without his mind flashing back to Alexandra. He fell asleep each night wondering where she was, what she was like now, whether she had forgiven Tom in their ten years of separation, but most of all, he wondered what her Aura had looked like.

He bought a box of colored pencils one day after practice and spent the following night drawing imaginary Auras in his journal. He made three of these drawings: one for who Alexandra had been as a teenager, one for who she'd been after meeting Tom, and one for who she'd been at the end of her year in East Parliss. Jeremiah paid the most attention to the second drawing, since he was the most curious about who Alexandra had been at his age. He expected that Alexandra was a lot like him: a naturally quiet person who wanted to be more sociable, sensitive even when she pretended to be tough, and shy even when she wanted to look strong and confident. She was suspicious of the world around her but did her best to trust, a rebel even when she knew it was best to follow the rules, and she strived for independence even when her fear of loneliness broke her down.

By the end, Jeremiah found that most of Alexandra's rings were magenta. It was the color of a person who dreamed of an invisible switch, as Howard would call it, the sort of person who was always stuck between who they really were and who they wanted to be, a person who could always see a better version of herself but couldn't quite reach her.

Jeremiah could have made a dozen more of these drawings if he had more time, and if he didn't have to spend all of Saturday rehearsing his lines. He went onstage the following night and performed his speech as well as he could. As expected, Alicia put on a better performance than any he could ever give, which was met with a chorus of applause twice as loud as the one he'd received. The comedian thanked them for a lovely week, and then left the pub after wishing them good luck with the rest of their stay.

Alicia almost went back upstairs to Mr. Zeeger's loft, but she stopped halfway through when Jeremiah called her name. He suggested they go for a short walk, now that they had some spare time. Alicia said that sounded like a lovely idea. She asked if Jeremiah wanted to go back to Littelbine Park, but he had something else in mind.

He stepped outside the pub and led Alicia a few blocks north along the eastern side of Corraine-Callister until they stopped at the entrance to the old Canmark Theater. The path leading up to the front door was smothered in weeds, loose branches, and crackling leaves, making it clear the place had been closed for a long time but was apparently too important to the Auralites to be torn down.

"Alexandra used to be an actress here," Jeremiah said. He didn't bother asking if Alicia knew who this was. Somehow, he already knew she did. "I've been wanting to come here this whole week. I thought you'd want to see it, too."

"It's so old-looking," Alicia said as she peered through the archway, staring at all the overgrown weeds and foliage that cluttered the entrance due to years of abandonment. "It's a bit of a shame. I'm sure it was very beautiful a long time ago."

"Yeah, probably," Jeremiah said, only half paying attention as he turned to face the opposite end of the Wide Road, as the comedian said it was often called. He sat down on the curb and looked across to West Parliss. He wasn't sure what to look for, but he was too curious to look anywhere else.

"Are you feeling all right?" Alicia asked as she sat down next to him.

"I think so. I've just been thinking a lot about Tom lately. Can I ask you something kind of personal?"

"Of course. What is it?"

"Why do you love acting so much? I mean, how does it make you feel when you get to be someone else?"

Alicia smiled for a moment. "Well, actually, for me it's mostly the opposite. I always feel like myself when I'm onstage. I've never played someone I thought was so different from me that I'd be lying if I said what they said. Being onstage just gives you the freedom to be what you want."

"So, you never feel like you're faking?"

"Not at all," Alicia said, shaking her head. "Offstage, I have to smile even if I feel sad, or be polite with people I don't like. That's where all the real acting happens. Being onstage just means you have the freedom to be whatever you want before you go back to the real world. Then you have to play by the rules again."

Alicia shrugged her shoulders while Jeremiah sat quietly. "That's just the way I see it. Someone else might see it differently. Why do you ask?"

"It's because of something I heard from Mr. Granzill," Jeremiah explained. He spent the next few minutes catching Alicia up on the comedian's stories, or at least the ones he could still remember. He could see them taking their toll on Alicia, who in the end was left with a lost, sad look in her eyes. She joined Jeremiah in staring across the Wide Road, not uttering a word.

In the past, Jeremiah always felt uneasy with long stretches of silence. His heart would race as the pressure swelled within his chest, urging him to blurt out a weather-watcher comment or two just to make conversation. Somehow, this time, he wasn't nervous at all. He wondered if Alicia felt the same way, if she was fine with their silence, if she was thinking about what was on the other side of the Wide Road, or if she'd spent just as much time thinking about Tom and Alexandra as he had for the last few days. It was a sad and somehow funny thing, that despite all their time together, Jeremiah still didn't know everything about her. The Aurascope gave him all the tools to strip her down to her nuts and bolts and build her back from a pile of scraps, and yet he was just now starting to see Alicia would always find some way to surprise him. He could live five times the length of a normal life and never know all he wanted, but he would try his best anyway.

"I think we should go look for her," Jeremiah suggested, after about a minute of sitting in complete silence. "Both of us, together. We have three more weeks to spend over in West Parliss. Maybe we can find something Tom didn't."

Alicia looked hesitant. "I'm not sure that's a good idea."

"Why not?"

"This is Tom's business. I don't think it's right to look too much into this."

"Tom wouldn't want us to stop exploring this place if that's what we wanted," Jeremiah argued. "That's what he did wrong last time. That's why he isn't keeping us from going to West Parliss. We're his second chance to make this right for him."

"How do you know that?" Alicia asked, as her voice started to crackle. "How do you know what he wants?"

"I don't. I don't have any clue. But I know it's important to me. I need to know what happened."

"Why?"

"Because I'm scared I'll end up like her if I don't."

A long pause followed after he spoke. His words rang like a gunshot, drowning out the surrounding noise until the whole world around them stopped. He looked away from Alicia, trying to hide the tears he felt building beneath his eyes while his friend sat by his side, wondering what she could say to make things better. He stayed at the cusp of crying for a long time until he finally drew a deep breath to steady his heart and numb the cold he felt in his chest. And then he spoke.

"I've learned a lot about her over these last three weeks," he said, turning back to look at Alicia. "I don't know everything, but I know she's a lot like me. I swear it's like I can see her standing next to me.

And what's worse is that she's a lot like what I could be in a few years if I don't get myself figured out. I can already feel it happening. It doesn't matter how much I talk to Tom, or how much my parents love me, or how lucky I am that I get to live in this great town and go to college. I'm still scared of getting out of bed in the morning and wondering what I'm about to screw up. I can't be that person, Alicia. I've already lost my chance to be a kid. I've lost my chance to be a teenager. I can't waste my chance to be anything else. I can't stay like this anymore."

"You don't have to," Alicia said, reaching out to pat Jeremiah on the back. "You're not as alone as you think. You still have me, right? Isn't that enough?"

"I know. You're right," Jeremiah said. "I'm a lot luckier than Alexandra ever was. I love having you as a friend. I know I haven't always acted like it, but I do. But that's also why I want us to look for her. For all we know, she's lonelier now than ever. Maybe there's something I can do to help, even if all I do is sit in a room with her and tell her I know how she feels. And maybe if we talk enough, I can learn how not to make the same mistakes she did."

Jeremiah turned away for a moment to look across the Wide Road again, and then looked back to Alicia a moment later.

"That's why I want to find her, and it would be really nice if I had you around to help me."

Jeremiah gazed into her eyes, waiting out the silence as she looked across the Wide Road. After a while, she finally smiled and gave Jeremiah a friendly jab in the side with her elbow. That was the only answer he needed. It had taken three weeks for them to spend some good time together, rather than sitting in Mr. Zeeger's loft trading stories about their separate adventures. From now on, they would stay together, stuck to one shared purpose for their last three weeks in Parliss County.

They sat together at the curb until they realized how dark the sky was starting to get, and decided it was about time they head back to the Broken Cottage. They would need a good night's rest for the long day that awaited them in West Parliss tomorrow.

161

PART THREE

WEST PARLISS COUNTY

Chapter Twelve

Six Single Voices

The Donnigan Boys would always meet up for lunch at a small hill at the south end of the field. When the bell rang, the doors burst open to a sea of teenagers pouring out of their classrooms to meet up with their friends for half an hour until they got back to work, and Jeremiah was often the last one out. Every day, he'd look out at the small hill at the edge of the woods and ask himself if this was a good day to join them or if he should wait for another day. Most of the time, he chose to wait.

"I've noticed you like to spend a lot of your lunch breaks with me," Tom once said, at a session that had taken place during Jeremiah's second year of high school. "Could you tell me why?"

"I don't have anywhere else to go," Jeremiah admitted, after he finished with his packet of pretzel sticks and wiped the crumbs off his lips.

"What about the rest of those boys from your year? Can't you sit with them?"

"Not really. It's complicated."

"How so?"

"I'm not really friends with them."

"I don't think sitting in here's going to fix that," Tom said with a light smile.

"I know, but like I said: it's complicated. I can't just sit down like

I'm part of their group. They'll look at me like I'm their weird little brother who keeps popping up when they don't want me. I have to get them to like me first."

"How so?"

"Just by talking to them during class, or something like that. Sometimes I can talk to them while we're doing in-class assignments. Sometimes they laugh at things I say, and they listen to what I talk about. I have to judge for myself whether I think they like me today or not, and if they do, then I sit with them."

"And what happens if you don't think they like you?"

"Then I just eat alone. Sometimes I come in here. Sometimes I'll just take pieces of my lunch out of my bag and eat while I walk down the halls so it looks like I'm going somewhere. That way, if people see me, I don't look so pathetic."

"Interesting strategy," Tom said with a solemn nod. "You've sure given this a lot of thought, but I have a feeling this isn't exactly how you'd like to spend your time. Is it?"

"No, it isn't," Jeremiah muttered. "I just don't know what to do about it."

"Have you tried talking to one of these boys individually?" Tom asked. "It's usually a lot easier to work your way into these groups when you make friends with one person first."

"I've tried, but it hasn't been working."

"Then let's see if we can figure out how to fix that," Tom said. Right on cue, he leaned back in his chair and unclasped his hands. It was around this time Jeremiah began to pay attention to the counselor's speaking habits. There was usually an increase in the amount of body language whenever he was about to dive into the core of their sessions.

"Do you remember when we talked about the Three Degrees of Conversation?"

"Yeah, I do."

"Can you tell me what they are?"

This was the subject of one of their earliest meetings, dating back to a late September day in Jeremiah's first year at Laronna.

"The first degree is called the Key," Jeremiah began, "which is what I say to you. The second degree is called the Response, which is what you say back to me. And the third degree is called the Consequence, which is what happens after that exchange is done."

"Exactly. So, let's look at this in a more direct scenario. Let's say you're talking with Ethan and you say to him: 'Wow, you did a really good job on your last math test. I didn't know you were that smart.' How do you think he'd respond to you?"

"He'd be upset that I said I thought he was dumb before."

"And what is the consequence of that?"

"He won't like me, and then we probably won't be friends."

"Exactly," Tom said. "These three stages are the mark of someone with good people skills. People who are good in social situations are able to think three steps ahead in any conversation, and they usually can do it automatically, like it's a reflex. Anytime you have trouble relating socially with other people, it will usually be because you're not following the Three Degrees."

"But I am following them," Jeremiah promised. "I've never said something like that to anyone, but none of them seem to like being around me, and I don't know why."

"Can you give me an example?" Tom asked. "Which of these boys have you talked to recently?"

"Roy Garson. We were sitting next to each other in English class once, and Ms. Meehan was quizzing us on some vocabulary words. They were all really complicated words that I've never heard anyone use before, like 'ubiquitous' and stuff like that. I made a funny comment to Roy about how weird it was to be tested on words we'd probably never use again. Then, just as a joke, we tried talking to each other with sentences that had these words in them. It was like our own private game. It lasted for weeks. But then I went to eat lunch with his friends and I used one of those words in a sentence, and he didn't even look at me. Then we just stopped doing it. Now he barely talks to me."

Tom nodded. "Do you think maybe this game of yours wasn't something he wanted his other friends to know about?"

"Why not?" Jeremiah asked. "He loved doing it before."

"I'm sure he did, but that was just when it was the two of you. People will usually act differently if they're worried about what six or seven other people might think of them, as opposed to just one person. You've spent a lot of time with these boys. Do they seem like the type of people who would get a kick out of language jokes?"

Jeremiah waited a moment before he spoke again, even though the answer was obvious. "No. They wouldn't. They'd probably think it was lame."

"Maybe that's why Roy never said anything," Tom suggested. "He looked three steps ahead and saw the Consequence. You always have to be more careful with a group than you are with a person. A group has rules, and the rules are stronger when there are more people there to enforce them. And usually it's a lot safer to follow them than fight them."

———— — — — ————

Jeremiah saw West Parliss every day he stepped outside the Broken Cottage. No one ever told him not to cross the Wide Road, but he stayed on the Eastern side anyway, obeying the unspoken rule of Parliss County long before he knew its history. Today was different. Today he slung his brown bag around his shoulder and left his seat at the dining table without a letter from Tom. He walked outside with Alicia, looked across to West Parliss, and they stepped onto the Wide Road.

He felt something yank at his heart as soon as the sole of his shoe pressed down on the cobblestone. It was like walking on a sheet of glass, each step more terrifying than the last, but he didn't slow down, and he didn't turn back. He felt the weight leave his body when he reached the sidewalk. He turned around and looked past his shoulder, seeing for the first time what East Parliss looked like from the other side. He admired the view for a split second, and then he reached into his bag and pulled out his map.

He led Alicia down a few streets and around a few corners until they arrived at the Fiatzi Café. This was a place Jeremiah learned about from one of Howard Granzill's stories, and where he figured their search for Alexandra ought to start.

"The candles are what I call a counter-motif. I say this to everyone I know who asks me about it," said a man in the café. He sat at a table in the corner with five other men, each one of them dressed in suits and sipping cups of hot coffee.

"The first act of the play, very first scene, you see Olivia up in her room looking through photos of her sister, wishing they could see each other again, and the script says in vivid detail that there is a candle on the nightstand at the opposite side of the room. The separation between Olivia and the candle is a representation of distance and isolation; the bed in the middle of the room symbolizes what is keeping them away from each other.

"So, it's an exaggeration of their reality, right?" another man said.

"Right, but here's where it gets tricky," the first man continued, adjusting his glasses and taking another sip of his drink. "Answer me this: what qualities do you commonly associate with fire? Suppose you see a painting of a candle. What does it make you think of?"

Jeremiah sat down with Alicia at a table near the center of the café, watching the five other men consider this question. It was the first man sitting at the high end of the table who grabbed Jeremiah's attention. His hair was dark, his nose was sharp and pointed like a beak, and as he spoke he moved his hands in waving gestures and shifted his voice in strange inflections, all while slouching back in his chair as the rest of the men sat straight.

"Passion, I'd say," said one of the other men. "Maybe love and kindness?"

"Ordinarily, you'd be correct," the first man said. "But Callingston knows better. He doesn't fall back on these old tropes of lesser storytellers. No, in *Candlelight Palace,* the candles aren't a symbol of sisterly love; they're an expression of sadness, loneliness—all the things our brains are trained to associate with cold colors. The candles don't represent love; they show the absence of love. See what I mean? Callingston took something that is normally a motif for warmth, love, and innocence, and flipped it into a sign of sadness. Hence my term, counter-motif."

Jeremiah had spent all morning wondering how he and Alicia would introduce themselves to this group of men. Walking into the café right in the middle of a discussion of *Candlelight Palace* was perhaps the most perfect excuse he could dream of. He could tell by the astonished look in Alicia's eyes how aware she was of their good luck. Without saying a word to each other, they got up from their seats and walked over to the other table as the first man's friends complimented him on his brilliant analysis.

"I'm sorry, I don't mean to interrupt," Alicia said. "We were just over at our table and we couldn't help but overhear your conversation. That play you were talking about, we actually did that show at our school. I was Olivia."

"Were you really?" the man said, his eyes wide as a sign of how impressed he was by this. "And did you agree with my interpretation?"

"Absolutely. I love Callingston. I'm so lucky I had the chance to play such a great character of his."

"It's quite an accomplishment for someone so young. I don't know many women as young as yourself who could read some of those lines. What's your name?"

"Alicia Scheinbach. This is my cousin, Jeremiah. We're here visiting our uncle for the summer and thought we should take a walk downtown and see what there was to see."

"You came to a good place. Would you like to join us at our table?"

"Oh, we'd love to. We won't be disturbing you, will we?"

"Of course not. You're perfectly welcome here. Isn't that right, gentlemen?"

None of the other men argued against this, but Jeremiah could see a puzzled look in their eyes as they slid up the table to make room.

"Thank you," Jeremiah said as he sat down. "And what's your name? Mister..."

"It's Doctor, technically, but I don't mean to be so self-indulgent.

Coffee houses are no place for titles and men who stand on pedestals. For most of the year while I'm teaching at Shemmer University, they call me Dr. Kennry, but here and now you may call me Jules. Plain and simple."

The other five men followed his precedent by introducing themselves with their first names, and mentioned they taught at a public high school in the same town.

"What's your uncle's name?" Jules asked. "One of us might know him."

"Ethan Kantzton," Jeremiah responded. "He lives a few blocks down over in the far west side of the county. He doesn't go out often. Work keeps him pretty busy most of the time."

"I don't think I've heard of him before," Jules said. "Is this your first time in West Parliss?"

"Yes."

"Have you ever been to East Parliss?"

"No. He doesn't want us to cross Cor-Cal."

"That's a lesson to live by," the professor said. "Pick a side and stick with it. That's the way to go."

"That's what he told us," Jeremiah said. "He said there was some woman who crossed the Road a few years ago because she wasn't happy on the other side. He said her name was Alexandra Cardor. Have you heard of her before?"

All the men at the table froze for a moment at the sheer mention of her name. One of them accidentally spilled some coffee on his lap, but Jeremiah pretended not to notice.

"What did he say about her?" Jules asked.

"Nothing," Jeremiah replied. "He told us it was none of his business, and ever since then, Alicia and I have been trying to figure out who she was and what happened to her."

"She came here when she was eighteen," Jules said after a short pause. "She had a very dramatic childhood—lost her mother to an abusive father, took up drugs, lost her virginity at a very young age. She was dealing with a lot of issues by the time she finished school. One day, she met a therapist, and Auralite, named Tom Berrinser, who thought he could help her. He brought her to East Parliss and taught her about personal balance. Did your uncle tell you what that is?"

"Yeah, he told us all about it," Jeremiah answered quickly, not wanting to waste time on a lesson he'd already learned.

"Then you know it was useless to her," the professor continued. "But old Tommy was too stubborn to admit he couldn't handle the job. Alexandra would've been much happier on this side, but by then it was too late. She was already part of the East, and no one on our side wanted her with us."

"Then why did she come here?"

"Because, like I said, West was the right place for her. She just didn't see that in time."

Jules reached into his coat pocket and took out an Aurascope of his own. Right as his skin pressed against the crystal-glass, Jeremiah noticed this Aura was different from all the others he'd seen before. There were no green rings. None whatsoever. Instead, his Aura was mostly made of rings in pure, unmixed shades of red and blue. The man was deep blue in confidence with no red for nervousness, independent without a hint of dependence, forceful but not submissive in any way.

He passed the Aurascope to his left, and the other five men followed his example and put one hand on the Aurascope. They all looked the same as the professor's, but with just a few differences. Jeremiah noticed they weren't as forceful or as independent as Jules, but apart from this, they might as well have all been the same man.

"Alexandra came to West Parliss for the same reason we did," Jules continued. "West Parliss is where people come to look for acceptance. Alexandra didn't come here hoping to find people to tell her she needed fixing, but people to tell her there was nothing to fix in the first place. She was a deeply sensitive young woman; neurotic, reckless, spontaneous, but also highly intelligent, and instead of living in a place that pressured her to be less of these things, she came to a place that would embrace her as she was."

"Then where is she now?" Jeremiah asked. "Do you know?"

"No, I do not," Jules confessed, "but I do know she left West Parliss after a year. She found some friends at the Terrinson Club, but not enough. I think coming here so late with such an East Parliss reputation was too much for her to overcome. It's a shame she didn't bother to come across sooner. I guarantee all the people who resented her for being Tom's puppet would have loved her. She left after just one year. None of us have seen her since."

Hearing this news left Jeremiah with a cold, aching feeling knotted up in his stomach and a chill down his spine. He'd only started looking for Alexandra a few hours ago and already there was nowhere else to go. He could visit this Terrinson Club and hope some of Alexandra's old friends could fill in the missing parts of her story, but if the professor was right and Alexandra was gone, his mission was already over.

"I hear it practically brought Berrinser to tears when he found out," Jules said, laughing as he spoke. "He left a few days later. No one's seen him since."

"That's awful," Jeremiah said. He widened his eyes to look as if he were hearing this for the first time, though the sentiment behind his words was real.

Dr. Kennry shrugged. "Serves him right, if you ask me. He needed to learn his lesson. Those folks on the East treat their precious personal balance like a word of gospel. Nothing's ever enough for them. You can always take one more step out of your comfort zone, aim a little higher, be a little better. Alexandra saw the truth. Tom was never going to let go of his ways."

"But isn't he right?" Jeremiah argued.

He wanted to take back his words the moment they escaped his mouth. The table went silent as the six men looked at him. He saw Alicia try to keep her distance by matching their expression, though he knew deep down she was just as anxious. He felt bad for putting Alicia in this spot, but he couldn't help himself. Bashing Tom and snickering at his misery was about the easiest way to make him angry. Dr. Kennry's list of offenses only grew worse the longer he slouched back in his chair, and the more he behaved like an arrogant leech, the sort of person who admired his own cleverness and laughed at his own jokes as long as he had the support of his entourage.

"I mean, I don't mean that as me disagreeing with you exactly," Jeremiah said, doing his best to look polite to help diffuse the tension. "I'm just trying to see both sides of this."

"Oh, no offense taken at all," Dr. Kennry said, though the cold look in his eyes and the stilted sound of his voice suggested otherwise. "The six of us agree on most things. It might be healthy to hear what someone else has to say. Especially since you're so…impartial to all this. Aren't you?"

"I suppose so," Jeremiah answered, still trying to act like Tom was a stranger to him. "I don't know much about the Auralites, but I know a few people like this Tom guy. I think I might know what he's talking about."

"And what is that, exactly?"

"Well, for starters, I'm an introvert," Jeremiah said. "For as long as I can remember, my parents have been looking for ways to help me be more social. They tell me to go outside more, that I shouldn't be afraid to go up to all the other kids at my school, and that I can't spend my whole life in my room reading books or out riding my bike by myself."

"And isn't it frustrating that they keep telling you what you should be like and why you aren't good enough?" Dr. Kennry asked.

"Well, yeah, it bothered me at first, but deep down, I also know they're right. I need to get better at that sort of thing. When I'm old enough that I start looking for jobs, I'll have to be personable enough so I can impress my interviewer. I'll need to get along with all my co-workers so we can do a good job and get promotions and all that stuff."

"So, it's out of necessity. Not because you want to. Suppose you didn't need to do that sort of thing to do your job? What then?"

"That's not how the world works," Jeremiah argued, thinking back to Tom's story about the bad singer.

"Not the way *your* world works," Dr. Kennry corrected. "The world out there is for the liars. Out there, you have to hide yourself, stay polite and shake hands with the people you'd love to sock in the face. But not here. West Parliss is a place of freedom, the place you go to meet people who take you as you are. There's no change necessary, so long as you find the right friends. That sounds like a pretty damn good deal to me."

"If you like living in a bubble your whole life," Jeremiah replied, turning up the tension once again as he watched the five other men look at each other, wondering what was about to happen. "What happens if you go somewhere else?"

"What if I don't?"

"I'm just talking hypothetically."

"So am I. Who says I have to go anywhere else besides here, my house, and where I work?"

"You work at a university. You have to deal with other professors at some point."

"That doesn't mean they're my friends," he sneered, leaning further into the table while taking another sip of his drink. "I can deal with all the nods and handshakes for a few hours on my way to the lecture and back to my office. Apart from that, I have no need for it. Once I retire, I plan on spending the rest of my life in West."

"That doesn't seem too fun to me," Jeremiah retorted.

"Is that so?" the professor said, speaking with a spiteful look in his eyes that had gotten worse in the last few exchanges. "You're saying you'd rather spend your time putting up with people you hate just because you have to?"

"I'm saying I'd have a lot more respect for a man with the discipline to grow up than a man who likes to do what's easy."

Dr. Kennry's response, like many of his others, was a mix of two contrasting emotions. He nodded gently, as though he understood and respected Jeremiah's views, but his eyes bore a sign of contempt sharp enough to cut through steel. He could see the professor's rage, and he tried his best to stifle the joy he took from it. He couldn't think of another time he'd been so bold to confront another person instead of staying out of trouble by nodding or smiling. He wished he could step back in time to behave this way around Ethan Kantzton or

Casey Marsley. He knew he couldn't, but he was perfectly happy to settle for Dr. Kennry.

He kept expecting Alicia to suggest that they leave, but he couldn't walk away just yet. He needed more time, but more importantly, he needed time away from the professor. He reached into his pocket to grab his cell phone and used it to call Alicia's. When it rang, he pretended it was a call from their uncle, and that they needed to go outside for a moment to talk in private. He led Alicia out to the sidewalk and stood away from the window so no one in the café could see or hear them.

"What was that all about?" Alicia asked.

"I'm sorry. I needed a way to talk to you without them hearing us. We can't leave just yet. I still have more questions."

"Jer, there's nothing else we can do here. Let's just head on over to this Terrinson Club. I'm sure we'll find a lot more there. Don't you think if they knew anything else, they would've said so by now?"

"No. I don't actually," Jeremiah said, taking Alicia by surprise. "I've been watching these guys carefully. Have you noticed that nobody else at that table talks when Jules is talking? They all wait for him to finish before they say anything. He invited us to sit at their table and they all went along with it. They're doing whatever he wants them to do."

"Why? Why would they do this?"

"It's because they're in a group," Jeremiah explained. He immediately thought of Roy Garson. "They're too scared of being the one person who doesn't match the others. They all rally behind him because he's the only one who makes the rules."

"Jer, I think you're reading too much into this. I think we should leave."

"I just need you to keep Jules out of the café for ten minutes while I talk to those guys alone," Jeremiah said as he reached into his bag and took out a box of playing cards he'd borrowed from Mr. Zeeger. "I have a plan to get him away but I need you to keep him busy. Ask him if he'll listen to you do a reading from *Candlelight Palace* and give you feedback on your acting. Maybe mess up a few lines so he can correct you—anything to stall time. Please? Just this once?"

Alicia sighed. "You promise you know what you're doing?"

He nodded.

"Fine. I'll do it. Ten minutes. Promise?"

"Promise."

He thanked Alicia and walked back inside the café with the deck of cards in his hands.

"Sorry about that," Jeremiah said as he sat back down at the table. "Our uncle wanted to know when we'd be back for dinner. Listen, I'm sorry if I was sounding rude earlier. I didn't mean to, but I think I have a way we can all relax for a bit."

Jeremiah held up his box of cards, and as expected, all six men looked nervous. When he asked if they wanted to play a game of Silent Captain, the man sitting on the professor's right said they'd stopped playing that game a long time ago. Jeremiah pretended not to know the reason why and allowed Jules to tell the story of the time he nearly lost everything he owned the last time he played. Ever since then, he'd withheld from playing cards, and the five other men had done the same out of respect.

Jeremiah offered his false condolences, and then suggested the rest of them play when Alicia asked if the professor would review her delivery of the monologue from the bedroom scene. Dr. Kennry agreed to help, but his enthusiasm faded once he stood up from his chair. The skeptical look in his eyes instilled Jeremiah with a sense of dread.

"You want me to go outside with her while you and my friends play Caps?" the professor asked. "Where exactly did you learn to play this game?"

"My uncle. I played a few games with him and I've learned all the important rules."

"All right. I'll step out for a bit. But before I do, could I ask for one small favor?"

"Sure. What is it?"

"It's been so long since I've been able to play this game, and, though I've stopped on account of my gambling addiction, I still have a deep love for it. Would you mind if I stay and watch you play for one round before I step out?"

Jeremiah could hear something foul in Dr. Kennry's voice, but he didn't show any sign of panic. He agreed to those terms, and the professor sat back down in his chair. Jeremiah volunteered to shuffle the deck and distribute the cards, and once everyone was ready, he prepared himself to make his first move. He thought back on all the rules he'd learned from the Jennabelle Kids, all his old mistakes and how to spot the good plays from the bad ones. He chose to play his first turn safely and remove his weakest card. As he did so, the five other men looked at him in confusion, and Dr. Kennry glared at him in disgust.

"Did I do something wrong?" Jeremiah asked, his heart beating faster as his muscles began to tighten. "Am I not allowed to do that?"

"Not here," the professor said. "I suppose you haven't learned yet that Silent Captain is played by a different set of rules depending on where in Parliss you are. Discarding on the first turn is only allowed in East, where you say you've never been to before. And yet these are the rules you know, which of course, means you lied to me."

With a single glance from Dr. Kennry, the two men sitting beside Jeremiah stomped down on his feet. The professor stood up from his chair and leered down at Jeremiah with a taunting but vicious look in his eyes. Alicia shot up from her seat like a bullet. None of the men tried to hold her down, but she knew she was hardly in a position to confront the four unoccupied men, so she stood against the wall and remained silent, trying her best to keep her distance.

No one else in the café seemed concerned about the commotion.

"So, what if I did?" Jeremiah protested. "Crossing over the Road isn't breaking the law."

"And yet you chose to lie anyway, which means you and your cousin are hiding something. So, I would like for you to tell me what that is, and if either of you is thinking of making a scene or getting the waitress to throw us out, it won't work. I'm a regular customer. I know the owner, all the servers, and I have five witnesses with the same credibility. Nobody here even knows your name, so whatever fight you start, I will win it."

"Okay, okay, you win!" Jeremiah blurted out. "I'll talk! Just please tell them to stop crushing my feet."

The two men did so at Dr. Kennry's request. Alicia stood silently by her chair, while the professor returned to his seat at the head of the table, where Jeremiah stared with an intense focus while all the other eyes rested on him.

"We came here looking to learn more about Alexandra Cardor," Jeremiah began. "That part was true. But what I didn't say before was that we came here because I heard a story a few days ago from one of your old friends—a man named Howard Granzill."

The professor's eyes popped wide open at the mention of this name. Jeremiah thought he'd make him stop talking, but he gave no such command, so the story continued.

"He told me he liked to play Silent Captain with this man from West Parliss who always visited during the summer, and always came to the Fiatzi Café in the morning. He told me you'd probably be surrounded by a couple other men in suits who didn't even know you two were once friends, or that you met Alexandra after a show at the Canmark, but that they would know the story of how you once lost all your money when you drank too much and gambled away everything you had to a stranger."

The professor's eyes sparked with fear. He looked around to the other five men who sat watching Jeremiah with a restrained curiosity, listening intently.

"Howard was close friends with Tom," Jeremiah said. "He was the best player Howard knew, even though he didn't play all that often. Tom had no idea who you were, but when you needed help, he talked that other player into a rematch and won back every cent you lost and gave it to you. I came here because I thought, out of everyone in West Parliss, you'd be the one to show him a little respect, and instead you sit here and laugh at his misery. Either that or you're just too much of a coward to disagree with anyone else and stand up for someone who saved you."

Once again, Jeremiah thought about Roy Garson.

"That's what he did. He saved you, not because he could but because he wanted to, and that says more about him than anything you can tell me."

A look of pure resentment found its way into Jeremiah's eyes, while the rest of the men fell into a silence so deep he could hear the sound of the dishwasher from behind the counter. The professor looked weak, vulnerable, rich with guilt and trying his best to hide it. Jeremiah glared into the professor's eyes, and then without another word, he stood up from his chair and walked out of the café with Alicia by his side.

Chapter Thirteen

The Terrinson Club

Part One

People often asked Alicia if she had any plans of acting as a career, and she would disappoint them each time by saying no. Instead, she dreamed of traveling overseas and exploring parts of the world she'd only seen in photographs, taking on jobs that let her work with animals or examine the art and history of other cultures. Then when the time was right, once she was past her time for adventures, she would return to a stable career and live a simple life for the rest of her days. She didn't want her future to be controlled by the stage, and yet that was the place where she felt happiest. She never understood why she felt so wishy-washy about one of her greatest passions, and now she finally had the chance to find her answer.

Alicia held the Aurascope and looked at the second ring, where blue light was a sign of a reclusive nature, and an adventurous one was marked in red. She expected to see mostly red, but was alarmed to find the ring was magenta, a perfect mixture of these two colors with no side surpassing the other.

"Second ring. I don't think I've seen that color there before," Mr. Zeeger said. He sat at his usual spot at the dining table, holding the Aurascope in one hand while clutching a bottle of whiskey in the other.

"Magenta is known as the color of conflict. It's the color you see in places where you feel lost and confused—like two halves of your mind are at war with each other. In this case, it means there's some part of you that wants to explore, but it also means there's some part of you that likes the idea of a home and having a place where you feel safe and welcome. My guess is that you aren't sure if traveling is right for you."

"That can't be right," Alicia protested. "I've always wanted to travel."

"Is that so?"

"Yes, it is. Ever since I was ten years old, I've wanted to see everything. I once spent a whole summer on a road trip through Europe with my parents. I made a scrapbook of all the local foods we tried and all the tourist attractions we visited."

"How exciting," Mr. Zeeger said, though his voice was so flat Alicia thought this might have been sarcasm. "Do you have it with you?"

"Well, no, I didn't bring it with me. It's back at home with my parents. But that's not my point. I love traveling. I've been doing it my whole life."

"Indeed, you have," Mr. Zeeger said, picking up his tone to appear slightly more invested. He even set his whiskey down on the table, which was a rare thing to see. "Tom said you moved here from Germany a few years ago. Is that right?"

"Yes, it is," she replied, nodding her head abruptly.

"And how excited were you to come to this country? Be honest."

"Well, I was obviously a little nervous when it started," Alicia confessed, "but once we started packing, I was incredibly excited about it. I really was."

"And what about when Tom asked if you wanted to come here? How soon did you decide this was something you wanted?"

Mr. Zeeger spoke as if he already knew the answer, and right as Alicia began to speak, she could see the trap she was heading into.

"I said yes, but I still didn't feel very good about it until just a week or so before we left."

"So, you hesitated?" Mr. Zeeger said with a cunning smile.

"It was different," Alicia protested. "This isn't like coming to a new country."

"No. I would argue it's much easier," Mr. Zeeger said. "You were only leaving for six weeks, you only needed to pack one bag, you had Tom and a friend of yours coming along with you, it took just one day to drive here in a car, and you'll be back with your parents in your own house in just a few weeks. But you were more scared of this summer trip than you were when you flew across the planet. Why do you suppose that is?"

Mr. Zeeger looked as if he already knew the answer. He marinated in Alicia's silence for a while before he spoke again.

"Did you have a good time at that school? Did you make any friends besides Jeremiah? Did you feel welcome while you were there?"

She paused before she spoke. "Not exactly."

"You traveled all the way across the country, and your new home didn't meet your expectations. Is that fair to say?"

"I suppose so," she muttered, her gaze falling somewhere between Mr. Zeeger and the carpet beneath her feet.

"Then I guess that's your answer," Mr. Zeeger said, looking to the Aurascope in Alicia's hand. "You might not see it yet, but your brain is already learning that moving to new places might not always be your path to happiness. Sometimes the small town life is all you need. What good is the rest of the world when where you are now is perfect?"

"Well, that's the trouble right there," Alicia said. "You don't know unless you look everywhere else first."

"I suppose that's true," Mr. Zeeger confessed. "I'm not trying to scare you away. I'm just saying the Aurascope doesn't lie. If you loved traveling as much as you say you do, I would be able to see it, and right now, I can't."

———————

Alicia knew there was nothing she could say to change Mr. Zeeger's mind, no matter how much she wished this ring would turn red just for a second. She had always thought of herself as a traveler, the sort of person with the courage to leave in the blink of an eye and run off to wherever she wanted. She refused to believe that could ever change. She would always be ready to leave home and go on an adventure, even if the Aurascope said otherwise.

When it was time to go to West Parliss, she left the Broken Cottage with Jeremiah as fast as she could to show Mr. Zeeger she wasn't afraid of exploring the unknown. She kept her head up high even as they left the Fiatzi Café, leaving a saddened, bitter Dr. Kennry leaning over his table surrounded by all his friends. She walked with her bag slung across her right shoulder as Jeremiah studied the map and led them right to the entrance of the Terrinson Club.

The man standing watch asked if they were members of the club or knew someone who was. When they answered no, he reached for his Aurascope and asked them to hold it.

"There are only two ways to gain access to the club," he told them. "One is to receive an invitation from another member, and the other is to impress the Judge. If I believe you belong here, I will let you in without question, but if I say otherwise, I will ask you to leave. If that is the case, you will leave at once, knowing it will be more for your sake than my own."

The Judge refused to let them know what he wanted to see in their Auras. He studied Alicia's Aura closely for a few seconds before giving her permission to go inside. He studied Jeremiah's for the same amount of time and told him to leave. Jeremiah went against the Judge's orders and started begging to go inside. He promised it was important, that he would only need an hour or two. He continued to make deals until the Judge threatened to ban Alicia, too, if he didn't stop. At that point, Jeremiah stepped away, but asked if he could have one quick talk with Alicia before they separated.

"Jer, there's nothing else we can do about it," Alicia said. "I'll just have to go in by myself. It's better than neither of us going at all."

"I know. You're right. I'm just a little upset, that's all. You sure you're all right with this?"

"Yeah, I'll be fine. I can handle myself."

"You know what to do, right? Just act innocent. You got here just a few days ago; you heard your uncle talking to someone about this girl named Alexandra and you just want to know who she is."

"I can manage it. I promise," Alicia said. "What are you going to do?"

Jeremiah sighed. "I guess I'll just walk around and see if I can find someone else who knows anything. Maybe I'll try another club, but this is the one we need to check. Someone in there must know something about her. They just might not want to admit it."

With one last exchange of goodbyes, Alicia made her way past the Judge and through the club doors, turning around for one last look as Jeremiah sauntered off down the road. It seemed rather funny how just yesterday she'd been against the idea of digging into Tom's past, and here she was not one day later as driven to the cause as if she'd planned it herself. Whatever tension she felt crossing the Wide Road for the first time disappeared the second she stepped into the club, but it came back as she entered a dark room where everyone sat under the dim lights at small tables, the air thick with the smoke of cigarettes and filled with music from the performers onstage.

A few heads turned her way as she sat down at a lonely barstool next to the entrance. She was the youngest one in the room by a wide margin. She remembered her first day at the Parryrose Club, though the dining hall looked nothing like where she was now. Her time with Bianca, while it may have ended poorly, was proving to be useful now that she once again was alone in the adult world and had to work her way into the fold.

The stress escaped her body the longer she listened to the beautiful singing of the woman onstage. She fell into a sort of trance from the melody of her lyrics, as well as the glistening of the stage lights shining down on her dark skin. Her dreadlocks reached far down past her shoulders and swayed from side to side as she strummed her guitar, and at the end of her final song, Alicia joined the rest of the room in their applause.

An elderly man with snow-white hair and a guitar of his own left a nearby table for his turn onstage, and the woman Alicia presumed to be his wife invited her to join their table now that they had an empty seat. Alicia sighed in relief at the woman's invitation, thankful she would not have to make the first step and could rely a little bit on the generosity of the other members. She understood everyone in the club had either impressed the Judge or was friends with someone who had, and if Alicia's Aura fit these same standards, there was a decent chance that most of the people here were like her in some way. She thought it would be easier to make friends in a place like this, but she began to second-guess herself when she sat down and noticed that the singer with the dreadlocks was sitting by herself in a dark spot in the club. A sullen look spread across her face, an odd expression to see on someone who'd just received a standing ovation.

"Who was that woman who was singing just a moment ago?" Alicia asked.

"They call her Charverra," answered one of the older women. "That's her stage name. But down here with the rest of us, her name's Charlotte Cawn."

"She's very good," Alicia said.

"Indeed, she is. She used to be one of the most famous performers the club ever had. Twice as many people would come each time she had a show."

"Used to?" Alicia said with a confused look. "What do you mean she *used* to be famous?"

"She left the club about nine or ten years ago," another woman answered. "It was the same time that Alexandra Cardor girl ran away. This is one of the first shows she's done since she came back to the county. All that time away has sadly made her less of a celebrity."

"Then why is she back now?"

"No one knows. None of us feel it's right to ask her. It's a bit of a sour subject. I've tried talking to her a few times but she doesn't say a whole lot. She keeps to herself and we all let her have some space. We let her sing, play her music, and do whatever she wants, and if she ever wants to talk, we'll be here to listen."

Alicia kept a steady watch over Charlotte as more musicians took the stage, and as the old women left their table one by one until she was all by herself. She looked around the room and saw that she and the singer were the only ones sitting alone. She wallowed in her newfound loneliness for only a moment before she turned around and locked eyes with Charlotte. It was for less than a second, half the time it would take to blink, but that was all it took to make the connection. Charlotte smiled and gestured for Alicia to come and sit at her table. Alicia sprung from her seat with barely a moment of hesitation, figuring there wouldn't be a better time than now to meet one of Alexandra's old acquaintances.

With a closer look, Alicia guessed that Charlotte was somewhere in her mid-thirties. She had a lean figure similar to Bianca's, with smooth, dark skin and a lovely pair of light brown eyes. They introduced themselves as Alicia sat down, and then remained silent once they turned their attention to the stage. Alicia wanted to speak up first, but she always found an excuse to wait for a better opening. About half an hour passed as Alicia watched the other performers take their turns in the spotlight. She caught a lucky break when the host announced they were taking a short intermission, causing Charlotte to turn around in her seat and look her in the eye.

"All right, you passed. Go ahead," the singer said, as the waiter returned with her martini.

"Excuse me?"

"We've been sitting here for just over twenty minutes and this whole time I could see how badly you wanted to ask me something, but you did the polite thing and kept quiet. Just for that, I'll let you ask."

"Oh, well, thank you," Alicia said. "I was just curious if you knew anything about Alexandra Cardor. Some women I was sitting with before told me you knew her quite well."

"I'm not sure if I can say they're right; there's a lot I never knew about her," Charlotte said. "That's the sort of trouble you have with Parliss: You learn the language of Aura, spend a few days looking at people's lights, and a week later you think you have them all figured out. That's what Tom Berrinser used to think. It's what I used to think. I just never dragged her down with my mistakes the way he did."

Alicia noticed a drop in the singer's voice when she mentioned the counselor, as well as the way her fingers gripped tighter around the edge of her glass.

"She had a big imagination," Charlotte continued, smiling in the wake of a fond memory. "That part of her never changed. She wanted to write children's books for a living; that was her dream. And she hated poetry. I don't know if I've ever known anyone who valued kid's books over poetry, but that was who she was. She thought poems were pretentious, that anyone could write twelve lines about wind, trees, rain, or something about the seasons coming and going, and stuffy old folks in suits and long scarves would say it was a work of genius when it was really just a bunch of nonsense. That's the way she saw it. I always thought that was rather funny."

"How did you meet her?" Alicia asked.

"Now there's a funny story," Charlotte said, leaning further into her seat and setting her glass down for a moment. "There's this pond a couple blocks up north where I like to go when I need to clear my head. I always sit at this one bench by the shore, just because whenever I stop by, there's never anyone sitting there. I'd been going to this place for years and I never saw anyone sitting on that bench; no one except her. She got up as soon as I sat down, I think because she wanted to give me space, so I apologized and told her it was fine for her to sit and that I could find someplace else. Then I started to leave and she insisted I stay. This went on for a while until we both realized there was enough space that we could share the damn thing. We started talking to one another to pass the time. One hour later, she was my best friend in the whole county."

"That's so sweet," Alicia said. "It really happened that fast?"

Charlotte nodded. "I didn't know who she was at first, and I'm glad I didn't. I never paid attention to that kind of gossip, but if I had, I probably wouldn't have given her a chance. A couple days after we met, I invited her to move into my apartment. We split rent and I would get her inside the club so she could watch me play and meet some of my other friends."

"Could she get into the club herself?"

"I'm afraid not. I'm not sure if it was who she was or just the reputation she had, but no Judge let her in. Honestly, it seemed to be for a pretty good reason. Most of the others didn't like her much either. It was like letting a stray dog into our house—like I was breaking some unspoken rule that all our friends had to be from this side of the county. But I didn't listen to them."

"Were you afraid of what they were going to think about you?" Alicia asked.

"There was nothing to be afraid of," Charlotte said, after taking another sip of her martini. "They could've booed me off the stage, broken my guitar, and I still would've stuck by her. Friends who pick your friends aren't your real friends. That's how I see it. You have to trust yourself more than you trust anyone else. That's what kept us together no matter how many times they said it was wrong."

"But why did she leave?" Alicia asked, afraid now that she was stepping onto dangerous ground. She waited for Charlotte to say she had asked too many questions, but the singer kept her usual calm, serene expression.

"We had a fight," Charlotte answered. "It's more complicated than it sounds, but that's what happened."

"And that's why you stopped being friends?"

"I told you, it's more complicated than that. We still care about each other. She still cares about me, wherever she is. I can't prove it, but I know it's true. I know because I was something she never had before, and you never forget what you only have once."

"And what was that?" Alicia asked. "What were you to her?"

Charlotte hesitated before she gave her answer.

"I was what she wanted Tom to be. Tom thought he was the one who could fix her. I just wanted to be her friend, and I stuck with her until she decided it was time for her to leave."

"How much do you know about Tom?" Alicia asked, once again noticing the way the singer's hand tightened around her glass at the mention of this name.

"I know he's a rat," Charlotte sneered. "That's all the information I need."

"But he was trying to help her," Alicia protested, trying her best not to sound defensive. "I mean, he might not have done a great job, but he was trying to be good to her."

"And he tried in all the wrong ways," Charlotte hissed. Her words were so sharp that Alicia fell back into silence. She realized defending Tom was a lost cause. There was no changing the singer's mind, at least not yet.

"Look, girl, I know you're new to this place and you're used to hearing a bunch of different things from different people about who's right and wrong, but I don't take any sides unless I know what I'm talking about. The people on the East, they like to fix things that aren't broken. They parade around with their speeches of self-improvement and reaching new limits, but that's not the right mindset for everyone. Girls like Alexandra, they've been through enough already. What she needed was a place where she could be with people who took her for who she was. That's what she could've found with me, with all of us, and I know if Tom had let her come to West, a lot would be different."

———— ———— ———— ———— ————

Neither one of them spoke as Charlotte took another sip of her martini. In their silence, Alicia could only sit and listen once again to the musicians onstage and the laughing and chatting of all the other people in the room, each of them sitting and smiling with their friends as though they could live at their tables. Not a single person aside from her or Charlotte looked lost. She wondered how much Alexandra would have loved this place if the old Judge had allowed her to enter, and if the other members had embraced her as one of their own.

She said goodbye to Charlotte when the time came to go back to Mr. Zeeger's place, and within the first few steps, she started to feel uneasy. She felt like she'd left something behind. She checked her bag and pockets until she was positive she had all her belongings. She wondered if maybe the feeling came from leaving the club itself, if she had already become so attached to this place that walking back to the loft was like leaving home. It would explain why the walk across Corraine-Callister felt twice as long, and the Broken Cottage felt half as full and half as cheery as it had been just that morning.

She told Jeremiah about Charlotte, about how she and Alexandra met on a bench by a pond, and how they'd lived together for almost a year, but she stayed away from mentioning the more personal comments that Charlotte would probably want to keep private.

"She was due for another show in a few minutes, so I didn't have the time to talk about anything else," Alicia said. "But I can tell she likes me. I think if I keep going back, I'll be able to learn a lot more."

"That sounds like a good idea," Jeremiah said. "I haven't found anyone else who seems to know as much about her, but I'll keep looking. Do you mind sticking around that place for a while?"

"No," Alicia said, surprised by how honest this answer felt, and how eager she was to skip past the next few hours and go back as soon as she could. "No, I don't mind at all."

Chapter Fourteen

The Terrinson Club

Part Two

Alicia never told her parents about the incident with the Sharing Circle. When they asked about her day, she pretended as though everything was fine, refusing to let even one tear drip down her cheek until she was alone in her bedroom. She felt hollow, as if something had been ripped from her chest and was now hanging above her head, casting its shadow across the rest of her body.

Even when Jeremiah apologized the next day and brought her to his private spot at Shangrin Lake, something still felt wrong. She decided to pay one more visit to the counseling room, hoping some advice from Tom would help. She stopped by his office the following Monday, once her final class of the day came to an end, and all the rest of her classmates were on their way home.

"Let me ask you a question that I think might help us get to the core of this problem," Tom said. "You started answering Ms. Meehan's question—said you would never go skydiving. You hear Jer laugh at you, you feel hurt by him, and you walk out of the room before anyone can see you cry. Right then, as you were walking out the door, who did you blame?"

Alicia didn't understand the question. "I'm sorry, sir, I'm not quite sure what you're asking."

"Did you blame Jer for embarrassing you, or did you blame

yourself for saying something he thought was embarrassing? And you can call me Tom. Don't worry about calling me sir."

Alicia paused. "Sir—I mean, Tom—are you suggesting this was somehow my fault?"

"No. I know what Jer did was wrong. The reason I asked this question is because I want to know how his mistake made you feel about yourself. Did I ever tell you about the Hero Bias when we talked about your birthday party?"

"I don't think so," Alicia replied, after scouring her memory for a moment. "If you did, I can't remember it properly. What is it?"

"It's this instinct we have to notice evidence that shows us we're good, decent people, and ignore anything that says otherwise," the counselor explained. "Let me give you an example. Let's say one of those girls, Gabby, hears you calling her a spoiled brat. Do you think she would instantly agree with you?"

"No, she wouldn't. She would tell me I was wrong, because all the other girls think she's nice. But what does all this Hero Bias stuff have to do with me?"

"It's because you and Jer seem to be the only two students in your class who don't have it," Tom explained. "I'm the same way. If someone said something nasty about me, I wouldn't shout back, knock them to the ground, and say they're wrong. My first reaction would be to stop and ask myself what I did that made this person hate me so much. I'm always the first person I blame, and I have a feeling you're the same way.

"Am I wrong about that?"

"No," Alicia confessed. She felt the hollow ache in her chest again, but she kept her face free of tears. Even if she was alone with the counselor, she would never let anyone see her cry.

"Has Jer apologized to you yet?" Tom asked, after a long pause.

"Yes, he has. He came to my house on Saturday. Then we went to Shangrin Lake together and talked for a while."

"He came to my house on Saturday as well. Did he mention that?"

"Yes, he did. He said you talked about the Donnigan Boys—I mean, the other guys from our class. That's what Jer calls them. He promised he was going to stop trying to be their friend, and that from now on, he'd start caring more about me."

"And what about you?"

Alicia frowned. "What do you mean?"

"Did you tell him you'd stop trying to be friends with the girls in your class?"

A long pause filled the room as Alicia sat with her mouth partway open, waiting for the right words to slip out. She wanted to say yes, that she would give up on her two-year quest and commit to a healthy, stable friendship with Jeremiah, as if the incident at the Sharing Circle never happened. She wanted to say yes, but something was stopping her. Luckily, she didn't have to explain it. Tom already knew the answer.

"You don't want to give up," he said. "You don't want to feel like a failure, so you keep trying to do the impossible even when it makes you miserable. I know that feeling. I've seen it before. I've felt it before."

Tom looked off to the side, trying to hide a sad look in his eyes that Alicia pretended not to notice. Something was on his mind.

"You picked a good day for a counseling session," he said, after a light sigh.

"Why is that?"

"Because I'm about to give you some advice I've never given to anyone. Not even Jer."

Tom paused again before he spoke, and with another long sigh, he continued.

"I had a patient many years ago—a woman, about the same age you are now—before I came to this school. At one point, I had a choice to make about what was best for her. I could keep her with me, help her work through some of her issues, and help her find the positive change she'd wanted for so long; or, I could give her a little more freedom, let her have some time away from me, so she could find someone who accepted her the way she was. In the end, I chose the positive change. I chose to keep her with me. I've spent my whole career encouraging people to ignore the Hero Bias—to look within themselves for what they don't like, and then try to become that person they wish they could be. But in this one case, at that particular time in her life, I think I made the wrong choice. Sometimes change is not the right answer. I don't think it was right for her at that time, and I don't think it's right for you now."

"Then what is right for me?" Alicia asked. "What should I do?"

"Ignore the advice I've been giving Jer for four years," the counselor said. "Tell yourself you're good enough just the way you are, and don't bother dealing with anyone who says otherwise."

"Like Gabby Milles, and all the other girls?"

Tom nodded. "You don't need them anymore. Jer likes you just the way you are—with or without a parachute."

Alicia smiled.

"He made a mistake. I know that. But trust me, Alicia, that pain you feel is only going to get worse if you don't find a way to forgive and move on. He thinks you're great just the way you are. Those are the people you need to stick around. They're not as common as you think."

——— ——— ——— ——— ———

A few more weeks would have to pass until Alicia understood who this mystery patient was, and just how much grief Tom had endured all this time. By now, she barely ever thought of the incident at the Sharing Circle. She'd become too distracted by Parliss County, the Parryrose Club, Besalbee Road, the Fiatzi Café, the search for Alexandra, and now by the Terrinson Club. She hadn't even spent a full week in West Parliss and yet the club was starting to feel like a second home, and Charlotte had become a close friend, as if they'd known each other for years.

Alicia came to the club as early as she could, leaving Jeremiah at the door and saying hello to the Judge on her way inside. She sat at any table she wanted without the fear of trespassing into a group of friends that didn't want her. Anywhere she went, the people of the Terrinson Club would welcome her, which gave her the chance to meet new people every day while Charverra performed onstage, and at the end of the song, Alicia would clap and cheer louder than anyone else.

They'd grown close enough to trust one another with their Auras. The singer, as Alicia expected, was an abstract thinker, imaginative, and deeply sensitive. These traits were all shown by red in their respective rings, along with her nervousness, tenseness, and shrewd disposition. Her Aura was mostly red, except for a noteworthy portion of pure blue in the outer two rings, showing herself to be reclusive and an introvert. The most curious part about the singer's Aura was the fifteenth ring, the second closest one from the center. This was the section where blue light was a sign of conscientiousness, a preference for following rules; and where red light was a sign of expedience, which was a fancy term that meant a willingness to break rules and defy expectations. This part of Charlotte's Aura was magenta, the color of conflict, which left Alicia wondering just how much was going on inside the singer's head. She often forgot how lonely Charlotte had been until the last few days, and how awful it must have felt to lose a friend and have to spend her time surrounded by happy people who couldn't see or feel her grief.

Alicia wanted to believe it would only take a few more days for the singer to trust her with these more intimate secrets, but she had a feeling this wasn't all that likely unless she took the first step herself.

"There's something about me you don't know," Alicia muttered. "I've wanted to tell you about it for a while, but I was always too afraid to say anything until now."

"Well, that's a fun way to start a conversation," Charlotte said, grinning as she took a sip of her martini. "You've got my attention."

"I know who Tom Berrinser is," Alicia confessed, after a heavy sigh and a long pause. "He works at my old school. He's a friend of mine, and he brought me here to Parliss County just a few weeks ago."

Alicia had spent the last several hours wondering how Charlotte would react to this news. Even as the words left her lips, she could feel her body stiffen under the pressure, and the dread of the fire she would see in the singer's eyes. Instead, Charlotte looked remarkably calm for a woman who hated the counselor so harshly, which would have made Alicia feel a bit better if she weren't so confused.

"I thought I heard a rumor he was back," Charlotte said. "I heard his name somewhere in the crowd when I finished playing last week. Some folks were talking about the old drunk man who owns the Broken Cottage, and that he was letting Tom stay there to cover his tracks."

"So, you already knew?" Alicia asked.

"A guy like Tom can't throw a rock into a pool this small and not expect to make a ripple or two," the singer replied. "I didn't think he'd bring someone with him, but I suppose I shouldn't expect him to learn too much, now should I?"

"No, I suppose not," Alicia said, averting her eyes from the singer to look down at the table.

"Why did you tell me this?"

"I wanted to be honest with you. You've told me a lot about yourself, and you've been really nice to me ever since we met. I knew you trusted me, and I didn't feel like I deserved it, so I thought I should tell you."

"That's awfully kind of you, darling, but it's not necessary."

"Well, actually, it sort of is. I didn't just tell you because it was the right thing to do. I was hoping that, if it's not too much trouble, you and I could talk about him."

"Why do you care so much about him?" Charlotte asked, speaking with a familiar bitter sound in her voice, and a spiteful look in her eyes.

"Well, I suppose two reasons, mostly. First, like I said, he worked at my old school. He worked there as a counselor, and from what I hear, he's the best they've ever had. I have a friend who looks up to him like a father. Tom's done a lot for him, and plenty of other students, and I've come to like him a lot now that I've spent some time with him. So, I suppose whenever I hear someone say nasty things about him, I might get a little defensive."

"And the other reason?"

"He loved Alexandra. He loved her like so many other people did, especially you, and I'm just now starting to see how much it's been hurting him all these years. I've seen what losing Alexandra does to people, and I've never been able to do anything about that until now."

"I don't need your help, if that's what you're suggesting," Charlotte answered. "I've spent ten years getting used to what it's like being without her."

"So has Tom," Alicia said. "He left Parliss, too. He tried to start over as a high school counselor because he couldn't stand to be here any longer."

"Because he's a coward," Charlotte snapped.

"Then what are you?" Alicia asked, starting to get a bit angry. "You left just like he did."

"I left for a much different reason. I was never afraid."

"But you were angry, right?"

"You would be too if you knew her like I did!"

"And you wouldn't be if you knew Tom like I do," Alicia protested. "He's one of the best men I know."

"I'm sure he's a wonderful man to a lot of people in that town of yours," Charlotte said. Her voice suddenly fell into a harsh whisper, like she was trying to scream but couldn't pick up the sound of her voice. "I really, really am sure of that, but you're not going to change the way I feel about him. It's too late for me."

"It's not too late," Alicia promised. "Is this what you think Alexandra would want? Do you think she would want you to be this full of hate for a man you've never even met?"

"Don't you dare act like you know what she'd want from me!" Charlotte yelled, her voice now loud enough that everyone from the neighboring tables turned their heads from the stage to see what was wrong. Her voice settled back down to a cold whisper, which to Alicia's ears was louder than the ambience of musicians, chatting people, and clanging glasses all at once.

"I think you should leave now," Charlotte whispered. Alicia didn't bother to say otherwise. It was clear by the piercing sting of Charlotte's eyes there was nothing to do but let the tension die with time.

It wasn't until Alicia was back at Mr. Zeeger's place that she wondered if she'd ever have a chance to make things right, or if she'd crossed a line and was past the point of forgiveness. It was painful to think about. She'd found a place in Parliss County she loved so much and she'd spoiled it in less than a week, losing a new friend as quickly as they'd met.

"Did you learn anything else about Alexandra?" Jeremiah asked when he came back to the loft. He sat down next to Alicia on the couch and hung his shoulder bag on the arm rest, tired after a long day of aimless wandering.

"Not really. Just a few things you already heard from Howard."

"We should probably look somewhere else then. I think we've learned as much from that club as we can."

Alicia felt a jolt in her chest. "No, not yet," she said. She almost shouted, but she managed to quell her voice down as Jeremiah turned to her with a puzzled look. "I mean, there's another person I think I should ask, besides that singer. There's a man there who people say used to be in love with her. He's a saxophone player. He's usually the second one to play in the show. I can talk to him tomorrow morning."

Alicia felt guilty for lying, but going back to the Terrinson Club tomorrow was more important now that she needed to make amends with Charlotte. She could see Jeremiah was curious about her sudden need to go back, but thankfully, he didn't bother to ask any more questions. Instead, he shrugged and said one more day probably wouldn't set them too far back. That was all Alicia needed.

— — — — —

She arrived at the Terrinson Club early the next morning. She expected the Judge to say she'd been banned from entering, but thankfully, she was allowed to pass. She stood by herself at the edge of the room, waiting for Charverra to come onstage. Minutes went by and Alicia didn't see her. Half an hour passed and she still wasn't there. She wasn't sitting at her usual table, or at any other table, and after another few minutes of scouring the room, Alicia knew she wasn't at the club.

Alicia stopped by three tables asking if anyone had seen Charverra, but no one knew where she was. She pushed past the crowds of people on her way to a fourth table before she suddenly realized where to look. She left the Terrinson Club and followed her map around a few corners until she arrived at Cattell Street. She hurried past a nearby souvenir shop and a small bakery, and finally found a sign pointing to a trail to a nearby pond. She followed the trail until she saw a dark-skinned woman with dreadlocks sitting down on a rusty old bench with a handbag by her side.

Alicia could see Charlotte's sobbing face buried into her hands. She sat down on the bench and draped her arm across the singer's back. She put Charlotte's open bag on the ground to make room for herself, and without meaning to intrude, she looked down and saw what was inside. She found torn scraps of paper with old lyrics etched into them, a dozen guitar picks along with a metronome and an old brass pocket watch with a dent on one side, but what shocked Alicia more than anything else was the gun, with only two bullets resting next to the barrel, waiting to be loaded.

"Come on, Charlotte. Let's get you home."

Alicia helped her stand up and walk away from the pond. Less than an hour later, Alicia was standing in what had once been Charlotte and Alexandra's apartment. It was easy to see why no one else bothered to rent this place for the last ten years. The room was a messy place with chipped walls and a lousy view of the town. It was dusty, dull, almost empty except for a single bed and a desk, and the only speck of beauty came from a white poppy flower in a vase by the window.

"It might not be the best place to live," Charlotte admitted. "But it sure means a lot to me. This is where we spent almost a year living together, and this is the last place I saw her."

"Why did she leave?" Alicia asked.

"I told you. We had a stupid fight," Charlotte said. She sat on the floor by her bed with her hand across her face and her back against the wall. "It was my fault. I was pushing her too much. She told me to stop and I just didn't listen."

"Listen to what?"

Tears began to trickle down Charlotte's cheeks as Alicia knelt down to look at her. They were quiet for a long time until the singer spoke again.

"Can I tell you a secret about me, now?"

"Of course. What is it?"

"She and I weren't exactly friends," Charlotte said. She held up her right arm, put her pointer and middle fingers against her lips then reached across to touch Alicia's.

"You were in love with her?"

Charlotte nodded. "She wasn't ready for people to know, so we kept it a secret. It didn't help much either that I was about five years older. We were nice and friendly down at the club, and we kept our kissing for when we were alone. That's how she wanted it, but I wanted something else. I tried asking if we could be public but she kept saying no. One day, she came back early and saw a song I was writing about the two of us. She thought I was going to sing it in front of the club, and she yelled at me about it when I came back a few hours later. I should've told her it was a mistake, but I kept asking again and again if we could tell people about us. One thing led to another and we just started shouting. We got angrier and angrier. I told her she didn't love me; she said I was putting too much pressure on her. She tore up my song, and I started cussing at her and telling her to leave, and that's exactly what she did. That was the last time I saw her."

Charlotte reached into her bag. She found a slip of paper with an address written on it and gave it to Alicia.

"I found this after she left. Some old woman lives there. They say she's the best therapist in all of Parliss County. When I stopped by, I figured out this was where she'd been living when she ran away from Tom, but before she met me. The woman told me Alexandra had come by the night of our fight and left Parliss County the next morning, and that she was never coming back.

"And it was all my fault."

"You can't blame yourself," Alicia said, patting Charlotte on the back once more as the next wave of tears ensued. "She shouldn't have run off like that after one fight."

"It wasn't just that fight," Charlotte said. "It was all the little ones, all the times I kept insisting she do things the way I wanted, and every day, she loved me less and less until she had no reason to stay. Now she's gone and I don't even know where she is or what she's doing. For all I know, she's dead and I'm holding out on lost hope that she'll come back."

"You don't need her to come back," Alicia said. "I know you don't."

She paused before speaking again. "Can I tell you something I heard the first day I came to the club?"

Charlotte nodded, not able to utter even one syllable on account of her sobbing.

"I was at this table with a group of older women," Alicia began. "When I saw you sitting by yourself, I asked who you were, and they told me you were one of the best performers the club had ever seen. They told me how loved you once were, so I asked why you were all by yourself, and they said it was because you liked to stay private. They left you alone because they thought you didn't want to talk to anyone, but do you know what one of those women said to me?"

Charlotte didn't answer, but Alicia kept talking anyway.

"She told me they would all be ready to listen if you ever wanted to talk. There are people in that club who love you. They love you and they've barely even talked to you. There are so many people who would want to be where I am right now. You just have to be brave enough to give them a chance."

Charlotte wiped away her tears and turned to Alicia. "You sure about that?"

"Yes, I am," Alicia promised. "The Judge let them in for a reason. These people are all your friends. You just don't know it yet. Please, Charlotte, if you give them a chance, I know they can help you. Just let them try."

A full minute went by before either of them spoke again, when Charlotte let out one last sigh and wiped away her final tear. "Okay. I'll try. But I need you to do something for me first."

"Of course. Anything."

"Do you see the two bullets inside my bag—next to the gun? I need you to take them, leave my apartment, and put them someplace where no one will find them. Please, don't ask why. I just need them away from me before it's too late."

Alicia tucked both bullets into her shoulder bag and left the apartment without any questions. She walked to an empty street and dumped both bullets down a storm drain, then hurried back to the Broken Cottage the second her hand was empty.

— — — — —

She stayed in her room while Mr. Zeeger was downstairs serving drinks and chatting with the customers. She wrote in her journal to pass the time, making sure she kept track of everything she'd learned during her time with Charlotte, promising she would never forget the pain she'd seen on the singer's face earlier today. She stayed in her bedroom until the sky started to go dark. She finished her latest entry then went outside and sat down on the curb. A minute later, she saw Jeremiah walking back.

"So, what did he say?" he asked.

"Who?"

"The saxophone player you told me about. Did he say anything?"

"Oh, right," Alicia said. "Um, actually he did say something interesting. Apparently, Alexandra also liked to date women, not just men."

Jeremiah looked shocked. "Really? She was bi?"

"Yeah, I suppose so. He told me that's why he had such a hard time getting a date with her. There was this other girl she liked at the time. She and that girl eventually started dating for a month or so, and he would try to impress her by writing songs for her and playing them at the club. That's all he said.

"What about you? Did you find anything?"

"As a matter of fact, I did," Jeremiah said, breaking into a proud smile. "I just learned about this club called the Ranchester. This man I met at a café said he used to be a Judge over there. He said he almost let Alexandra in one time but ended up turning her away. We should go by tomorrow. If she got lucky with another Judge, someone inside might have met her once."

"Are you sure about that?" Alicia asked, stuttering a little as the words came out. "People don't usually get accepted into more than one club. If Alexandra got accepted into the Terrinson, she probably didn't get accepted anywhere else."

"But she didn't get accepted into the Terrinson Club," Jeremiah said. "You told me she only got inside because she was friends with that Charlotte woman. She was a guest."

"Oh, right," Alicia said. "Are you sure that's what I said?"

"It has to be—I wrote it down in my journal. Let me see if I can find it."

He pulled his journal out of his bag then flipped through the pages until he found the right spot. "See, right here."

"Oh, well, sorry. I must've forgotten. But, either way, I can't go to that other club tomorrow. I have to stay at the Terrinson, at least for a while."

"Why?"

"Charlotte needs my help."

"With what?"

"She just needs a little company, that's all."

"Why? What's wrong with her?"

"Oh, for God's sake, stop asking so many questions!" Alicia snapped, finally losing her patience. She stood up from the curb and looked Jeremiah square in the eye. "This isn't any of your business!"

"Whoa! Alicia, what's your problem?" Jeremiah blurted out, raising his own voice. "I'm just trying to help."

"No, you're trying to figure out a way to help her that's quick and easy so I can get back to this stupid scavenger hunt of yours! That's what you want, right?"

Alicia didn't mean to sound so harsh. She was just as stunned by the sound of her voice as Jeremiah. She couldn't remember the last time she'd ever spoken so impulsively to a friend, or another time she'd yelled at someone other than Bianca.

"Is that what this is about?" Jeremiah asked, in a weak voice that was barely more than a whisper. "Do you not want to do this anymore?"

"There's nothing else we can do," Alicia said, settling her voice back down to its usual tone. "She's gone. She left ten years ago and no one knows where she is. There's nowhere else we can go. I don't understand why you're so obsessed with her."

"I told you why."

"But have you thought about Tom? Honestly, Jer, do you really think Tom would want you snooping around like this? This isn't what he wants; he even said so in his first letter. He just wants us to find a place we like and enjoy the rest of our summer."

"Like the Terrinson Club?" Jeremiah said.

"Is that so bad?" Alicia asked. "I love it there. It's amazing."

"Well, I'm sorry I wasn't good enough to get inside!" Jeremiah spat. "Go figure I'm still not special enough to get accepted! God forbid everybody gets a pass except me!"

"Charlotte can invite you in," Alicia said. "I know she would. I just have to ask. Please, Jer, do yourself a favor and put this Alexandra nonsense aside and just have fun for the next two weeks."

"I can't!" Jeremiah said, shouting one last time before his voice settled down. He lowered his head, the way he often did when he was depressed. He dropped his bag at his feet and sat down at the curb, while Alicia stood and looked down on him.

"I can't do that," he muttered. "And I'm sorry if you think that's selfish, but I can't give up on this. Not now. I have to know who she was and what she did wrong, or one day, I'm going to be just like her.

"I started this, and now I have to finish it."

Alicia somehow knew Jeremiah wouldn't change his mind, no matter what she said or how wrong she thought this was. She could see how obsessed he'd become with Alexandra, how tightly he clung to his journal, and the notes and drawings he'd made over the last few days. It was all tearing him apart, whether he saw it or not, but it was no one's choice to make but his own.

"Then you'll have to finish it without me," Alicia muttered. She looked away as Jeremiah glanced up at her, not wanting to see her friend's reaction. She walked back to her bedroom, afraid of what might happen if she stayed outside any longer.

———— —— —— ——

Her own words towered above her as she lay in bed, casting their shadow across her body. She tried to fall asleep as the sound of her own voice and the memory of the lost, shattered look in Jeremiah's eyes kept her awake long into the night. She took the Aurascope out of her bag and studied it under the sheets. She gazed into the magenta-colored ring, and she heard Mr. Zeeger's voice echo inside her head while she wondered if she'd made the right choice. It was a choice she would have to make again and again for many years to come, a choice between finding a home and scouring the globe for new adventures. She wanted both but could never have them at the same time, and that would never change. This one ring would most likely stay the same color for years until the slow passage of time and the wisdom of adulthood made it green. It would never be blue, never be red, but that did not have to be a problem. As long as she had Charlotte, Tom, her mother, her father, or anyone else who loved her on her side, she would find a way to be happy. Hopefully, with time, she could add Jeremiah back to that list.

Alicia didn't stay for breakfast when she woke up the next morning. Instead, she grabbed a peach off the kitchen counter and rushed down the stairs, and then walked across Corraine-Callister alone. She wasn't ready to see Jeremiah again. Her memory of last night stung even as she stepped back inside the Terrinson Club; seeing him again during breakfast and eating in their tense, awkward silence was too much to handle for now. She had to stall their next meeting for as long as she could, even if it meant starting her day without a stack of Mr. Zeeger's pancakes and a glass of milk.

Charverra was back onstage at her usual time, armed and ready with nothing but her guitar, her words, and her magnificent voice, but that was all she needed. As always, the crowd erupted in applause when she finished, and Alicia was the loudest of them all. It was a performance like any other, but the rest of the day would be different. Instead of walking back to their private table, Alicia insisted they both sit at one in the center of the room, and she introduced Charlotte to some of the other members she'd befriended over the last few days. Within minutes, they were all talking; within hours, they were all laughing; and within the day, Charlotte looked and felt happier than she had all week long. She looked like a new woman, and Alicia was ready to devote all her time and focus to making sure this didn't change.

"Can you do one last favor for me?" Charlotte asked, once she and Alicia were alone.

"Of course. Anything."

"Could you stay with me—just as long as you can until you go home? You've been very helpful to me. I haven't had a friend like you in a long time, and I would love nothing more than if I could have your company for as long as I can."

Alicia reached out and gave the singer a hug. "I promise I won't leave until I have to," she said, smiling as she looked around the Terrinson Club. "There's no place I'd rather be."

Chapter Fifteen

The Mask Chamber

Her name was Betty Westridge. She was the daughter of a widow, seventeen years old with a dream of becoming a figure skater, a dream that faded more and more each day she came home to the same tattered house and found her mother stressing over the bills. She had worked all through high school, either by waiting tables or washing dishes. Her closest friends were an elderly woman she sat next to on the bus, and the cigarettes she would smoke whenever her mom wasn't watching. She'd stopped caring about sex and dating after a false pregnancy scare when she was only sixteen. The only men she concerned herself with were the ones dating her mother, the ones she thought might make for a good stepfather and the ones she wanted as far away from their home as possible.

And she was one of Alexandra's favorite characters.

Tom had been in the audience for each of Alexandra's plays. He'd watched her play a single mother, a prostitute, a killer, a drug addict, and the abused wife of a wealthy diplomat, but he never considered until now how much Betty and all of Alexandra's other roles had shaped her. He could have written a book about Alexandra's childhood, her years as a struggling high school student, and all the time they'd spent together roaming around East Parliss, but her time in Canmark was the one part of her life the counselor knew nothing about. He'd spent nearly four weeks held captive in Mothcatcher's empty theater, learning about Alexandra's experiences with the Canmark actors, finally seeing the conflict she'd hidden so well for so long.

The Cardorians hadn't been around since the night Tom arrived at the theater, allowing him and Mothcatcher to speak in private. Through these lonely talks, Tom learned Alexandra had been petrified with fear simply by holding a knife, as it brought back the memory of her mother's death, and she could only carry it once she'd been desensitized to the violence by watching another actor stab a dummy. Her distrust of men and intimacy became a problem when she had to play a prostitute and practice by kissing the older male actors. Once a month she was given sheets of paper along with a box of colored pencils, and they would ask her to draw the Aura of her newest characters, to look inside their minds and their histories until she could take them apart piece by piece and put them back together onstage.

"You asked me a few weeks ago how it was Alexandra and I came to meet," Mothcatcher said. He sat in the same place as the night of their first meeting, at the head of the table, shrouded by scarlet candlelight in the room beneath the theater. "Can you remember what I said to you?"

"You want me to tell you something we both already know?" Tom asked.

"Not for the sake of my memory, but yours, Mr. Berrinser. Remember, you're the one who needs to know all this, not me. If you can't remember a simple story, then frankly this has been a waste of our time. It's your turn, by the way."

Mothcatcher insisted that each night they play a game of chess while they spoke, as a way of training Tom to listen under constant distraction. Tom made his move as quickly as he could, studying the board for a moment before moving his knight to the center to guard his queen.

"You used to be an actor here at Canmark," Tom began, "way before Alexandra came to Parliss. You were never in a show with her, but you were always in the audience. You saw something special in her, something that always drew your attention away from the rest of the stage whenever she spoke. One day, she noticed the way you stared at her from the audience. She found you after a show, and that's when you introduced yourself. She asked why you retired from the company, but you didn't tell her, and from then on, she started worrying if there was something she didn't see about Canmark that you did.

"A few days went by and she saw you at a café one night while I was off at the Parryrose Club. You two started talking. You told her more about your past and she identified with a lot of your acting experiences. From then on, each Saturday night when I was at the Grand Burnett and I thought she was rehearsing late, she was actually with you. That's when you started calling yourself her second counselor. You'd started to replace me, even before she knew it."

"We still met even when she ran away to West Parliss," Mothcatcher said. "Just at a different café. She slept at my old apartment in one of the spare bedrooms. It wasn't ideal, but there was nowhere else for her to go, and I couldn't leave her out in the cold by herself."

Mothcatcher pushed his king's side rook down in an attempt to threaten Tom's queen. It was a move so reckless that Tom didn't have to think long to make his counter. He slid a nearby bishop into the crossfire to help protect his strongest piece.

"You have quite the respectable memory," Mothcatcher said, sliding his next piece into its new position without hesitating. In a flash of panic, Tom watched the remaining black knight land within one move of capturing his queen. He scoured his options but found no solutions. Whatever he could send into the firefight would be taken in two or three moves at best, and securing a crack in one spot would leave a crack in another.

"You impress me still as an impeccable listener, but you're a rather disappointing player."

"Chess isn't really my game," Tom confessed.

"I hear you're quite good at Silent Captain," Mothcatcher said. "I heard you once saved some poor college professor from a pretty serious debt. That's what you're good at. That's what I wanted you for. You can make all the right reads and guesses at just the right time; see things others mean to hide and make the calls others shy away from. Those are your skills, but not mine. I excel in the world of the obvious, and in games of nothing more than thinking two or three steps ahead, and where everything you need to know is right at your fingertips. I leave no room for guesswork. To win, I simply look ahead and trust the enemy won't do the same."

They continued to trade moves as Mothcatcher went on speaking, and as the statement came to an end, Tom watched an opposing knight sweep his queen off the board. A loss this severe was reason enough to forfeit, but as long as his king stood alive, he would go on playing. Within the following turns, Tom cleared out most of his first row and castled, staying safe behind a wall of lowly pawns in a corner.

"You can see clearly into shadows but show consistent blindness to all that is obvious," Mothcatcher said, infuriating Tom even more with another amused expression. "I knew what Alexandra wanted weeks before you even knew what to look for. I knew she would leave East months before the thought even crossed her mind. Would you like to know how?"

Tom rarely walked away from these discussions without wishing he could sock Mothcatcher in the jaw. It was sinful how much pleasure this man found in his grief, but Tom understood he could do nothing about it. Until he had Alexandra's journal in his hands, Tom would stay and suffer through the arrogance and snide remarks, and he knew Mothcatcher understood the power he held. He could do and say whatever he pleased and never suffer the consequences.

"Tell me, Mr. Berrinser, which section of the Aurascope is the one that deals with Neuroticism vs. Stability?"

"The seventh ring," Tom answered. "Red for neurotic; blue for stable."

"And what would you say are the advantages of emotional stability?"

"Well, it helps you handle pressure, it makes you a better leader, it keeps you from making rash and impulsive decisions, you're less susceptible to stress, and, in general, it helps you live a better life."

"Fair enough," Mothcatcher said. "And what would you say are the advantages of being a neurotic person?"

"There aren't many. That's why I try not to be."

"And yet you're an advocate of East Parliss. If personal balance is so great then why do you cling so tightly to one end of this spectrum?"

"Ring seven has always been one of the exceptions," Tom replied.

"That's because nobody can answer my question," Mothcatcher said. "And neither could she. There is no logical reason why you would ever prefer to be neurotic when you have the chance to be sensible. She knew that, and yet here she was living in a place where any change from red and blue was a good thing. She couldn't see why. Nobody had an answer for her. But I did."

"And what was your answer?"

"Well, to put it simply, neurotic people are more interesting," Mothcatcher replied. "They're better characters, better at starting drama and grabbing our attention, better at landing themselves in odd or comical situations that are more entertaining to watch."

"They're good qualities for an actor," Tom inferred.

Mothcatcher nodded. "That's the greatest distinction between the world and the stage. The theater is a place for the interesting. Fiction is where we want our drama, our tension, our suspense, to see people have their lives thrown into war, misery, and action. The real world is a place for consistency, where we feel safe and happy, and it disturbed Alexandra to realize she was living in a place that mixed the two up. She saw what I had seen, how the people of Canmark and East Parliss cared more about putting themselves through challenge after challenge instead of living a safe, happy life. From then on, I could see the rest of what was to happen. I saw her leaving the actors months before she did. I saw her walking over to West Parliss before she was even sure what it was."

"But she left that place, too," Tom said. "She lasted just as long in East as she did in West. How do you explain that?"

Tom's voice had risen out of frustration. He'd always been

defensive of East Parliss, the place that had been his home for many years and supported his faith in the importance of personal growth. He had only just begun to wonder if he'd been wrong this entire time. Half of Parliss County thought he was. A lot of Auralites lived in West, Auralites he trusted to be wise, thoughtful people who wouldn't have made their choices without a good reason.

Tom hadn't fallen asleep for the last few nights without whispers of doubt clouding his weary mind. He wondered if East had ever been the right choice, for him or Alexandra, for Jeremiah or Alicia, and whether his trust in the importance of the green Aura was an old belief he was too stubborn to leave behind.

"I know as little as you about that," Mothcatcher said. "That's mostly what I hope to learn for myself once you open the box. My best guess is that she never found enough people on the other side she connected with. That was all she really wanted, now wasn't it? Connection. Community. She didn't have it with her parents, or with her aunt and uncle, or any friends she had in school. She would always dream of clubs, she told me. She wanted to be a part of something, but I suppose they didn't want her. So, she left."

"There must've been someone over in West who liked her," Tom said. "She couldn't have stayed there for a year just by herself."

"There was one woman she told me about," Mothcatcher said. "Some singer she met on a park bench who performed at the Terrinson Club, but that's the most I know."

"Who was she?" Tom asked, suspicious of how Mothcatcher suddenly knew so little when before he'd been an expert in the most insignificant of details.

"Alexandra never told me her name," Mothcatcher said with a reserved look in his eyes. Tom noticed this was the first time this man had looked away to avoid making contact. Tom had seen this sort of look many times before back at his office, when he asked troubled students what was bothering them, when they said everything was fine but their faces said otherwise. Something didn't feel right.

"So, you're telling me Alexandra told you about a woman she met on a bench and revealed she was a singer, became friends with her, but didn't bother to tell you her name?"

"I might've simply forgotten it," Mothcatcher replied. For a brief moment, Tom observed a look of gaping uncertainty in his eyes, as if he'd made a mistake and was trying to hide it.

"Mr. Berrinser, are you suggesting I'm deceiving you in some way?"

"It just seems unreasonable to me that you could forget something so simple as a name when you've been so clear on everything else. What about the old woman?"

Mothcatcher looked puzzled. "What about her?"

"You told me two days ago about that old woman who lives in a house in West—the house Alexandra ran off to when she left East Parliss. You knew the old woman's name, you knew she was a therapist, you knew the house address, how old she was, the names of all three of her brothers, and now you're telling me you can't remember the name of the one real friend Alexandra had for a whole year?"

"If you're accusing me of something, Mr. Berrinser, I would like for you to tell me directly."

"Well, either your memory isn't as good as you say it is, or you're hiding something from me."

"I think we've already established I prefer to exist in the world of the transparent, Mr. Berrinser," Mothcatcher sneered, looking back to the chessboard.

"Everyone makes exceptions now and then," Tom said. "No matter how clear something seems, there's always room for a little distraction."

Without redirecting his gaze, Tom slid his knight into place and took the opposing queen. The score was even again with a single move and a brief loss of focus, and Tom basked in the glory of his opponent's desperate search of the chessboard for any sign of cheating. He tried to hide his rage behind a façade of confidence, but Tom could see past it.

"Right you are," Mothcatcher growled. "We all face moments of weakness, and I suppose you've exposed two of mine."

"Any chance I'll find another?"

"I wouldn't feel so lucky if I were you," he sneered. "Compared to you, my record is spotless—stainless and blank as though I'd never touched it. You think you're so brilliant? Or that all I have is talk? Haven't we made it clear you had countless opportunities to keep her from leaving, and only through your blatant negligence did she slip through your grasp? You are a child compared to me."

"Don't you ever talk to me like that!"

"How can you call yourself an expert on the minds of young people when you fell into the most obvious trap there is?"

"And what's that?" Tom asked. His voice simmered down to a somber tone. Mothcatcher's did the same. A haunting silence crept back into the room as the echoes of their yelling died between the narrow walls, and as the wax of the candles dripped from the burning fires.

"Let me put it to you in context," Mothcatcher said. "Outside this room, past the stairs and down the hall, you'll find a door, a door with a silver handle that leads to a place we call the Mask Chamber. Suppose I tell you, right now, this room embodies one of the last few remaining mysteries in Parliss County, something only a fraction of us will ever see and even fewer will understand. Now, suppose I tell you, that you are now and forever forbidden to go into this room, and then I left you alone. What would you do?"

"I wouldn't go into the room," Tom replied.

"Exactly. Now, what would a teenager do?"

Tom said nothing. He opened his mouth to give his answer, but the words escaped him the second he understood what Mothcatcher was trying to tell him. He thought about Jeremiah, the reckless curiosity that drove him to open the cabinet, the same ambition he could see in Alexandra as the memories came back one by one.

"It's a simple case of the reactance principle," Mothcatcher explained. "You tell someone not to do something and it becomes exactly what they want to do. Tell a kid to go to bed by ten, they'll stay up 'til eleven; tell a kid they're too young to ride a bike, they'll go out of their way to prove you wrong; tell a kid not to cross the road and stay by your side at all times, then walking across is all they can think about. Alexandra was destined to leave for West Parliss the moment you told her she couldn't. When you never gave her a reason, what other way could she find out?"

A cold chill rushed down Tom's spine when he saw how right Mothcatcher was. He felt even more discouraged at the sight of the chessboard. Since capturing the queen, he'd fallen back in numbers and lost his momentum. Mothcatcher slid his last bishop into place and declared checkmate, and in a desperate act to deny him his victory, Tom scoured the board for some way to save his game. All hope seemed lost until he saw his two remaining bishops and placed one between his king and the other bishop, blocking the check and keeping the game alive for a few more turns.

"She's special to you, Mr. Berrinser. She's special to me as well, but in many ways, she was still no different from anyone else her age. She was young, and with youth comes stubbornness. When we tell them what they should do, they find ways to do the opposite. When we tell them who they are and strap a label across their backs, they find ways to tear it off. When we make rules, they find ways to break them. I'm not a rule maker. I don't live with rules because I have seen how pointless they all turn out to be. I never fell into that trap with her, and I will not do the same with you. And I know just how to prove it.

"Come. Have a look inside the Mask Chamber with me."

Tom rose from his seat as Mothcatcher grabbed a nearby candle, lighting their way down a dark and tattered corridor so long Tom suspected it was more than the length of the auditorium. In the distance, he spotted the door with the silver handle, and soon after he found himself standing in a round room. A vast collection of decorative masks hung from the wall in a circle, each one immensely different in shape and color from its neighbors, and in the center of the room was a large mahogany desk topped with wine bottles.

He looked around as Mothcatcher described this room as a relic of a forgotten past, a tomb of old ideas and theories from the Old Practice about the foundation of personality, many of which had died out of popularity, but still maintained a niche of loyal enthusiasts.

"The Mask Test was based on an old idea that personality was easy to predict even without the use of Aura," Mothcatcher explained. "To test this theory, members of the Old Practice invited a sample of fifty people and asked them to choose one mask that appealed to them the most. What the subjects did not know, however, was that each mask had been carefully designed so that it would appeal to people with a specific set of traits. Introverted people, for example, would theoretically be drawn to masks with darker colors, while extroverts would be attracted to masks with vibrant colors and lavish designs. Once a mask was chosen, the experimenters would study the subject's Aura. They predicted that each subject had chosen a mask that corresponded with their Auras. In the end, only five subjects had chosen the right mask. The experimenters were wrong."

"So, this was a failed experiment," Tom said. "Then why did you bring me here?"

"To help you see the truth about the Auralites you've ignored for far too long," Mothcatcher said. "We are not gods. Our knowledge is limited. Even those we love the most can still find ways to surprise us. You believed you knew Alexandra well enough to predict her every decision, but you proved you were wrong. And now, you'll prove it again."

"How?"

"By failing my version of the Mask Test," Mothcatcher replied. "I invited Alexandra into this room once to choose her mask. I want you to find the one she chose."

The challenge seemed impossible. The sheer chance of finding the right mask from dozens of choices was massively out of his favor, and getting it right on the first try would be more of a miracle than a testament of his skill. Ordinarily, Tom would have shrugged his shoulders over such a meaningless test and picked one just to spare himself from wasting time, but he shuddered at the thought of making a mistake so absurd that Mothcatcher would mock him for it every night until he left. Even worse, Tom remembered the box, and how a week from tonight he would have to make precise assumptions about the answers to Alexandra's questions. His odds then would be even worse than now, and if choosing a simple mask was too hard, he would fail the most important test before he even started.

Tom began pacing around the room, grabbing masks and putting them back several times over and over before he finally made his decision. The mask he chose was golden yellow on its left side, and blue on its right. It was perfectly split down the middle, creating an invisible line that cut through its nose and lips.

But the test wasn't over. Mothcatcher revealed he'd built an extension of this old test just for this occasion. He led Tom to the mahogany desk in the middle of the room and gave him a bottle of wine with the number thirty-two written on the label. Tom saw the same number written on the back of the mask.

"What's in the bottle?" Tom asked.

"Red wine, if you chose correctly," he answered. "If you chose a mask she never even touched, you will taste poorly seasoned wine, laced with salt and herbal spices that will leave a bitter taste in your mouth for hours. But if you picked the mask that was expected to be her choice, according to the research of the Old Practice, then this bottle is filled with poison."

Tom was certain this was a lie, but as his doubt grew stronger he made sure to keep his panic hidden. He knew the odds of this being the poisoned bottle were drastically in his favor, while a cautious voice inside his mind echoed on and on, reminding him of the slim chance he was wrong, and that a show of bravado could lead to his death.

"How bold do you feel?" Mothcatcher asked, his sly demeanor bearing no signs of fading.

"This isn't poison," Tom insisted. "None of them are. You wouldn't risk me dying. You need me."

"I need someone who knew her well enough to open the box," Mothcatcher said. "If you can't survive this, you were useless to me from the start. I'd rather know how useful you are before I waste any more of my time with you."

Every part of Tom's body ached with fear and resentment. By refusing to drink, he would not only prove himself to be a coward, but confess he wasn't the great counselor so many believed he was. He would never be rid of Mothcatcher's special brand of condescension, the mocking look in his eyes, and the wry smile that would stick with him forever.

"You don't have to be right," Mothcatcher said. "You just can't be wrong."

Tom opened the bottle and drank, swallowing down the most vile, putrid substance he'd ever tasted. Clearly, he hadn't picked the right mask, and he could only hope that was the worst of his bad luck. Mothcatcher counted down while Tom waited, a tear trickling down his cheek as he felt more and more certain he was about to die. By the final ten seconds, Tom felt his stomach churn, his vision fade, and in the final five he expected to fall to the ground writhing in pain.

But he didn't. He was still alive, or so he was for now.

He held his breath, waiting for death to take him the moment he let his guard down, but it never came. Second by second, he felt his life return to him, though his relief wasn't strong enough to close the hole in his chest when he looked at the bottle, and remembered he'd still failed.

"You weren't right," Mothcatcher said. "But you weren't as wrong as you could have been. We still have work to do before you're ready. We're done for tonight. We'll talk again tomorrow."

Chapter Sixteen

The Dogs of Club Culture

There had been a time when Jeremiah thought he had an excellent memory, and now looking back on the last few years, he wasn't so sure. There were some moments he could still see in clear detail, while others had gotten lost with time. He remembered the day he'd gone out to Shangrin Lake with Alicia in her father's boat, but he couldn't remember a single word they'd said to each other. He remembered asking her about her favorite books and movies, but he couldn't remember their names. He even struggled to remember parts of the stories she'd told about her old life in Germany, the very stories that built the foundation of most of their talks. These were the things he ought to know about his best friend, and somehow most of them had slipped away.

"The human memory is a tricky thing," Tom said during a counseling session that had taken place earlier in the year. "I'm not sure I know enough about this field to give you the right answer, but I do have one theory."

"What is it?" Jeremiah asked, leaning into his seat.

"When I was just starting high school, a few months before my parents got divorced, I remember being upstairs in my bedroom studying for an algebra test when I heard my parents fighting with one another down in the kitchen. I tried to ignore them, but a few harsh words slipped through the walls no matter what I did. I remember hearing my father slam the front door shut when he went to spend the night at my uncle's place, and my mother throwing a frying pan across the room and accidentally leaving a dent in the wall. The very next day, when I had my test, that was all I could think about. All I heard all day long was the sound of my parents fighting. It followed me everywhere, and I couldn't think about anything else. I got a C-minus on that test a week later."

Jeremiah didn't see how this connected to his problem, but he didn't interrupt Tom's story. Somehow, he knew the counselor would tie it all together.

"I learned that day that bad memories are a lot stronger than good ones," Tom continued. "I don't have any research to back this up, but I can speak from experience that it's hard to remember what day the Treaty of Versailles was signed when you spent three days that week with a marriage counselor. I was fixating on my parents, and it got in the way of everything else. I think something similar is happening with you. I think you're having trouble paying attention to Alicia because you're spending too much time trying to impress the rest of your classmates."

"You think so?" Jeremiah asked. He hoped this wasn't true but felt in his gut that it probably was.

"Well, let's put it to the test," Tom said. "Do you remember the first session we had together once you started school? Do you remember what you were upset about that day?"

"It was about Ethan Kantzton," Jeremiah answered. The memory came back instantly. "We were playing capture the flag. We'd just been divided into teams and Ethan was on mine. We were walking over to our side of the field and I was talking to some people about some cool move I made the last time we played, when I outran two of my chasers by going up over the hill and zigzagging a lot. Before I could finish talking, Ethan shouted out that no one cared about what I was saying."

"And what about the baseball game?" Tom asked.

"I was put on the same team as Ethan again," Jeremiah said. "I saw him look at me and the rest of our teammates, and I heard him mumble to himself that he was going to lose because he was stuck with a bunch of wimps."

"And what about the cast party?" Tom asked. "You'd all just finished the last show of *Candlelight Palace* and Casey's parents invited your whole class to their house to celebrate. You came to this office the following Monday. Do you remember why?"

Jeremiah nodded. "The guys were all hanging out in the backyard. I decided to tag along with them, just because all the girls were inside trying to decide what song they wanted to play. Casey's older brother was out with us, and they were giving him updates on all the gossip. They started talking about the girls from our class, and I heard Ethan call Alicia retarded. Then Mike did an impression of her and went on talking in this high-pitched voice and making up some fake story about his time in Germany."

Tom nodded. "Okay. Now let's see how well you remember one of Alicia's stories."

The counselor leaned in closer, looking Jeremiah right in the eye.

"What do you remember about the turnip story?"

Already, Jeremiah knew he was in for a bumpy ride when he needed a moment to understand what Tom was asking, and even once the smoke cleared, the struggle was far from over. The question was referring to a Sharing Circle that had taken place a few months ago. Ms. Meehan had left earlier in the week to attend her nephew's wedding, so Tom had volunteered to take her place. As their final question, the counselor had asked them each to tell the class about the best day of their life. By now, Jeremiah had forgotten most of their answers, as his classmates had surely forgotten his, but he was sure they all remembered Alicia's.

"It was a family picnic; that was her story," Jeremiah said. "She went hiking with her family up a hill, and when they got there, they took turns cutting some special turnip with a knife."

"And what was so special about it?"

"I'm not sure. I just remember her talking a lot about the way they cut it. It was either a special turnip or a special knife, or some special cutting technique her parents knew about. It was something like that,

I'm sure. I just can't think of it."

"Do you remember any other details?" Tom asked. "Where did they have their picnic? What country were they in? Who from her family was there besides her parents? How long ago did it happen?

"Do you remember anything?"

The answer was no. He didn't say this right away, but he knew it was the truth. This one word stung so much that before he even parted his lips he felt his heart sink deeper into his chest. Tom was right. He didn't remember the good. He only remembered the bad.

"No," he finally admitted, lowering his head to stare at the carpet. "I don't remember anything."

— — — — —

Alicia was already gone when he woke up. He tried his best to find relief in dodging another tense encounter, but as he helped himself to his breakfast and looked to the empty seat, he wished he could see Alicia there with him, even if she kept her head down and remained silent until she left. Mr. Zeeger's company wasn't the same. He ate slowly, trying to stall as much as he could before he finally grabbed his bag and returned to West Parliss.

The Wide Road didn't scare him anymore. When his feet left the sidewalk and hit the cobblestone, he felt the same as he had for the last few days, which meant he felt nothing at all. His face was void of any expression, which anyone could've seen if he didn't walk with his head so low. He trudged along until he saw the Ranchester Club, and the Judge standing at the foot of its large, ornate doors.

He noticed it was a different Judge than the one who'd denied him access the last time. For a moment, he considered trying out for a second time, but he changed his mind a second later when he realized it was hopeless. No Judge would ever let him in. No one ever wanted him.

He looked to the other side of the street and went inside the nearby diner. He wasn't hungry whatsoever, but he thought maybe a little extra food or a drink would help him get in a better mood. He ordered himself a glass of lemonade then sat down at a table by the window, granting him a perfect view of the Ranchester Club.

He knew Tom would have advised him to sit somewhere else, but Tom wasn't with him. Neither was Alicia. By now she was probably sitting around her new friends, swaying her head to the tune of Charlotte's music, waiting until they could reunite offstage and spend the rest of the day telling stories while he stayed outside.

"Hey, excuse me?"

Jeremiah turned and saw someone standing by his table.

"Hi, I don't mean to be rude or anything, but would you mind moving? I've come to this diner every day for a few years now and I've gotten used to this table. I really don't want to sit anywhere else."

Jeremiah didn't care where he sat. He would've graciously moved to another table if an idea hadn't come to him right as he was about to speak. He looked at the young man in front of him. They appeared to be about the same age, though Jeremiah was a little taller. His dark, unkempt hair hung down across his forehead, and reached so far down it nearly covered his light hazel eyes. He looked lonely, the same way Jeremiah knew he looked to the rest of the diner and anybody else who'd seen him for the last few days, and here he saw the chance to fix both of their problems.

"What if we sat together instead?" Jeremiah suggested. "You're not meeting anyone here, are you?"

"No. I just usually eat alone."

"How come?"

"I just like having time to myself, that's all."

"So do I. But we all need company now and then, don't you think?"

"I guess so," he replied, a concerned look still draped across his face. "I don't have that many friends, though."

"Sitting by yourself won't help that," Jeremiah said, gesturing to the empty seat. "We don't have to talk if you don't want to, but that doesn't mean we have to be alone either."

Jeremiah hardly ever found himself in this position. Moments like this were so rare that if it hadn't been for Alicia's first few days at

Laronna, this would've been the first. He was the Judge of his own club. He had the power to welcome a lonely stranger into his company or seal the doors and make him try again with someone else. Even this small amount of control weighed on him as he imagined how good it would feel to claim the table for himself, but he would never do that. He wasn't a Donnigan Boy, despite his lack of trying. So instead, he waited patiently until the young man sat down across from him.

He said his name was Cody. That was all he said for the next ten or so minutes while they sat in perfect silence. He wouldn't so much as look at Jeremiah. Instead, his focus was either down at his food or at the window, staring out across the street to the Ranchester Club.

"Have you ever been in there?" Jeremiah asked.

"Been where?"

"That club across the street. The Ranchester. Have you ever been in there?"

"Not ever," Cody replied. "Frankly, I don't even want to anymore. I hate that place."

"How come?"

"I tried getting in there once; the Judge didn't let me in," he said. "That's all it was, really."

"I'm sorry about that," Jeremiah muttered. "He didn't let me in either. He took one look at my Aura and told me I was too quiet for a place like this."

"He told me the same thing," Cody hissed. "He told me this was the place for the chitchat types; that was what he called them—the sort of people who always look like they're having a good time and always have something to talk about. I didn't think I'd get in, but you can't say I didn't try."

Silence fell over their table while Cody leered out the window once again, as Jeremiah had done moments before. His eyes burned with the same intensity while the rest of him looked stiff and dispassionate, the way Jeremiah figured he looked to everyone else these days. It was like looking into a mirror, and the resemblance only grew when he reached into his bag and pulled out his Aurascope.

They were both introverts, restrained and reclusive young men whose worlds didn't extend very far beyond their own inner worlds. They both fell on the side of suspicion, nervousness, and neuroticism, the sort of qualities that didn't seem desirable but cemented their bond even further. The only difference between them seemed to be the tone of the colors. Jeremiah's were near the middle of the spectrum while Cody's rested on the extreme ends of sharp reds and sharp blues, like most of the Auralites who lived in West Parliss.

"What does the Ranchester look for?" Jeremiah asked.

"Not this, I guess," Cody sneered, glaring down at the Aurascope as if he wanted to smash it with a hammer. "You've got to be red on the outer two rings; that's the most I've figured out. Having blue down there's a deal breaker."

Jeremiah almost fell back into the same angst-ridden state he'd been in earlier, but when he looked at Cody and saw the same cold visage, he stopped. It did neither of them any good to drown in their frustration. He'd known this before, but now he felt a sense of responsibility. If Cody was having a rough day, it was up to him to make it better.

"Maybe it's a good thing we didn't get into the Ranchester," Jeremiah said, trying to raise his voice to a more optimistic vibe. "I mean, think about it. Would you really want to be surrounded by people who are so different from you?"

"That's what the Judge told me," Cody replied, not looking any more pleased. "That's what all the Judges say when they turn you down. They pass it off as some kind of favor instead of a punishment, like they're doing you a service."

"Aren't they, in a way?" Jeremiah argued.

"If you want to look at it that way, then sure," Cody spat, "but I'd rather be disappointed by something I thought I would love than never have the chance in the first place. That's the problem with people like us: we don't get that many chances to prove them wrong. We have to work harder all the time, and they never notice it."

Cody finally took some time away from the window and glared down at the table, resting his eyes on his plate of macaroni while

225

Jeremiah sipped some more of his lemonade. He tried thinking of something else to say, something that might make Cody feel better, but nothing came to mind.

"Have you ever seen *Candlelight Palace*?" Cody asked.

"Yeah, I have," Jeremiah answered, confused by the abrupt change in subject matter, and stunned by how many times this play had been referenced during the last few weeks.

"There's a scene I always think about whenever I walk by one of those fancy clubs. I think about Edward Donnigan, him and all his brothers, that night they have that big party at their house. He's standing out letting guests in, and this one kid—I can't remember his name—the baker's helper."

"Andy," Jeremiah said. That was the character he'd played.

"Right, that's it. Anyway, the Donnigan brothers are all outside when he gets to the door. Edward steps out and says Andy can't come in because he doesn't know anybody here, and the only way into the house is to get invited by someone in the family. So, Andy looks at them and asks: 'Well how can I get an invitation from someone I have to meet at a party that I can't get into?' Then all the brothers look around and don't know what to say, so they just tell him to go away."

"Yeah, I know that line," Jeremiah muttered, remembering a few chuckles in the audience on the day of their first show.

"I always think about that scene when I walk by a Judge," Cody said. "I always wonder if maybe I'll learn once I'm inside—if something in me will snap once I start chatting with some of those people. For all I know, all those people behind those doors would love me if I could just get inside, but I can't. There's always a Donnigan brother in the way. If they don't like what they see, they'll let you rot on the street like a stray dog before they give you the key. Once they send out their invitations and come up with their rules, there's nothing else you can do.

"They never change their minds. Not ever."

— — — — —

226

Jeremiah could still hear Cody whispering in his ear when they left the diner and went their separate ways. Sometimes, he thought he could see Cody's face when he thought about Alicia, or when he walked past one of the clubs, or when he let his mind drift away to memories of high school. All of Cody's dissertations on the culture of exclusivity dug into him like nails embedded in his skull. A single word was all it took to drag his former classmates back into his new world, and a single memory of Ethan Kantzton was all it took to make him angry. Each time this happened, he took a moment to breathe and center himself, and then he kept walking. He still had work to do.

Jeremiah took out his map and made note of all the remaining clubs in West Parliss. He planned out his route and decided to visit each location, playing the odds a few Judges would let him in. With any luck, it wouldn't be long until he happened upon a club whose criteria fell in line with his Aura. Maybe he'd even find a place he loved as much as Alicia loved the Terrinson Club, and he could end his summer with proof there was a place for him after all.

He tried his best to stay optimistic as he approached the first of his seven stops. The Judge studied his Aura for about a minute before turning him away.

He could hear Cody whisper in his ear: "They don't want you."

He made his way to the second stop and asked the Judge if he could go inside. This time, the Judge only took ten seconds to inspect his colors before sending him away.

He could hear Cody whisper in his ear: "They don't want you."

The next stop was a half hour away, but Jeremiah trudged along anyway. He was nearly out of breath by the time he arrived, but once he did, the Judge looked at his Aura, then told him to leave.

He could hear Cody whisper in his ear: "They don't want you."

The sun was starting to set when he met the fourth Judge. This one took a full two minutes to study his colors, and just when Jeremiah found a spark of hope, he was asked to leave.

He could hear Cody whisper in his ear: "They don't want us."

The fifth Judge said no, and left Jeremiah walking away beneath the dim evening sky.

He could hear Cody whisper in his ear: "They don't want us."

The sixth Judge said no, and left Jeremiah walking away beneath a pitch-black sky.

He could hear Cody whisper in his ear: "They don't want us."

He could hear Ethan whisper in his ear: "We don't want you."

He could hear Alicia whisper in his ear: "They just want me."

If anyone had seen Jeremiah walk away from the sixth Judge, they might have said he looked like a man who'd lost his house and his job on the same day, a man so deprived of food and sleep that he could collapse at any moment. He walked so slowly and his face looked so weary. But as Jeremiah looked around, he realized no one was watching him. They were all too busy chatting with their friends and looking up to admire the stars in the sky, while Jeremiah passed them by like a ghost, holding no one's attention even for a moment. His skin and bones felt like ice. His skull and chest felt heavy. He nearly turned around to go back to the Broken Cottage, but he didn't. He kept on walking, and when he arrived at his last stop and found the seventh Judge, he promised himself this was the one. It had to be the one. This had to be the one.

Jeremiah approached the Judge and touched the Aurascope.

"Can I come in?" he asked.

The Judge looked at him. "No."

It was slow at first. Right as the word cut through his ears, he felt nothing. He was numb to this pain, like a boxer who'd taken so many hits during his life that a punch to the face meant nothing, but as he walked away, once he took his first few steps away from the door, he felt the fire rising. His blood burned like acid as those seven faces flashed before his eyes. His hands curled into fists when the doors opened behind him, letting the sounds of music and laughter flood the street and drown him in his stolen life.

He felt his mind drift as he wandered back to the Broken Cottage. The Donnigan Boys were walking toward him. They were on their way to the seventh club, knowing the Judge would welcome them, wearing their privilege like a badge of honor, taking their status for granted as they always did. Their voices grew louder as he kept walking, getting closer with every step, and when he was close enough he kicked Ethan Kantzton right in the gut. The blow was so hard that Ethan fell to the ground. The others stood by, too paralyzed by fear to fight back. He kicked him again, in his back, in his knee, in his arm, in his face, not letting up no matter how many times Ethan begged him to stop.

When the moment passed, when Ethan and his friends vanished into thin air, the anger went away. It was like driving a car and slamming the brakes right before he crashed into a wall. He felt nothing but shock and horror over what he'd witnessed—what he had done. The image was so clear and fresh in his head that he needed to look around and confirm that he was alone, which he was, or so he thought until he heard someone shouting. He was in pain. He needed help.

But this was not Ethan's voice.

He carefully followed the sound until he arrived at a nearby alley. He turned the corner and saw a tall, blonde young man, roughly his own age, lying down on the ground in agonizing pain, with blood dripping from the left side of his head. Another young man stood above him, with a blank, fear-stricken look across his face and a brick in his right hand, covered in blood.

"Cody? What are you doing?" Jeremiah shouted.

"It-It's not my fault," he stuttered, dropping the brick and staggering back in shock. "I didn't try to do this, I swear!"

"What did you do to him?" Jeremiah shouted. He crouched down and wrapped his sweatshirt around the wound to try to stop the bleeding. The guy was still breathing. His eyes were halfway shut. His nostrils flared as he gasped for air. Jeremiah didn't recognize him until he got a better look at his face, and suddenly remembered seeing him earlier today. He'd seen him through the window at the diner. This guy was a member of the Ranchester Club.

"It's not my fault; he deserved it. He had it coming!" Cody said, although the panic in his voice was proof he knew this wasn't true.

"We have to get help! Find someone!"

"I can't! I could go to jail for this!"

229

"This isn't about you, dammit! Hurry, we have to get him to a hospital!"

Cody ran away from the scene before Jeremiah had the chance to say anything else. Without Cody, he had no clue how to find a hospital, and if he left the alley to chase after him, the Ranchester guy would bleed to death. To make matters worse, his cell phone was out of power.

Jeremiah wrapped the guy's arm around his shoulder and helped him walk to the Broken Cottage, his free hand pressing firmly against the head wound. He screamed as loud as he could for help but the streets were as desolate as they'd been just a moment ago.

He looked up and saw a man smoking by the corner of the street, his entire body silhouetted by the lamppost against the night's darkness. Jeremiah called out for help but the man didn't come. He continued to stand still and release puffs of smoke into the cold air, not taking so much as a step. And once Jeremiah got a better look at his face, he understood why.

"I figured I would see you again, sometime sooner or later," Dr. Kennry said with a smug grin. "The world is not so convenient a place that those who disagree can live in peace away from each other. But we try our best here on this side, do we not?"

"Sir, please, he's hurt! He has to get to a hospital!"

"I'm not that kind of doctor. I'd be as much help as you are."

"Please! I think he's going to die! Just do it for him! Help me get him to a hospital!"

"He's not my problem," the man said. "I'm sure you'll manage just fine without me."

Dr. Kennry sauntered off down a nearby road with one final puff of smoke and not another word. Jeremiah stood fixed where he was in disbelief at how a man could be so cruel at a time like this. He might have screamed and cussed out the professor for a minute or two if someone weren't dying in his arms, so instead, he rallied himself again for his march to Mr. Zeeger's home, as the Ranchester boy continued to bleed and gasp for breath.

In a stroke of good luck, the only one he'd had all day, Alicia was sitting outside the Broken Cottage on the curb. She had never been back this early since her acceptance into the Terrinson Club, and had no reason to be sitting outside when she could be upstairs in her bedroom. Thankfully, tonight was an exception. At this one crucial moment, she was barely within earshot of Jeremiah as he called out one last time for help.

She quickly ran inside to call for an ambulance. When Jeremiah finally stumbled in through the doorway, she and Mr. Zeeger were ready with a packet of ice and some towels to stop the bleeding. Together, they laid him down on a nearby table while the rest of the customers looked around in horror. Mr. Zeeger did his best to calm them down as Alicia ran upstairs to fetch some more towels. Jeremiah stayed by the table, promising everything would be fine.

"Thank you," he said, shivering as if he'd just been pulled out of a frigid lake.

"You're going to be okay," Jeremiah promised. "What's your name?"

"Reese. It's Reese. What's yours?"

"You can call me Jer, okay? Short for Jeremiah. Can you hear me?"

"Yeah. Yeah, I hear you," he mumbled.

"Can you tell me what happened?" Jeremiah asked. "Do you know why that guy attacked you?"

"No," he said, after a long pause. "No, I don't know why he did it. But I guess he remembers something I don't."

Chapter Seventeen

The Birdhouse Garden

Mr. Zeeger went back to his drinking right as the ambulance drove away with Reese. Within minutes, the pub was filled with cheerful sounds of laughter like nothing had happened, as if the world had only stopped for Jeremiah but went on spinning for everyone else. He could never fall asleep tonight. His mind was too restless for his body to be still, and if he ever shut his eyes, the surrounding darkness would drag him back to the alley. He would be back to the desolate roads, back to the cries for help and the blood on the ground, and as soon as he fell asleep he'd wake up again.

"Alexandra used to get in fights often," Alicia said. She sat down next to Jeremiah on the edge of the sidewalk. "Charlotte told me that a few nights ago. One time, when she was in high school, she wrestled some guy to the ground because she thought he was cheating on her. Other times she would scream and say nasty things, but at some time or another, she would always run away. That's why Charlotte wanted her in the Terrinson Club so badly. She wanted to be the one to welcome her when no one else would, but nobody else wanted her."

Jeremiah could see Alexandra where he'd been moments ago, by herself on the dark, empty roads as lonely as she'd ever been, her face drenched in tears despite how much she would try to look strong and resilient. There was nothing he could have done to help her. Smarter, more patient people had already tried, and one by one they'd all failed.

"I should have listened to you," Jeremiah said.

"It's fine," Alicia said with a light smile. "You don't have to apologize."

"Yes, I do. I was the one who convinced Tom to invite you here. I asked him 'cause I wanted you and me to do something special—something just the two of us could share, and I got distracted again, like I always do. First it was the Donnigan Boys; now it's Alexandra. I always find ways to put you second, and I should know better by now. You're my best friend, Alicia. You're the best person I know, and it's about time I started acting like it."

Jeremiah wished he'd said this months ago, when they were still in school, when the Donnigan Boys would be out by their hill and the Donnigan Girls were off gossiping somewhere else, when he and Alicia could have been together. They would talk about the things that mattered, instead of his usual weather-watcher comments. He imagined them leaving school at the end of the day, riding off on their bikes to his favorite spot at Shangrin Lake, away from all the false expectations he'd wasted so much time trying to fit. He knew the truth now. There had never been any rules, nothing to stand in his way apart from the walls he'd built himself. He could have left their spot on the hill to sit with Alicia whenever he wanted, but he never did.

"We still have a week left before we go home," Jeremiah said. "Let's go—you and me—together. We can go back to Littelbine Park. I can teach you how to play Silent Captain—the East version, anyway. We can do anything you want. Just tell me what you want and I'll do it."

"Jer, I can't now. Charlotte needs me. It's more serious than you think. I can't leave her just yet."

"What if I came with you? If she could get the Judge to let me in, maybe I could help in some way."

"It's too late for that now," Alicia said. "It wouldn't be right if I brought someone else to talk with her. Would you want to be in a counseling session with Tom if he brought a complete stranger to come watch?"

The silence that followed was a better answer than anything he could put in words. He of all people should know to respect the privacy between a patient and a counselor, no matter how alone he would be because of it. There was nothing he dreaded more than loneliness. He couldn't survive another seven days and nights of wandering down these streets, letting everyone else go about their lives while he watched from the sidewalk. He needed Alicia, now more than ever, but Charlotte needed her more. He still had a life for himself in Pritchard Haven, a life with years ahead to mature and make the right choices, while people like Tom and Charlotte had already made mistakes they could never undo. He was too young to grieve so easily. They would spend the rest of their lives without the person they'd once loved more than they'd ever loved anyone, and nothing he'd endured or experienced could compare to that pain.

"You said a few weeks ago that we're Tom's second chance," Alicia said. "Well, now I'm hers, too. I didn't plan this, but that's what happened, and now I have to be responsible. You and I will have next summer when we're back from college. She only has seven days. Don't you think you could wait that long for her?"

Jeremiah looked across the Wide Road. A long, heavy sigh burst from his lungs as he sat in silence, asking himself if he had the strength to give up his last few days with Alicia so someone else could be happy. For a moment, he shut his eyes and covered his face with his hands, and when he had his answer, once he was ready, he turned back and looked at Alicia.

"Yeah. I can do that," he said at last. "I'll be all right. She needs you more than I do. Seven days to myself isn't as bad as ten whole years. I have to keep my problems in perspective. I get that."

Alicia reached across to hug Jeremiah around the shoulder with a single arm. She stood up from the sidewalk like she was about to leave, but stopped before she took even one step toward the pub.

"I just remembered something I wanted to give you," Alicia said, as she reached into her pocket and withdrew a tattered sheet of paper with a house address scribbled in red ink. "Charlotte gave me this. She told me it was for a place the Auralites call the Birdhouse Garden. I don't know much about it. I just know it's where Alexandra lived when she first ran away to West Parliss, and it's where she ran away to after her fight with Charlotte."

"I don't care about Alexandra anymore," Jeremiah said. "I've given up on that."

"I know you have, but that's not the reason I'm telling you. There's a woman who lives in that house. I can't quite remember her name, but Charlotte told me she's the oldest person in Parliss County. She's a therapist. Some people here even say she's one of the best in the world. She's the last person Alexandra spoke to before she left Parliss for good. I figured, with Tom gone, she might be a good person to talk to. At least consider it."

The scrap of paper hung from Alicia's hand for a moment before Jeremiah finally took it. He tucked it into his pocket right as Alicia said goodbye, wished him luck, then went back inside. He was alone, just as he'd been for so many days and would be for another seven. There was nothing left to do with the time he had but wait. He sat with his body hunched over his legs, but then shot to an upright position when he noticed his shoulder bag was missing.

He looked around until he remembered dropping it on the ground when he ran to help Reese in the alley. He considered whether it was worth the trip back to get it. In his mind, the summer with the Auralites was over, and the Aurascope and everything he'd written in his journal had lost any value. He decided to stay put at first, but he changed his mind when he realized the cops would most likely arrive at that alley soon, and after hearing the rumors of a young white man fleeing the scene, finding his bag alongside a blood-stained brick might cause a lot of problems.

The longer he waited, the more he was at risk. He had already given up any hope of going to sleep, and soon enough he'd be bored of sitting and go on a walk to clear his head anyway. He figured at least the missing bag gave him a purpose aside from his usual wandering, and now that Mr. Zeeger was nice and drunk, he had a perfect chance to leave without anyone noticing.

He found his shoulder bag resting on the sidewalk. He grabbed it by the strap then quickly ran off to another road before anyone could see him. He sat down at a bench between two lampposts. He reached inside the bag and found his journal. He opened it up and flipped through the pages until he saw all his drawings and his notes about Alexandra. He reached inside for the Aurascope, checking one more time to see if his colors had changed, if any magentas, cyans, or yellows had been replaced with greens, or if he'd somehow become more social and less tense in the last few days, but everything looked the same.

He wanted to break it. He wanted to throw it on the ground, watch it shatter right by his feet and kick the shards across the road until every last piece of it was gone. He wanted to tear out every page in his journal and flush them down the nearest storm drain. He shut his eyes and imagined taking everything in his bag and setting it on fire, holding his breath and closing his hands into fists as he watched the fire rise, leaving nothing but dust and ash in its fury.

And then he felt the tears around his eyes. The fire went away, and he started to fall. He saw nothing but darkness. He felt nothing but the icy touch of cold water around his skin as he sunk deeper and deeper. He didn't mind drowning. He didn't mind the silence. He welcomed the escape, the peace that came with knowing he would never wake up and face this again. He let himself fall, and then he opened his eyes. He was back in the real world, and he couldn't leave.

"What if it's always like this?" Jeremiah whispered to himself, the way he did when no one was around to hear him.

He almost closed his eyes a second time, but he opened them as soon as he felt his skin turn cold again. He wouldn't welcome any more thoughts of death. He couldn't. He had to stay, and he had to keep going. But he couldn't do it alone.

He looked at the address on Alicia's scrap of paper. He checked the map to see if he could find the house, and he realized it wasn't so far away from where he was now. He put everything back in his bag and made his way toward the Birdhouse Garden.

He walked to a part of West Parliss he'd never been to before, away from all the clubs and diners and all the other downtown hotspots. He followed the map until he saw a sign for Weatherfield Lane, and he kept on walking until he got all the way to the end of the street. He looked up at a small white house. As he might have expected, the place was surrounded by many colorful birdhouses, each one bolted to either the house itself or to one of the many nearby trees. He was surprised to see the lights in the house were still on, proving the old woman was still awake.

He held his hand in the air for a second before he finally knocked on the door, and he immediately heard the sound of footsteps trotting down the stairwell at a pace he considered strangely fast for such an old woman. He staggered back as the door swung open, expecting to be scolded for coming to her house at such an inconvenient time, but all the tension passed away when he saw the old woman's face. She had long, white hair that glistened with a faint trace of auburn. Her face was pale but smooth, and there was a youth in her eyes Jeremiah hadn't seen in people even a quarter her age.

"Hello. How may I help you?" the old woman asked.

"Um, hi, my name's Jeremiah. Sorry to bother you so late. I was wondering if I could set up some sort of appointment with you, so I could talk to you later?"

"Would you like to talk now?"

Jeremiah never would have expected this kind of response. Even Tom would have asked that he save this for a more appropriate time, and he would have been perfectly in the right to usher him off the doorstep without a shred of guilt. Instead, he followed the old woman into a small room next to the kitchen, a private room with a single door and two chairs, but no windows. Behind the old woman's chair, he saw a cabinet filled with books and old jazz albums, and as he sat down in the smaller chair, he noticed a stack of private journals resting on a mantle, with old ticket stubs stuck between the pages as bookmarks.

"It's not so often I have visitors so late in the night," the old woman said, reaching into a drawer and taking out a bottle of pills. "I suppose it's a thing with teenage boys. You seem a little cold. Do you want one of these?"

"No thanks," he responded.

"Are you sure?" the old woman asked, taking one for herself with a swig of water. "They're not prescription. You can buy them at any store without a doctor's note."

"Thank you, but I'm sure I'm fine," he repeated.

"If you say so," the old woman said, setting the bottle back into the drawer. "They'll be here if you change your mind. Don't be shy to ask. There are people here who claim I'm the best therapist in Parliss County but none of us can read minds, now can we? I can only know as much about you as you are willing to tell me."

The old woman pulled her hand away from the drawer, this time with an Aurascope tight in her grasp. He could see the old woman's confidence, her trusting nature, and her relaxed, stable disposition, each marked by crisp blue light. In the red rings, he could see her bold imagination and abstract ways of thinking. Not a single trace of magenta could be found. Instead, the vast majority of her rings were made from the green light of Personal Balance, a color Jeremiah had yet to see from someone who lived in West Parliss. She was as much of an introvert as she was an extrovert, a woman who understood the value of rules but knew when to break them, who lived a quiet life in a house cut off from most of the county but had a skill for talking with people and a passion for adventure. The youth Jeremiah saw in her eyes made more sense now that he could truly see her as she was: an old woman with the soul of a girl, and perhaps the smartest girl he had yet to meet.

"They call me Madame Josephine around here."

"That's a pretty name."

"Thank you. It's rather funny. I didn't like it at all when I was younger, but I suppose age has a way of changing these sorts of things. Surely you're much different now than when you were a child."

"Yeah, I am," Jeremiah said, despite how much he'd felt like his younger self during the last several days. He thought of reaching into his bag for his own Aurascope, but he shut this idea from his mind the moment it crept up. He knew better than to rely on the Aurascope now that he could only use it for another week. He had to learn to use his words to explain his problems, and there was no better place or time to practice than here and now.

He stammered a few times in his attempts to explain what was troubling him before he began his story right when it had truly started. He took Madame Josephine through the last four years in as short a time as he could. He told her everything she needed to know about Alicia, the Donnigan Boys, his obsession with Alexandra Cardor, and his history with Tom Berrinser.

"Tom came to my hometown after he left the county. He told me it was a place people came for change, that I could meet people who were like me, and I could learn more about them while I looked at new parts of myself I never knew existed—that type of thing."

"That was a very kind and bold thing for him to do," Madame Josephine said. "Not many people go so far out of their own way to do what's best for someone else, especially if it means coming back to a place with so many bad memories."

"I know," Jeremiah replied, nodding in recognition of the counselor's good nature. "He's the best man I know, and he always will be. But there's something that's been troubling me ever since he invited me to come here, and I can't stop thinking about it."

"And what's that?"

"Tom's been a counselor at Laronna for ten years," Jeremiah began. "Before my class, before the Donnigan Boys came along, all of the other students were like me in some way. Some were shy and liked to be by themselves, some would talk too much and annoy the other kids, and some would always screw around in class and not listen to the teachers. They all had something they needed to work on, just like me, but somehow, out of all those kids, Alicia and I were the only ones Tom thought needed to come here. Now, Alicia's found her place at the Terrinson Club and she's happy. I'm the only one of the whole bunch who couldn't do it."

"Alexandra said the same thing to me," Madame Josephine said. "She felt like a failure, not just to herself, but to everyone else who knew her. Is that how you feel?"

Jeremiah nodded. "I've spent a lot of my time here learning about Alexandra, and the more I do, the more I start to see myself in her, and that really scares me. It's stuff like this that gets me wondering if it's always going to be like this for me. No matter where I go or what I do, something doesn't seem to go my way, and I've run out of ideas about what I can do."

"Then you came to the right place," Madame Josephine said. "I've lived here longer than anyone else. I've spent a lifetime standing with people like Alexandra when no one else would, from strangers I've met only once to people in my own family. Are you sure you don't want any medicine? You look like you're catching a cold."

"I'm fine, I promise," Jeremiah said. He wasn't sure what was so off about his posture that he'd been asked this question a second time. The room was already heated above a normal temperature, and the summer air was hardly cold enough to warrant any fear of sickness.

"I need your help," he said. "Please. Just tell me anything."

"I do have something to say that I believe will help," Madame Josephine said, after a short pause. "But I must warn you, it will either be just what you want to hear, or it will make you feel as if you've wasted your time with me. But it is the truth. Before I say what this is, there is a question you need to answer. Tell me, why did you come to Parliss County?"

This was a question Jeremiah expected to be easy, and yet he had no idea what to say as soon as he opened his mouth. Each response that came to mind felt more important than the last, and by the end he decided he couldn't pick just one.

"I wanted something to be different," he answered. "I wanted to stop being so quiet. I wanted to stop being so anxious. I wanted to learn how to say all the right things and learn how to get people to like me. I wanted to meet people who dealt with all this kind of stuff when they were younger and learned how to change for the better. And I wanted to be with people who liked me as I was, so I didn't have to lie or act differently just to be a part of their group. I just wanted something different, and I thought Parliss County was a good place to start."

"So, you came here to meet people who would welcome you as you were, but you also came because you wanted to be different?" Madame Josephine asked, raising her eyebrows.

"I know. It doesn't make a lot of sense," Jeremiah confessed, looking down at the carpet beneath his feet.

"Actually, it makes all the sense in the world to me," the old woman said. "Those are the same reasons we all come here. That's why Parliss County was built."

Jeremiah looked up. "What do you mean?"

"The Auralites are a lot of things," Madame Josephine said. "But more than anything, they are seekers of change. The only difference is where they want it. People come here to the West side when they feel the rest of the world doesn't want them. They come here to look for a second home, with people who are like them, and will welcome them as they are without any change to themselves.

"And there are people who go across to the East side, the place we go if we want to be better people. It's where people go when they blame themselves for their failures, when they berate themselves for being too quiet, too loud, too much this, too much that, and try to find some kind of balance that lets them rejoin the world once they're done."

"It's all about blame," Jeremiah said. "One side is where you go when you blame yourself; the other side is when you're mad at the world and want to blame someone else. You can pick a side, but you can't pick both."

The old woman nodded. "People come here to look for the change they want, a way to make things perfect, but they don't always find it. That's the great lie of Parliss County. It wears the mask of some great answer, but one way or another, it always finds a way to fail, and the rest of us pay the price. Some stay for weeks. Some stay for months. Others stay for years. And when they fail, they always put the blame on themselves for not finding what was never there the whole time. Only the people who live here know the full truth, that whatever side we pick, we will lose something we may find on the other. Some days it will all feel like an act, some lie we tell ourselves about how who we are today is the best version of ourselves there is, but our minds never stop asking what might happen if one ring was a different color. Doubt always finds its way back to us, even if we were at our happiest just the day before. All we can do is learn to handle these days when they come and look for a better tomorrow."

Jeremiah felt as if he'd heard this sort of lesson before, either from Tom, his mother, or his father, but it wasn't until now that he believed he finally understood what it meant. He saw it as he looked back on all his four years of high school. The blame never stayed in one place. Day by day, he'd go from pointing the finger at his wretched classmates to himself, hating them for locking him out of their club before he punished himself for not being good enough to earn their respect in the first place. Some days he wanted to be better, and some days he wanted his classmates to pick up the slack instead.

He wondered if the Auralites were the same way. He wondered if Howard Granzill ever wished he could lament his failed wedding in front of the crowd instead of hide the pain with jokes, or if the Jennabelle Kids ever wished they could abandon their group when memories of their past betrayals popped into their heads like a bad dream. He wondered if Gretchen ever took a break from missing her family and allowed herself to enjoy her lonely life in her small house with the rocking chair. He looked back on his summer and wondered if any of his teachers had truly reached the end of their journey, if Parliss County had wiped away their scars forever, or if it had only kept them hidden.

"The Auralites can't fix people," Jeremiah said. "That's what you told Alexandra. You were the one who told her to leave."

The old woman nodded. "There was no place for her here, and she thought that was her fault. She believed she was a failure, when really, it's just a natural truth about Parliss County. It can't fix your troubles, but it will make you think it can. This disappointment has led so many people right to this house, and I give them all the same lesson I'm giving you. You can stay in Parliss or you can leave Parliss, but there will always be days you feel weak and there will always be days you think the world has failed you, but there will also be days you love yourself and feel welcome where you are. You just have to find those days however you can."

Jeremiah unleashed a deep sigh as the stress in his body passed away. He didn't exactly feel happy, but he could feel his chest swell with a tender feeling of hope, the sort of feeling he would expect to have if a family member died a few months ago and he was just now starting to feel a glimmer of joy again. He was stuck somewhere between doubt and confidence, and he was okay with that.

"Does it ever get easier?"

"Not always," Madame Josephine said, "but that doesn't have to be a bad thing. It's the days that feel the worst that make you better tomorrow. If you trip walking down the stairs, you learn to step higher. If you lose a race, run faster in the next one. And if you aren't happy where you are then find a place out there that's better. Always keep trying. Always keep looking. That's about the most any of us can do, but usually, that's all we really need."

There was nothing else Jeremiah had to say other than what could be told by the nodding of his head, a sign he'd listened to each and every word and would keep the old woman's advice with him through his final days in Parliss County, and many more after. He thanked Madame Josephine for her time, and finally agreed to take one of her pills before he left, thinking it was the least he could do to show his gratitude.

He stood out on the road to take one last look at the Birdhouse Garden, and he began walking back to the Broken Cottage when he saw the lights turn off.

Chapter Eighteen

The Last Session

Reese was alive and on the mend. That was all Mr. Zeeger said when they sat down for breakfast the next morning. No one knew where Cody was, but more than likely, he'd run away from Parliss County and would never come back. Jeremiah hoped this was the case. He could still hear the whispers when he let his mind drift, like a ghost standing behind in his shadow, dragging him back to the alley, the screams, the blood, the anger, and Jeremiah had to ignore all of it. He couldn't let hate into his heart, even on his worst days. He'd fallen into that trap once. He would not let it happen again.

He did his best to find joy in the little things: eating breakfast with Alicia for the first time since their fight on the curb, walking alongside her on their way to the Terrinson Club, and seeing her again in the evening when she returned for dinner. In the afternoon when he was alone, he kept himself busy by reading some of the books in Gerald's collection or by wandering around West Parliss some more, taking in all the sights while he still had time. His days with the Auralites were running out, and he had to make the most of them.

The thought of going back to Pritchard Haven never crossed his mind until he watched the sun go down on Saturday. Tomorrow was his last full day in this strange place, and then he'd be on his way home the next morning. He decided to visit the Birdhouse Garden one more time to say goodbye to Madame Josephine before he left.

He knocked on the door and thought he heard a second voice from inside, which meant she was probably busy with another visitor. The old woman welcomed him inside with a cheery smile, and she asked once again if he was feeling cold and would like some medicine.

"No thanks. I'm fine," Jeremiah promised. "I just wanted to say goodbye since I'm leaving in a few days. Is this a bad time? I thought I heard someone else inside."

"Thank you very much," Madame Josephine said. "Actually, you couldn't have picked a better time. Would you wait here for a moment while I check on something?"

The old woman came back after a brief talk with her anonymous visitor. He followed Madame Josephine into the windowless room he'd visited just a few days earlier. He stepped in through the doorway and nearly staggered back in utter shock at the sight of Tom sitting in the patient's chair.

Seeing him now after all this time left Jeremiah standing with his eyes and mouth wide open, like someone had slapped him on the back and knocked the breath out of his lungs. He took a few steps to get a better look. He saw Tom hunched over in his seat, hanging his head above his lap while resting his clasped hands on his knees. His hair was so unkempt and messy that Jeremiah wondered if Tom had spent the last hour tugging at it, or at the very least, hadn't bothered to brush it in a long time. He had never seen Tom like this, bending over in his chair, numb and cold as if he were a statue.

Jeremiah flinched when Madame Josephine shut the door, sealing him in this room with the counselor. The two of them were alone, and somehow, without any directions, he knew just what to do. He sat down in the old woman's chair, the one by the cabinet with all the books, jazz albums, and medicine jars. He asked Tom what was wrong. He could tell this question would be met with a much longer response, and he was willing to sit as long as he needed to hear it. He'd waited nearly six weeks to learn where Tom had been. Now was the time for his answer.

Jeremiah listened as Tom took him back nine years ago, when he found a mysterious letter in his mailbox from a man named Simon

Falzoga, who had since adopted the name of Mothcatcher. He told the full story until they were caught up to the present, sitting right where they were in the Birdhouse Garden, with one day left before they returned home. The counselor sunk back into his chair as Jeremiah took the time to process what he'd heard, leaving the room completely quiet for a long stretch of time until either of them bothered to speak.

"Madame Josephine is the last person who saw Alexandra before she left," Tom said. "She's the one person who might know something neither of us did. That's why this is the one place I've been allowed to visit since the night I left you, and honestly, I'm scared of going back. It's taken me almost six weeks to see it, but I'm starting to wonder if this has been worth it."

"Is there another way you could open the box?" Jeremiah asked. "Break it open, or something?"

"I'm sure I could if I tried," Tom muttered, "and if I were dealing with anyone else but her, I would have done it by now. But it's not just about what's inside that matters to me. It's about proving I can open it. I suppose Simon feels the same way; he wouldn't have waited for so long if he didn't. It's all a test to see if I ever knew her at all or if I was always as blind as I feel now."

A heavy sigh unleashed from Tom's throat as he looked down at his feet.

"I know it might not make sense," he confessed. "I know I can't expect you to understand. I know you're doing your best to see this my way, but it's not something you can feel until you're older, when you're a father or have someone you feel the need to care for. I'm just asking you to accept that I need to do this."

Jeremiah sat while nodding his head, his eyes turned away to the side so he could avoid the unpleasant sight of Tom's sullen eyes until he was ready to speak again.

"She's like a daughter to you."

Tom nodded. "And it's been eleven years since the last time I was with her. That journal is all I have left of her. It's my only chance of finding out where she went, where she might be now, or whatever it was I did wrong. It could be the key to every question I've spent a decade trying to answer. Or it might not be. I might not be able to open the damn box at all, and this would have all been a waste of my time. Frankly, I'm not even sure which would be worse. I'm scared of them all. I really am."

Tom sat with his head turned away, with his eyes on the brink of tears while Jeremiah struggled to find anything to say. He felt helpless, like it was his responsibility to comfort his old counselor, but he didn't have the skill or the wisdom he needed. Tom was right. He had no way of knowing the full reach of this misery, for the simple reason he was only eighteen years old and had yet to experience a loss this severe. For all his complaints about the Donnigan Boys and his lonely life, he was still better off than plenty of other people he'd met this summer, and now it was his responsibility to be strong for someone who needed his help.

"I've learned a lot about her these last few weeks," Jeremiah said in a hushed voice. "Your friends told me what they knew, or, at least, the stuff they didn't mind sharing. I learned about her family, how she was as a teenager, how she met you, the things she did at the theater and why she left, but it still wasn't enough for me. So, when I came to West Parliss, I tried looking for people who knew where she was or where I could find her, and it's taken me until now to see what a mistake that was."

"What do you mean?" Tom asked.

"I shouldn't have been doing this," Jeremiah replied. "The whole reason I asked you to invite Alicia was because I wanted another chance to be a good friend to her, and I got distracted, just like I always do. She's the most important person in my life and I never act like it, and I think that's what's happening with you. We spend so much time thinking about the things we did wrong in the past that we don't focus on what we're doing wrong now."

Tom sat up in his seat, as if he were impressed by this observation. "You think so?"

Jeremiah nodded. "You've been at Laronna for ten years now. You've watched hundreds of kids leave the school after you've spent so much time with them. You don't miss them this much, do you?"

"It's not the same. She was like family to me."

"Was I?"

The silence that followed this simple question cut the deepest of all the others that came before, and the tension only grew the longer Jeremiah waited stiff in his chair for the counselor's answer. He often forgot that he was not the only one at Laronna who came to Tom for advice. He had always believed he and Tom shared a special bond that transcended that of a counselor and a patient, but he might have been wrong all this time, and Alexandra was at the top of a pedestal he could never reach.

"Am I like family to you?" Jeremiah asked again.

"Yes, you are," Tom said, speaking with a sincere look in his eyes that made up for all the silence. "You're more of my family than anyone else I know today. You've been very important to me these last few years, and I'm sorry it's taken me this long to tell you. I'm not as good of a talker as most people think I am. I'm not good at saying goodbye; I never have been. I talk a lot about how my time as your counselor has to end one day, but I think I say it more for my sake than yours. That school is all I have left, and it's going to feel very empty next year without you."

"It doesn't have to be that way," Jeremiah said. "I'm not the only kid at that school who needed your help. Maybe they won't be just like me. They might not have all the same problems, but one way or another, they'll all need someone like you to pick them up on a bad day and help them get where they want to go. They'll need you, and as soon as they leave that office for the first time, they're going to love you.

"Doesn't that sound like something you should focus on more than her?"

After four long years of speaking with Tom in the counseling room, all this time observing his strength and confidence, Jeremiah finally saw his old counselor cry. He bent down in his seat, his hands covering his face while tears streaked across his skin and fell into his lap, his hair in more of a tousled mess than it had been just minutes before. Jeremiah almost reached across to pat him on the shoulder, but he stopped himself. He needed to keep this moment as private for Tom as possible, give him as much time to cry on his own until the tears ran out, because when he eventually picked himself up, he would feel much better.

Jeremiah waited patiently in his seat, promising he would wait all night long if he had to, but he only needed to wait a minute before Tom looked up. There was a hint of acceptance in his eyes, so subtle it would've been invisible to anyone who wasn't used to his expressions and mannerisms. The misery was there, but the sense of hope was rising, growing stronger as Tom looked ahead to next September and saw the life he had waiting for him back home. Second by second, Jeremiah watched him regain his strength, and then he moved in for the final blow.

"There's a lot of good in your life right now," Jeremiah said. "And there's even more waiting for you next year, and every year after that. What happened in the past doesn't have to matter all that much."

"So then, what should I do tonight?" Tom asked, nodding his head and wiping away the last of his tears.

"You should go," Jeremiah said. "Try to open it. Try once, or twice—maybe three times if you want a good number, but stop after that. I know there's a lot you want to know about her, but if there's anything I've learned this summer, it's that there are just some things you can't learn. You can spend years with someone, think you have what it takes to pick them apart and put them back together, and they can still find ways to surprise you. Even if you open it, you still might not get all the answers you wanted, but that's okay. Try your best, do what you can, and just have faith that wherever she is, she's happy.

"That's all you can really do, but it's all you really need."

Jeremiah watched as Tom unbent his posture to an upright position, his head nodding as the red in his face faded away, and as the sides of his mouth rose to form a delicate smile. The counselor would have looked happy if his eyes weren't so sullen, staring off to one side of the room as if a sad memory was still in his mind somewhere. He looked to be in peace and in misery all at the same time, the expression of a man at the edge of making a right but difficult choice and trusting it would be best for him in the end.

"Have you ever thought about being a counselor one day?" Tom asked.

The sudden change of topic took Jeremiah by surprise. A quick gap of silence filled the room as he adjusted, and then he gave his answer.

"Not really. I haven't thought that far ahead yet."

"Think about it. I have a feeling it might be a good job for you."

Chapter Nineteen

The Wings of Solace

Tom stood by the kitchen table as he watched Jeremiah leave the house through the front door. Once they said goodbye, he sat down and stared out the nearest window as Madame Josephine poured them each a glass of milk. The old woman took a seat, and together they drank in almost perfect silence, all alone with nothing but the birds outside to keep them company.

"You were the last person she came to before she left," Tom said, ending the silence after his fourth sip. "Do you know why?"

"Why she left, or why she came to me?"

"Both, I suppose. I have a feeling they might have the same answer."

There was a pause as the old woman considered this response. She took another sip of her drink, and then she set her glass down and spoke.

"My time in Parliss County has taught me that we all have two identities: who we are, and who we want to be. Sometimes these two identities are the same, but sometimes the two don't match. That's what leads to insecurity. That's why quiet people wish they could be more social, why sensitive people wish they could be tougher, why anxious people wish they could be more confident—the list goes on. Those are the ones who come to Parliss County in the first place. That's the sort of person she was. I think she knew a lot of people who understood who she was but didn't see what she wanted, and I think she believed I was someone who knew what she wanted."

"And that's why she came here?"

The old woman smiled. "A home for the homeless. That's why it's called the Birdhouse Garden. People come here when there's nowhere else, and I take care of them as best as I can until they're ready to go. That's the only reason people come here. I imagine it was the same for her."

Her guess was as good as any Tom could have made by himself, and while he made his way down Weatherfield Lane, the old woman's words echoed on in his mind. A strange feeling overtook him as he turned around for one last look at the Birdhouse Garden, thinking back on how respected he was at Laronna for his work as a counselor, when compared to this old woman, he had the insight of a newborn child. He didn't know why, but it felt strangely nice to know there would always be someone better at his craft than he was. A higher standard had been laid out for him, and he had several more years left in his life to achieve it.

The sky was dark. He was less than an hour away from the moment he'd spent more than a month preparing for. A gust of wind shook the nearby trees and spun the weathervanes on the nearby houses. He felt Alexandra holding his shivering hand, her warm, smooth skin against the tips of his fingers. They were about the same height, so when the wind blew, her long, tangled brown hair would brush against his face, and when a strand of hair landed in his mouth, she would laugh as he spit it out. He could hear her footsteps marching in tempo with the music they heard from the nearby clubs, almost as if she were dancing.

When they reached the end of West Parliss, they stepped off the sidewalk and strolled down the middle of the Wide Road. He could see the sign for the Broken Cottage off in the distance, dangling in the wind as he and Alexandra made their way north, hand in hand until he looked off to the side and saw the entrance to the Canmark Theater. And then they stopped. He looked down the dark pathway, and then he felt Alexandra let go of his hand.

"Don't worry about me," she said.

She turned around and walked back the way they came, heading south down the middle of the Wide Road until she vanished.

Tom felt his heart beat faster as he began his walk to the Canmark Theater. His thoughts switched back and forth with each step. In one breath he would inspire himself with words of encouragement and in the next he would feel hopeless, in full remembrance of all his past failures. He nearly turned back twice but managed to continue his march down the promenade, through the entrance, and across the stage, until he arrived at the door behind the curtain. He wrapped his hand firmly around the handle, and with a deep, cleansing breath, he pulled the door open and began his walk down the eerie steps with a sputtering confidence but a righteous ambition.

He entered the room under the stage. Mothcatcher stood by the side of the painting. The Cardorians sat along the table, once again with their faces shrouded in darkness, away from the glow of the candlelight. A quick glance at an empty chair led him to believe one of them was missing, but this became of little importance when he looked to the end of the room and remembered what he had to do.

Every eye in the room set itself on him as he made his way to the other end of the table, his head hanging low to avoid the unpleasant sight of all these people waiting to see if their faith in him was misplaced or not. He stood by as Mothcatcher grabbed the edge of the painting and pulled it toward him like he was opening a door. It was as beautiful as it had been the first night, and Tom felt a sudden need to study it again before he started. It was a picture of a young girl in a green dress, lying down on her knees on a field of lush grass, reaching out with both hands to release a purple sparrow into the sky. The girl's face showed no emotion, making it hard to see whether setting the poor creature free made her sad, happy, or something in the middle. He looked to the bottom right-hand corner, and he read the title of the painting: *The Wings of Solace.*

Mothcatcher set Alexandra's box on the table. Then he tore the list of questions out from the backside of the frame and gave it to Tom. He offered Tom his seat at the end of the table to do his work but the counselor said no, promising he'd be more focused if he stood. He studied each question, looked up for a quick glance at the young ones in the room, then turned back to the painting one last time.

"I do have one question before I start," Tom said, looking to Simon.

"And what might that be?"

"You've had this box for over ten years. How many times have you tried to open it?"

"More than I can remember."

"And what makes you think I could do in one night what you couldn't in almost a decade?"

"You are a very astute man, Mr. Berrinser," Simon answered. "I thought perhaps you might see something I didn't."

Tom hoped that would be the case. He placed one hand on the box, and with the other, he grabbed the parchment and read the first question:

What happened at Tyler's party?

Even after all these years—fourteen, to be exact—Tom could still remember the day Alexandra recounted this story. All the little details returned in a flash, dragging him out of the room and dropping him next to Alexandra, where he listened to this story a second time.

"We started dating about two months earlier," she'd said, sitting with her head down and mumbling as she spoke, which was rather normal of her. "When I heard there was a party going on at his place, I wondered why he didn't tell me about it. I figured he just forgot, so I decided to go anyway. I found Tyler standing outside, and I knew he wasn't happy to see me. It was like shining a flashlight in his eyes. He was scared, and I knew he didn't want me to take another step forward, but that didn't stop me.

"Anyway, I tried to act nice at first, just to give him the benefit of the doubt. I tried to walk inside but he kept blocking the door. He tried to keep me outside by asking me about work, or school, or anything he could think of. I knew he was hiding something. It was so obvious. I just didn't know what it was."

At this point in the story, Tom had asked what she believed Tyler was hiding, and then fell silent to let her speak.

"I thought maybe he was cheating on me with some other girl who was at the party and didn't want us to talk. I also thought maybe he was trying to hit on some other girl and didn't want me to ruin his chances. All my ideas were basically just about him and other girls, which I know is kind of petty of me, but that's just where my mind went.

"Anyway, when I looked past his shoulder, I saw some of Tyler's friends looking at me and laughing. It was one of those oh-my-gosh-guys-this-is-about-to-be-super-embarrassing kind of reactions—it's hard to put it in words. I knew they were getting ready to watch me get humiliated, and I just snapped. I turned around and slapped Tyler across the cheek. It was so loud that everyone around us stopped what they were doing to look. I started yanking his hair, and then I wrapped my arm around his neck and wrestled him to the ground. I didn't stop until some of the other kids pried me away. They pulled Tyler inside and told me to go away before they called the cops."

Tom remembered he'd almost made a joke about the unforeseen consequences of calling the cops to a house filled with high schoolers drinking alcohol, but he chose to stay quiet. Humor wasn't appropriate at the time. Instead, he'd promised Alexandra he wouldn't judge her for her actions, and then asked how she could have handled the situation in a nonviolent way.

"I wish I just talked to him longer," she'd said. "I always assume the worst in people, especially with guys. I could've asked him why he didn't invite me, and if it really was because he was cheating, I could've just called him out in front of everyone and had the last laugh. Then I could've left the party with a few good curse words just for good measure, if I really felt like I had to lash out at him. That would've been better. I really wish I'd done that instead."

This imaginary story of Alexandra backing down from a fight, unmasking Tyler's lies in front of their classmates, and walking away with a few good parting shots, was choice number three on her list of answers. The incident as it had actually happened, in which she slapped Tyler across the face and wrestled him to the ground, was choice number eight. This was undoubtedly the answer Simon had chosen in all his attempts to open the box, but as Tom knew, Simon had failed every time.

Tom set the first dial to three instead of eight. He turned around in time to catch a glimpse of Simon's skepticism as he looked down at the box. He seemed unsure about this choice but stayed quiet, which was not a common thing to see, but Tom welcomed it all the same.

The counselor was alone in the room, alone in the sense that he did not see anything else but himself and the box, and a world of false memories of a life Alexandra wished she had lived. He closed his eyes and took himself back to the stories she'd told him, what had happened and what she might have done differently with the wisdom she had from being a few years older. Instead of an actress, she would be a children's author. She never lost her virginity at fifteen, and instead decided to wait until she was older. She never tried to run away from her new house at the age of twelve, and instead learned to trust her new guardians to take good care of her. She had always been a reasonable girl, coping with her struggles through patience and meditation instead of getting angry when something didn't go her way. She had never been so quick to end any of her old friendships after a rough moment, and instead was willing to compromise and admit her mistakes as her friends had done for her. Second by second, minute by minute, a new layer of her new life pealed its way through Tom's mind until he turned his attention to the eighth and final question.

"Who is the person I needed the most?" Tom said. Every person in the room shifted their attention toward Tom in slight surprise, since this was the first anybody had spoken in a long time. Each option was a name written next to a number. Alexandra's mother, Emma, was listed next to zero. Her aunt and uncle were listed as numbers one and two. Three was Howard Granzill. Four was Madame Josephine. Five was Charlotte Cawn, a name Tom didn't recognize, but he assumed it belonged to a woman she'd met in West Parliss. Number six was Simon Falzoga, with Mothcatcher written in parentheses. Seven was Gretchen Salcott, eight was Bianca Bellanessa, and nine was Tom Berrinser.

There was nothing Tom wanted more than to roll the last dial to nine, pull the lever, and watch the box open. Any other number in this last slot would disappoint him even if it were the right one. He could see Simon wanted the same for himself, peering from behind his shoulder and staring intently at the number six, and the counselor felt an uneasy stir in his body as he wondered if this wretched man would beat him.

Tom set his hand on the last dial and began turning it to nine. He reminded himself of all the good he'd done for her, the help he'd offered and advice he'd given, and as he felt the carvings of the number nine against his fingers, he believed with the utmost certainty that of all the names on the list, he was the one who had changed her life the most, and he was too stubborn to believe anyone else could take his spot.

He took his hand off the dial and thought he heard a snapping sound from the box, like a hatch had come undone. His heart pounded as Simon peered anxiously from behind, and the young Cardorians stood up from their seats to watch as Tom clenched the lever and pulled.

The box did not open.

The Cardorians sat back in their seats, disappointment in their eyes while Simon sighed in relief. Tom had never felt so angry and so miserable as he did now. He clenched his fists and pressed them down against the table while a tear trickled down his face. He wanted to scream. He wanted to throw the box against the wall, and he may have done exactly that if it weren't for the sound of Jeremiah whispering in his ear, telling him to stay calm.

Simon reached out to turn the last dial to six, but Tom pushed his hand out of the way like he was swatting at a fly. He was not changing the number on the last dial. He'd suffered too much to believe another person could fill his old slot. He stubbornly examined the other seven questions, trying to find one he might have gotten wrong his first time.

He took a second look at question six, which asked what Alexandra believed was the most important value for a person to have. This was perhaps the simplest of all the other questions. Each answer was only a single word, while most of the others described events that had taken place during her childhood and adolescence. The dial was set to the number eight, for loyalty. He chose this because of a conversation that had taken place during Alexandra's third week in East Parliss. He'd taken her to dinner at the Parryrose Club, and a woman named Sofia Agniss had asked them what it was they valued most in other people. Alexandra chose wisdom. Bianca and another old woman mimicked her answer, but when it was Tom's turn to speak, he chose resilience.

He would have given the same answer if Sofia asked him the same question again today, but he wondered if maybe Alexandra would not. He wondered if maybe she'd changed her mind, that with all the time she'd spent running from place to place, she now believed resilience was the best way to keep her moving through doubt and disappointment.

Tom turned the dial to change his answer from eight to five, then studied the combination one last time before his second attempt to pull open the hatch. Once again, the rest of the room looked to the end of the table as Tom wrapped his hand around the lever and pulled.

The locks on the edge of the box came undone with a clicking sound that echoed through the room like a gunshot, and the counselor fell to his knees in tears of joy. Tom kept his hands pressing down against the top of the box, refusing to give anybody else the privilege of being the first to look inside. He stood up from the floor, turned his head to the side, and saw Simon at the brink of breaking down in tears as well, but a man like this would never show any sign of frailty while someone was there to see him. He asked Tom to open the box, and the counselor took hold of the lid and slowly pried it open.

Tom still had no clue what he would find inside, whether this really was the end of his journey or just a piece of a bigger puzzle. He could feel the anxiety build in his chest until he remembered what Jeremiah had said tonight, and then he felt all right again. He had already come further than he'd ever come before, and if this was the end of his road, that would not be such a bad thing.

This proved to be the right sort of mindset for him to have, since Alexandra's journal was not inside the box. All Tom found was an unofficial copy of *Lola and the Berryserpent*, which was just sheets of paper from Gretchen's rough draft stapled together rather than a published book. Simon frantically wrestled these pages away from Tom's hands to look for some sort of clue, but not before the counselor pried away a sealed envelope that had been tucked between the pages. He pulled out the letter and read it aloud:

To the reader of this letter, whoever you may be,

If you found this letter, chances are you were looking for something else, and if you made it this far, I hope it means something to know you came further than anyone else ever has. But this is as far as you can go. What you're looking for isn't here. I've taken it, but not for myself. I've sent it far away from me, to the person who, right now, I trust more than anybody else. I have sent my journal to the person I need to stay close to in some way or another, since I might not see him or her again.

A day never goes by when I don't look at myself and reflect on how I have touched the people around me, whether it's been for the better or the worse. I have been told by some that I am mature for my age, and I have been told by some that I am a petty child in a woman's body, and if there is something I take from that, it's that I still have plenty more growing up to do. I thought Parliss County would be the place that could fix all my problems, but now I can see it was only a first step in the right direction.

That's why I'm leaving Parliss County. I've done all I can with the time I've had. So, I've gone away, far away, and even if I never come back, I couldn't leave without leaving something behind to say goodbye. There are too many important people in my life for me to leave without some final words, and since I only have one letter, I suppose I'll have to put all of them here.

For Tom:

I was a stubborn little girl when you first found me. I always found ways to say no, run when I needed to walk, and scream when I needed to talk. You came to me when everyone else had given up, and if it weren't for you, I might not have made it anywhere in the world outside my own doorstep. You are my father. I'm not your blood and you didn't marry my mom, but I'm your daughter, and that's how I'll always see it. You taught me there's always a healthy way out of a bad situation, and if it's hard then that's when you know it's the right one. So that's what I'm doing. Just know, wherever I end up going, I'll find a way to be happy.

For Gretchen:

When you told me you'd written a book and used me as inspiration for your main character, I didn't think I could see so much of myself in her. Now she's a part of my life I can't live without. You told me once that, as a journalist, you measure your success not by the number of articles you print, but by the number of lives you touch. I see how right you were now. My life has been forever changed by your work in the best way possible, and your legacy will not end with me. I am not married at the moment I'm writing this letter, but any children I have will grow up with Lola the way I wish I had. I'll be the first one to buy it when it's finished, and the last one to ever put it down.

For Howard:

I was taught growing up that you should always show strength, that those who were confident, happy, beautiful, and blessed with pleasant lives would always be more desirable than the people like us, the unlucky ones from broken families who have to keep the deeper, sadder parts to ourselves, and hide behind pretty smiles so nobody says we're begging for attention. You're the only one I know who probably has any clue what was going on in my mind when I was a kid. It wasn't until I met you that I had someone I didn't have to hide from in that way. You were the one who heard me the loudest anytime I fell back into that place, and more importantly, you helped drag me out of it. I don't know how you do it, but you always find a way to pick yourself up when you feel at your lowest. That's what I learned from you. I wish I could say that I changed my mind about performing, but it's not what I want to do. That being said, I'll always be grateful for what you did to help me find my own strength. I'll never be able to thank you for it, but hopefully, this letter will count for something.

For Charlotte:

My aunt had an old saying that I tell myself every now and then. She said it's better to be born on the ground than to be born with wings and have them taken from you. I didn't quite understand what she meant until I ran away to West Parliss. At the time, I thought coming to live with the Auralites would somehow fix everything I thought was wrong, and when that didn't happen, when I lost faith in Tom and I was alone in West Parliss, it was worse than anything I'd felt growing up. I never told you this before, but the day you found me sitting on that bench by the pond, I was thinking of drowning myself. I had mixed painkiller meds with my drink because I thought it would help make it easier. I'm not sure if I would have done it. I might not have, but it didn't matter in the end because you sat down next to me when I thought I had nothing left. I'm not a huge believer in things happening for a reason, but the day I met you is one of the exceptions. I love you, more than I ever told you in person, and I'm so incredibly sorry for what I did to your song. Hopefully you still think of me well, and maybe one day I'll get the chance to hear it.

For Azubuike:

Our time together on Besalbee Road was something I will always cherish. Even when I began to doubt others in my life, my faith in your love and kindness never faded. You helped me find the good in the world at a time when I only saw the bad, and when I got too cynical for my own good, I could always count on you to show me a brighter side. While my time as an actress didn't quite go how I wanted, my time as a painter, as your student, was nothing short of empowering. I felt more alive with a brush in my hand than I ever did on that stage. *The Wings of Solace* says more about who I am than any character I've brought to life, and it only exists because of you. For that, I thank you, and I hope even though I left East Parliss, you can still find a way to see the good in me.

For Bianca:

I miss my mother every day. While I don't remember much about her, the memories I do have still help me smile even when I know I'll never see her again. When you told me about your own mother, the way she dragged you into the pageant world when you were only ten and put you on your first diet at twelve, I thanked my lucky stars I got to spend a brief amount of time with the wonderful mother I had. Not all childhoods are equal. I've certainly come to realize this now that I've seen more of the world. I appreciate how honest you were with me, since I know this is one of the many secrets you like to keep because you're afraid of what will happen if everyone knows the truth. I know there is nothing I can say to change the past, but I know from experience that you will never be happy if you live your life thinking everyone is out to get you. You're not as difficult to like as you think you are. Even after all that's happened, I still love you, and when the time comes I know you will make an excellent mother.

And for Simon:

I've saved you for last because what I have to say to you is the last thing I want you to hear before you set this letter down. Out of everyone I've met in Parliss County, you're the one who I thought was the most like me. I suppose that's why I was so interesting to you. You were good to me, and I could tell despite how boldly you carried yourself that you cared for me in a way you hadn't cared for anyone in a long time. I said things to you I never said to anybody else, because I knew you would understand. You were as cynical as I was, and it only grew worse the longer I stayed with you. Day by day, I could see your grief and anger tearing you apart, and I would only stand, watch, and wish there was something I could do, but I couldn't. I'm not Chelsea. As much as I wish I could, I cannot bring your daughter back, and I will never be able to replace her no matter how much you want to believe I could.

I'm not telling you this to sound cruel. I'm telling you because I get the way you think, and I'm the only one you'll listen to. I don't know where you are now, what you're doing, or whether you still have this box you gave me, but if you're anything like the way you were when I knew you, then there's nothing else you can do in Parliss County. You need to leave, before you get too lost, and if there are others like me who have looked to you for wisdom then they need to leave, too. As my uncle would say, you ought to think to the future, see in the present, and forget about the past. Whatever happened in this place is only as relevant as you make it, and there is plenty more you can do if you leave now and never come back. I know for certain there is something better out there for you, like there is for me. We just have to be willing to look a little harder than others.

Always keep trying. Always keep looking.

For my final words, I want to thank you all one last time, and I trust the person in possession of my journal to do whatever he or she thinks is best.

Love, now and always,

Alexandra Cardor

Tom looked up from the letter once he finished reading. The silence that filled the room stretched so thick that the loudest sound he heard was that of his fingers rubbing against the paper. He turned to look at Simon, who after listening to Alexandra's letter looked like a completely different man. He had the look of a scared child who'd just spotted a dead animal on the side of the street, his body shaking as if he could collapse at any moment. Tom couldn't tell if he was angry, depressed, baffled, or frustrated by not finding the book he'd waited so long to hold in his hands, but Tom found himself harboring a stunning level of pity for this man he could never have felt just five minutes ago. He folded the letter back into the envelope and tucked it in his coat pocket. He set Gretchen's makeshift book on the table for Simon to keep, then made his way to the door.

"Where are you going?" Simon asked.

"I did what you asked," Tom replied. "There's nothing else I can do. It's like she said: this is as far as we go. That's good enough for me. I can only hope you feel the same way."

Tom left the theater without saying another word. He didn't turn around once as he ascended the stairs, as he made his way down the promenade, down the Eastern side of the Wide Road, remaining silent with each step. He didn't stop walking until he sat down at a bench in the center of Littelbine Park, where he stayed until he finally saw the sun rise up from the horizon.

He had one day left in Parliss County, and he knew just what to do with it. He would go see Bianca, and Gretchen, and Howard, and Azu, and then perhaps he'd spend some time looking for Charlotte. There were a lot of people who still needed to read this letter.

Chapter Twenty

The Turnip Girl

The shortest route to the far west point of Parliss County was to go down Harrison Road, pass the town square, pass the bookstore with the cracked window, and go down a hiking trail that began at Bassetty Park. The trail would take him to the edge of a shallow creek, and a keen eye would be able to spot a silo off in the distance across a field of lush grass that would be ripe with wildflowers this time of year. Part of this Jeremiah knew from Mr. Zeeger, who'd reminisced about this place a few days ago while under the influence of red wine. The rest he learned from the map, which he'd read many times over the last few days so he could visit as many places in Parliss County as he could before he left.

Jeremiah planned to go to this spot on his final day in Parliss, to stand as far west as he could go while still being within the invisible line that kept the Auralites from the rest of the world. Then he would turn right or left, whichever he preferred, and take one last walk around the whole county and return to the creek by the end of the day. He couldn't think of a more perfect way to end his summer. The Judges had done their best to make walking his one and only option, and he planned on turning their punishment into an adventure. It would be the last of his many private walks, and one of the few he would spend relaxed and happy instead of lonely. For once, the thought of being alone didn't bother him. He almost felt like a new person, a grown man who'd finally caught up with the rest of the world, even though the Aurascope said differently. The lights hadn't changed. At his core, he was still the same as he'd always been, and days would come in the distant future when he would feel lonely and out of place again, as would everyone else at some time or another. He couldn't change into a whole new man in just a few weeks. It would take months, possibly years. His three weeks in East Parliss had only been a first step. Three weeks in West Parliss had been a good second, and a walk around the whole county might be a decent third.

He could hear the distant echo of Madame Josephine's voice in his head: "Always keep trying. Always keep looking."

He left the pub with Alicia on the morning of their last full day in Parliss, trading weather-watcher comments while they walked until they parted ways at the Terrinson Club. He heard a voice call out his name from a block away. He didn't recognize who it was until he turned around, and saw Reese standing just a few steps away. Thankfully, the side of his head was no longer covered in blood, and any wounds or scars were kept hidden by his tousled blonde hair. With a closer look, Jeremiah knew he'd find a few stitches on the side of his face, but from where he stood, Reese was a picture of fine health, as tall and handsome as he'd always been.

"I came by the Broken Cottage to look for you a few days ago, but you weren't there," Reese said. "I wanted to say thanks for what you did for me."

"You're welcome," Jeremiah said, unsure of how to respond. "I just did what anybody would have done."

"Right," Reese said, who looked unsure of how true this was. "Anyways, I wanted to make it up to you. Have you ever been inside the Ranchester Club?"

The sheer mention of this name made Jeremiah's eyes swell open with intrigue. He could already tell what Reese was about to say, and as expected, he offered to take Jeremiah into the club as a show of gratitude. A sense of pride took over his whole body as he imagined strutting past the Judge with a smug, cheery look in his eyes, full of power as he stepped through the door and joined the ranks of Parliss

County's most popular residents. It was an unmatched feeling of bliss and excitement that slowly passed away the more Jeremiah imagined himself in his new role, a part of the very same culture that left so many people out on the street like stray dogs. It wasn't a place for a person like him, and suddenly the thought of walking inside didn't feel so good.

"Thanks, but I don't really think that's the right sort of place for me," Jeremiah said, after a long pause. Reese looked disappointed, but he nodded his head gently as if he understood what Jeremiah was thinking. He offered instead to buy Jeremiah a snack or a drink of some kind, insisting he couldn't leave without repaying the favor in some way. Jeremiah took him up on his offer. He let Reese buy him a vanilla milkshake at a diner near the corner of Harrison Road, and they sat together at an outdoor table.

Reese offered to show Jeremiah his Aura. Like many of the people in West Parliss, his was composed of sharp, vibrant colors of red and blue with no green. He was an extrovert, deeply adventurous, and deeply carefree, as shown by the bright red in his first few rings. The bluest parts of his Aura were signs of his relaxed and trusting tendencies. He was also very confident, as Jeremiah would expect from someone so handsome, but two areas of his Aura struck Jeremiah as being unusual. One, he was very sensitive, which might explain why he was so visibly distraught from his experience in the alley. Second, he was very dependent, which told Jeremiah that his membership to the Ranchester Club was crucial to his sense of worth. He was clearly the sort of person who was used to having a lot of company, men and women alike, but he likely wanted their approval in a more desperate way than they might expect.

"We went to high school together," Reese said, after a long stretch of silence. "We took the same bus, from the same spot down at the end of our neighborhood. He would get a seat and save the next one for me. He did the same thing anytime we had class together. I guess he liked me, or thought I was his friend, but I just didn't feel the same way. We were really different. You would see that if you listened to us talk to each other, but for some reason, he didn't see it even as we got older. I would always find a reason to sit somewhere else, and when my friends asked why he kept trying to talk to me, I'd make a joke about him. I didn't think he'd ever hear about it. I guess I was wrong.

"Anyways, at some point, he just disappeared. I never heard anything about him for years until just a few months back. I was inside the Ranchester. One of the servers came to my table and said a kid named Cody was at the door and asking for me. I could have let him in, and it would've been easy, but all I could think about was him coming up to all my friends and embarrassing me, and all night I'd have to play babysitter for him. I knew he'd hate the place, too. Guys like him always do. They try to get in 'cause they hear how cool it is, or how special it makes you feel, but one minute with all those voices and all that talking and he'd wish he was off somewhere else. That's what I told myself when I said not to let him in. I told myself I was doing the right thing, and someday he'd know that. I guess I was wrong again."

"You can't blame yourself for what he did," Jeremiah insisted, raising his voice to help his point stick. "You never could've seen this coming."

"Maybe not," Reese muttered, shrugging his shoulders. "Someone else, maybe, but not me. I've spent most of my life with the same sort of people. I'm a pretty social guy. Most of my friends are the same way. My buddies and I give each other a hard time now and then, say things we don't really mean, but we always laugh it off and find a way to keep having fun. I've never been on Cody's side of things. I guess it's just hard for me to see what it's like through his eyes."

"Well, now might be a good time to find out," Jeremiah said, as he reached out to touch the Aurascope.

He let Reese take a good, long look at who he was, from his preferences, his habits, his limits, and all his strengths and weaknesses, adding up to an Aura that displayed a strong resemblance to Cody's. He could see Reese making this connection as he studied the pattern of his Aura one ring at a time, and Jeremiah didn't feel the least bit bothered by it. He never imagined a day would come when he felt so safe with a person like Reese, who would've fit right in place with the

Donnigan Boys and have the admiration of every girl in school with his good looks and charm alone, and yet there was no place he would rather be right now than by his side, wherever that might be.

———————

Jeremiah led Reese down the trail in Bassetty Park and stopped when they arrived at the creek, and together, they gazed out across the long plain of grass to the ambient sounds of chattering birds and rustling leaves. For days, Jeremiah had dreamt of coming to this place by himself, to admire the surrounding beauty and be with his own private thoughts while he stood and walked along the trail, but having Reese by his side made for a better experience than he could have hoped for.

He could hear Tom's voice in his head, reminding him that having the courage to embrace change and welcome others into his company was the true mark of maturity. It was only once he and Reese began their walk around Parliss that Jeremiah questioned whether this was actually one of Tom's little sayings. He couldn't remember a place or time the counselor had said this to him. He wondered if this had come from Gretchen Salcott, or one of the Jennabelle Kids, or even Dr. Kennry. He scoured his memory until he and Reese arrived in East Parliss, then wondered if maybe he'd come up with this little saying on his own. He dismissed this idea about two or three times during the rest of their walk, but always found a way to keep wondering if maybe he was right. He thought of what Tom said to him the other night at the Birdhouse Garden, about how he would make a great counselor one day if he gave it a shot. If Tom of all people could see that sort of potential, then maybe this wasn't so far from the truth.

He talked with Reese about his life in Pritchard Haven. He didn't mention his connection with Tom Berrinser, but for this one secret he repaid Reese with stories about his time in high school. He mentioned the Donnigan Boys once or twice, but he tried not to focus on them too much. Instead, he mostly talked about his friendship with Alicia. He told Reese about her adventures in Germany, or at least, the parts he could still remember. He told him about the Skydiver Incident, the turnip story, and any other moment he felt was worth mentioning. He finished telling every important story from the last four years by the time they were standing back by the creek at the west edge of Parliss County. They walked back to the main part of the town mostly in silence, exchanging a weather-watcher comment every few minutes, and they were about to go their separate ways at the door to the Ranchester Club before Reese turned around for some final words.

"Those Donnigan Boys you were talking about before," he said. "Be a little patient with them. In a few years, once they grow up a little, they might surprise you."

"I'm sure they will," Jeremiah replied. He meant what he said, but he wondered if he would have the discipline to act on it. Whether they knew it or not, the Donnigan Boys had been the cause of all his distress and self-doubt. Even if they all got down on their knees and begged for forgiveness, he might not be able to give it. As calm and pleasant as Jeremiah felt now after his time with Reese, he knew there would be a day in the distant future when a rough experience would bring back all the memories he'd tried to repress. In his rising bitterness, he would come to resent Ethan Kantzton as badly as ever, and in a few days, he would forgive him all over again. That was the sad and funny thing about aging, Jeremiah thought, that any lesson he learned would be forgotten and remembered over and over again. The circle would never break. Bad days would always come, but good days would be waiting just around the corner. He just had to be patient, and he would get there eventually.

Jeremiah walked past the Terrinson Club on his way back to the Broken Cottage. He imagined Alicia sitting around a table, surrounded by all the friends she'd made in the last few days, chatting away about their hopes for next year while they listened to the music. He saw Charverra singing her final note and taking a bow to the sound of roaring applause and the sight of all her adoring fans and friends, the happiest she'd felt in ten years of loneliness, and it was all because of Alicia. He wanted to run past the Judge and step inside the room, not because he was lonely, not because he wanted company, but so he could have one moment to see Alicia with everything she deserved, and to have proof he was no longer the only person in the world who saw her greatness. No one but Alicia could have done this—step into someone else's life at just the right time when everything felt wrong and bring them happiness in such simple ways that most people wouldn't even notice.

He remembered the story about the turnip. He saw Alicia with her parents, her aunts and uncles, and maybe a few of her cousins, hiking up some trail to the top of a hill so they could enjoy a simple family picnic. That was all she needed to make the greatest day of her life: friends, family, and some good food for them all to share. He saw Alicia crouched down on the blanket, cutting away at the lone turnip with her loved ones close by, and he smiled.

He lay down in his bed when he returned to his room and opened his journal to the next blank page. He remembered when he tried writing a story about Ethan Kantzton, and only managed to scratch down two words before he tore the page out. He tried to write about Alicia instead. He tried his best to remember the turnip story, scouring his mind for every detail he could find, and then made up the rest as he continued to write. He didn't need everything to be exactly as it had happened. As long as he gave Alicia her friends and family, that would be enough.

He wrote for nearly two hours straight, building his own version of the story so he had a memory to hold onto. When he finished, he returned to the first page and wrote down the title at the start of his story. He named it *The Turnip Girl.*

———— —— —— ——

Jeremiah didn't see Alicia again until the next morning, when he woke up to the sound of Tom's voice and Mr. Zeeger's hearty laughter. He dressed himself as fast as he could and joined them all in the kitchen for their last breakfast in Parliss County. It occurred to Jeremiah while he ate that this was the first time Alicia had seen the counselor in the last six weeks, and he could see the curiosity present itself in the concerned, distant look in her eyes when she asked where Tom had been all this time.

The counselor told his story while they ate, while Jeremiah went on acting as though he were hearing this for the first time. He was grateful that Tom seemed to recognize this and abstained from mentioning their time together at the Birdhouse Garden so Alicia wouldn't feel like she'd been kept out of a secret. He kept his story fixed to the events at the Canmark Theater, the man named Mothcatcher, and the old box that had once belonged to Alexandra. He was however able to join in Alicia's curiosity when Tom revealed what had happened that night, when he succeeded in opening the box after just two tries but found the journal had been sent away. All he'd found was a makeshift copy of *Lola and the Berryserpent* and a kind farewell letter, but that was all the counselor said he needed.

The drive back to Pritchard Haven was mostly silent. They listened to the music from the radio as the wind blew through the open windows, and a weather-watcher comment came up once every few minutes, but from the moment they left the pub and said goodbye to Mr. Zeeger, they were each trapped in their own worlds, thinking back on their time in Parliss County, living each memory for a second time. Jeremiah could see the Jennabelle Kids playing Silent Captain in the park. He could see Gretchen in the rocking chair with a copy of her book. He could hear Howard Granzill's voice as if they were sitting right beside one another. With each passing minute, a new memory came back into focus, all the way until the familiar sights of Pritchard Haven came to view from beyond their windows, and the real world came to push them back.

Within seconds of climbing out of Tom's car, he was standing in his own bedroom, with his mother and father making plans to go shopping for school supplies. He would be off to college soon. He only had two weeks to get ready, two weeks left in Pritchard Haven before he would be on the road again, and he had to make the most of the time he had.

He rode his bike to Alicia's house three days later, and suggested they go to Shangrin Lake for a third time before they left. He prepared a picnic for the occasion, and kept all the food and utensils in a basket he'd strapped to the back of his bike. He even packed a turnip for them to share, hoping he could recreate this memory of hers in a way he could be a part of. For the second time this year, they were back at his favorite spot by the edge of the lake, where the Smoothing Rock was still resting in the shallow water.

"I think I've finally realized what it is I like so much about you," Jeremiah said, while he nibbled on his third slice of turnip.

"What's that?" Alicia asked, chewing on her second.

"You don't have rules," Jeremiah said. "Or at least, you don't have that many. Most people have too many. With everybody else, you always have to do something the way they want it. Some people want you to talk a lot, and others want you to stay a little quiet. Some people like it when you tell dirty jokes, and others think it's gross. Some people think you're cool when you talk about this, and others think you're lame if you do. There's always a way to be too much and a way to be too little, and everybody draws the line in a different place. But with you, all I had to do was introduce myself, say hi whenever I saw you, listen to your stories, and just like that I had a new best friend.

"That's what I like about you."

Jeremiah hoped Alicia would say something similar about him, some brief but thoughtful deconstruction of what she thought of their friendship, but instead, all she did was smile and get back to her food. She'd been unusually quiet, just as she'd been on the drive back from Parliss County, and Jeremiah wished more than anything else he could see what she was thinking. He noticed the way her eyes stayed away from him, drifting off to the side and looking out to the lake as if she were daydreaming.

"There's something else I wanted to tell you," Jeremiah said, trying as best as he could to end the silence. "It's a bit of a confession, I suppose."

"What is it?" Alicia asked, her eyes finally drifting back to him.

"I went to the Birdhouse Garden, on the night with the ambulance, and I met the old woman who lives there."

"How did it go?"

"Great. She was wonderful," Jeremiah said. "But there's more to it. I went back for a second visit, just to say goodbye, and Tom was there. It was a complete coincidence—I didn't plan on it—but he told me about what he'd been doing all that time in the theater, and how he was trying to open that box. He told me everything."

Alicia looked confused for a moment until she slowly put the pieces together. "So, when Tom was telling this story over Mr. Zeeger's breakfast, you already knew?"

Jeremiah nodded. "I didn't know if he actually managed to open the box or not, but I knew everything else," he admitted. "I wasn't trying to keep it a secret; I just thought it was a private issue for Tom and I didn't think it was right for me to say anything unless he wanted me to, so I kept it all to myself. I'm just letting you know today because I felt guilty about it."

"Oh, no, that's quite all right," Alicia said. "I would have done the same if I'd been in your position. As a matter of fact, if you don't mind, I have a bit of a confession myself."

"What is it?" Jeremiah asked, trying to gauge from the look on her face how nervous he ought to be.

Alicia didn't look afraid, or guilty. All Jeremiah could tell from the placid look on her face was that the information at her disposal carried a lot of weight. She reached inside her shoulder bag, which had been resting right beside her this whole time. He watched Alicia dig through the contents of her bag, reaching past the Aurascope and past the map until she grabbed hold of Alexandra's journal.

Jeremiah had no words to describe the amount of shock he experienced at the sight of this book. His disbelief was best expressed in his own silence, the way his body froze stiff, the way his eyes remained wide open. He stopped chewing his food, utterly speechless in a way he'd never been in his life while he wondered how this was even possible.

"Charlotte gave this to me the day before we left for home," Alicia explained. "She called me into her dressing room, and she told me how much help I'd been to her these last few weeks. She told me she almost did something terrible, but that because of me, she found the strength to let go of her anger. She thanked me for saving her, and she gave this to me as a token of her gratitude. She told me what this book was, that it was all she had left of Alexandra, and that she felt it was time to leave that part of her behind. She told me I was the only person who deserved it, but I'm not sure if that's true."

"What do you mean?" Jeremiah asked, finally ready to speak again.

"I want you to have it."

"Me? Alicia, I told you, I don't care about Alexandra anymore."

"But you should," Alicia said. "I know I said you shouldn't, but that was a different time."

Alicia stayed quiet for a moment while she thought of how she could make her point. Jeremiah sat patiently until she was ready.

"Do you know what I like so much about you?" Alicia asked.

"No. What?"

"You give a shit."

Once again, Jeremiah had nothing to say. He had never heard Alicia use a curse word before, whether as an insult or just for some dramatic stress when nothing else would do the trick. The rest of their old classmates would be speechless if they'd been around to hear it, jaws dropped with their eyes wide open, looking around to their friends and wondering what had gotten inside the German girl's head.

"You actually care, about a lot," Alicia said. "You're the only one in school who ever listened to anything I said. You didn't just nod and let me talk. You asked questions. You wanted to know more about me. You took the extra step when nobody else would. That's what I like the most about you. And I don't want to be the only one you do that for. What if you read this and learn the one thing about her that no one else knew—the one thing Tom couldn't find—and then meet someone else just as screwed up as Alexandra and help them get better?"

"I couldn't do that," Jeremiah protested. "I'm not Tom."

"Not now," Alicia said. "But maybe one day you could be."

Jeremiah remembered what Tom said to him at the Birdhouse Garden. He reached out for Alexandra's journal, his fingers shaking as if they were cold, but he moved his hand back right as his skin touched the cover.

"I shouldn't," he said. "She gave it to you. It's not for me."

"She gave it to me and said to do what was best with it," Alicia said. "Giving it to you is the best thing I can do. Please. Take it."

Jeremiah left his arm dangling in the air again, his hand shaking above the cover as he wondered if he deserved to have it. He finally took the book from Alicia, held it with both hands and set it down in his lap. He stared down at the cover as if he were cradling a newborn baby in his arms, already thinking about when he would start to read it, and what he could do with it once he flipped over that final page.

"There is one condition to keeping it," Alicia said. "You can't tell Tom about this."

"I know," Jeremiah said. He felt guilty about keeping this a secret, but he knew just as well as Alicia that it was the right thing to do. It had taken more than a decade for the counselor to heal from losing Alexandra. He'd lived with so much guilt and regret for so many years and had finally reached a healthy state of mind where he could accept this young woman would no longer be with him, but also understood he had a full life left to live as the counselor of Laronna. There was no good that could come from letting him get distracted again, and Jeremiah wouldn't be the one to give him that chance.

When it was time to leave, Jeremiah wrapped Alexandra's journal in a tablecloth and tucked it inside the picnic basket. He left Shangrin Lake and stayed with Alicia for as long as he could until they rode off in separate directions down two different roads. They promised to stay in touch with each other during the year, and to meet up again for a second picnic once they were back for the summer. He waved goodbye and kept on riding his bike, but he still wasn't quite ready to go home just yet.

He went to the northwestern part of town to see Tom's house again. He wondered what might happen if he broke his promise with Alicia and left the journal on the counselor's doorstep. He wondered what might happen if he gave Tom the chance to live in his old world, and when he looked into this future, he didn't feel so guilty about keeping this one secret. Tom didn't need the journal anymore, and so

Jeremiah left it tucked away in his basket, promising to keep it where it could never do any harm, but had a chance to do some good.

He looked across to the other side of the road and saw a sign by the red house saying it had been sold. Apparently, Tom's reclusive neighbor had moved away while they were in Parliss County and left this old house behind for someone else to take. Hopefully, this new neighbor would be better company for Tom. For a man who was so used to watching people leave, having a friend right by his house was the best gift he could ask for. Sometimes the best way to let go of the past was to say hello to something new, even if it wasn't always clear how long it would stay around.

Acknowledgements

Alphabetical Order by First Name

Amelia Fraik: Volunteered to read a draft of my story and provided positive feedback. I consider her to be my first fan.

Audrey Baker: My lovely sister whose sharp wit and tenacity always kept me on my toes growing up.

Chersti Nieveen: Edited my revised draft and provided the last round of critiques before I wrote the final version.

Christina: An old friend of mine who inspired Alicia and was the highlight of my first few years as a teenager. I've kept her last name hidden, as I suspect she would prefer to stay anonymous. I wish her nothing but the best for her future, wherever it may take her.

Claire Allen: Edited a revised draft of this book and caught a number of grammar and spelling errors that were not as rare as I would like to think.

David Baker: My incredible brother who inspires me every day with his creativity and his boundless positive energy.

Deborah Baker: My loving mother who edited many drafts of this book and provided excellent feedback. Also, she raised me.

Dr. Jennifer

Manlowe: Edited the initial draft of this book back when I barely knew what I was making and helped me hone my writing skills and sort out my many wild ideas into a story with a clear set of themes and motifs.

John Baker IV: My wonderful father who taught me to work hard for what I want, and who helped raise me alongside my mother.

Kris Van Gieson: Volunteered to read an early draft of my story and helped me develop the earliest rules and guidelines for Aura that would eventually develop into how it is seen in the final version. He also introduced me to the Myers Briggs Type Indicator when I was twelve, sparking my fascination with personality and psychology that would define most of my adolescent life.

Lydia Harrison: Tutored me from elementary school all the way through high school, along with my brother and sister. It is because of volunteering for her summer activity camp that I was able to meet Michaela and her lovely family, and it is because of her generous nomination that I was one of the two recipients of the Bob Satterwhite Award for Compassionate Acts in 2014. I probably would not have graduated high school if it weren't for her help. Harrison Road, which is mentioned in the final chapter, is named after her.

Dr. Melanie

Henderson: One of my psychology professors during my time at Ohio Wesleyan University who helped me decide how to organize the 16 rings of the Aurascope into their final positions, and for answering plenty of other personality-centric questions that further helped me develop this story.

Michaela Rossi: My dear friend who inspired me to pursue a career in counseling. Her kindness, friendship, and spirit sets an example I can never hope to match, and I will love her like my sister forever.

Raymond Cattell: The great British psychologist who developed the 16 Personality Factor model that was used to create the sixteen rings of the Aurascope.

Ron King: A fellow author and friend to my mother who provided feedback on the first four chapters of this book.

Suzanne Selfors: A fellow writer who provided me with many of the resources that led to my novel's publication.

Thomas Zuzelski:A science teacher at Bainbridge High School who taught me about the relationship of colored lights that would ultimately spark the concept for how an Aurascope would work.

And to all my other friends, whether or not I've already met them.

About the Author

John Baker grew up as the oldest of three siblings in the small town of Bainbridge Island, Washington. He began writing at twelve years old but would not finish a complete draft of his first novel until the summer of 2016, when he was twenty. He graduated from Western Washington University in 2018 with plans to pursue a career in mental health counseling. *The Cardorian Complex* is his first book.

More information can be found at jtaylorbaker.com

Made in the USA
Las Vegas, NV
03 September 2021

29539200R00162